HILL
112

ALSO BY
ADRIAN GOLDSWORTHY

The Vindolanda Series

Vindolanda
The Encircling Sea
Brigantia

The City of Victory Series

The Fort
The City
The Wall

Non-Fiction

Hadrian's Wall
Philip and Alexander
The Eagle and the Lion

HILL 112

ADRIAN GOLDSWORTHY

HEAD
of ZEUS

An Aries Book

First published in the UK in 2024 by Head of Zeus,
part of Bloomsbury Publishing Plc

9 7 5 3 1 2 4 6 8

A catalogue record for this book is available from the British Library.

ISBN (HB): 9781801109017
ISBN (E): 9781801108997

Cover design: kid-ethic

Printed and bound in Great Britain by
CPI Group (UK) Ltd, Croydon CR0 4YY

Head of Zeus Ltd
First Floor East
5–8 Hardwick Street
London EC1R 4RG

WWW.HEADOFZEUS.COM

HILL 112

A NOVEL OF D-DAY AND THE BATTLE OF NORMANDY

This is a novel based on fact. The Glamorganshire Regiment and the 165ᵗʰ RAC are fictional, but all of the key actions and nearly all the little incidents reflect what actually happened, if sometimes on a different day and in a different place. I have done my best to make the characters act and talk like their real-life counterparts. Many of the soldiers who landed on D-Day and afterwards were very young. This is a story of a few such men – or boys as we would be inclined to see them now. It cannot be the story of all who took part in the Normandy campaign. The Canadians, who played a vital role in the Battle of Normandy, punching above the country's weight as they did in the air and at sea appear only on the margins. The Americans barely appear at all. This is simply because the story is told from the perspective of three young men from the same town in South Wales and is not meant in any way to denigrate the contribution of others. A novel like this has little to do with strategy and cannot include all those from many lands who fought in the war. Soldiers who do the fighting do not see the big picture.

D-Day, Tuesday 6th June, 1944

*07.00 hrs Double Summer Time,[1] in the English Channel,
three miles off GOLD Beach, King Sector*

'WILL YOU LOOK at that?' Lance Corporal Collins tended
to speak loudly, but even he had to shout to be heard
by the men beside him. Gun after gun was firing, pounding the
shore, the sound drumming against their ears. 'Bloody hell,'
he added after a moment, whether in sheer awe or simply for
something to say.

He and the other three were standing on the back of their
Sherman tank, which, like the other vehicles on the landing
craft, was chained down to keep it in place during the voyage.
The LCT – or Landing Craft Tank Mark IV to those who had
not been formally introduced – was just over one hundred and
eighty feet long, less than forty feet wide and shaped like an
open box, with no concern for elegance, style or anything other
than utility. As the name implied, it was designed to carry tanks
and trucks across water and with its flat bottom run onto the
beach and let them off on the sand. The men who would drive
those vehicles were an afterthought, expected to make do as
best they could. There were meagre quarters for the LCT's own
crew, under the bridge at the square stern, but the passengers
were left with the main deck, sheltered a little by the sides, while
always open to the sky.

---

1   Two hours ahead of Greenwich Mean Time.

Most of the regiment was further back on a couple of big
LSTs,[2] which the tankmen's imagination had turned into pre-
War liners of almost decadent luxury. The only disputes were
over which men to envy and resent more, although the ones
assigned to the American ship, with all the bounty of that
golden country where rationing was unknown, were ahead in
the stakes. 'Greedy bastards' was the general verdict, 'they'll be
stuffing themselves all the way'. Still, American ships were dry,
for reasons best known to their strange transatlantic cousins,
and there was a good deal to be said in favour of Royal Navy
rum.

These discussions, surprisingly detailed and fervently
contested, had been before they left the Solent. After that the
LCT had begun to pitch and roll like a fairground ride, getting
worse the further they went, and all conversation had soon died
away and thoughts of food and drink became a torment rather
than a dream. The copious issue of 'bags, vomit' were soon
filled, mostly blown away as fragile, exhausted men emptied
them over the side. An early shower left everyone damp, and the
spray soon completed the job, adding to the sheer misery for the
retching, shivering men, for whom the threat of collision, mine
or torpedo became too distant to register.

The deck still stank of vomit, mingling with the smell of
salt and that lingering combination of grease and petrol that
always hovered around tanks. James Taylor found that he kept
smelling it even when he was on leave, in the same way the
scent of a stable, of old leather, dung and horse sweat, lasted so
long in the nostrils.

James had grown up beside the sea, had spent a lot of his
childhood in and around boats, and had always considered
himself a good sailor with a strong stomach. That was until last
night. He was not the first to succumb, and even when the LCT

2   A Landing Ship Tank was capable of carrying some 500 tons of
vehicles and equipment and landing them directly onto a beach.

was tossed and rolled by the waves, he had just about managed up on the bridge. Then he had gone down to the deck to check on his men, as a good officer should, and the stench, and maybe not being able to see out, had grabbed him and suddenly he was bent double, retching, the vomit spraying onto the wheels of his own tank. For a moment he had wondered whether that was lucky, for they said that aircrew peed on the wheel of their plane before a mission as a ritual. The thought did not last long, for he had soon lost all the will and energy to wonder anything. Even the shame of speckling his overalls with his own vomit had meant nothing anymore.

Daylight had helped, and surely the logistics of the digestive system, since there could have been nothing left to throw up, and back on the bridge he had recovered. Yet duty was duty, and James had felt trepidation coming down onto the deck again, but so far, so good. A few of his own men and others from the Recce Troop stood or leaned against the tanks, but most were up on the vehicles so that they could see out. Thankfully no one was still puking, for he was not sure that he could cope with the sound or the fresh smell of vomit.

James wandered up and down, exchanging a few half-audible words and more nods and smiles. No one saluted, for this was an armoured regiment and such formalities were kept for when they were needed. Then he went and stood beside his own tank looking up at his crew. A Sherman was a big piece of metal, and very high even compared to other tanks. His place, in the main hatch of the dome-like turret, was a good nine feet off the ground, and even though the boys were standing on the engine deck, their boots were almost at eye level, and they were able to see over the grey painted side of the LCT. He wondered about putting his foot on the track and hauling himself up to join them, although what with the tall hoods added to the exhausts there was not a lot of room.

Then the air was split by appalling crashes, each running into the other so that it was almost one noise, followed by a distinct whistling as the shells punched through the air overhead. They were close to HMS *Belfast*, and the cruiser must have let fly with its dozen 6″ guns.

'–ck me!' Trooper Whitefield's voice carried in what seemed almost like silence for a few moments. 'Like cracks of the Devil's whip.'

The Londoner was inclined to be sullen, was quick to anger, but he did have these rare, poetic moments, and James knew what he meant. You expected battleships, or even the big cruisers like the *Belfast*, to sound like rolling thunder when they fired. That was always the way in the newsreels, a deep rumble, very loud and full of purpose, before the camera would turn and show distant spouts of water as the shells landed. The cinemas made everything so clear, whether it was a report with the clipped tones of the narrator explaining or inspiring, or a picture where the target was a model ship in a studio tank and you knew that it would all turn out alright in the end. This was a much sharper sound, and far louder. The whole bombardment was simply bigger and louder than anything he had ever heard, even when there had been live firing on exercises.

The barrage had started once the Sun came up, pausing only to let the bombers have a go. The tankmen had seen some of the planes pass overhead, twin-engine mediums, white stripes bright on their wings as they passed in and out of the clouds. For half an hour the airmen had dropped their bombs, and once they were out of the way, the ships opened up again. Now they were joined by field artillery, self-propelled guns placed in LCTs like this, but on special mounts, so that they could fire from the decks onto the shore. Then there were other landing craft, specially converted, so that they sent up volleys of big rockets. The beach had become a mass of dark smoke and dust, with tiny sparks of explosions, but no sense of pattern.

'Will you look at that,' Collins said again, shaking his head in wonder. 'Just look at it.'

'There can't be much left.' Trooper Albright was the

youngster of the crew, a thin, gangling lad with the slow accent of Wolverhampton. The LCT was circling, following the one ahead of it, and was carrying them further from the *Belfast*, so that the next volley was less overpowering, otherwise James doubted that he would have caught what the lad was saying. 'I mean there can't be, can there? After all that shit poured onto them.' He sighed, before adding, 'Poor bastards.'

'Poor bastards, nothing,' Collins replied. 'They're bastard Germans waiting there with their eighty-eights and Spandaus to carve us up. Pour it on, boys. Flatten the sods! Every last one!'

'There can't be many left by now,' Albright told him. 'Just wasting ammo.'

'You bloody paying for it?' Whitefield snarled. 'Blow 'em all to buggery I say.' He did his best to mimic a posh accent. 'Spare no expense – and home, Philips, and don't spare the 'orses.'

Albright shrugged. 'I was just saying, we might as well go now, there can't be any of them left.'

'Hark at ruddy Monty here.' Whitefield's quick temper was rising. 'What the bloody hell would you know? Them Jerries is snug down in concrete shelters, twenty fucking feet thick. My dad was on the Somme. They told him they'd just have to walk across into what was left of the Jerry front line. Guns would have killed 'em all, they said. Fuck. Off they walked and all them little Huns pop up with their machine guns. Only three men left out of Dad's company at the end of the day. Three! That's your fucking artillery and your fucking Navy!'

Collins happened to glance back and noticed the officer standing beneath them. His boot nudged Whitefield, and he gave a sheepish grin. The Londoner's eyes remained belligerent, but he said no more.

'Alf's giving us a history lesson, sir,' the lance corporal explained.

'Splendid.' James called up, smiling back. 'I love history.' Which was true enough, not that it mattered. He was the 3 Troop commander with the all the intoxicating power of a

second lieutenant's single pip on each shoulder, and had enough
sense to know how little that really meant.

'Are we going soon, sir?' Albright asked.

James pretended not to see Whitefield rolling his eyes.

'Be a while yet,' he replied. 'You know the plan. The assault
waves are ahead of us. They'll be going in soon. A few hours
yet, lads, then at least we'll be back on dry land.' All save
Albright were older than him, but no one was likely to object
to the 'lads'. Five months shy of his twenty-first birthday, so not
yet old enough to vote, Second Lieutenant James Taylor was
supposed to care for the men of his Troop, even the ones with
far more experience of life, which was just about all of them.
School and the Army only taught so much and he had known
nothing else.

'Hoo-bleeding-ray!' Collins called cheerfully. 'If I'd wanted
to float about, I'd have joined the ruddy Navy.'

'If they'd have you,' Whitefield said as James nodded and
turned away. 'And you,' Whitefield went on, 'what's this "when
are we going ashore, sir?", eh? Haven't you learned anything
about the Army yet, boy?'

'He's just keen, that's all,' Collins said. 'A good lad wanting
to do his bit. Not a Cockney git trying to skive off.'

'Skive off? And us going in with the supports?'

Collins scoffed. 'Better than going first, mate.'

'You reckon? By the time we get there, Fritz'll have his big
guns zeroed in. That's what we'll get, matey, fucking big guns
right on top of us. Nah, the best place is right at the back, but if
you can't have that, go out in front and get to cover quick. The
poor sods in the middle always get the worst.'

'Really, better write to your MP,' Collins assured him. 'You
can swim back with the letter and get us shifted.' He laughed.
'Miserable git. At least Billy-boy here' – he nodded to Albright
– 'is cheerful... And after a while you get used to his smell. Well,
after a while...'

A fresh salvo drowned the rest, and James nodded and left

them to it, heading back towards the bridge, swaying as he walked, for they must have turned against the waves as the LCT followed others in yet another wide circle. Filthy water rolled across the deck with every motion, pooling on the far side until the craft shifted again and it set off on another journey. The stench almost made him gag, so he hurried as fast as dignity allowed.

At least the men were moaning again, and ribbing each other, which made everything seem more normal, for the anguished silence of the last night had been as disturbing as it was understandable. The sea was no calmer now, perhaps even worse, but there was more to see, certainly more to think about, and they all seemed to be coping.

They – not just 3 Troop, but plenty of others if you had a mind to think that way – were attacking Hitler's Atlantic Wall and liberating France. That was the idea anyway. Whether they went first, last or in the middle, the LCT would take them into the beach eventually and they would land and drive inshore, and the Germans would try to stop them, with their Spandaus and 88s as Collins had said. The machine guns would not matter as long as they were inside the tank, but the 88s... The German eighty-eight millimetre gun had become a legend in the War. Designed to pot aircraft flying several miles high, it fired a big shell very fast and very straight. Rommel, the same German general who was said to be planning the defence of France, had worked out years ago that such a gun could be just as deadly against ground targets and especially tanks. No protective armour – at least none yet made by the Allies – would stop a shell that big and fast. Collins was right, the Germans would be waiting and they would be no pushover. The bastards weren't about to pack it in any time soon. So that meant someone had to convince them to quit, and this invasion was meant to do just that, once and for all.

It was the thing that they had all been training for, some for four years, and even he had been a soldier for getting on half that time without ever having anyone shoot back at him. Their Regiment, 165th RAC,[3] was a new one, raised during the War and until now never sent overseas. Apart from a handful of veterans posted to them in the last few months, none of them had ever seen battle – until now, and they were only on the edge of it at the moment. It was bound to make even the least imaginative think, and it was better to chatter away and gripe than to brood in silence. James had gone down onto the deck telling himself that this should encourage the men. He had no idea whether he had managed to appear confident and unconcerned, and if he had, whether this had done any good. What he did know was that he felt better from having seen and heard them all. He trusted them, even if he was none too sure about himself.

07.25 hrs

'H-Hour,' Captain Symonds told him when James climbed back up to the open bridge.

'God help them all,' the Navy Lieutenant in command of the LCT said fervently.

A salvo of rockets hissed screaming into the air, the flames behind each one a rare splash of colour in all this drabness. Otherwise, it was a world of grey – grey sea, save for the white caps to the breakers, grey ships and landing craft and goodness knew what else, all under grey cloud with barely a break in it to show the sky above. Even the drably painted tanks seemed more grey than green in this light, and the men's faces were not much better.

Yet what the scene lacked in colour it made up for in sheer scale. There were craft everywhere as far as the eye could see, warships and landing ships and landing craft of all shapes and

---

3   Royal Armoured Corps.

sizes. Ahead James could see rows of LCAs[4] running in towards the beach. They were tiny open boxes, so small that they had to be carried this far by bigger ships, then lowered into the water and each filled with a platoon of thirty of so. Some of the men would have climbed down scrambling nets to get into the wildly pitching little assault craft and he did not envy them at the best of times, let alone with this swell and every man laden down with equipment. One slip and that would be it – sinking like a stone, if you weren't pulped between the side of the ship and the LCA. No, he did not envy them, and for all its discomfort he felt better off in a vessel that would take them close enough to drive ashore.

Symonds was staring through his binoculars at the beach. The barrage should be shifting aim inland as the first wave went ashore. James lifted his own glasses, but could see very little at this distance and with all the lingering smoke and dust.

Symonds glanced down at his watch. 'The Dragoons ought to be ashore already, before the infantry get there. Don't think I can make them out. Let's hope the damned things worked as advertised.'

The 165th were brigaded with two other armoured regiments, the Dragoons and the Yeomanry, who were leading the attack. For that reason, those regiments each had two of their three squadrons equipped with one of the new secret weapons, the DD or swimming tank, where canvas screens and propellers driven by the engine were supposed to turn thirty tons of Sherman tank into a boat. It worked, *mirabile dictu*, for James had spoken to several officers from the other regiments and glimpsed a few of the DDs on exercise. So it was safe enough, as long as the canvas did not tear or the waves were not higher than a few feet, and all that was before the Germans started paying attention. James continued to scan the sea towards the beach, but could

---

4   Landing Craft Assault were small and designed to carry the three dozen or so men of an infantry platoon.

not see any of the swimming tanks. There were lines of LCAs, the ones in the lead stationary, so presumably landed, others behind, as well as LCTs at wide intervals, probably carrying engineers in their special tanks designed to clear minefields and bridge ditches. There were some tiny dark shapes on the sand, which meant that some were already ashore.

There was a pattern to all this activity, and, in many ways, it was a familiar one, for they had spent months practising for this moment. Time after time they had driven set distances to a harbour, and even embarked, gingerly reversing the Shermans onto LCTs. At first, they usually came straight off once all was loaded, and then drove another set distance and route to simulate landing and pushing inland. A few times they had even put to sea and landed somewhere for real. One sergeant in the squadron had had the pleasure of invading his home town in Dorset, driving off the beach past the little cottage that he and his wife rented, until she was forced to leave when the War Department had cleared civilians from the area.

No one could say that the preparations had not been thorough, with drill after drill, exercise after exercise, as the intricate plans were formed, adjusted and refined. Landing craft and barrages were nothing new to any of them anymore, but even so this was different, in sheer scale as much as anything else. The seas were crowded with more vessels than he had ever seen before, even on the biggest exercise, and the barrage was far louder, bigger and lasting longer. The sky seemed almost as full as the sea, whenever you could glimpse it, with Allied aircraft everywhere, some fighters swooping low to pass at little more than wave level. It was simply staggering, past grandiose or awe inspiring, almost beyond words. This was GOLD Beach, the one in the middle of the landing. A few miles to the east was JUNO, where the Canadians were going in, and beyond that SWORD to complete the British sector. The Americans were to the west on two beaches, and they should have landed an hour ago because the tide came in earlier over there.

At the main briefing they had been told that more than seven thousand vessels were taking part in the landings, and staring around him he could believe it. This LCT was one of around eight hundred, all part of a constant stream heading from Southern England to France – and then back again, returning with the wounded to take on fresh troops, equipment and stores for the beaches and so on and so on. It was gargantuan, the cost of it all too appalling to contemplate.

James lowered his binoculars and stared up. A Spitfire flew over them, the pilot waggling his black and white striped wings enthusiastically.

'Makes you humble, don't it?' Symonds said as he watched the plane. 'All of this laid on for our benefit.' He sighed. 'I thought Alamein was big, but this...' The commander of the regiment's Recce Troop was one of the veterans, an old Desert hand sent as leaven to the 165th. 'Can make a fellow feel quite humble. ... And give him a blasted headache.'

James nodded, unable to speak, for at that moment he felt more insignificant than humble. What were they all, but tiny cogs in a vast, complex machine? The fate of the world was being decided, so the newsreels said, and that did not give the world or the Heavens much time to consider the fate of James Taylor. He realised that his right hand had come up to touch his breast pocket, or at least near to it. Like most of them he had his one-piece tanker's overalls on top of battledress tunic and trousers – and was still cold and wet. That meant he could not touch the pocket, let alone what was inside. Even so he felt guilty and embarrassed and quickly grabbed his binoculars again with both hands. No one seemed to have noticed, and there was no likelihood that they knew his secret, but he worried about looking strange, and then about seeming furtive.

Symonds did not seem to have paid any particular attention. 'Have you ever been to France?'

'Yes. Well, in a way. My father is fond of mountains and hiking, so we took the boat train a couple of times, but didn't linger. He was keen to get to Switzerland as soon as he could.' For some reason James chose not to mention earlier holidays to the Tyrol. 'I did not really see anything. At least I was spared the embarrassment of trying out my schoolboy French on the natives!'

'Always dicey, and I'm not sure that the conceived wisdom of speaking loudly and slowly is all it's cracked up to be.'

No one in the regiment knew much about Symonds, and even his age was unclear because there were lines around his grey eyes, and his once fair skin was tanned dark, but that was true of a lot of former Eighth Army men. It was known that he had had three tanks shot out from under him in the desert and had walked away without a scratch. There were rumours of wildness, which might explain the lack of any decoration, and more talk of an adventurous career before the War, with stories that he had been a professional card player on liners. It all made him sound like a cross between Raffles and the Saint.

'I love France,' Symonds said, his tone a good deal more serious than usual. 'Paris, of course, but also the coast. Spent a lot of time in Deauville...' The captain's voice trailed away and he seemed lost in thought. James had heard of the resort town and its famous casinos, which fitted well with some of the stories about Symonds. The captain came across as an educated, well-spoken and stylish man, who wore his uniform with a casual air that was only just acceptable – not least because the wearer was who he was. The 8th Army types were notorious for their individualistic and deliberately unmilitary costume. Yet the impression everyone had got of the new captain was that he was not a rich man, or well connected, at least anymore, none of which mattered because he certainly knew his job and was readily likeable.

'Good to be back,' Symonds said loudly, breaking the silence, or at least the steady drumming of the guns. He checked his watch. 'We're due in at H+120 at the earliest. Still another hour and a half to go.'

'Maybe.' The RN Lieutenant sounded sceptical. 'No one planned for this wind. We're being carried closer to the beach all the time.' They were still circling, one of half a dozen similar LCTs waiting their turn. At the moment they were heading towards the beach, but would soon veer away. Ahead of them was another craft bearing the rest of the Recce Troop, a Sherman or two and some scout cars. They were to land together, and advance together, all under Symonds' command, linking up with a company of infantry. The latter were to ride bicycles, adding a bizarrely primitive touch to all the complex ships, equipment and machinery deployed for the invasion. James still felt surprised at this part of their orders. You would have thought that the factories of Britain and the USA could have done better than pedal power at such a critical moment.

Symonds nodded to the sailor. 'Well, that was the plan, for what that's worth.'

'Tell that to the weather.'

'So, I presume we'll be going round the lighthouse a few more times before the man with the megaphone tells us that our time is up?'

The RN Lieutenant smiled. 'Something like that.'

Two spouts of white water shot up from the sea five hundred yards away to starboard, just in front of a line of LCAs heading for the beach. James just managed to stop himself from blurting out that some bloody fool was dropping rounds short as the realisation sunk in. This was the enemy.

Another two shells landed, behind the LCAs this time, close enough to drop spray onto one of them. He did not know who was in them, whether supporting companies of the assault battalions or the first of the reserves. James had lots of friends scattered around the Army, and some from childhood, especially the old gang from home. He knew that two of them, Mark Crawford and gloomy old 'Toby' Judd, were in the same battalion. He did not think they were with the Division on GOLD Beach, but then they might be.

The next salvo missed with one round and landed the other shell smack onto the deck of an LCA. The little craft disintegrated, pieces of metal and wood flying into the air with the spray. They were too far away to see the men shredded in the explosion, but, in an instant, nothing was left, just debris floating on the churning sea.

No one said anything. What was there to say? A platoon was gone, thirty or so men killed by high explosive, shrapnel or drowned, because no one was able to stop or reach them in time. The other LCAs kept ploughing through the surf towards the shore, and the next shells were nowhere near as close.

James focused his glasses and could see no trace at all, not even a patch of oil. There was nothing, and perhaps one of his friends had been aboard. If not, then they were surely men much like them, wearing much the same uniforms. He looked inshore, and there was an LCT turned side on to the beach, with dense black smoke coming from its stern. Another was stationary, far short of the beach, whether because of damage or having hit a sandbank or obstacle. On the sand itself he saw the little squat shapes of tanks, although he could not tell whether they were Shermans or Churchills. Focusing his binoculars, he had just decided that one was a Churchill when it exploded, the gout of flame vivid in the gloom.

'Our turn soon,' Symonds said beside him. He was not looking at the beach, and instead was staring up as another pair of fighters flew overhead.

08.55 hrs, somewhere in Sussex

Private 649 Judd was cold and lying out on the damp grass, the butt of the Bren gun comfortably tucked into his shoulder. His right hand was on the pistol grip, the left steadying the top of the gun just ahead of his cheek. The bipod at the front was steady, and Griffiths, his number two, was on his left side, ready to replace the magazine, or even change the barrel if they kept on shooting and the metal got too hot. To their left were the other two Bren teams from 9 Platoon.

The drizzle had not stopped, and Judd had to blink to clear his eyes and make sure that he was lined up with the target. His Christian name was William, usually Bill or Billy these days, although back in prep school he had been 'Toby' Judd, to boys who were untroubled by strict accuracy when it came to a good nickname. Bill's ears had stuck out impressively when he was young, and it was years before his head grew enough to catch up. Still, there were not many of those lads left anymore, and likely to be fewer still by the end of the year as the War dragged on.

Judd squeezed the trigger, relaxed, squeezed again, giving steady, three-shot bursts that made the canvas target quiver as the rounds struck home. The Bren was a precise piece of machinery and Bessie – the name he had given this one, not that he had ever, or would ever, admit it to anyone – was especially well behaved. Empty brass cartridges fell out from underneath the breech onto the grass.

The magazine was empty, and Griffiths must have been counting, for he plucked it away, and locked a fresh one into place, tapping Judd on the helmet to signify gun loaded. Before he could cock the weapon, a whistle rang out.

'Cease fire!'

Griffiths took off the loaded one and replaced it with an empty. Judd pulled the cocking handle to eject any round left inside, not that any were there. The sergeant duly inspected each weapon to make sure that it was safe, and then they were dismissed to join the rest of 9 Platoon.

'Get some tea and a wad, lads.'

There was a light truck parked at the back of the range, with a couple of the cooks to serve them.

'It's on, boys,' one of them assured them as they queued. 'Already started. They went in at dawn.'

'That's what you said last week,' Griffiths told him. 'And the week before.'

'Second Front now!' someone called in a high pitched voice, like one of the crazier speakers in Hyde Park.

'Gospel truth,' the cook insisted. 'You heard the planes overnight.'

They had, but there were so many big raids that it need not mean much. Everyone had been waiting for so long that it became ever harder to believe that the training really would come to an end.

'Alright, if you're so clever, where?' one of the men asked.

'They're saying Holland,' the cook said. 'That's what I heard, anyway. We'll be off soon.'

'Aye, aye, what's this we?' Griffiths asked. 'Don't reckon you'll be out in front.'

'I knew a lass who was out in front,' someone chipped in. 'Never had to use her hands to open doors.'

'We'll be with you, sonny boy,' the cook went on, ignoring the interruption. 'All the way.'

Griffiths grimaced. 'Christ, as if fighting the Germans wasn't bad enough, we'll still have to eat your food. Still, I might get poisoned and work my ticket that way.'

'What!' The cook waved his arms in mock anger, spilling tea from a mug he was holding. 'That's all the thanks I get. And me having worked at the Ritz.'

'That's right, the Ritz Café in Bognor,' someone suggested. 'Run by the Dung Brothers.'

'You spit in his tea, next time, cookie,' came another voice.

'Nah,' the first man said. 'Might make it taste better.'

'Come on, come on,' the sergeant barked. 'Get a move on. Fifteen minutes to get it down you and then we're off.' After an hour at the range, A Company was due for a route march.

Griffiths and Judd each collected a mug and a corned beef sandwich and carried them over to where the rest of the section were sitting on their packs to stay off the wet grass. They talked a little of the invasion, and whether or not it was happening, but mostly they talked and joked about nothing in particular, and there was more debate over what was showing in the camp cinema that night than the prospect of a Second Front.

10.35 hrs, a few miles away

'Great big spiders crawling up your arse!' the voices sang as the hob-nailed boots hit the tarmac of the road in time. The 1st/4th battalion of the Glamorganshire Regiment still had a substantial Southern Welsh component, testament to its origins as a Territorial unit, even though like most wartime battalions they now had men from all over the country. Perhaps that gave the singing a trace of melody, but only a trace, and there was more the sense of a boisterous crowd at a big match than of a trained choir.

'We had to join! We had to join!' They were at the chorus again, and Mark Crawford bit his lip to stop from joining in. 'We had to join old Churchill's army!'

The boots pounded against the road. No one ordered the men to march in step on a long haul like this. It simply happened, out of habit from men called up and chivvied to do everything in time – or at the double – morning, noon and night for months or years of their life. Even men out on a pass tended to fall into step without noticing whenever they strolled side by side. On a march it was easier, and helped too, because otherwise a man could easily tread on the heels of the one in front. So, without orders they went in time and in step, at least when on a good flat surface like this.

'Ten bob a week,' they sang and their ammunition boots rattled as they hit the ground. The rhythm was steady, almost hypnotic, and as mile followed mile, all you saw was the pack of the man in front and all you heard was the clashing of the boots. Mark was off to the side of his platoon, less enclosed than they were, but still he felt the almost trance-like mood of a long march. Even the Welsh did not talk much after the first mile or so, so each man was left to think, until even that was too much effort.

'Fuck all to eat!'

The boots pounded down again and again, and Kipling had got it right even if the man had never marched anywhere himself – boots, boots, boots, mile after mile, until there was nothing else in the world.

'Great big blisters...'

There was a rest every hour, just a short one, and then on they went, mile after mile.

'On yer bleeding feet!'

On and on, the unending clash of boots like a clock ticking away. A man had to empty his mind to stand it, but that made it all too easy to fall asleep, especially the longer the march went on and the more tiredness embraced them. Mark noticed that his batman, young Evans, was blinking, eyes not quite focused.

'Keep up, Evans,' Mark called as the men drew breath for the great crescendo at the end of the verse. The lad's head twitched round in surprise, but he was awake again.

'Churchill – yer bastard!'

At times in the Mess, Mark had heard the second in command angrily condemning the entire Education Corps as a bunch of 'damned Reds', but he did not think that there was anything especially political about the song. Sometimes it was not the Prime Minister but one of the officers whose legitimacy was challenged.

'We had to join!'

If they sang because they were browned off, as soldiers usually were, they really sang because they had to if they wanted to ward off sleep. A man who passed out was lucky if he simply slammed into the road, for more often, as he fell, he met the iron shod boot heel of the man in front, and that could break a nose, snap teeth, or shatter a jaw. Mark had seen it happen, and nearly fallen prey himself more than once back when he did his Basic Training.

'We had to join!'

The words did not matter too much, and it was easier to remember something funny and subversive. He recalled the old boys talking about the words put to hymn tunes back in the Last War – 'Wash me in the water that you washed your dirty daughter' and the like. Just sing anything, and stay awake, and keep going.

They reached the top of a hill, and the Sun broke through the clouds, bathing the South Downs in light. It was a pretty scene, one to make a man linger in peace time, but this was a route march not a hike, and they were not due another break for half an hour.

'We had to join,' they sang, and the boots thumped down again and again. At breakfast there had been rumours that the invasion was on, had already started, but no one really knew anything, and there were no fresh orders for them, so the routine continued. Weeks ago they had moved to this camp of Nissen huts and tents, all fenced in and closely guarded. There they waited, and trained, and waited, with all leave cancelled and special permission needed to leave the camp for any reason other than for exercises like this one.

First thing in the morning, the news had been exciting, and a little unnerving, but the long miles and clash of boots had driven all those thoughts away. No doubt he would learn more at the end of the day, and that was time enough.

'Churchill – you're barmy!'

Mark must have missed the last verse and that made him worry that he might faint. He halted, letting his Platoon pass by. He was very proud of them all, and determined to do his best when the time came.

There was Dalton, his platoon sergeant in his proper place at the rear, striding along like the countryman he was, not visibly hurrying, yet covering the ground fast. The sergeant was new to them, a regular who had served with the first battalion in Tunisia and Sicily, winning the MM in the process. He was supposed to carry a Sten gun, like Mark and the other officers and senior NCOs, but instead had a rifle, one of the old ones with its stubby muzzle and long sword bayonet. That little blue, white and red striped ribbon of the Military Medal on his tunic gave a man some leeway when it came to regulations, and his marksmanship on the range was uncannily good. A Sten was ugly, cheap, but very effective at a short distance. It was not made for accuracy, but then Mark was no more than an average shot with anything, although he had a knack for lobbing a grenade just where he wanted it to go. Thank cricket for that.

'We had to join, we had to join.'

On and on they went, down into a valley, where they were to loop around to come back parallel to the way they had come, so eventually back to camp. Yet the main road they were to cross was filled with traffic, truck after truck driving steadily south. The Company sat on the grass and watched them, happy to rest, especially now that the day had warmed up. They jeered at the men in the lorries who jeered at them, but everyone knew what this meant. It really was on.

12.25 hrs, GOLD Beach, King Sector

This was the third time the LCT had tried to land. The first, at the time they were due to go in, had ended when a cutter appeared, signalling frantically for them to turn around.

'There isn't room!' the RN officer on board yelled over to them, before making the line of LCTs turn about and go back. Shells fell among them, without doing more than send spray onto the decks.

'Hurry up and wait,' Symonds said, giving a wry smile. It was a familiar slogan in the Army, where a man always seemed to be rushing to catch up or hanging around with nothing happening.

Somehow James had expected a battle to be more efficient, or at least on time. Not that most exercises were either of those things, but all the drills for the crossing had been so thorough that he had wondered whether this would be different.

After a while, they were signalled to go in again. Shells were still dropping, and an LCT coming out from the beach was hit and set on fire, slewing around broadside to the shore and almost colliding with the one carrying the rest of the Recce Troop. Narrowly, with a grinding of metal, they scraped past, only to run onto some obstacle under the waves. There was an explosion, dull and not especially loud, and water shooting up against the bow.

'Signal says their ramp is wedged shut,' the RN Lieutenant told them as they kept going, more easily steering past the burning landing craft ahead of them.

'Tommy Price will be angry,' Symonds said, referring to the subaltern who was the only other officer in the Recce Troop. 'Never the most patient of men.'

'At least they should be alright,' James ventured, just as a couple of shells straddled the damaged LCT, which was now backing water very slowly.

There was a judder; James felt himself stagger and almost fall as their own craft came to a sharp stop. He held his breath, waiting for the mine to detonate, but nothing happened.

'Sandbank?' Symonds suggested. They were a couple of hundred yards from the sand of the beach.

The RN officer merely grunted, and ordered full astern.

'Move, you bitch,' the man at the wheel muttered. Their engine complained noisily, but they did not move. A shell landed, just behind them, and James felt the rush of fear because this might be a ranging shot, but no more came, or least no more shots anywhere near them. Up ahead the beach was crowded with vehicles, some burning, some on their side, and lots of people milling around. He could not see any German position still firing at them, and wondered whether all the observers able to call in artillery and mortars had been dealt with. On each side of the wheel was a mounting with a 20mm rapid fire cannon, with the sailors manning them obviously eager to let loose. They could see no targets, although it was not for want of searching.

As suddenly as it had struck, the LCT lurched back, and James staggered again, grabbing hold of Symonds' arm to stop himself from falling.

'Sorry, old boy, my dance card is full,' the captain drawled.

'Oh well, next time.'

'Bloody pongos,' the RN officer said and then gave orders for the coxswain to take them back and then head more to port and find a route that was clear.

This time they went straight in, past several other craft wrecked or stranded on the iron girders and other defences. There was debris in the water, especially timber, lifebelts, and more than a few shapes that could only be corpses or body parts floating in the surf.

'Nearly there,' the skipper assured them.

'Then we'd better go,' Symonds said, and was halfway to the ladder when he turned. 'Thanks for bringing us here. Look, this is rather embarrassing, but I seem to have left my wallet at home...'

'Bloody Army.'

The crews were already aboard the tanks. Symonds' Stuart – or Honey as he insisted on calling it, like all the Eighth Army men – was on its own in the prow, the others in pairs behind, first the other Stuarts and then the four Shermans of 3 Troop. As he ran forward the captain circled his arm to tell the drivers to start up. Not that the drivers could see him, but each crew had a man up on the turret who shouted the instruction. Engines coughed, banged and spluttered into life. The American-made Shermans ran sweetly once they were going, smoother and quieter than the British tanks, but they were noisy starters, and clouds of black exhaust smoke came from the hoods on the back of each tank. James almost felt he would be sick again, but held back.

There was a jolt, lighter than before, and the LCT came to a halt. James clambered up, using the top of the track as a foothold. Collins grinned from the turret hatch, then ducked down into the gunner's position. James clambered inside, grabbing the headset and pulling it on over his black beret. There was a helmet designed for tankers, but it was uncomfortable, and his was stowed in the big box fixed onto the rear of the turret along with their blanket rolls and all the other stores and luxuries tankmen had the chance to carry. Up ahead the ramp was lowering. James had to hope that it was going down on the sand itself or at least water shallow enough for them to drive through, for he could not see.

James switched on his headphones, but kept one ear uncovered for the moment. In the other was the all too familiar hissing and clicks of static, the constant companion of a tank on operations. After a long exercise it was days before he really felt that he was no longer hearing it, for it lingered just like the odour of the vehicles.

Symonds was up in the turret of his Honey and he gestured with his arm in the signal to go forward. Then he started off down the ramp. The other four light tanks followed one by one, exhaust fumes still dark and stinking and engines noisy. Back in '41 the Stuart had been a good tank, as well armed and armoured as anything British and a good deal more reliable. The design had not changed much, and it was a bit like a miniature Sherman. It was still about as fast as anything else on tracks, but that was about all to be said for it, and they were now used for reconnaissance, to find the enemy rather than to fight him. That was why 3 Troop was attached to them for this task, to offer a bit of muscle. James was not quite sure whether it was a mark of faith in him and his men or a sign that they were expendable, or, knowing the Army, simply their turn had come up on some list at HQ.

'Driver, advance,' James said into his microphone, for the last of the Stuarts was down the ramp. 'Take it easy,' he added. Whitefield was a very good driver, but inclined to show off, and this was not the moment to bang against the side of the exit, let alone come off the ramp.

They went forward, then Whitefield locked one track for a moment to turn and centre the Sherman ahead of the way out. The tracks were noisy on the metal deck, which was still slick with water, but the Londoner was good and thirty tons of tank went neatly out onto the ramp then into the water. Symonds and two of the Stuarts had already covered the short distance onto the uncovered sand through surf that did not come higher than their wheels. James glanced behind to see the next Sherman following him.

'Shit!' That was Collins, his head out of the gunner's hatch. James turned to see that the Stuart just ahead of them had gone a little to the right rather than following the one in front directly. It was now at a weird angle, tilted at thirty degrees, its right side sunk into the water. As he watched, it fell, like a man slipping on ice, dropping to the side and almost vanishing into what must have been a crater. The commander had ducked down into his hatch rather than jumping out, and he disappeared as the tank turned over completely, its tracks and wheels still turning, all that was visible over the water. They must all have passed close to the crater, probably left by a bomb for it was surely too big to have been made by the cruisers' shells, but only this one tank had edged further onto it, so that the sand and shingle gave way and it toppled over.

'Keep moving!' A man with the white stripe of the beach group on his helmet was yelling at them, waving them on. 'Don't stop!'

Whitefield edged them a little to the left to be on the safe side, without waiting for the order. A man appeared in the water next to the upturned tank, flailing around and spluttering for breath. Soldiers were running over to help.

'Keep going!'

James did as he was told, and with a last splash the Sherman was out of the surf. He was trying to remember whether the Stuart had a hatch underneath the hull, like the Sherman, because otherwise he could not think of a way the rest of the crew could escape, but he did as he was told and followed the four remaining Stuarts.

The beach was a cross between a Bank Holiday at Brighton from the number of people, Piccadilly Circus at rush hour before the War for the vehicles, and a stinking rubbish dump where someone was burning rubber tyres. The tide was on its way out, but slowed by the brisk wind, so that the strip of sand was narrow, making it all the more crowded. Engineers were working on the beach obstacles, some of the men up to their waist in water as they defused mines and set charges to demolish the frameworks of girders meant to stop landing craft and tanks. There was a dressing station in the lee of a pillbox, its concrete sides pockmarked from strikes, and not far away rows of bodies with all save their boots covered by blankets. A huddle of men in drab grey and shapeless caps sat down, guarded by a rifleman with a bandaged head. Everywhere men were running around shouting orders, asking questions, as the Beach Masters' teams tried to keep some sort of control over the situation. Now and then a shell landed, flinging up a fountain of sand. The ships were firing well inland and less constantly, and with the distance their noise was less. Now and again James' uncovered ear also caught the sound of small arms, but always some way away and invisible.

They waited a long time, queuing behind the half-tracks, trucks and self-propelled guns of an artillery battery, until at long last they were chivvied off the beach and up a road through the village.

So this was France, and more specifically Normandy, and for all the confusion they had landed mere yards from where they were supposed to be. The briefings had been astonishing in their detail, with maps, sand tables and plasticine models and dozens of photographs. James remembered one showing nervous German soldiers running for cover amid the rows of big girders forming obstacles. Others were surely postcards or holiday snaps from before the War. He recognised without any trouble the row of houses they were passing, just the same as a postcard except that the one on the end was missing half its roof. Everything was where the briefings had said it would be, and presumably they had been just as accurate when it came to marking the enemy positions.

'Bugger me, the Japs are here,' Collins said over the intercom as they passed a row of prisoners, hands clasped behind their bare heads. A pair of them in the lead were definitely Asians, and not what he had expected of Hitler's Master Race. None of the others were up to much either, seeming old or very young, and with baggy uniforms that fitted even worse than those of the sergeant major's nightmares that they were all used to seeing in the British Army. All were covered in pale dust, adding to the sense of age and fragility.

They did not look very frightening or formidable, but the blanket-covered corpses they had passed on the beach told another story.

14.45 hrs, behind the beach

They were waiting again, the tanks, four Shermans and four Stuarts, parked – or laagered as they said in the RAC – in a walled field half a mile inland. The infantry had not yet appeared.

'Probably had a puncture,' Symonds remarked. 'Still, we must wait a bit longer for our bicycling beauties... In the desert I would...' He trailed off. 'Well, that doesn't matter. Let's be ready when they come, hair brushed, trousers pressed, bunch of flowers in hand, other essentials in inner pocket in case they prove to be not such nice girls as we thought. Either way, we must look our best.'

Which was one way of saying that the crews needed to strip the tanks. They had spent days at the start of the month waterproofing each one, preparing them to land in far deeper water than they actually had. The big hoods over the exhausts were part of it, as well as shapeless brown covers over the gun mantlets, protecting them, but at the same time blocking all the vision ports and sights. Then there was resin gel, foul smelling, sticky stuff made by Bostick, which they had had to rub into every joint and every line on the metal to prevent leaks. All of the crews, James included, still had gritty black dust clinging to their fingertips, for the stuff would not wash off, even in petrol. Some of the wading gear came off quickly, blowing free when they set off a small explosive charge designed for the purpose, but the rest took a while, especially to make sure that the covers came off the guns without upsetting them. James was just wondering whether there was time to check that the sights were zeroed in accurately, when an officer appeared in the gateway to the field.

'Who the hell are you?' he shouted at them.

'One hundred and sixty-fifth RAC,' Symonds called back. The man was a major, a rather stout major, red of face and agitated of manner, and with considerable quantities of vegetation decorating the netting on his helmet. 'We've tea if you care for some,' Symonds suggested, in a spirit of hospitality.

The major did not move, and appeared lost for words, until he eventually managed to croak out, 'Don't you realise you're in an uncleared minefield!'

'We're bloody not,' Symonds responded. He did not swear often, but was never too impressed by authority, especially unfamiliar authority.

James stared nervously at the ground. Surely something would have gone off by now, after they had driven in and then wandered around, sorting out the tanks. Whether light stuff set off by a step or the heavy stuff designed to wait until something big drove over, they ought to have come to grief by now if there really were mines here.

'You bloody are, it's on my bloody map. Clear out!'

Symonds wore a khaki sweater, green corduroy trousers and fawn desert boots, and had no badge of rank, other than his manner and tone, which left the major uncertain of his seniority.

'We're waiting for someone,' Symonds explained. 'Leaning on a lamppost as it were.'

'Then you can damned well wait somewhere else. My sappers are due to clear this patch and they won't risk it with you there.'

'Oh well, anything to oblige.' Symonds gave the major a languid wave. 'Dear, dear, the people one meets,' he added under his breath. 'No manners at all... Well, young James, let us mount up and be on our merry old way.' He tipped his cup upside down to empty it. 'Let's clear up and be going,' he called to the crews. 'And just to be on the safe side, try to back out the way you came.'

That was easier said than done, not least because a driver could see nothing behind him with the tank itself in the way. Still, they did their best and no mines went off, and before long they were back on the road.

'Silly man's got the wrong ruddy map.' Symonds' voice came over the radio before he realised that he not only had spoken aloud, but had his microphone switched to the group setting rather than just for internal communication in his own tank. He coughed. 'Ah, I mean that a splendid member of that distinguished Corps, His Majesty's Royal Engineers and firework merchants, has acted in our best interests and in the finest traditions of the service. Splendid.'

'He's a card, isn't he.' Collins had made sure that he was on the internal link, so only the rest of the crew could hear him. James decided to let this comment about a senior officer pass.

'Ahem, Item to all stations,' Symonds announced formally. 'Our two-wheeled companions are still not here, so there is no sense in hanging around any longer. We'll do the job ourselves. Follow me.'

James could see the captain standing, waist up out of the hatch on his Honey. Most of the other commanders were a bit lower, but they all needed to see and the vision ports and periscope inside the turret were very limited in the view they gave. Each member of a tank crew had his role and relied on the others to do theirs. James remembered one of his instructors saying that the commander was the eyes and brain – and also remembered the muttered 'God help us,' from the back of the lecture room.

Symonds was probably right to press on. Their task was to head inland for some time and then turn east, following a road in the hope of linking up with Canadians coming from JUNO. The main link-ups would be elsewhere, but this was a decent road by local standards, and someone had decided that it was better if there were no Germans running up and down along it between the beaches. Symonds was probably right to press on in the circumstances, even though it would be nice to have infantry support. Whether right or wrong, it was his decision, and not up to James.

'Item to Baker Three.' That was James' call sign as commander of 3 Troop from B Squadron. 'I'll lead off with Recce and you keep close behind. Keep it tight. I don't want to get split up in all this traffic.' The road was jammed with the RA[5] battery and all its vehicles, as well as carriers and trucks and some of the big Churchills AVREs,[6] with dustbin sized stubby mortars instead of normal guns.

They kept together, gradually working their way through. At the first junction there was already a military policeman,

---

5   Royal Artillery.
6   An Armoured Vehicle Royal Engineers was a modified Churchill tank crewed by engineers rather than tankmen and designed to bridge gaps, cover soft ground and perform other tasks.

armband, blancoed gaiters and all, directing traffic. Eventually they were through and able to go faster.

'Item to all stations – eyes open, my tiddlywinks. There be Injuns out there, the varmints.'

'Mad bugger,' Whitefield muttered admiringly.

They drove inland. The Sun was out, with little cloud left, and the wings and canopies of the many Allied fighters over their heads glinted whenever the light struck them.

17.30 hrs, Officers' Mess, Camp B43, Sussex

Just about all the officers of the Glamorgans not on duty were crowded into the Mess, listening to the wireless. There was a lot of discussion and excitement, although even after all these hours the BBC were offering little detail. The invasion had started, the Allies had landed in Normandy, with parachutists, gliders and divisions coming in by sea, and it was all going well. Eisenhower had made a speech, as had plenty of others.

Perhaps the evening editions of the papers would be different, but the rest had gone out too early for the announcement, so the front pages were full of the fall of Rome and 5th Army chasing the Germans north, which was all marvellous, but as troops waiting to embark in support of the invasion of France, that was almost as distant as Burma. Mark had picked up a *Daily Mirror*, without really concentrating on the news from Italy. Inside, there was a rumour that Roosevelt might soon visit Britain, which was well enough and good luck to the old boy, but did not seem important. Still, near the back, *Jane* was undressing to take a bath, which was nice, and he could concentrate on that, which made picking up the paper worthwhile.

Officially the battalion had been told that there would be no move before noon on 11th June, so there was no immediate hurry to do anything they were not already doing. Thus life would continue as normal, at least for the rest of the week.

There was post, although disappointingly only two for him, both from his mother. Nothing from Anne again. By the sound of it, this would be the last post for a while, and, as soon as the thought came, he regretted the expression. Could be Last Post for him and all of them soon.

Still, there was no sense in brooding, and when they joined the great expedition was not up to him. They would go when ordered, and that was that, but just in case they were now cut off from the outside world. For two weeks no one had been allowed to send anything out of the camp, which at least had meant that he was spared the task of censoring his men's epistles. That was a nasty job, making him feel dirty, almost like a sneak eavesdropping on conversations. Most of it was dull, but to be honest some of the more passionate offerings from a couple of the married men were disturbingly candid. He was not always sure he understood, but guessed that such matters were of little concern to fifth columnists and enemy agents. Corporal Brown was such a nondescript little man, but in his letters he was Errol Flynn, not simply to his wife, but to a couple of girlfriends. Pretty good corporal though, whatever his morals.

Mark put aside these thoughts and settled in a chair away from the radio so that he could read his letters in some sort of peace. His mother wrote of the usual little things of life back home there on the Bristol Channel. It was still a small town, and even with all the comings and goings of wartime, the ships in and out of the docks in town and in Cardiff and the other nearby ports, everyone still seemed to know everyone else – or, as his mother would surely say, everyone who mattered, albeit in her case that was less about money or class and more about what she considered proper and decent.

There was not much news of his brothers. John was definitely a prisoner of the Japanese, which meant at least that he had not been killed, even if the stories coming out about the brutal treatment of POWs was bound to make you worry. Chris was still at the hospital where they were doing their best to give him back a face more than two years after his Hurricane went down in flames. Apparently, he still hoped to return to active duty and Mother was torn between wanting him to be well enough and fearing for what might happen if he was.

Mark was the youngest, not so tall, handsome or confident as his older brothers. On the rare occasions his father bothered to write to him, he encouraged his remaining active son to play his part for King and Country, while always leaving the impression that his expectations were not high. Mr Crawford was very keen on England and the Empire and loved to read in the papers of victories. In the Last War he had worn uniform, but never left Britain, although from the confidence with which he spoke of the world and war no one would have guessed. His father was impatient for victory and gave the impression that Mark and everyone else in the Forces was not really pulling their weight. In contrast his mother asked about his health, hoped that he was keeping warm and staying out of draughts, and was regular in his bowel movements.

She also gave him news of friends, not that there had ever been many, at least really close ones, and not simply fellows he quite liked and who quite liked him. Deep in his soul, Mark felt that 'quite' summed up his life so far. He was quite good at school, quite pleasant, quite good looking – at least according to the mothers if less so their daughters – and quite good at sport. He was a decent cricketer, even more than decent, and had been lucky enough to fall in with a crowd of genuinely good players, at least by schoolboy standards. Their prep school was small in their small town, with a few boarders among the day boys, but for a couple of years they had beaten every single one of the bigger schools, whether public or grammar, winning the regional trophy. Good old Jimmy Taylor had led them, batting at three and often carrying the innings, as well as adding some cunning off spin to the tempestuous pace of 'Toby' Judd, who had always been hefty and tall for his age. Some of Mark's dearest possessions, displayed on the little mantelpiece of his room back home, were a miniature of the trophy and a photograph of them all in whites, blazers and caps. All in all, he had never been happier, and certainly never had better and closer friends, than in those days. Jimmy, Toby and Ed Fellowes had shared common interests as well as the sport and they had spent a lot of time together.

Then they had all gone their separate ways, most to board in far flung parts of the country – James first, along with the other boys who were in that class ahead of them. Mark had made an effort to keep in touch, writing short, rather naïve letters and keeping on writing them until the other lads replied. His mother was good at hunting out news, and he used to pass it on to everyone else. The War came soon enough, and initial fears that it would be over before they got their chance turned in time into certainty that they would play their part. They had too, all of them, because – well, because they were such a decent bunch of fellows.

His mother's second letter informed him that Naughton had gone down with a corvette somewhere in the Atlantic, and that Fellowes was missing, his bomber seen to fall over Germany. There might be a chance, but then there might not, and according to his mother the family were keeping a brave face on it all.

That left three of them, Taylor, Judd and himself, as the only ones left from that winning side from '37. Just three, and the others had all done their bit, and from all he heard – and knew of them – done it gallantly.

Now they were gone. One had married, but not had time to have children before he was posted overseas and died of typhoid fever somewhere in Burma. Their families mourned and remembered them, but they had had so little time to make a mark on the world. Mark tried not to wonder whether he and the other two would get a chance.

Judd was in the battalion, ironically enough, if in a different company, and since the fellow was in the ranks it did not give them much chance to mix. On leave it was a different matter, and Mark was sure he did not show any side, even when it came to their joint pursuit of the lovely Anne. A mean part of him wondered whether she had written to Private Judd when she had not written to him, but he fought down such an ignoble thought. Anne was in the Wrens, so was surely as busy as they were, and she had given no special sign to either of them. Damned fetching in her uniform though. The Wrens certainly had the trimmest outfits of any of the women's services.

They were called for dinner, so Mark folded the letters neatly and put them away.

18.45 hrs, inland from GOLD Beach

At first everything went well. They pushed on, at times alongside other troops doing the same thing, each with their own objectives. They even passed a few dozen men on bicycles, although not from the unit assigned to work with them. The maps they had been given were pretty good, especially the final versions issued within the last couple of days and with the real names in place of the codewords used before.

Away from the beach there was less sign of destruction, and this was pretty country, with ripening fields of green wheat and barley, lots of walled orchards, some still with traces of fading blossom. In some ways it reminded James of Devon, not so much the hilly north coast so often visited during summer holidays, but further south where it was flatter. All in all, it did not seem so very foreign, and there was almost the sense of being back on exercise. Even the crumps of artillery and the snappier cracks of rifles and machine guns did little to break the spell, for they still seemed always to be some way off. He almost expected to see umpires with their armbands, waiting to declare a road as blocked or a vehicle or unit as knocked out.

'Item to all stations, Edinburgh up ahead.' That was the codename for the crossroads where they were due to turn east. 'Looks like there has been some trouble. Keep your eyes peeled. Out.' That was a surprisingly formal message for Symonds.

James noticed that the light tanks ahead of him were swinging their guns to cover arcs on either side, just able to see over the walls lining the road. This was a main route, wide enough for traffic to pass in both directions. There was a sack of old clothes by the wall on the right – no, not mere rags, but what was left of a man, a German from his grey uniform. As they passed, James saw his face. It was like a waxwork, human shaped, but wholly lifeless and with a greenish hue. There was no sign of any wound, and it was almost as if someone had tossed a mannequin from a shop window by the roadside. His mouth was wide open, a black circle as if locked in a last scream of horror or pain.

'Item to Item stations, I'll go straight across. Able, you go left, Baker and Charlie, you go right. Halt and take a look around. Baker Three, you stay back, over.'

'Baker Three to Item, understood. Baker Three, halt behind me.' James switched to the intercom. 'Driver, halt.' They were taught not to use names in action, but to stick to roles. He was scanning what he could see of the crossroads as the Stuarts surged ahead, flinging up more than the usual dust from their tracks. There was a shape at the junction, big and square, and after a moment he realised that it was one of the Sherman DDs, the lowered canvas sides giving it an enlarged and unfamiliar appearance.

'Item to all stations, seems quiet. Anyone see anything, over?'

Each commander in turn reported in to say that they could see nothing dangerous.

'Item to all stations, looks like the party here is over. Let's go. I'll lead again, out.'

The Stuarts sorted themselves back into order and Symonds led them along the road to the left. James brought 3 Troop behind them. As they came to the crossroads, he saw that the DD tank was knocked out, a neat round hole in the side of the turret. On the far side of the crossroads was a German truck, windows all smashed, sides and cab riddled with holes and tyres flat. There were a couple of bodies beside it with the same waxy shade as the other one. Behind was another vehicle, equally shot up. This was not like an exercise anymore, and something was nagging at the back of his mind, something odd and wrong, and it was only as they turned and he read the name on the wooden sign that he realised.

'Road signs,' he said aloud without meaning to.

'Sorry, sir, didn't catch that.' Collins was back inside the turret, ready on the gun.

'They've still got signs to tell you the way,' James explained. Back home everything had been taken down early on in the war. It was rather like blackouts and window glass covered in tape to stop it shattering: things you had become so used to that their absence was distinctly odd.

'It's as if they wanted to be invaded,' Albright said, getting a laugh from the others. The lad had a gift for irony.

They went steadily down the road. This was the very edge of the GOLD sector, and nearly everyone else was busy pushing further inland rather than heading to the east. Symonds halted when they approached a bridge, in truth little more than a culvert, with a few houses on the far bank. He ordered 3 Troop off the road, into a field to the right where the ground rose slightly, so that they could offer supporting fire if necessary. Only when they were in place did he move, crossing the bridge and driving past the main row of half a dozen buildings. Another house was separate from the rest, a couple of hundred yards beyond.

'Item to all stations, follow me across,' Symonds said after a while. 'No trouble here. The natives say the Boche have gone.'

The bridge was narrow, but proved strong enough to take a Sherman's weight, and they pushed up behind Symonds, who was chatting away to a rather dour old man wearing a flat cap and shabby black coat. One of the houses had a great gash torn in its roof tiles, presumably from a stray round from one of the ships, because there was no other sign of damage. That most likely explained why, apart from the old man, all they saw were nervous faces at the windows.

'All stations, let's go,' Symonds said, then turned to grin back and wave at James and the other tank commanders. Then the captain's neck exploded in a great gout of blood.

James saw – or thought he saw – the tiny flash before they heard the smack of the bullet and crack of the rifle.

'Gunner, thirty degrees left, house on left of road. Sniper in top window.'

James was not really thinking, simply reacting, the words coming out as a formula, even as he saw Symonds drop down into the hatch, blood still spurting from his neck. The commanders in the other Stuarts were jerking back down at the same time, and the second bullet just missed the head of one sergeant.

'On,' Collins reported. 'Clear shot.'

'Co-ax,' James ordered, wanting to make sure that they were not about to shoot their own.

The gunner had two buttons on the floor in front of him, one for the big 75mm main gun and the other for the machine gun next to it and aligned to the same target. Collins must have stamped on the wrong one, for the big gun boomed, shaking the Stuart only a few yards in front.

His aim was good and the shell went straight through the open window, then exploded, punching bricks out of the wall and bringing down half the roof. The co-axial machine gun started to chatter, as Collins realised his mistake and the bright red tracer went into the dust and smoke.

'Give him another to make sure,' James ordered. 'Baker Three to all stations,' he said switching to the radio network, 'reckon we got him, but there might be others. Spread out into the field to our left and keep your eyes peeled. All stations acknowledge, over.'

Once they reported in and started to move, James continued. 'Item, how is Sunray?' The army's odd codename for a commander seemed all the more incongruous at the moment.

There was hissing, garbled noise across the airwaves, before a Scottish voice answered. 'Bad sir, really bad... Oh Christ, hold him, man.'

'Do what you can, out.'

There were no more shots, no sign of other enemies, and James had to wonder at the courage or folly of a lone soldier willing to take on eight tanks with just his rifle.

James waited and nothing more happened. Still, they could not be sure. 'Pass me the Sten and a couple of grenades,' he said over the intercom. 'Collins, you do the same. Co-driver, come up and take over the seventy-five.' He was about to order some of the other crews to dismount when he saw a corporal climb out of one of the Stuarts, sub machine gun in hand. Other men in the other Recce tanks were doing the same, and now that they were outside he could not reach them over the radio. Instead, he jumped out to join them, keeping the hull of the Sherman between him and the house. His back was already slick with sweat, for his clothes had dried out and having overalls on top of the battledress was proving to be very hot. He licked his lips, found himself touching the spot over his breast pocket, although since he had a Mills bomb in his hand he could not feel anything at all apart from the metal pressing against him.

Five minutes of cautious movement brought them to the front door of the house. Collins kicked it open; James jumped through, Sten gun ready, rather than a grenade, because he had made up his mind that there were no more enemies and feared that he might kill civilians. His boots crushed shattered glass from a window and the air was thick with dust. No one was in the hall or any of the rooms. Upstairs, in the remnants of a bedroom, was what was left of the German soldier, head missing, along with his right arm and most of his shoulder. Flies already buzzed over him, and over the blood spattered across the bed clothes.

'We got the Jerry,' Collins said nervously, his boot prodding at broken china on the bare floorboards. Next to it was a framed picture of a rather severe looking couple, neither smiling as they stared at the camera.

James had seen bombed out houses during the Blitz; the destruction, the chemical reek of explosives mingling with the musty smell of torn apart furniture and walls was all very familiar. Yet never before had he been responsible for smashing up someone's home. It did not seem real even now.

'Right, back to the tanks,' he told Collins and the others. One of the Recce men was carrying a pillowcase stuffed with something or other, and James supposed that he ought to stop any looting, save that he knew that he would be a hypocrite after ordering Collins to shoot the house up. He did nothing, mainly because the realisation was at last coming home. With Symonds down, he was in charge.

Symonds was still alive, at least so far, but had lost a lot of blood and there was probably more coming out in spite of the two dressings they tied around his neck. James sent him back on the rear deck of his Honey, the loader cradling the captain in his arms, while the gunner took command and guided the driver. They went at high speed, for the Stuarts had an engine originally meant to power a fighter plane, and whatever else you could say about them they were fast. They vanished down the road, a plume of dust marking their progress, but at best it would be three or four miles before they were likely to find a dressing station, and they might have to go all the way back to the beach. Symonds had been so pale, unable to speak or move on his own, that it was hard to see him lasting.

'Baker Three to all stations. Form up on me. Three Troop behind me and Item behind them. We had better push on.' James felt that he ought to go first, although that was not what their training taught. He could sense how on edge everyone was. Symonds had seemed indestructible, and now he was gone, and their lives were all in the hands of a twenty-year-old subaltern. 'Keep your eyes peeled, out.'

James had adjusted the commander's seat so that he could sit and have just his head out of the hatch. Less, and it was hard to see. He had also fished his helmet out and put it on. It was designed to fit with headphones, but it was still heavy and uncomfortable. Glancing back, he noticed that several men were wearing them.

'Driver, advance,' he ordered Whitefield.

The Sun was lower in the sky, but this was June and the days were long. There were still pairs of fighters roaming around above them, but they seemed higher up now than earlier.

The tanks went steadily, slower than before. Even so their tracks still churned up plenty of dust from the unmetalled road.

19.55 hrs, Camp B43, Sussex

'See you there, Billy?' Griffiths asked.

Judd nodded. 'Just want to finish my tea.'

There were in the NAAFI, and the hubbub of low conversation told of men contented after an ample dinner and copious amounts of tea. Say what you like about the Army – and given the opportunity most of them could say plenty – it fed you. One of Judd's chief memories of the years before he had joined was of hunger – constant, insidious hunger. Soldiers ate better than civilians, at least in terms of quantity. There was not much flavour in powdered egg and whatever mysterious ingredients had gone into the pie they had had this evening, but there was plenty of it and the chips had been good. That was something even Army cooks could not mess up.

Judd felt full and he felt well. All in all, after over a year of training he was a little taller and certainly heavier, but the weight was all muscle. He doubted that he had ever been as fit in his life and he had always taken training seriously, whether for cricket, tennis or in later years boxing. The discovery that he had a good record at these things meant that the battalion had got him to play rugby, which he just about understood, as well as football and hockey, which he did not. Army logic was that if you were good at one sport, you must surely be good at everything else. He was not, but that did not seem to matter and he was still chosen no matter how badly he performed.

'I'll see you there,' Griffiths said. 'You've got twenty minutes. Don't want to keep Rita waiting, do you?'

Judd smiled dutifully. The cinema was showing some new American musical, in colour no less. It was bound to be full of the sentimental songs that the rude and licentious soldiery lapped up – and it starred Rita Hayworth. What was it someone said preoccupied the British soldier: the 'Three Fs' of food, football and – if you wanted to be polite – females. 'I'll be along. Keep me a seat.'

The NAAFI was clearing, with most heading off to see the picture. Others were clustering in one corner, starting seriously on the beer, but they were still fairly quiet and for the moment the place was calm. Peace, quiet, and least of all solitude, were not something the Army was good at. Judd liked films, even if musicals were not his favourite, and even if all the cigarette smoke in the air would mean that everyone watched the screen through a haze. For the moment, if he tried hard, he could almost ignore the tobacco scent here in the NAAFI, and the tinny music in the background, and revel in as much quiet as he was likely to get. He cherished these moments.

'Hullo, Judd.' One of the staff was coming round to mop the tables. A short, plump woman who was always chattering away, Judd could not remember her name, although knew her by sight. 'Did you hear about Evans? Mr Crawford's batman in C Company?' NAAFI staff got to know the troops on a base very quickly.

Judd shook his head.

'Caught deserting... Poor kid. They shouldn't call up weak little things like that. I mean, how's he going to cope fighting the Germans? Couldn't fight his way out of a paper bag that one. And now he's in... Oh, pardon me for living, I'm sure,' she said as Judd sprang to his feet and turned away.

'Sorry, lass. Just remembered I'm on guard,' he lied.

'I'll forgive you this once.' She gave him a wide grin. Her teeth were not a good colour. 'Don't you get put in jug as well!' She laughed. 'That's good that is. Judd in jug!'

'Send it in to ITMA,' Judd suggested over his shoulder, boots echoing on the polished floor as he hurried away. He was worried, for a few weeks ago he and Evans had been left out in the wilds during an exercise, tasked with guarding a broken down carrier. That was an important task, for no doubt a black market in Bren gun carriers was thriving these days, but orders were orders, even though whoever had given the order had promptly forgotten about all them, so that it was not until the next day that someone showed up to relieve them. He had never met Evans before that, but with so much time inevitably they had talked a fair bit, and gradually the lad had opened up and told Judd things he had never told anyone else. He could not help thinking that this all might have something to do with some of the dark stories the boy had told.

There were clusters of soldiers chatting and smoking outside the NAAFI and Judd searched the faces for the right person.

'Hey, Billy-boy, got a fag?' Hutton from HQ Company was fond of the joke, as well as being someone who always seemed to know what was happening. He was perfect, and did not need any prompting.

'What, no? Mean git. You heard about three seven four Evans? Tried to do a runner. Well, can't blame him, what with the invasion. You must have heard that on the news? All those bombs, all those ships blasting the shore. Hell, someone could get hurt. Odd thing is he took a revolver with him and a dozen rounds.'

'Maybe he doesn't want to wait for us to be sent,' someone suggested. 'He's off to call Hitler out.' The man switched to what he felt was an American drawl. 'See here, pardner, this here Berlin ain't big enough for the both of us. Go for your iron.' He mimicked a quick draw, his thumb coming down a few times as if his hand was a gun, then raised it and blew imaginary smoke away from the tip of his finger. 'Evans, the fastest gun in the Valleys.'

Judd nodded and ignored their calls as he hurried off. He knew he was right, and the lad was not running from anyone, but had probably wanted to do the bravest and most terrible thing he could imagine.

Mark Crawford was a good friend, one of the best, and a decent fellow. He was also Evans' platoon officer, and that was the point. Mark was an officer while Bill Judd was a humble private, although he had never really mastered the humble bit. Officers and other ranks, that was how the Army worked, with a divide almost as strong as a Hindu caste. In a sensible, reasonable world, he could just call on his old friend, explain what he knew and help Mark make sure that the authorities understood. Instead, this was the Army, and apart from that the world was busy tearing itself to shreds so could hardly qualify as sensible.

Proper procedure was to see 9 Platoon's sergeant and request to see the officer, leading to an interview with the lieutenant, a request to see the Company Commander, and then eventually get permission to speak to Crawford in C Company. It would probably happen, for most of the men involved were sensible, and a soldier had his rights, but at best the process would only start in the morning and would take hours at the very least, especially as they were due to go on another route march. Judd wondered what to do, then saw a tall, stately figure striding across the track ahead of him.

Judd worried about a lot of things, and one of them was whether or not he would be brave when the time came, and whether he would let anyone down. Even at nineteen, childhood dreams of heroism struck him now as thin and unlikely. Yet somehow he walked forward, stiffened his shoulders and turned the walk into a march, before halting and coming to attention.

'Permission to speak, sir.' Judd was a praying man, at least at times during his life, but this was akin to slapping the Divinity on the shoulder with a hearty, 'How are you, me old mucker!'

The Regimental Sergeant Major stopped and stared at him. There was a faint trace of surprise and perhaps a raised eyebrow, which was more emotion than RSM Roach usually displayed.

This was madness, pure madness, and Judd knew that he was quivering as he stayed to attention, the muscles in his thighs twitching. He noticed Griffiths and a couple of others from the section off in the shadow beside a Nissen hut. Their mouths were hanging open.

'Well, Judd, what have you got to say?' Roach rarely spoke very loudly, though his shout was believed to carry for miles and be capable of uprooting trees.

Judd tried to answer. His mouth was dry, his tongue like sandpaper. 'Yes, sir,' he croaked, fully expecting to be put on a charge or at least told that if he had nothing better to do with his time then the sergeant major would soon find something for him. He had visions of a blunt knife and a mountain of potatoes, or a little flannel and orders to clean the latrines.

'Out with it, lad.'

'Sir, it's about Evans, sir. Three seven four Evans, sir. I think I know what this is about. Please, sir, it's important, sir. It's not what everyone thinks.' He was on the edge of hysteria, picturing his younger self in the headmaster's study. 'He's not running, sir.'

'Go on.'

'No, sir. He just wants to shoot his father.'

The eyebrow went up a fraction of an inch.

'Come with me, lad, but first, straighten your ruddy hat! Now then, forward march, left, right, left, right, get those arms up – who do you think you're waving to!'

21.50 hrs, inland from GOLD Beach

The sky to the west was a blaze of reds and golds as the Sun started to set. Soon it would be dark, although they were not so far from home that this would happen too quickly and instead the light would fade gradually. James could not remember for certain, but he thought that there was no Moon tonight.

Tanks were not supposed to operate in the dark. In the daytime it was hard enough to see out, even with the hatches open. At night it was impossible, and at the same time the tanks were big shadows, easy for anyone on foot to spot against the sky. They were vulnerable, terribly vulnerable to infantry with bazookas or bold enough to climb up and drop a grenade into a hatch.

Their little force had not reached its objective. No, that was not quite fair, for James was in charge and he had decided not to try. As he led the column, they had come to a rise and just as his Sherman was breasting it, there was a snap in the air above his head as something steamed past at high speed. Bullets were pattering against the gun mantlet and just ahead of him.

'Driver, reverse,' he barked as he ducked his head down, and only then did he hear the boom of the gun and the mad, tearing sound of machine guns. Whitefield must have sensed the order before he spoke, because he shifted straight into reverse and they went back. Thankfully, everyone was keeping to proper distances, so there was plenty of space behind them. In seconds the Sherman was back behind the low rise, and James could no longer see the wooded hill half a mile to the north of the road. There was an anti-tank gun up there, along with infantry, and he was lucky that the enemy had fired too soon because, if they had waited, they would have had a much better target.

Luck only went so far. The other LCT had carried an observation tank, with powerful radios so that the Royal Artillery officer riding in it could call in the batteries, but it had not got ashore after the collision. He had no other link with the gunners, let alone the ships' guns, who could easily have pulverised the wood where the enemy were positioned. There were fighters overhead, fewer now that the day was ending, and none appeared to have seen the ambush. If they had had infantry with them, as had been the plan, then he reckoned that there was a good chance that they could have cleared the ridge. Without them it was hopeless, little more than suicide.

James gave up on the objective. He had no idea whether or not the Canadians had got there to meet them, for no one had thought to give them a common frequency on the radios. Hopefully they were not left out on a limb by his failure to rendezvous with them.

They pulled back a few hundred yards to a walled orchard, and spread the tanks out so that they formed a box, guns over the top of the old stone wall. The Germans had not followed them, not yet at least, and did not seem to have mortars or guns on call. One man from each crew went outside to act as sentry, doing a two-hour stag[7] before being relieved. Another was given a turn to sleep, while the rest sat in their positions inside the tanks, waiting in case of attack. It was going to be a long and nervous night.

His own Sherman was in the corner of the orchard closest to the enemy, overlooking a paddock where five mares were grazing and rolling in the dust. As dusk was falling, another horse appeared from somewhere, a stallion.

'He's a big 'un,' Whitefield commented. 'Probably a bit slow, but might be decent over the sticks.' James suspected that the

_____

7   Slang for sentry duty.

HILL 112   47

Londoner could not tell one horse from another, let alone mare from stallion.

Collins was trying to sleep in the driver's position, Albright was on guard outside, so Whitefield had come up to man the gun with the co-driver, Miller, as loader.

As they watched, the stallion proceeded to mount each of the mares in turn, and, apart from murmurs of wonder and admiration, Whitefield said little.

'Like a Yank in Piccadilly after dark,' he said when all was over.

It was a strange way to close the first night of the invasion. Later, with the night, came German bombers, or at least so James had to assume. Behind them, the darkness over GOLD Beach was filled with tracer arcing up into the sky. There was no way of telling how many bombers there were, whether they hit anything, or if any were brought down. Still, it was a more colourful and restrained display than the morning's barrage.

D+1, Wednesday 7th June

05.35 hrs, Normandy

A JUNE NIGHT was short, even when you were lucky to get an hour's sleep, propped up as best you could in the driver's compartment. Whitefield had the knack of bending himself into a pose where he could relax and snore his way to peace and contentment, but James could not master it. He made himself stay there when it was his turn, worried that to get up would hint that he did not trust Sergeant Dove to keep an eye on everything, or that he would make everyone believe that their lieutenant was nervous and fussy.

He must have dropped off once or twice, because he shifted and cracked his head on one of the many pieces of angular metal to be found inside a tank. It could not have been for long and, if anything, he felt even more weary and stiff when his watch confirmed that the hour was over and he could give someone else a turn.

James also felt cold, in spite of his uniform and the overalls on top. When he jumped down from the Sherman his feet hurt when they struck the ground. They felt numb, and it was an effort not to shiver. Normandy was as cold as England often proved in the early hours while out on exercise, if not quite as bitter as North Wales. Back in the autumn he and a lot of other officers from armoured regiments had been sent on a course based near Snowdonia, where they had spent weeks on route marches, assault courses and long runs. No one ever explained how this was supposed to prepare them for controlling a troop or more of tanks in the field, but 'theirs was not to reason why' and so on.

Thankfully the night had been quiet, so perhaps the Germans were few in number or under orders to defend rather than attack. Either way, if any patrols had come to look at the tanks then they had done it well, not being seen by anyone.

Before dawn James had ordered a stand-to, something normally left to the infantry, who ought to be out in front ahead of the vulnerable tanks. For an hour they were all awake, one crewman out as sentry to see better and the rest in their positions.

It was cold. When it came down to it, a tank was simply a big metal box on tracks. James groped back in his mind to science lessons at school, where they had talked about metal as a conductor. In practical terms that meant that a tank was damned hot in the Sun and damned cold in anything else. They were also cramped and uncomfortable, and if the Sherman was better designed than many, there was still very little space.

Albright and the other wireless operators had checked that all radios were on the same net, and the steady crackle and occasional whine filled everyone's ears as they waited.

Slowly the day came, bright red at first as the Sun rose before climbing into the low cloud. There was drizzle in the air and a heavy dew on the ground. Not a good day to bat, James found himself thinking, even though he tried to stay focused on spotting any threat before it struck.

No one spoke very much. There was a brief alarm when Sergeant Dove reported movement.

'False alarm,' he reported a few moments later. 'Just one of those horses.'

'Bloody hell, that bugger at it again,' Whitefield said on the internal link. 'I should have half his strength.'

In fact, as the light grew, there was no sign of the stallion, which suggested that the field opened onto another, perhaps somewhere beyond the point where the hedge turned and blocked their line of sight.

The stallion was not there, nor, more importantly, were any Germans, and with full daylight and the hour complete, James stood them down. He kept the turrets of half the tanks manned, with one sentry provided by each of the other crews, while everyone else began the morning routine. Some made tea or prepared the last tins of self-heating soup, while others checked that everything was in working order.

James was not sure what to do. He guessed that he ought to advance again, simply to make sure whether or not the enemy were still blocking the road. It might be possible to outflank them, leaving the road and approaching from an unexpected direction, because after all tanks were designed to go cross country. Yet that would mean leaving the road open, and his job was to prevent the Germans from using it. With just seven tanks, he really did not want to divide his force. Ultimately it came back to his lack of infantry. Without them, it was hard to do anything.

He had made up his mind to move at 06.30, and to lead again, because he did not feel he could ask anyone else to do that in the circumstances.

Dove was unimpressed. 'Not your job, sir. If you get brewed up right at the start, then where are we?'

James grinned. 'Well, you would be in charge, so I'd hazard the Troop would be better off.' Part of his mind was wondering why British tankmen talked about a tank being destroyed as brewing up, the same expression they used for making tea. He could not work out why he had never thought of it before.

'No, sir,' Sergeant Gordon of Recce Troop insisted. 'I'm senior, so I would be in command. But I am also Recce, sir. It's our job to go in front – and clear off sharpish if we meet trouble. I should go first, a good hundred yards ahead. That's what we're trained for.'

Neither sergeant was a veteran or a regular, although both

had been in the Army since early on in the war and were with the regiment when it was first formed. James guessed that each man was in his middle to late twenties, so not really that many years older than him, yet they seemed so much wiser, so much more assured. He did not know much about Gordon, but knew Dove was married, with two little daughters, and had been a working man before he was called up. Perhaps that explained the air of capability he had. Responsibility was nothing new to him, whereas James had never really been responsible for anything important before he went into the Army. Even then, the Army told you what to wear, what to do and drummed routine into you from the very start.

'Very well,' James conceded.

In the event, the sound of engines and the clatter of tracks approached from behind them before they were ready to move. They could not see who it was, so all mounted up and switched on engines. They were just turning two of the Stuarts to face that direction when a scout car appeared, drab green in colour, and with a man wearing a very British beret in the open hatch. As it came closer, they could see the fox badge of their brigade and the unit number 998 painted on the front of its hull. Behind it came a Sherman, followed by more.

James let out a sigh of relief. The regiment had caught up. In some small way, even here in France, they were home again.

09.35 hrs, near Camp B43, Sussex

Judd and the rest of A Company were on another route march. There were limits to what could be done in the way of training when the whole county, and most of Southern England, was crammed full of camps, depots and stores waiting to support the invasion. The coming days would be filled with lectures, and sessions checking weapons and equipment, because there simply was not space for any manoeuvres. There was PT as well, but really only these marches helped to keep them in some sort of trim as they waited for the summons to a port.

Talk at breakfast had mainly been of the invasion, for the papers were full of it today, and there was a little more information on the wireless. The Allies had landed on the French coast in Normandy and were doing well, having taken both Bayeux and Caen. This afternoon there was due to be a briefing for the whole battalion on the current state of things over there, which ought to be interesting. Judd was struck by the parallel with 1066, for this seemed a Norman conquest done in the other direction. Still, Henry V had also landed in Normandy and that had gone well. He had seen the new film only a few weeks ago, and liked the way they had started off as if it was all in the theatre. The rest of the section sitting alongside him had sniffed at the 'load of pansies mincing about', but as it went on he could feel them being drawn into the story.

Army life was full of surprises, and one of many had been listening to Griffiths chatting in detail about it all afterwards, about the Scottish and Welsh captains, Ancient Pistol and the rest.

'It's a bit like music, isn't it?' Griffiths had concluded. 'The words, I mean. You don't always catch all of them or know what they all mean, but somehow it goes straight to the heart.' No one seemed that bothered about the stage Welsh of Fluellen, which he thought would have annoyed them.

'Well, what do you expect from the bloody English,' was all that was said.

Yes, his fellow soldiers often surprised him, whether in a good way or bad.

Evans' story was one of the bad things, although it was about life outside rather than inside the barracks. It made him realise that for all the disappointments and hardships of his life, in many ways he had been lucky.

Last night the RSM had taken him to one of the huts used by Headquarters Company, and left him there to sit down and wait while he made things happen; no one in the battalion, or probably any battalion, could make things happen as fast as its senior warrant officer. After a while, officers appeared, first Mark Crawford and Major Jackson, CO of D Company, and then, a moment or so later, in strolled Judd's own platoon commander, Mr Buchanan, who gave him a nod and said that he was there as 'prisoner's friend'. All of them must have come from the Officers' Mess, which was in an adjacent building, for none had caps or belts. The RSM came last of all, and stood in the background.

'Now then, Judd, explain what all this is about,' Major Jackson had asked.

Judd struggled at first, not because of all this authority, but because it really was such a ghastly tale. Evans came from the Rhondda, his father a well-known and prominent union man in the local pit. Evans had shown him a family picture, which showed a big, immensely broad man, his face set in a wide grin, a watchchain prominent on his waistcoat. Mrs Evans was almost as tall, very thin of waist and limbs, and with an even thinner smile. Beside her were a boy of ten – presumably Evans himself some years ago – and a waiflike girl about half his age. The picture and the family did not seem so very unusual, and there must be thousands of similar pictures sitting on frames in as many houses. Mr Evans had that dark black hair so common in the area, and had let it grow into a beard so thick as to be almost Victorian.

Mr Evans also drank, especially on Friday and Saturday nights, which again was nothing unusual, least of all in those communities where so many men worked long and very hard hours in the gloom under the earth. Drink made him angry and violent, and sometimes he fought outside the pub, or more often came home angry. During that long day and longer night guarding the abandoned carrier, 374 Evans had spoken of his childhood in that little two up, two down, terraced house his mother kept so spotlessly clean. At least once a month, sometimes more, his father would come home and at the slightest thing – or for no reason at all – would hit his mother, or the children if he saw them. Then he would take her, whether she was willing or not, sweeping the table clean and throwing her on top.

Well, such stories could be told in a fair few households as well, and were just the way of things, even if deep down you knew that things should not be so. Life was hard, and sometimes a man was not strong enough to cope and became bitter and vicious.

Yet there was worse, for every few months, Mr Evans would bring home a couple of his drinking cronies and closest mates from the mine. Then he would watch as the friends took turns and raped his wife on that same kitchen table. Judd could remember the flatness as 374 had spoken of it, his eyes glassy, emotionless, as he told of her pleas and screams that had carried to the little bedroom upstairs, and how he had buried his head under the blanket. Once, when he was about twelve, he had gone downstairs yelling at them to stop hurting his mother, and seeing things no child should have to see. His father had grabbed him and tanned his hide so hard that there was blood, then sent him to his room. The next morning Mr Evans seemed repentant, and his mother had made the boy promise her solemnly never again to come down. 'She said it was just what grown-ups do, and not to worry,' the soldier had hissed. 'Not to worry.'

For a while Mr Evans had behaved, but it did not last and soon he was back to his old ways.

Evans had lied about his age to join up at sixteen. 'Best thing, my love,' his mother had assured him. 'Get out, now.'

'She was worried the old bastard would make me like him,' Evans had told Judd. 'Reckoned joining up was safer. Dad didn't care. Don't think he really likes me much.'

Judd had told the officers what he knew, seeing in their faces the same shock, incredulity, then sheer horror as the truth of it all sank in. He had felt just the same. Even the RSM grimaced, although Buchanan simply smoked his pipe and remained impassive. Judd's own revulsion had not diminished with time. If anything, it was worse, for he had moved in political circles, which for anyone of intelligence living in Wales meant various forms of socialism and doctrines even more extreme. He had been taught to put miners and good union men on a pedestal, as ideals of manhood, which made this all the more contemptible.

'Evans said that his mother was growing more and more worried about Evans' sister,' Judd had concluded. 'She's thirteen now.'

The major said something under his breath, too soft to catch, but blasphemous from its tone. He shook his head. 'Well, Judd, I have to thank you. This puts a very different complexion on the whole business. Now, run along – I'm afraid you will have missed much of the film, but there you are.'

Mark was expressionless, although perhaps that was from shock at the grim nature of the business. As Judd passed Mr Buchanan, the lieutenant removed his pipe, gave another curt nod, and said, 'Well done, son.'

This morning it was as if it had all been a dream, for he was back with his own platoon and company. Whatever they were doing with Evans, he was not summoned to be part of it. Buchanan had said nothing unusual to him, simply led 9 Platoon off on this march. Still, that was nothing out of the ordinary, for the officer was a man of few words. He was one of three Canadians sent to the battalion as part of the CANLOAN scheme, because the British were short of trained officers and the Canadians had a surplus. Buchanan was thirty or even older, elderly for a subaltern, and there was a story that he had dropped a rank to volunteer, having been a captain in the artillery. Rumour also said that he had been a Mountie, just like in the flicks, and after last night Judd suspected that it was true. In his limited experience, policemen were less shocked than everyone else by the viciousness of others. No doubt they had seen too much to have many illusions left.

Buchanan was tall, rangy, and while very military in his

manner, there remained a hint about the way he walked that suggested a man more used to riding a horse than being in a car. That, and good looks more than a little resembling Gary Cooper, and a laconic manner of speech had soon earned him the nickname of 'Coop'. He was not quite restricted to 'Yep' and 'Nope', but was never a man to waste words. When 'Coop' said anything to the platoon, they knew that it was worth listening to closely and obeying. He never fussed them, never shouted unless it was really necessary, and gave the impression that he trusted his men to follow and held them in respect. Everyone in 9 Platoon had taken to him very quickly, and were rather proud of their unusual officer.

10.30 hrs, Camp B43

Mark was not sure what would happen. The colonel was away, summoned to a briefing, which meant that the second in command was in charge, and Major Probert was known to be a stern, fiercely regimental and rather bitter man, not given to smiling or to showing any sympathy to others. That was in stark contrast to the colonel's almost paternal attitude towards his men.

They had to coax Evans to tell his story. The private did not appear frightened of them or the trouble he was in, and instead was resigned, almost empty. He looked even younger than usual, and it was easy to believe that he had concealed his age to join. Mark had not paid enough attention to the records to know that Evans was a volunteer, simply having assumed that he had been called up like just about everyone else apart from the few surviving pre-War territorials still serving with them.

Eventually, Evans began to talk, and to Mark's surprise it was Probert who got the most out of him, perhaps because the major showed no emotion at all, whether sympathy or anger, apart from raising his voice slightly to demand answers. Habit took over, and the young soldier did as he was told by authority; no more and no less.

The story was much as Judd had described to them the night before, and Mark was glad to have been prepared to hear it because it was so appalling. He would be the first to admit that he still had much to learn about women, and just about everything to learn about sex – the word itself rarely used in that sense except by the more fashionable and pretentious novelists and critics. He had had little experience of the former and none of the latter, and as far as he could tell the same was true of most of his friends, although most, like him, aspired to learn.

Mark had been raised to revere women. As a boy it had been drummed into him that he must never, *never*, strike a girl, because they were weak and as a male he was strong. Boys and men were there to protect the weaker sex, to do the hard work and risk danger on their behalf. That was why they went off to fight the war – not that many plucky girls like Anne were not also playing their part and doing it very well. Strength was the difference, not courage, and surely there was a rare courage on the part of Mrs Evans to survive such bestial behaviour and still protect her children.

For Mark, a woman, most of all a true lady, was to be raised on a pedestal, and if a chap tried to peek up her dress when the opportunity came, that did not mean that he did not admire and respect her. It was up to him to win her heart and do the decent thing. There was something he remembered being told at school that seemed to sum it all up rather well. When you heard about an engagement, the proper thing was to wish the bride well, while congratulating the chap, because he was the one who had got the catch, while she deigned to accept him.

Last night, when he had learned why Evans had tried to go absent without leave with a revolver – Mark's revolver no less – he had more than half wished that the boy had got away with it and shot his father dead. Mr Evans was vile, worse than an animal, and surely the world would be a better place if someone blew off the man's head. He had even had a wild thought of slipping away, travelling to Wales and doing the job himself.

That thought came back when Evans told them that he had received a letter from his mother the day before.

'She's terrified, sir, terrified,' the lad explained, reporting to Major Probert as if he was talking about something routine. 'He's been boasting to his friends that our Sal is now all grown up. Promising that one day soon he'll let them have a go at her.'

'And that was why you took the gun and tried to go home?' Probert asked.

'Yes, sir. He's got to be stopped.' Suddenly Evans broke down and began to sob, body shaking like a child.

'Very well. You can wait outside, Evans.' The major gestured to the NCOs to help the boy out, then turned to the other officers sitting alongside him. 'I think that this is something we can keep in the battalion,' he said. This was not a court martial, for it had not yet got to anything so formal. Evans had been caught at the guardhouse, where he had produced a hand-written note and claimed that they were orders sending him out to the nearest village to shop for his officer. It had not been the most imaginative of excuses, and then the revolver had dropped heavily onto the wooden floor as it fell from the pocket of his greatcoat.

'If he had been brought back by the MPs,' Probert continued, 'then that would have been another matter and out of our hands, but as it is we can be lenient and give him twenty-eight days in the guardhouse, or as much of that as lasts until we embark. After that he can be under open arrest. Any objections?' There were not, so Probert ordered Evans brought back in and informed him of his punishment. 'Do you accept this?'

Evans came feebly to attention. 'Yes, sir.' As a prisoner, he had no cap, so could not salute. It was his right to seek judgement from a higher authority if he refused to accept punishment at this level. 'But, sir,' he pleaded. 'What about my sister?'

'We will do all we can,' Probert told him, then dismissed the soldier, who was escorted away.

'And all we can is probably bugger all,' one of the other officers said bitterly. Mark shared the sentiment.

'We cannot do more than our best,' Probert said gnomically. 'And ghastly though this affair is, there remains a war to be won. So, gentlemen, we had better get on with preparing to play our part.' He stood. 'Time to be about our duties.'

15.30 hrs, Normandy

'Gunner, traverse right. Range, fifteen hundred yards, the field behind those trees. There, that's it. On.' The hedge in front of them was lower than some they had seen, allowing the gun to clear it, and they were on a low hill, which meant that they could see over another hedge halfway to the target. Still, Collins might have a few leaves obscuring his line of sight. As commander, his head just out of the open hatch, James was higher and could see clearly. 'Load HE, and keep your eyes peeled, but wait for the order. There are our people over there as well, so we need to be careful.'

So far as anyone knew, there were German infantry with a gun or two in the woodland and perhaps in the village beyond it – James could see no more than a few rooftops and a church tower topped by a steeple. No one had seen any sign of tanks, but you could not be too careful. A day after the landings, the Germans knew where the Allies had attacked, so they were bound to want to counter attack while the invaders were few in numbers and not fully prepared. It was a race now, between the Allies shipping everything across the Channel and the Germans driving and travelling on trains – or even walking – towards the beachhead.

James was back with the regiment, or at least part of it, and that was reassuring, and on the whole the news was good, which was even better. All five of the invasion beaches had been taken, in some cases after bitter fighting. Elements of their own brigade, with supporting infantry, had almost got to their objective of Bayeux last night, and ought to have gone in by now. Men from GOLD had linked up with the Canadians at JUNO yesterday, and further inland today, including along the road they had been meant to cover yesterday. The Canadians had been where they were supposed to be, and to his great relief had not come under attack.

While that was going on, 3 Troop had been ordered to fall back and restock with fuel and ammunition. They did not need much of the latter and only a little of the former, which was just as well because most of 165th RAC was still landing on the beach. Supposed to come in last night, the congestion on the beach and the high winds had prevented that from happening. Apart from Symonds' little force, only C Squadron had come ashore. James and his men were part of B Squadron, but for the moment were attached to the other unit and put in support of infantry tasked with clearing this village and the woods outside it. As far as anyone could tell, this was an isolated position, a company or so of stubborn men dug in and refusing to pull back. It reminded James of the lone rifleman who had shot Symonds.

The attack was going in from the north-east, and most of C Squadron and the Recce tanks were there to offer fire support. James and 3 Troop were to act as a cut-off, waiting to cover the Germans' likely line of retreat if they could be forced out. They were in position, engines switched off, and had the assurance of a couple of sections of infantry to protect them. James once again had lifted his headphones off one ear, and for the moment it was fairly quiet, although there was muffled gunfire from the east. By the sound of it, the Canadians were having a fierce fight over in that direction, although the sounds were too distant and confused for him to make any sense of it.

Shells and mortar bombs started to land in the wood. Through his binoculars, James saw the treetops quivering.

Sound reached them later, coming as a series of deep crumps. There were twenty-five-pounder guns supporting the attack as well as the infantry's own mortars, and for twenty minutes they pummelled the target, until it was lost to view in a haze of dark smoke. Then it stopped abruptly, like a switch being turned off, and over the net they could hear C Squadron offering covering fire as the infantry began their advance. The signal was intermittent, even at this distance, and they had no contact at all with the infantry.

The other three tanks of 3 Troop were lined up along the same hedge, waiting to play their part. There was not much chatter in his own tank, nor did any of the commanders call him, so they waited. In each tank the driver and co-driver sat near the front of the hull, unable to see anything apart from the hedge in front of them. The loader was no better off, for the designers of the Sherman had not felt the need to give him a periscope, since his job was to feed the gun and tend the radio.

They waited. Without the barrage, the battle was less noisy, and only now and then could they hear machine gun fire or the crack of a tank gun. Judging from the radio, C Squadron were shifting targets and the attack was making progress.

James woke just in time to stop his chin from hitting the rim of the cupola, the rotating ring mounting vision blocks which surrounded the main hatch. He must have dropped off, although he did not think it was for long, probably just an instant. The day was not warm, for there was no sign of the Sun, but then he had always found it harder to stay awake on dull days than bright ones. He smelled tea, and realised that Whitefield must have brewed some using one of the little stoves. It was strictly forbidden to use one inside a tank, but few of the crews paid much attention.

'Would you like a mug, skipper?' the driver asked.

'Thanks.'

They waited. The tea had done him good and he felt less

sluggish. He had never been that fond of tea before coming into the Army, but now he craved it. He rested the mug on the top of the turret to scan the wood and the field behind it. There was still nothing.

Ten minutes later, James had just finished the tea when he lifted his binoculars again and saw movement in the field. He tried to make sense of it, and thought that he saw tiny dots as men ran out of the wood.

'Baker Three to Baker Three Able and Baker, target infantry retreating from wood, range one thousand five hundred yards. Open fire,' he ordered, then switched to the internal link. 'Gunner, both guns, open fire.' His own tank and the others started their engines.

Collins pressed one button and the co-axial machine gun chattered into life. There were tracer rounds in the belt, and the glowing specks seemed to go slowly as they looped up and then down onto the distant target. Once the gunner was happy with his aim, he pushed down on the other button and the main gun thundered. James sometimes thought that he could see the shell leave the muzzle as a black blur, although that might have been his imagination.

'Baker Three to Baker Three Charlie, keep a lookout for hornets, out.' Hornet was the code for hostile tanks and self-propelled guns, and he had stationed Sergeant Philips' tank on the far left, facing to the flank to protect the others. Just because reports knew nothing of enemy tanks in the area did not mean that there were none out there and it was better to be careful.

The three tanks hosed the machine guns across the field, punctuating this with rounds from the 75s. Bursting shells flung up gouts of smoke and muck.

After five minutes James ordered them to cease fire and scanned the field with his binoculars. There was no sign of movement.

They waited again, until orders came for them to move to C Squadron's position. The village had been cleared, the wood taken, and presumably that meant a little bit more of France had been liberated. Men had died and been maimed in the process, both German and their own, but they had seen none of it.

There was still the murmur of battle to the east, which faded as they drove around to join C Squadron. One of its tanks had been knocked out, losing a track, but no one was injured, and the Sherman ought to be repaired in a few hours, once the fitters came up. However, a corporal commanding another tank had been killed by a sniper.

20.30 hrs, Camp B43, Sussex

Mark did his best to take in the news of the invasion. There was more of it now, the papers offering maps and considerable detail, some of which might even be reasonably accurate. He remembered reading that Napoleon had relied on *The Times* to find out what his own armies were doing in Spain, the London paper of his enemies getting the news faster than French despatches could reach Paris. These days, the Government was a good deal more careful, and you did not really learn what had happened until much later.

Still, it all seemed to be good. The Allies were ashore in considerable numbers – some 120,000 according to the reports – and Mark knew that he ought to feel happier. It could easily have been a disaster, or at least far more difficult and deadly than it seemed, and it had not.

He could not lift his spirits, and his mind kept going back to Evans and his family, to that little house where a frail woman waited in fear, no longer for herself but for her daughter, still just a child. His anger threatened to boil over and the paper ripped apart in his tight hands. Major Jackson was sitting in an armchair nearby and raised a quizzical eyebrow.

'Sorry.' Mark was not sure what he was apologising for, but his upbringing had made this an instinctive response. He worried that this was not a good thing for a soldier and leader of men.

Jackson smiled and stood up. 'Try this, old fellow,' he said, handing over the *Daily Mirror*. '*The Times* seems to be upsetting you.'

'Thank you.' What else was there to say. Jackson commanded a company of infantry, but that did not mean that he could change the world.

'Well, no rest for the wicked,' Jackson went on. 'With Jack Probert away, I'm in charge.' He noticed the surprise, suggesting that he had been expecting it. 'Jack's a queer old stick, but knows a thing or two. He's gone to see what can be done. So have patience, dear boy.'

Jackson headed off and Mark did his best to be encouraged. Yet what could they do? He made some headway with his new paper, before his mind wandered again. The invasion seemed more distant than ever before, even though it was finally under way. *Jane* was off for her bath, a plump and lecherous landlord taking too much interest, which made her bolt the door before disrobing. Mark was not sure how he felt about that either.

23.45 hrs, near Bayeux

'So, gentlemen, we will have a busy few days ahead of us.' Colonel Leyne had gathered the officers of 165th RAC in the shelter of a barn. The regiment was at long last fully landed and gathered together in one place, more than sixty tanks and as many more other vehicles laagered in a couple of fields around this farm. Their brigade was not far away, along with several battalions of infantry.

'The situation is essentially this,' the colonel went on, 'we're in France.' The laughter was natural and unforced.

Tim Leyne was a small, dapper man, who had been a lieutenant in Egypt when the War began, a captain of a scratch squadron when Tobruk was first besieged, a major at Alam Halfa, and had since come back to command his own regiment. He was twenty-eight, with a DSO, MC and bar, and the air of a man who did not give a damn about anything unless it was important or to do with making his regiment the best there was. A shell splinter at Beda Fomm back in '41 had given him a scar next to his mouth so that he always seemed on the verge of a smile.

'The invasion has begun,' he went on, pointing at a map. 'All five beaches are secure. Our Twenty-First Army has joined their three beaches together, and we're now just about in touch with the American First Army to the west. Every hour more and more men and material are landed. It's a good start, but that's all it is.

'As you might guess, the Hun is none too pleased to see us!' He waited for the laughter to subside. 'He will attack because that is what he always does. Lob a brick at him and he charges like a bull.

'And he has to attack, because otherwise he's beaten. His job is to throw us back into the sea, and the only way he can do that is rush all his panzers here and hit us before we are so strong that we cannot be knocked down. So, they are coming, gentlemen, as fast as their little jackboots can run and their little tanks can drive. They tried on D-Day and Third Div. stopped them. Earlier today they halted the advance of the Canadians to the east, then tried to drive the Canadians back and got cut to ribbons. Score one for the Maple Leaf. They'll keep attacking there and they'll soon be attacking here, because this is the best place for tanks and they know that only their panzers can do the job.'

James rubbed his eyes. He really wanted to sleep, but this was important and afterwards there would still be a lot to do. Back with the regiment, its support vehicles were there and that meant 3 Troop could be restocked with everything, and the tanks checked to make sure all was in working order. Whatever instructions the officers received, he would have to pass on to his tank commanders, at least as far as their role in the wider scheme was concerned. He blinked to focus, then licked his pencil to be ready to make more notes.

'We could wait for the Hun, but that lets him choose the time and place of his attack and that's never good. On balance, I don't think we'll do that.' Colonel Tim spoke as if they were talking about whether or not to go to the theatre. 'No, we are going to hit him first. That way he doesn't get the chance to organise.

'The BBC announced that we took Bayeux yesterday, as well as Caen. Well, as usual, they're talking through their hat. One rule of war, gentlemen – never believe anything the BBC says until you have a dozen independent witnesses.' There was more laughter. 'We took Bayeux today, as you know, and tomorrow we will drive south. The whole operation is being set up as we speak, but these are the bare bones. Our Brigade, along with a battalion from Fiftieth Div., are to drive south.' He pointed to the map, tracing the route. 'Two columns leading. We're here on the left...'

James forced himself to concentrate and note down the details, of routes, map references, timings, orders of march and phases, but he was so very tired that he did it automatically, almost as if he was watching himself from some high place.

D+2, Thursday 8th June

THE REGIMENT WAS where it should be, but apparently others were not as yet, so that the advance was postponed. 'No move before twelve hundred,' James said, passing on the order to 3 Troop. He felt refreshed, even though he had had no more than three hours' sleep. They had fastened a canvas sheet to the side of the tank, which offered shelter, and simply being able to lie flat had made a difference. This morning was chilly, the drizzle faint but persistent, yet still he felt well, not least because he had stripped to the waist to wash and then shaved. He felt clean, reasonably rested, and content that for a while they would not be required to do anything.

Post had arrived along with a few newspapers – yesterday's newspapers, but it was still staggering that any had come at all. They were passed around, and he was surprised at how many men were excited to read about the invasion.

'The start of a great crusade, General Eisenhower announced,' Collins had read out loud. 'That's you, Trooper Albright, so straighten up and try to look like a ruddy crusader!'

He had two letters, obviously from Penny from the round, childlike handwriting addressing them, and had saved them until now, when he had the time to read them at leisure. Going back to the tank, he sat on his bedroll, accepted a mug of tea from Whitefield, and fished the first out of his pocket. Then he sensed a presence hovering nearby.

'Beg pardon, sir, but Major Scott would like to see you at Squadron HQ.'

There was a change in the order of march and the route to the start line, some additional codes for the radio net, and other minor details. Thirty minutes later, James sat down again, sipping at his cold tea, and began to read.

My dearest, most beloved, I hope you are well. I have your picture in front of me as I write, your ring on my finger...

The engagement was new, from his last leave only six weeks ago, so that he was still half surprised about it. Part of him was guilty that he did not think about it or her every moment of every day, as she assured him in both letters was the case for her. There was a lot about how wonderful he was, how little she deserved him. James had propped up a mirror when he shaved, and failed to see anything very remarkable about his face. There were three pages in each letter, every one filled with adoration apart from a few snippets of news from home. Penelope Stevens wrote as she talked, only more so, the words spilling out in a rush. She had less restraint in a letter, although he could imagine her blushing when she wrote that she was longing to be crushed in his great arms.

In a way it was all too much, almost false like a comic opera, if he had not known her. This was a deluge of love, overwhelming, unquestioning love of a sort he could not imagine ever feeling for anyone. Sometimes that had made him feel guilty, even treacherous, like some rake out to rob a girl of her innocence – and again he was back to comic opera or melodrama, for that was how Penny seemed to see the world.

Reading the letters now, in a field surrounded by tanks and soldiers, all parts of the same military machine, he felt a rush of relief that he mattered to someone, and mattered so very much. If he was lucky there was time to write a quick note in return. He realised that his hand was over his breast pocket again.

12.15 hrs, Camp B43, Sussex

Judd sat on the floor, the blindfold tight enough to stop him from seeing, but not giving that much sense of darkness. The whistle blew, and his fingers began the familiar task. Find the bolt, pull it back with a click, pull the trigger to let off the action, another louder click, find the body locking pin. This was not Bessie, but another Bren gun used for training, and assembled and reassembled so often that the thing probably fell apart if you looked at it. Butt group slides back, pull return spring to the side, and out comes the breech block and piston all in one piece, and so on and so on, until the gun was laid out in pieces on the groundsheet folded and placed on the floor for that purpose.

'Well done,' Sergeant Holdworth said a moment later. Judd may have been the first of the three men to finish, but it was not by much. 'Ready?'

Mr Buchanan blew the whistle again, and Judd started to put it back together, bipod and body first, then the barrel nut. Everything was designed to be simple, only to fit one way and in the right order, and it was all so familiar.

'Good,' Holdworth announced. 'Blindfolds off, put them on the next man and raise a hand when they're ready.' Once they were, the whistle blew and the process began again.

Bill Judd did not dare think how many times he had stripped and put back together a Bren gun, or a .303 rifle for that matter, or filled and then emptied a magazine. He had done it in lecture halls, in big tents, out in the field and even at the bottom of a trench they had just dug. Before that had been the lectures and demonstrations, beginning with the laborious, almost soul destroying basics, 'the naming of parts' as the instructors called it, going through one by one every bit of the gun and telling the recruits what to call it. It worked, he had to admit that, and now he not only talked but even thought without prompting, in terms of gas regulators, piston rings and flash eliminators.

Blindfolded or not, day or night, fingers numb with cold or slick with sweat, he could take a gun apart as fast as almost anyone and put one together. That was what the Army wanted, a soldier always able to make his weapon function in any circumstances, and by and large that was what they got.

Then there were stoppages. That was another sort of session, just as familiar, which almost inevitably followed practice at stripping and assembling the guns. Today was no exception. Judd and the other gunners lay behind each Bren, and the sergeant tapped on the floor.

'Gun fires a few more rounds and then stops.'

One, pull back the cocking handle. Two, remove magazine, the kidney shaped magazine peculiar to the Bren. Three, fire the action. Four, replace magazine – a new one, not the one before the stoppage. Five, cock and fire.

Another couple of taps on the floor.

'Gun fires a few more rounds and then stops.'

That meant it was not something simple, like an empty or badly filled magazine, so the drill was to shift the position of the gas regulator and so on.

So much of the Army was about repetition, everything pared down, made as simple and mindless as possible, whether it was on the drill square, making your bed, putting creases in your trousers or arranging your kit, everything had to done the Army's way, and done again and again, until it was a habit. Judd was convinced that there had to be a better way of teaching, but had had the sense never to suggest that to anyone. The Army's way worked, and it brought all save the utterly handless and hopeless – and there were usually a few of them in every unit – to the required standard, so no one was likely to be in a hurry to make changes.

Not much seemed to have changed since the Great War or probably since the Crimea or Waterloo. The Glamorganshire Regiment had been at both, and in India, Africa and right through the Great War. He wondered whether those men had been just as bored, just as fed up. There should have been an urgency about it all now that the invasion had begun, a greater sense of purpose and belief that the training mattered and might save his life. Instead, it still seemed unreal, just more pointless Army bull to keep soldiers busy and make sure they never had time and energy to think for themselves.

'Gun fires a few more rounds and then jams.'

This time, the routine was to remove the barrel and replace it with a new one. Judd went through the process smoothly and quickly, almost as if watching someone else doing the job. His conscious mind was elsewhere, wondering for the thousandth time whether it might be different in the RAF, or if he had not failed to pass selection for commissioning, or to transfer to the parachute regiment. RTU was stamped on his documents each time – Returned to Unit. So here he was, the lowest of the low, and it was not up to him what he did each day. A man could protest and refuse, but that meant the glasshouse and he certainly did not fancy that prospect.

Judd finished reassembling the gun and reported, 'Gun ready.' The others spoke at almost the same moment.

'Open fire,' Holdworth ordered.

Judd pulled the trigger and the action worked smoothly with a decisive click on the empty chamber. Of course it did, since there had been nothing wrong with it in the first place.

'Cease fire. Make safe.' Holdworth gave them a nod. 'Well done. Now, next men, up you come!' Three more soldiers appeared to take the gunners' places. Judd sat back down with the rest of his section, all of them cross-legged like schoolboys. After this they were due for lunch, then more lessons. He could remember that one would be on grenades, another on the Sten gun, but after that he was not sure. The only thing he could be sure about was that it would be nothing they had not done before.

14.15 hrs, Normandy, between Caen and Bayeux

'Driver, advance,' James Taylor said into his microphone. Whitefield had his hatch open, his seat adjusted so that his head was clear of the hull. The Sherman was American made, which meant that it was left-hand drive, unlike British tanks. The co-driver, Miller, was on the right, manning an additional .30 calibre Browning machine gun. He also had his hatch open, although in his case only eyes and the top of his head were visible between the edge of the hull and the rim of his pudding bowl shaped tanker's helmet. Whitefield was in his black RAC beret. Collins, as gunner, did not need reminding to be careful and give warning before he traversed the gun, which was mere inches above the two men's heads. If ever they were hit, one of the gunner's jobs before abandoning was to shift the gun so that the heavy 75mm was away from the two lower positions. If it was not, then neither driver nor co-driver would be able to lift their hatch enough to open it and escape. That assumed that the gunner was not dead or maimed, and not so terrified that he did not stop to think because he knew that within seconds the ammunition and fuel might ignite and turn the metal hull and turret into a furnace. The solid armour that protected the crew could trap them if things went wrong.

The tank ahead, Sergeant Dove's, sent up a spray of muddy water as it went through a puddle. There had been several heavy downpours during the morning and the sky suggested that more was on the way. Somehow that added to the sense that this was all an exercise up on the Yorkshire Moors like the schemes they had done back in the winter. Everything was going well, and the concentration of the regiment, not too far short of its strength of some seventy tanks, gave a sense of confidence and power, reinforced by the knowledge that the other two regiments of the brigade were nearby. Even Taylor's own 3 Troop seemed to him more formidable, now that it was back with the rest of B Squadron.

An hour ago they had crossed the N13, the big trunk road
linking Caen to Bayeux. The 165th RAC led the left-hand column
of the brigade, with B Squadron in the middle of the column.
While they were waiting, a platoon of infantry had ridden past
them on bicycles, which took his mind back to D-Day itself. The
last news was that Symonds was still alive, even if no one could
quite understand how, and that the doctors were on the verge
of cautious optimism. The wounded captain was already back
at a hospital in England, which showed how well everything
was working and that he had been stable enough to move. Yet
already James found that he was not thinking about Symonds
at all unless prompted. In the Forces people came and went, and
you dealt with those on the spot, almost as if everyone else had
ceased to exist.

They drove on, occasionally in bright sunshine, but more
often under heavy cloud. So far, they had not heard any firing
or seen sign of the enemy apart from a few corpses no one had
had time to bury. Early on they had driven past two shot up
and burned waggons, the horse teams lying dead in the traces,
bellies bloating and covered in flies.

Colonel Tim had warned them to expect more opposition
as they pushed forward. 'The intelligence wallahs believe that
Twenty-First Panzer is more to the east, in front of Caen. I know
Twenty-First from the Desert. They're good soldiers, tough as
any, but decent enough by Hun standards. We might meet them,
we might not – intelligence wallahs don't know everything and
Caen isn't far away as the crow flies or panzer drives. Rommel
likes to do the unexpected.

'Still, more likely we'll run into some new boys. There's
Twelfth Panzer Div. They're SS and call themselves the Hitler
Youth, so chock full of young fanatics and bristling with all the
latest kit. Some of them were here yesterday, fighting against the
Canadians. On the way is another new formation, the Panzer
Lehr Div. – but these are different. It's been formed from all the
demonstration units at their training depots. These fellows will

be good, experienced and very well practised and again with all the newest stuff.

'The Germans are good, and these are top units by German standards. That means we have to be even better,' the colonel had concluded. 'Fortunately for us, we are, but because we're English we are far too modest to say that. I'm half Scots, so it's easy for me!'

The laughter among the officers had been genuine and unforced, whether or not anyone – including the colonel – was convinced. The Germans had spent the last few years fighting bitter winter and very determined Russians in battles whose sheer scale and horror seemed worse than anything likely to happen here, worse even than the Somme or Passchendaele in the last lot. A lot of Russians were dead, which was dreadful, as were a lot of Germans, which was better, but the ones who were left must have seen a lot of fighting and have become pretty good at it. By the sound of it, these units they were facing were some of the best they had, and that was enough to make a man think. James still felt confident. The regiment was good and he was pretty sure that they would win in the end. He just doubted that it would be easy.

However, as another shower blew in, things were going so well so far today, that maybe the colonel was right after all. The 165th were following a route codenamed ISEL, heading towards Brouay, which was spelled differently on their maps, but clearly the right place.

'Standards of education in French schools are not high,' Colonel Tim had explained.

After that, their next stage was to take them to Point 102, which was not even a place where anyone lived, but a trig point marking some high ground on a map. The other column was heading for the conveniently named Point 103, giving a coherence to the operation. After that they were both to press on south, ultimately towards Villers-Bocage, seizing as much ground as they could before the Germans were in place to stop them.

'So far, so good,' James said under his breath as they crossed the railway line outside Brouay. In spite of the thick cloud, the rain had moved on and fighters were buzzing overhead, mostly heading south to hunt for the enemy.

16.45 hrs, near the village of Putot, Normandy

'Baker Three, this is Baker.' That was Major Scott, B Squadron commander, calling James. 'Move up on the right of Baker Two, over.'

'This is Baker Three, acknowledge, out.'

They were in a wide field of green wheat, leading up to a thick hedge and a wood about half a mile away. James and 3 Troop had brought up the rear of the squadron when it was ordered off to the east, away from the main line of advance. Someone from Recce Troop had bumped into Canadian infantry who were facing a big German counter attack. B Squadron was sent to help, driving towards the village of Putot. James could not see any of the houses from where he was, and there was even less chance as he brought his tanks to join the end of the line.

'Baker Three to Baker Three Able, you take station on the far right next to me. Three Charlie, you come next to me on the other side, and Three Baker on his left alongside the closest tank of Baker Two, over.'

The three commanders acknowledged as they drove to take position. B Squadron had its four troops in line facing the hedge and wood, with the three HQ tanks a little behind, along with another carrying an observer for the artillery.

'Baker, this is Baker Three, we are in position,' James reported. The cupola around the hatch rotated, so that he could turn to look around him without turning the whole turret, all the while keeping the two raised hatches on either side of him as protection. Sergeant Dove was in Three Able over on James' right. On the left was Sergeant Powell, in Three Charlie, and beyond him Corporal Bell in Three Baker.

There were four Shermans in each troop. Two were just like his own, armed with the stubby 75mm gun that had been in use since Alamein. It fired two main types of shell, the high explosive, or HE, which blew up, shattering and spreading a swathe of jagged metal over a wide area, and armoured piercing or AP. Those did not explode – even if in the movies every shell back to the days of cannon balls always went off with a big bang. In a sense these were like the roundshot of Nelson's and Wellington's day, for they were solid lumps of metal although they were shaped like a bullet. Travelling at high speed, giving them momentum, they were meant to slam into the armour of an enemy tank and with luck punch through, spreading red hot fragments of themselves and bits of the armour and anything else scything and bouncing around inside. That was a lethal combination in a space as confined as any tank, packed as it was with highly combustible ammunition and fuel, and fragile human flesh and bone.

Back in 1942 the Sherman's 75mm had been as good a gun as anything mounted in a German tank, but since then the Germans had built larger and heavier tanks with bigger guns. To help deal with those, someone had come up with the idea of taking a long seventeen-pounder anti-tank gun and cramming it into the turret of a Sherman. Somehow it was made to fit, although only by extending the turret at the back to make room for the recoil and provide space for the wireless set. Another sacrifice was the co-driver, whose position was removed to give enough space to store the much longer and heavier shells needed by the gun. Twice as long as the 75mm, the barrel of the seventeen-pounder stuck out far ahead of the hull, and needed a heavy counterweight at the rear of the turret to make it manageable at all.

They called it the Sherman Firefly, and it was new, so new
that they had only begun to arrive with the armoured regiments
in the last weeks before the invasion. James had never seen one
fire before they got to Normandy, and was still to see one take
on a German tank. Although it could shoot a decent HE shell,
its main role was to fling a heavy AP round further and harder
than anything else they had and to give the panzers a nasty
surprise. It was their secret weapon, although as Whitefield had
commented, 'How can a bloody great gun be a secret?'

So new and so secret was it, that drivers and commanders were
still having to learn how easily the great long barrel would bend
if it struck a tree, telegraph pole or wall while they were moving.
Fireflies were a lot more awkward than normal Shermans. At
a higher level, there was not yet an official Army way to use
them, in part because not every regiment had received the same
number of them so far. In their brigade, the Dragoons and the
Yeomanry had not been issued very many, partly because the
long gun meant that it was impossible to turn a Firefly into one
of the swimming DDs. The ones they had, they had grouped
into a separate troop in each squadron, holding them back as
a reserve. Colonel Tim had other ideas, in part because he had
connections with the units in the Armoured Divisions who had
priority for supplies. They were adding a Firefly to the three
ordinary Shermans in each troop, so that was what the 165th
RAC had done. Troop commanders, like James, were given this
extra punch and trusted to make best use of it.

'Baker to all stations, there are friendly infantry on our left
near the village. Hostiles ahead of us, perhaps close. Keep your
eyes peeled, out.'

James glanced to the left, but could not see anything apart
from the row of tanks, each thirty or so yards apart. A machine
gun opened up from that direction, the regular tap-tap-tap of a
Bren gun, which meant that it was one of ours. More joined in,
as did rifles. Mortars crumped distantly.

The Sherman rocked back as the ground erupted just to the

right between them and Sergeant Dove's tank. Earth pattered down, one small clod hitting James on the head. He had given up on the helmet, deciding that the weight meant his head moved too slowly. With just a beret he could dodge and glance quickly, just like being back at the crease.

More shells landed around them, the Sherman shuddering whenever they were close. Whitefield and Miller slammed their hatches shut, adjusting their seats lower. From now on they would only be able to see out through a narrow vision port, almost as cut off from the world as a medieval knight in his helmet.

'Bloody hell, it's raining,' Whitefield complained.

'Was it something we said?' Collins asked and there were chuckles.

James crouched low so that only his eyes were clear of the cupola. A shell landed right in front, so that he saw the flash before it vanished in the dark smoke. These were mediums by the sound and size of the bang. Big enough, if not the biggest that could be thrown at them, and lobbed by a battery of guns miles away and out of sight. An observer was calling them in, correcting the aim, but they were still pounding an area and not shooting at him or his tank personally. It still felt pretty damned personal. Still, even a direct hit would be unlikely to get through a Sherman's armour, although it might cripple the tank and give them all one hell of a headache. The only danger was that one in a million fluke of a shell coming down smack into his open hatch.

The tank shook again and James ducked down, pulling the hatches shut above him. Albright gave him a grin, his face just visible over the breech of the 75mm. It might have been a grimace rather than a grin, and the boy looked pale. James wondered whether he was paler still for his heart was pounding. He felt the pocket of his tunic. Collins had a rabbit's foot hung up on the wall of the turret and most of the crew, probably most of the regiment, had their lucky charms. His was just... well...

'Baker to Baker Three. Push forward a hundred yards and see what you can flush out. We'll cover you, over.'

'Baker Three to Baker, acknowledged.' James hesitated, planning in his head how to do this. 'Three Able, you and I will lead, Three Baker and Charlie cover. Take it slow and watch the long grass, over.'

'It's wheat, sir, not grass,' Collins the countryman pointed out. 'Good wheat as well by the look of it. Ought to be a decent harvest if the weather is kind.'

'Three Able acknowledged, out.' Sergeant Dove started forward.

'Or some sod doesn't drive his tank over it,' Whitefield chipped in.

'Yes, there is that,' Collins conceded. 'Who invited the bloody *anglais* over here.'

'Pipe down,' James hissed. 'Driver, advance.' He was trying to watch the field through his periscope. The view was narrow, and shifting it as he turned the cupola around made it still easy to miss a patch. With some reluctance he opened the hatches again. He had not heard a shell for a minute or two, and he wanted to see.

Sergeant Dove's tank opened fire with both its machine guns, tracer whipping into the corn about two hundred yards ahead of him.

'Baker Three Able to Baker Three, I saw movement.'

'Roger, Three Able.' James switched to the internal loop. 'Gunner, can you see anything?'

'Nothing.' Collins had traversed slightly so that the 75 and the co-axial machine gun were covering the same spot.

The air above James' head snapped as he felt a bullet flick past just inches above his beret. The crack of the rifle came only a moment later.

'Germans!' Miller shouted over the intercom and began to fire his Browning from the hull. He was hosing the tall wheat barely fifty yards to their left. James switched to the wider net to warn Dove. 'Baker Three to Baker...'

Something dark and trailing flame rushed at him

'Oh Christ...' James screamed and ducked down, hands clasping his head. The missile was already passing them, a rocket from one of the German bazookas, and it had missed because there was no crash, no searing fire shooting through the armour into the tank.

He dared to sit up. Collins fired the 75 and the range was so close that the burst was instant. James looked up and saw a human torso, one arm still attached, flying high. Collins stamped on the other button adding his machine gun to Miller's and the other two tanks from 3 Troop were joining in, so that the long wheat twitched and jerked as if struck by a cyclone.

Two men sprang to their feet, their helmets and jackets a camouflage pattern of whirling dots. They were running, sprinting like startled rabbits away from the appalling violence unleashed by the tanks. One dropped a moment later, a great hole ripped in his back. The other seemed immune, until the tracer from two machine guns found him. Like a puppet with its strings cut, his limbs flailed as he was flung this way then another, until his corpse was torn into shreds.

If there were other Germans in the wheat then they kept down and were hidden by it. A machine gun clattered from the hedge on the far side of the field, and there were pings as rounds sparked off the Sherman's hull. James ducked again, so that only his eyes were visible, but the chattering gun had moved on. It sounded so much faster than any of their own weapons.

'Baker Three to Baker, am in position. Have engaged some infantry. The rest must have gone to ground, over.'

'Don't blame 'em,' Collins muttered.

'Well done, Baker Three. You halt there and I'll push Baker Two forward. Nice and easy. Our infantry friends are too short-handed to accompany us, so we need to be careful.'

'Baker Three acknowledged, out.'

'Oh, and Baker Three. Remember to follow correct RT procedure.'

'Sorry, Baker. Will do my best.'

'Thought you'd got religion, out.'

'Halle-ruddy-lujah!' Whitefield said over the intercom.

'Hark at that from a good Catholic boy like you,' Miller told him. 'It's a wonder that rosary doesn't wear away the way you play with it.'

'You ought to be more worried about wearing away what you play with, mate!' Whitefield assured him. 'It's a wonder you're not blind already.'

'Cheek.'

James did not pay much attention. He reckoned a silent crew was too likely to brood, and chattering did not seem to stop any of them from doing their job. In his mind he was thinking of how they had torn apart those Germans a few moments before and now were joking. Perhaps that was what you had to do. Better than thinking about what might have happened if the rocket had struck home. He guessed it was a panzerfaust, and those had a short range and were dropped once they had delivered their one shot. If the German had just waited until they were closer... Yes, better not to brood.

'Pass me up an apple, will you,' he said. Collins reached into a bag in which they carried grenades and a couple of apples. 'Thanks.' He switched the setting on the microphone to tell Three Baker and Charlie to come up level with them and for everyone to keep a close watch.

For half an hour B Squadron crawled forward into the big field. Small arms fire came at them often, salvos of medium guns or mortars less often. Now and then they saw movement, and took to plastering every patch of wheat that looked at all suspicious with everything that could bear on it, just to be on the safe side. Sometimes it was simply the wind stirring the wheat, sometimes simply nerves, and sometimes there were panzer grenadiers in camouflaged smocks crawling forward, trying to sneak up on the tanks. Either they did not have many of their panzerfausts – James wondered for a moment what the German ending of the word would be and could not remember anything much from school – or they could not get close enough to use them effectively.

Nearer the village, the Germans came on in waves, in the open, trying to beat down the company of Canadians just managing to hold on. The nearest troop and some of HQ went to help, massacring the enemy with their firepower, backed by batteries of artillery called in by the observer. The Canadians took prisoners and reckoned that they were facing at least a regiment, nearly ten times their numbers, mostly from the Hitler Youth Division with a few from Panzer Lehr.

'Shit,' someone said when Major Scott passed that news on over the net. Whoever had forgotten to switch off his mic remained anonymous, but had probably expressed the general feeling.

The lieutenant commanding 1 Troop was shot through the head as he peered from the turret and died instantly. A sergeant in another troop was either standing taller or luckier, because the sniper's bullet took him in the shoulder, wounding rather than killing him. Then in a flurry of mortar rounds, Sergeant Powell in 3 Troop's Firefly was hit by shrapnel and there was a good chance that he would lose an eye. James sent Collins over to take command of the Charlie tank, and had Miller come up to man the gun. Their own artillery was hammering the hedge and the woods behind it, which seemed to keep the enemies' heads down, because there was no incoming fire while they made the changes and a half-track evacuated Powell.

'Baker to all stations. Our little friends say that they have seen an enemy hornet nosing around that wood, out.'

A panzer. That would be the real test. So far, they were managing well enough against unsupported infantry, but the Germans had done so well in these last years by using tanks, guns and infantry all together. It was the way of modern war.

James scanned the hedge with his binoculars and could see nothing at first. Without a co-driver they had one less pair of eyes to watch the corn and shoot at the first sign of trouble.

'Gunner, traverse left, by the tall tree. Think it's an elm.' He expected Collins to correct him then remembered that Miller was in his place. 'On. See anything?' The gunner's periscope was powerful, better probably than his field glasses.

'Maybe, sir.' Miller did not sound confident, then his tone picked up. 'Yes, there's something.' That was all James could see, something that looked straight and angular, something not natural, but man-made.

'What are you loaded with?'

'HE, sir,' Albright reported.

'Never mind. Follow it with AP. Gunner, wait for the order, then put some tracer on that spot, then fire the seventy-five.' James adjusted the switch. 'Baker Three to Able, Baker and Charlie. Target hornet, half left, next to the tall tree in the hedge. Observe my fire and then fire at will, out.' He switched back. 'Gunner, co-ax.'

Miller's foot went down on the button and the bright tracer went almost lazily towards the target. It was always strange how slow it looked when going away from you. The 75mm boomed, and the other three tanks joined in with machine guns and then their main guns. The tree's trunk cracked and fell; Miller sent another shot, AP this time, for Albright had loaded very quickly.

The explosion was huge, a great jet of red and orange flame shooting up from behind the hedge.

'Bugger me,' Miller said.

Surely that was too much for a tank, even if all its shells and petrol went up in one instant.

'Must have been an ammunition lorry,' James said, wondering why anyone would drive such a dangerous cargo so close to the enemy. He glanced around the troop and out of the corner of his eye saw the briefest of flashes from a spot on the hedge well to the right of the explosion. He saw, or thought he saw, the wheat parting in a line, heading straight for them, then the Sherman staggered as there was a brilliant flash of light from inside the turret and his legs and stomach were splashed by something hot and wet. Smoke and dust made him cough.

'Bail out,' he shouted, hoped he was on the intercom not the net, but there was no time. He glimpsed Miller through the murk, and the man was still sitting in the gunner's seat in front of him, fingers around the pistol grip that allowed him to traverse the turret. He just did not have a head anymore.

James unhooked his microphone and hauled himself out of the hatch. Albright was behind him, face white as a sheet, and James reached down to help him and the boy flinched as his arm was grabbed. James' hand was wet with more blood, for Albright's right arm was slashed open and bleeding profusely, but he got the lad out.

The other tanks were firing at the hedge line, trying to locate the gun or the tank or whatever it was, but more high velocity guns were firing at them, and someone had the sense to start letting off smoke to hide them until they could sort themselves out. Whitefield appeared, taking Albright by the other side, and they managed to lower him off the hull to the rear, keeping the Sherman between them and the enemy.

'Dusty?' Whitefield asked, for Miller had the inevitable nickname.

James shook his head. 'Let's get back in case it goes up.'

Albright shook them off, determined to walk, so Whitefield followed behind like an anxious mother watching a toddler take his first steps. James pointed to the far edge of the field. 'Take him back!' He ran towards the Firefly, then flung himself down as his own Sherman suddenly erupted, a gout of flame shooting up out of the open hatch. He was twenty yards away and the heat felt as if it was searing his skin. The smoke screen in front of them was thick now, helped by the rest of the squadron.

The Sherman burned, flames coming out of the turret hatch

and the driver's hatch Whitefield had left open after his escape. Above the flames was a dense column of black smoke. In the storage box behind the turret, and stored wherever they had found a good place, were most of his and the crew's possessions, all now slowly being incinerated. Along with the remains of Miller. The thought came, sudden and treacherous, and James wanted to vomit. His hand squeezed tightly against his breast pocket and that seemed to help.

James also wanted to go with Whitefield, but his job was to command 3 Troop, and that meant being in a tank. It also meant evicting Collins, who was the most junior and inexperienced commander, so the obvious one to replace. Collins was not impressed: his reluctance to leave the safety offered by three inches of hardened steel was obvious. James felt an exactly opposite reluctance about getting into a tank again with his last one burning so fiercely and so close.

'Baker Three, this is Sunray, I am now in Baker Three Charlie.'

'Baker to all stations Baker, we're pulling back. The infantry have done all they can, but cannot hold out any longer against these numbers. And we'll be sitting ducks in the open without them. Withdraw to the road. Artillery will cover us.'

James heard the whistle of shells passing overhead – a lot of shells. The smoke was still between them and the hedge and woodland, so they could not see the deluge of rounds landing there, but the rapid succession of booms were loud even with headphones on. So many shells were falling that it was almost like the barrage covering the landing.

As they pulled back, he saw Collins and Whitefield helping Albright onto one of the half-track ambulances. The two men climbed onto the narrow back of a scout car. Collins raised an arm, perhaps a salute or simply a wave. James did the same.

Half an hour later they were ordered back to re-join the rest of the regiment as it continued its advance.

20.45 hrs, Camp B43, Sussex

The Mess remained rowdy, even if the early enthusiasms brought on by the absence of the colonel and the dour Probert had subsided. Mark Crawford felt something in his hair and reached up to evict a little piece of bread, legacy of a wild bombardment of bread rolls over dinner. He was also nursing a very sore leg courtesy of a game of indoor rugby. The papers offered little distraction, even though they were full of news about the invasion, and not simply because a group of subalterns were singing strongly and badly in one corner, while in another a poker school, formed by their three Canadians and joined by any Britons willing to become poorer, seemed to be getting louder by the minute.

Mark had never thought that he would miss the presence of Major Probert, but the situation of Evans and his poor mother filled his mind, making it difficult to feel much interest in anything else. *Jane* had all her clothes on and did not say anything particularly funny today, so that offered no real distraction. Post – both into and from the camp – was to resume from tomorrow, presumably on the basis that now that the invasion had happened no one could give the secret away anymore. Mark wondered whether he ought to write home and whether it would be too bold to write to Anne, and perhaps a mistake before she replied to his last letter. Most of all he wondered whether Probert's absence had anything to do with Evans. Surely something could be done? They were all devoted to the task of overthrowing one tyrant and a powerful state in Germany; it must be easier to squash a petty tyrant in a little Welsh village.

'Thinking great thoughts, young Mark?'

The adjutant had appeared beside his chair without Mark noticing. David Hopkins was not a tall man, but bristled with military efficiency and smartness and was good at his job as the CO's extra eyes, ears, and as his general dogsbody.

'Any word on our move?' Mark asked.

'Nothing new. Assume that Sunday's cricket match will be cancelled because we will be on our way. Wish we could cancel Saturday's football tournament. Always get more casualties from football than anything else, even rugby. Still, all that healthy body, healthy mind stuff must be right, even if old Martial probably did not have in mind the shin-kicking propensities of 916 Williams.'

'Juvenal,' Mark said without thinking.

'Really, his parents christened him Juvenal Williams? That can't have gone down well in Maesteg. No wonder the fellow is so angry. Dear, dear... Anyway, that is beside the point. We have a fresh draft due in tomorrow, so there may be a change or two to your platoon and others. Just wanted to give you warning.'

Mark nodded, although he did not like the thought of losing anyone he knew to get strangers in their place. There was another worry. Every battalion selected officers and men from each company and held them back as LoB – left out of battle. The idea was that initial losses to the battalion could be replaced by men already familiar with the unit and its ways of doing things. A few weeks ago the selection had been made for these first line reserves, who were taken from the Glamorgans to a Reserve Holding Unit. At the time, Mark had been terrified that he would be chosen, as one of the newest subalterns in the battalion. Some of that was genuine keenness, more the desire to keep the platoon he knew and have Sergeant Dalton beside him. He did not fancy waiting to fill a dead man's shoes – or a wounded or captured man's shoes for that matter.

'Oh, one more thing. The colonel is due back late tonight and called to tell me that he would like a word with you in the morning. Ten hundred hours.'

Mark nodded again, his heart sinking. Perhaps they had decided to hold him back after all. The adjutant departed and Mark remained in his chair, paper held up in front of him. His eyes did not really see the words or pictures, as he tried to think whether there was any hint that he was not going be picked for the first team, the ones who would land together. Only later did he realise that he had stopped worrying about Mrs Evans. He felt guilty about this, but it was still the fear of being left behind that consumed him and later robbed him of sleep.

D+3, Friday 9th June

09.30 hrs, south-east of Bayeux, Normandy

THE PLAN HAD changed, as plans did, even on exercise, where the umpires had a fondness for setting a new problem as soon as the first phases were complete. James had managed to get almost three hours' sleep, for there had been so much to do the night before when they had laagered back with the rest of the regiment. There was an Orders or O Group, explaining what had happened, and what was likely to happen tomorrow, then another one just after dawn this morning to fill in the details.

The drive south to Point 102 had failed, blocked by enemy forces too strong to barge aside, at least quickly and without heavy losses. However, to the west the brigade's other column was doing a little better, heading for Point 103. That suggested that the Germans were weaker in that sector, so the 165th RAC and an infantry battalion were to swing round even further to the west and outflank Point 103. There was a lot to arrange, both with the infantry battalion and the artillery who would follow close behind with their self-propelled guns. James was too junior to be involved in all of this, but even troop commanders needed to know what was arranged and how their tasks fitted into the wider picture. There was a lot to take in, maps to be marked and timings set down.

A new Sherman was not available, although one was promised by tonight along with replacements for Miller, Albright and

Sergeant Powell. James decided to command 3 Troop from the Firefly, rather than disrupt either of the other crews. B Squadron was at the head of the column, and 3 Troop second, and behind them 1 Troop in front of HQ. Corporal Bell led in Three Baker, the Firefly came next and Sergeant Dove followed.

Half a dozen infantrymen clung to the back of each tank, for the aim was to go faster than men could walk. Most were Geordies, stocky men who grinned and smoked and chattered. The rain was constant and the soldiers were soon drenched, as was James, who stood so that he was half out of the open hatch, partly to see, but also to be sociable with the infantry lieutenant who was riding with him and was eager to talk.

James was soaked, his battledress collar rubbing against his skin no matter how much he tried to adjust the silk scarf around his neck. His overalls were so stained with Miller's blood and brains that he had taken them off as soon as he could. They had gone to be washed, but he rather hoped that he would never see them again. His gear had burned along with the tank, and although 3 Troop had done a good job scrounging and begging replacements for him, and for Collins and Whitefield, there had not been time to get much. He had slept in Sergeant Powell's blankets and shaved with a borrowed razor, but for the moment in other respects owned just what he stood in. As they drove along, his legs were warm, comfortably inside the fusty interior of the Firefly's turret, but his torso was wet and cold, and his face numb from the rain. It did not feel much like summer, even though he and the infantry subaltern talked at length about the contrasting merits of off and leg spin and the best way to play them.

Progress was good, in spite of the weather, which soon meant that they were all being sprayed with dirty water from the tank in front. No main road, or even a half decent minor one, ran in the direction they wanted, so from early on they followed narrow tracks when they could, and more often were in open fields, going up and down slopes, across ditches and banks. It

was a bumpy ride, and quite a few times he called to the infantry
to hang on, but there was something immensely exciting about
it. Shermans were fast, by the standards of most tanks, and at
times it felt like riding a point-to-point on a good mount.

'My corporal has just told me he reckons this is a canny way
to travel,' the infantry lieutenant told James.

'Is that good?'

'Highest praise. Still, I wouldn't swap places with you once
the shooting starts.'

'No?' James was surprised. 'There is something reassuring
about being behind armoured plate. This' – he pulled at his own
clammy battledress tunic – 'won't stop a bullet.'

The subaltern rapped his knuckles on the top of the turret.
'Ow. That was a damned silly thing to do.' He massaged the
fingers with his other hand. 'Still, it's all very well, but they have
to see us to shoot us. Hard to hide in one of these infernal
machines. And they tend to throw a lot bigger shells at you than
they do at us. No thanks, you can keep your tin cans.'

'Tin! What a cheek. This is best quality Meccano all tied
together with boot laces.'

James had one ear uncovered, the other filled with the hiss
and crackle broken by periodic transmissions. He had long
since realised that everyone in the Army, while they might
moan and bitch about their equipment and role, was never
keen to swap with anyone else. If asked, he would say that he
was happier in a Sherman than any other tank, and knew from
experience that the men in the fast Cromwells or the slow and
heavily armoured Churchills felt exactly the same about their
own tanks. Infantrymen always swore that the thought of being
cooped up in a tank terrified them, while tankmen thought the
same about the idea of walking towards the enemy without any
protection whatsoever. Either the Army was good at finding
the right people for each role, or even a little time in a unit
convinced you that this was the best place to be, given the likely
other options. Of course, lots of men joked about working

their ticket out of the Army, or transferring to some cushy billet hundreds of miles from the enemy, but few did anything to make it happen. If it was enthusiasm, it remained well hidden, and if was pride, then it was an angry, even sullen pride. He could not help thinking that it was more about innate stubbornness.

'Well, as I say, no offence meant.'

James smiled. 'Hold on again, this next bit is going to be bumpy!' The tank followed Corporal Bell's Sherman down a steep slope, over a low wall, already half demolished and crushed by the vehicles ahead, then surged up another hillside and over a low bank topped by a hedge. The Sherman had to climb steeply, then crashed down on the far side once the weight tipped it over. They thumped to the ground, and one of the infantrymen yelled as he fell off the back. He was not hurt and ran to catch up, his mates laughing and catcalling as he came after them.

'Bit like the Keystone Kops,' the subaltern suggested.

The country was much closer than the open field of yesterday's action and it was hard to see far in any direction. Most of the lanes were like tunnels, the trees on either side meeting overhead. Fields were small, each surrounded by hedges on top of a bank of packed earth and even stone cleared from the farmland over the centuries. Some were higher than the tanks, although as far as possible they avoided these. Even the smaller ones meant that a tank rose up high as it climbed, exposing its underside, the most vulnerable spot with the thinnest armour since no one expected an enemy to be able to shoot at it. Thankfully, each time it happened there was no enemy waiting to send a shell through the Sherman's floor and blow them all to oblivion.

Indeed, there was no sign of enemy at all, or even of the war, for these fields had not been fought over or bombed. Intelligence appeared to have guessed right, and there were no enemy troops here – at least not yet.

The earpiece crackled into life. 'Item One to Sunray.' That

was the Recce Troop under its new commander. 'Have reached Morningside. No sign of hostiles.' Morningside was the code for a hedge line about a thousand yards short of Point 103. 'High ground seems clear.'

James passed on the good news to the subaltern. 'You'll soon have to start walking again.'

'Probably. Hard to find a cab these days.'

10.00 hrs, Camp B43, Sussex

Colonel Davis was very popular in the battalion. He was a Welshman, short and stocky like so many men from the south, but was not simply good with others from the region: all the men under his command liked him, for although he was firm and could be acidic in his criticism when he was not satisfied, he was predictable and that counted for a lot. They knew that he cared about their welfare and they knew that he treated them with an avuncular kindness. They also knew that he wanted his battalion to be the best, and worked flat out to make them so, driving them when they needed it, and wheedling and tricking every little benefit he could get from higher powers.

This morning he was as smart as ever, save for the bushy moustache which never quite obeyed orders. In parts it remained the raven black of his youth, but like his hair it was now heavily speckled with grey. The effect, combined with his air of friendly aggression and enthusiasm, was of a mature terrier. In fact he was both, just short of his forty-sixth birthday and a former territorial who had been with the battalion for as long as anyone could remember. He had seen action in 1918, arriving at the front just in time for the big German offensives, had got mentioned in Despatches twice, somehow survived unscathed, and then left the Army to study for the bar. Since then, he had built up a highly successful law practice in Cardiff, while spending his weekends and summers with the volunteers.

There were not many territorials commanding battalions these days, and he was old by the standards of the modern army, so that more than once fears had grown that he would be replaced. Yet he was still there, fighting for his battalion, looking after them all. It helped that he was very persuasive, and it was easy to imagine him holding forth before a jury.

'Come on in, my dear fellow.' The colonel gestured towards the chair. No one else was in the little room used as an office. 'Now how are your chaps doing?'

'Just fine, sir. Although I think they'll be happier once we're off.'

Davis' moustache twitched as he smiled. 'Yes, of course. Waiting is hard on everyone.' A Welsh speaker, he spoke slowly and from the back of his throat as many did. 'Now, I suppose you are frightened that I'll send you to the RHU?'[1]

Mark could not stop himself from jumping in his seat.

The colonel chuckled. 'Well, don't worry. Like the rest of us, you will get your chance for the Hun to have first crack at you. Division wanted me to take half a dozen new subalterns in place of established men even at this eleventh hour.' Davis was lying, but understood a thing or two about men. 'I told them – very politely of course – to go and boil their heads. I do not intend to lose any good men at this late stage. God knows where they'd send you from RHU if some other fool battalion gets shot up. So, young Crawford, here you are and here you stay.'

'Thank you, sir,' Mark managed to say as relief flooded over him.

Davis smiled again. 'I'll remind you of that when we're in France being mortared!

'No, there is no need for you to worry. I wanted to see you for two reasons, both about Private Evans. First, to say well done for finding out what was happening. Secondly to pass on some

---

1   A Reinforcement Holding Unit consisted of men held back to replace casualties.

news so that you can tell the lad yourself – I think it would be better coming from you.

'Major Probert went to the family home. It's on our patch, so the regiment has friends, and so do I – as does the major and several others. He took a couple of MPs, arranged things with the local JP and the constabulary, and went calling on this Evans fellow. Said they were searching for his son, who had deserted, and they had a warrant to make it all legal. They went late, and the fellow was half cut, and if I know the major, he was deliberately provocative. The result was a policeman with a black eye, Mr Evans with a broken arm and under arrest for assaulting a rozzer. The magistrates are friendly, and with luck he'll get six months. In the meantime, Mrs Evans and the daughter have been brought to my father's place down in the Gower. They're desperately short of help, as everyone is these days, and it's a big house, so the mother has been taken on as housekeeper, the daughter can earn a few bob as a maid, while finishing her schooling if she wants. Might help her to have a better life. Either way, they are out of it, somewhere safe and away from that bounder.' Davis frowned as if surprised to find himself using the word.

Mark struggled to find the right words. 'Thank you, sir,' he stammered. 'That is wonderful.'

'Well, it's help come very late in the day for that poor woman. I can only imagine what she's been through. And as to thanks, the major deserves the most. Pity he couldn't have just shot the bugger, but even I cannot think of a way to twist the law to make that legal… And it's supposed to be laws and decency and all that, that we are fighting for after all.

'But that is the best we could manage. A regiment is like a family. There are good ones and bad ones, just like other families, but most are pretty good and try to look after their own. Never forget that.

'Now, I suggest you inform Evans. And tell the lad that he's coming with us when we go, arrest or not.'

Mark stood up and came to attention. 'Thank you, sir.'

'Well, run along. Oh, and young Mark?'

'Sir?'

'Try not to leave your revolver lying around in future.'

'Sir.'

12.30 hrs, Point 103, Normandy

James stood with his back to the hedge, signalling for the Firefly to come on. Croucher, the driver, had his head out of the hatch to see, because this was delicate if they were to avoid the ditch to the side. The rain had stopped, but the grass was slick underfoot and the field was muddy, made worse by the churning of tracks.

At the last minute, James moved out of the way, letting the tank edge as close to the corner of the field as it could. The ground was sloping down, which meant that the long barrel of the seventeen-pounder cleared the foliage without them having to cut a gap in it. Ahead, the landscape of Normandy rolled away, rising and dipping, a patchwork of fields and woods, with a scatter of farms and a few villages surrounded by orchards. They were on the south-western corner of the high ground called Point 103, near a patch of more open country. The squadron was in defensive positions, ready for fuel and reinforcements to come up and for Brigade to plan the next step in the advance. Until then, they would wait, and see whether the Germans were inclined to put in an appearance.

The whistle came first, and James ran, bounding up the sloped front of the tank and onto the turret. The first shell burst before he got there, fifty yards away, so that the shock of its explosion was no more than a gentle punch. Even so, little pieces of shrapnel pinged off the rear deck of the hull. James scrambled in, saw Dove and Bell doing the same, for both commanders had dismounted to guide their tanks forward. A quick exchange over the wireless confirmed that no one was hurt, then everyone sat, hatches closed, for a long five minutes as the shells rocked the tanks.

'Our poor paintwork,' Lance Corporal Greene said as they heard little strikes against the armour. He was the gunner, sitting in front of James. Flynn, the loader, was on the other side of the immense breech, and the turret felt even more cramped than in an ordinary Sherman.

'Could be worse,' Flynn said.

'Well, it's still early, give it time. I'm just worried about Mickey.'

All tanks in the regiment had markings of the brigade low down on the front and back of the hull, along with the regimental number. On either side of the turret was a dark blue hollow square for B Squadron. Near the rear of the hull there was the serial number for the tank, and further forward its name. B Squadron tanks in the 165th had names beginning with H. The Firefly was *Hopeful*, Sergeant Dove had *Halifax* and Corporal Bell was in *Hythe*. James' old mount had been *Hector*. Lots of extra markings to do with weight and loading had been chalked on before they crossed the Channel, and these were still more or less in place. However, on the LCT James had noticed that *Hopeful* also had a neat little painting of Mickey Mouse in front of the tactical sign. He had noticed, but then decided that this was something it was better not to notice formally, so had said nothing. Once again, he felt that a lot of an officer's job came in not seeing or reacting to things according to regulations. He still hoped this did not make him a bad officer.

'He's a cartoon. You can touch up the little bugger if he's scratched,' Flynn insisted. 'That's if the Jerries don't use him as an aiming point. Some gunner could send an eighty-eight right at your little mouse and your bloody head just behind him.'

'Nah, they'll see him and laugh. Everyone likes cartoons. Even Jerries.'

'Don't think he's Aryan though,' Croucher cut in. 'They won't like that.'

There had been no shelling for a few minutes, and James decided to open the hatches again. He peered out, breathing in deeply. The air smelled of wet grass, mud and petrol fumes with a faint hint of cordite, but it was a lot better than the fusty air inside the tank.

'Mind if I empty the po, sir?' Flynn asked. The crew were still not sure of him and his little ways, so tended to be formal.

'Fine.'

The loader opened the square hatch above his position and appeared, carefully holding a brass shell case. It was an empty, fired off yesterday or the day before, and now used to urinate into when it was too risky to get outside the tank. Flynn theatrically held up a finger to test the wind, smiled because there was none, and flung the contents over the side. He turned it upside down and tapped the bottom of the shell to force out the last drips.

'Down in the sewer, shovelling up manure...' Greene sang over the intercom. So far they had not had to do anything more than piss into the empty case. Even so, it added to the stench of grease, sweat, damp woollen battledress and sheer concentrated humanity inside the tank.

James saw something in a valley about a mile and a half away, so raised his binoculars, adjusting the focus.

'Baker Three to Baker, there is movement to the south-west.' He grabbed his map and gave a grid reference. Other stations called in to say that they could see something, but were not sure what it was. The heavy rain meant that there was no dust to betray vehicles driving fast, but there should not be any friendlies over there.

'Baker One to Baker, I can see tanks. Figures one zero, range three thousand, repeat three thousand yards, moving north-west.'

'Bearing Baker One?'

'Sorry, Baker. Oh, they're south-west of us at the moment. Bearing oh... two twenty degrees?' That was Charlie West, commander of 1 Troop, who always sounded like a minor character from a musical comedy set in a country house. James could not see the tanks, because his view in that direction was blocked by a line of trees.

'Baker to all stations Baker, be more precise in reporting. It saves time.'

'Sorry.' James always expected West to follow each comment with 'Anyone for tennis?', but the lieutenant failed to oblige.

Major Scott must have spoken to the Royal Artillery observer, because soon the FOO[2] called in a barrage to pound the area. So the day continued, mainly heard rather than seen, as reports came over the net of suspected enemy movements and the artillery responded. Sometimes James could see the shells erupting in the distance and sometimes he could not. Now and then the Germans responded with guns or mortars, and sometimes the salvos landed around 3 Troop and sometimes they did not. The squadron was spread out, and all save a few tanks hidden by folds in the ground, or hedges and trees. Radio chatter was almost constant, for the regiment was in one place, which meant that someone nearly always had something to report.

As far as he could, James kept his hatches unbuttoned, wanting to see as much as possible, only ducking down and closing up when the shells were close. That was fine with the big guns and their distinct whistling approach. Mortars were cruder, lobbing bombs high in the air and falling gently, almost soundlessly. One landed between his tank and Sergeant Dove's when both commanders were busy standing tall, staring out through their binoculars. The explosion was not as loud as a shell, the fountain of earth smaller, but it was so sudden that James panicked, jerking down and pulling on the hatch so hard that the heavy steel thumped him on the head.

---

2   A Forward Observation Officer was a Royal Artillery officer with a radio team allowing him to direct the fire of batteries miles to the rear and unable to see the target.

If it had caught him a fraction of a second sooner, it might have broken bone, but as it was it caught the band of his headphones and simply pushed him hard onto his seat. He blinked, trying to focus. It was like being caught on the head by a bouncer.

'You alright, skipper?' Flynn asked. The informality was a sign of his concern.

'Bit of whack on the head.' James managed to grin. 'Least it wasn't anywhere too important.' His head throbbed and he hoped that the Germans would keep on shooting for some time and give him the excuse to sit there for a while.

After another six explosions the mortars stopped, but from then on that became the pattern. Sudden flurries of fire, one or two rounds from each gun or tube, first in one spot, then in another, feeling and probing the front slope of Point 103, like the fingers of a blind man searching for something. The Germans were shooting by map, unable to see the British positions, simply trying to work out where they might be. Now and then, there was an airburst from a bigger gun, the crack appallingly loud, as the fuse detonated the shell before it hit the ground and spread wickedly sharp fragments over a wide area.

James' head still hurt, and he suspected that there would be a bruise and a sore patch for days, but somehow he made himself open up as soon as things were quiet. There were infantry around somewhere, but he could not see them, and the field on the other side of the hedge was pasture, the grass too low to hide a man, so the Germans could not creep up on them easily. Still, he needed to see and report, and spot any threat in time to do something. His eyes kept being drawn to a field, nearly a mile away in front and on a hillside, the green broken by tiny white dots as cattle grazed. With his binoculars he could see them like toy animals, apparently unconcerned by the madness of men.

Half a dozen mortar rounds dropped some way to their left, the dull crumps reaching them a few moments later.

'Baker, this is Baker One.' That was Charlie West's call sign, but not his voice. 'Please send assistance. Sunray down, out.'

A few minutes later shells landed further back, reaching behind the ridge, then it was the mortars again, and somehow James sensed it was coming and crouched down so that his head was below the rim of the cupola. The bombs landed just ahead of them in front of the hedge, and only a few fragments struck the gun mantlet.

If the Germans were clever, they might change the pattern and drop some more in the same spot after a slight pause, so James waited a little longer before bobbing his head up again. Nothing happened, which did not mean that they would not be clever next time. He spotted some more movement in the distance and reported it. The messages over the net made it clear that the Germans were moving in force and with plenty of armour to the north-west, away from Point 103. If they kept on going they could get behind the brigade and threaten the whole position. There were supposed to be infantry in the path, so it was to be hoped that they would stop the panzers.

So far, the Germans were not coming at 103 head on, but kept on shelling the area, while the British sent back even more shells anywhere they thought the enemy were moving or concentrating. There was no sign of the RAF or American planes, which might mean that the heavy rain had not yet cleared back in England.

James scanned the land ahead of him, coming back as always to the field of cows. He suspected that he was smiling, for there was something reassuring about such a pastoral scene.

A shell burst among the white dots, then another, sending up great fountains of earth. He could not tell whether the shells were ours or theirs, or whether barrels were worn, charges defective, the number one commanding each gun was not paying attention or the officer in the command post had his map upside down. When the dust cleared half the dots were no longer moving.

James sighed.

14.45 hrs, Camp B43, Sussex

'One cannot expect the world to be perfect,' the Education officer explained, pushing his horn rimmed spectacles back up onto the bridge of his nose. Why did nearly every education officer not only wear glasses, but wear the same style, and have lean, ill featured faces like a caricature of a schoolmaster in *Punch*? Presumably when a man was called up, the Army took one look and posted everyone like this to the Army Educational Corps. Or maybe the universities were to blame? Whatever it was and whoever was responsible, it was a surprise when AEC officers did not look like Mr Crenshaw, did not have a supercilious air, or left leaning political views.

Judd did not object to any of these things in themselves. He would be the first to admit that he was far from classically handsome, and knew his hair more naturally went to the shape of a wind-blown haystack than anything else. He wore glasses, if only for reading; it was that or hold a book out at arm's length. He suspected that had he needed them to see the rest of the time then he would not be an infantryman – signalman, engineer, tankman, perhaps, clerk or storeman, certainly, but you hardly ever saw anyone in a rifle platoon who wore spectacles. It was different for officers, as were so many things, and these days there were a few of them who wore specs.

Judd longed to go to university. There had been much about school he had not liked, the pettiness and regulation – although as it turned out these were marvellous preparation for the Forces. Judd loved books and reading and ideas and arguments. History was his passion, a common one with friends like Crawford and Taylor, followed by poetry and Shakespeare. At prep school they had had wonderful masters for English and history, men who made both come alive. He still remembered the thrill of classes where they took turns to act the parts of all the great plays.

Memories of grammar school were less kind. The money had run out, so he could not go off to boarding school. A new boy, he was resented, and his sadness about so many things had made him volatile and resentful in turn. He broke rules, got caught and punished, and did not make close friends. Relief when he left at fifteen was followed by deep disappointment when he started work in a chandler's office in Cardiff docks. There was the excitement of the Blitz, the sight of battered and scarred merchant ships coming in, but in the main there was drudgery and boredom. Lists and accounts, more lists and more documents to copy, and the oppressive control of the stern old men who ran the place and had no time for the chatter of a boy. They had the authority and he did not, and his mother needed the pittance he earned to help pay the rent and buy them enough to eat – a struggle even with rationing. So every day he cycled to work, spent the long hours in the dusty and cold office, unless the siren went and they moved to the shelter, and at the end of each long day he cycled home.

'The world is not perfect,' Crenshaw insisted, repeating his point. 'If one points to the more brutal aspect of the Soviet regime, they must be seen in context. This is a state born of revolution and civil war, one that had to fight for its very existence.'

'Sir, didn't we send some of our boys to help fight the Reds?' a soldier asked.

'Yeah, we did. The regiment was there,' another confirmed.

'Imperialist lackeys,' Douglas chipped in, although through habit more than commitment. He was an older man, at least thirty-five, and rumour said that he had served with the International Brigade in Spain. 'Trampling on the oppressed.'

'Well, that is one way of putting it.' Crenshaw gave a toothy grin. He desperately wanted to encourage humour in these sessions, feeling that a lighter tone helped his audience to react and think more deeply about the topics in question. Sadly, the things that made him laugh rarely seemed to strike the same chord with anyone else.

Friday afternoons were one of the gentler moments in the Army's week. Whenever they were in camp, it was a time for lectures and discussions, whether led by AEC officers or nervous and hastily prepared subalterns, with everyone inside, allowed to smoke and sit at ease. The War Department encouraged such things as good for the soul and perhaps for morale, and topics were wide ranging, from religion to politics, industry and the economy, plans for a better Britain after the war, and most of all the reasons why we fought and would prevail in the end. This afternoon's theme was 'Our friends, the Soviets'. Crenshaw was beginning to regret the choice, especially since Judd was here, for the bloody man asked too many questions.

'As Private Douglas points out, if a little, shall we say, bluntly' – the hoped for laugh did not come – 'no one is without sin or blemish. After all, the Empire covers a quarter of the globe, more or less. The British are imperialists since we have an empire – and not everyone who lives within that empire is automatically happy with the situation.'

'But Stalin did a deal with Hitler to carve up Poland back in thirty-nine,' Judd pointed out.

'Yes, yes, but that was before he understood the true nature of the Nazis. And before the Russians were ready to fight. Like us, they appeased to gain time, and since we are without blemish we should not cast stones.' Crenshaw was an atheist, but tended to become Biblical whenever he was on the back foot. There was simply a power in the language.

'Rough on the poor bloody Poles, though. And they're good lads,' someone said.

'And boy, can they drink!' another added.

Crenshaw rallied. 'But the borders of countries in central Europe were fluid, the product of politics after the Great War rather than what people there really wanted. Some of them just didn't want to belong to the state put in charge of them. So it's not simple, but very complex...' He trailed off, sensing that this was weak.

'Sir, isn't that what Hitler said about ethnic Germans in other countries?' Judd asked.

Bastard, Crenshaw thought. He wondered about using his rank to close the debate, before deciding against it. It may not have been what he wanted, but the whole idea was to get the men talking and thinking. Things would be much worse if the assembled soldiery simply sat in silence staring at him until the two hours were done. Instead, he beamed at them as if delighted by this show of knowledge. 'Indeed, that is the excuse the Nazis used for their conquests, which illustrates how we must be careful with the claims made by any state. And...'

'Including our own, sir?' Judd tried to make the question sound as innocent as possible.

'That's it, get him Judd-boy,' came softly from somewhere at the back.

'No. ... Well, yes, but that's why we have free elections to choose our leaders.'

'But we can't all vote,' someone said, who like many of them was under twenty-one.

'No, but...'

For a while Judd said nothing as others took over. Part of him was sorry for Mr Crenshaw, who was a decent enough man in his way and only doing his job. Still, he was part of the Army, of the powers that ruled their lives – definitely them and not us.

More than that he liked arguing, and it had become a deep habit, not that he was daft enough to try it when they were doing anything serious. Friday afternoons were a time to relax, and most of the men were content to let it be at that, to daydream and sit in silence for a short while. Only a handful were earnest and a few more simply wanted to be awkward.

Judd was both. His mother was a devout chapelgoer; his father had loved her so much that he had made every open sign of adherence and participation in the life of the Gospel Hall. Judd was not sure, and they had never had the chance to speak as one adult to another, but suspected that his beliefs were vaguer, but also very deep. His father had once said that he had seen too much in life not to hope that there was some great force for good behind everything and something better to come, which meant that he chose to believe in God. Judd would have liked to have known his father better, but TB had taken him in the end, slowly wearing his lungs away, killing him from the inside.

His mother's faith remained staunch through all the trials and sorrows; not the satisfied, complacent faith of those who had never had anything bad happen in their lives, but it was sincere nonetheless. Judd could not match it. He struggled to believe and to be so sure of anything, for the world seemed so far beyond his control. He had gone along to chapel and to its Sunday School and later the various youth clubs and services. They sang, talked, listened more, and played table tennis when it was wet or cold and outdoor sports when it was better weather. It provided plenty of entertainment, and as they grew older there were plenty of girls. Mark Crawford's parents were stalwarts of the place, where his stern father was an even sterner elder of the Assembly. Even James Taylor joined in a lot of the clubs to play sports and spend time with some of the lasses. There were two pairs of sisters in particular who drew him and many others for the thrills offered by safe flirtation.

Yet Judd could not help asking questions whenever there was an opportunity and whether or not he actually believed what he was saying. He liked to find out how someone coped, especially the men who talked as if they had the answer to everything, or the ones who told him simply to believe and not think. There were complaints and he was ejected from one or two meetings. Old Mr Rawlings, a retired ship's master, was the one who persisted with him, listening, answering and reasoning with the patience of a true saint. Judd often felt guilty thinking back to the sheer bloody-mindedness with which he questioned the old man, seeking every way possible not to agree.

At fifteen, his father's death still a fresh memory and the bombers overhead many nights, Judd decided that he could not believe in a God who would let so many die so very horribly. It also shocked some of his more pious schoolfellows to challenge their ideals and he enjoyed that. By the time he had left and started work, he had decided that politics offered better hope for the future than religion. He went to the library and read everything they had, even ploughing through Marx, and that caught the eye of Miss Prentice, who worked in the office. She was tall, with the build of a hockey player, a narrow, almost sharp face, with dark blonde hair cut short and pinned up to keep it under control. She talked to him a few times, then took him to party meetings.

Judd fell in love. Not a stylish dresser, Clara Prentice was very obviously a woman, and an intelligent, well-read one who took him seriously. For a while he behaved very well, listening, starting to speak at some of the sessions, but always saying what he knew they wanted to hear. They spoke of change, of a better world, where workers were respected and treated fairly, and decisions were made for the good of society as a whole and not simply the rich and privileged. Clara sometimes wore slacks instead of a dress or skirt, and he found this wonderful. She smoked too, not just cigarettes, but now and then long cigars. She was like no woman he had ever known – admittedly that was a very small field – and even when she mocked him, he continued to follow her like a puppy. She had an arrangement with one of the senior men, much older than her and more often away than present, but once or twice, her breath smelling of gin, she cuddled Bill Judd and let him touch her.

Judd was angry because the cause demanded it, and happy all at once. Yet after a year he started to ask questions again. He could not understand why the Unions and still less the party did not wholeheartedly back the war against the fascists. Someone else raised the question of the alliance between Stalin and Hitler, and after that he read as much as he could, trying to understand it. The questioner was a one-armed veteran of Spain, so a man who had proved his devotion and could not be easily dismissed, but that did not stop everyone else from trying. Men too precious to the party to be allowed to volunteer for that war and in reserve occupations for this one, assured him that it was part of the wider picture – that the world was not perfect, just as Crenshaw was telling them now.

For once, Judd had decided not to say what was expected. He argued that the pact was wrong, that Stalin was a fool and the system around him vicious and cruel, and only had itself to blame for being so nearly overrun by the Nazis, for by this time Hitler's invasion of Russia had begun.

Judd was not popular, but he kept attending and speaking. At one meeting he was punched, the blow catching him by surprise and knocking him down. He got up and punched back harder and more skilfully, for he went twice a week to the boxing gym whenever he could. Clara laughed.

That night, she asked him to come home with her to help draw up some pamphlets. Her landlady was away, but still they went to Clara's room to work there. She gave him a drink, which made him cough and he did not like, although he did his best to be polite and finish it. Her manner was strange, and she finished the bottle as he worked on the text. Suddenly, she leaned forward and kissed him, and her arms were around his waist, pulling him close, and the world became very wonderful for a boy not yet seventeen. Sometimes it felt like wrestling, for she was only a little shorter than him and strong too, and it was a while before they both were free of their trousers.

Twice more she invited him back to help with a pamphlet,

until her landlady returned. Judd still hoped, but then Clara's man came back from wherever it was he went on party business, and something seemed to have changed and would not change back. She no longer sat near him, avoided touching him, and barely spoke to him. At work she was formality personified, even cold. After a few weeks, they chanced to be alone in a side office during lunch hour, when everyone else had gone out. She was tidying up a vase of flowers perched on top of a bookcase filled with ledgers.

'These have been dead for weeks,' she said to herself, her back to him. She wore a deep red dress, long in length and years out of fashion. Judd came softly behind her and slipped an arm around her waist, pressing close.

'Darling,' he gasped. His other hand grabbed her dress and began to lift it. It was snug fitting and did not come easily, and he was little more than a child, clumsy and unpractised.

She arched her back, but said nothing. He was doing better now, lifting the hem of her dress and her slip over her drab woollen stockings. With rationing, she could not afford anything better, but the office insisted a woman cover her legs. Anything else was unladylike and quite unsuitable for the firm's reputation.

Judd's fingers touched her warm skin. She had on a slip, but there did not seem to be anything else underneath. He could smell her. He started to make little grunting sounds he could not imagine making in any other situation.

Clara lifted the jug and tipped the dirty water over his head. He sprang back, shocked, not sure whether this was something lovers did.

'Never again,' she told him. 'Never.'

'But I love you,' he begged, with all the immense self-regard of an adolescent. He lunged forward and she slapped him very hard across the face.

'But…'

Her eyes seemed full of contempt and then she did something

worse than anything else to a boy like Judd. She laughed at him – a woman of twenty-three mocking a sixteen-year-old. The bitterness remained strong, even all this time later, when he could see their brief liaison for what it was, a bored, rather angry and lonely young woman seeking a brief diversion. What was it Kipling had said, 'And I learned about women from her.' He had, learning the hard way, in bitter sleepless nights of self-pity. He did not weep. He had wept for days when his father died and promised himself that he would never again cry at any lesser grief.

Judd still had a lot to learn, but at least he had those few memories of their passion. He did not miss her, did not think he would even like her very much if they met now, but there was the memory of the feel of her body, of the wonderful release as they were joined. No wonder a lot of other poets spent so much time talking about it, or at least of the stages that got you there.

'… So I hope that answers all your questions satisfactorily,' Crenshaw ended what must have been a long speech. Judd had not been paying any attention, as his mind had wandered. The lust and its fulfilment was a good memory, and the rest was by now distant enough not to bother him too much. 'I trust that you agree, Private Judd.' Most officers did not insist on using a man's rank at every opportunity.

'Yes, sir. Absolutely, sir,' Judd said in an enthusiastic tone. Crenshaw stared at him for a moment, wondering whether this was sarcasm and deciding not to make an issue of it.

17.10 hrs, Point 103, Normandy

The reports and orders over the wireless network were constant, for with the regiment in one place there were sixty or seventy different stations on the net. Men spoke over each other, blotting out both messages, and at other times a signal was weak, half the words garbled. No exercise had ever been so confusing and it was very hard to follow.

For the last hour, as well as the periodic flurries of shell and mortar fire, the Germans had started to bring high velocity guns to bear on the gentle ridges that made up Point 103. These were tank killers, 75s or even 88s, some of them towed guns, some the same guns on tracked chassis, and some in tanks. The panzers were out there, at ranges of one and half to two miles, and they were searching for targets. Each side tried to see the other first, and at that distance a tank was a tiny thing to see, and most guns even smaller.

'Baker Three Baker to Baker Three, there's something on the edge of that orchard.'

'Baker Three Able to Baker Three, I think I can see it. Where the wall dips a bit.' Sergeant Dove had always had keen eyesight.

There was a snap in the air, and a thrumming sound as a solid shot passed between the Firefly and Bell's Sherman to bury itself deep in the earth on the gentle slope behind them.

'Got the bastard,' Dove said. 'Firing to mark target.'

'Gunner, watch the fall of shot,' James said. The immensely long barrel was already traversed to cover the spot.

There was a distant puff of smoke in front of the orchard.

'Baker Three Able, I'm too short.'

'Oh I don't think Sergeant Dove is too short,' Croucher said over the intercom. 'A fine figure of a man.'

'Anyone looks tall to you, short-arse.'

'Baker Three to Three Baker, try a shot.' James said over the chatter.

At this distance an AP shell from a Sherman's 75mm was unlikely to do much. Instead they were firing HE, which might be enough to slaughter the crew of a gun or even an open topped self-propelled gun. It was unlikely to inconvenience a tank unless some fluke knocked off an aerial or shattered a vision block.

James focused his glasses on the target. He could see the wall and just make out the spot where some of the top was broken off, the dip Dove had seen. Was there a flash? An instant later Bell's shell burst right on the wall, the dust hanging in the air, but before that a dark blur came rushing towards them, striking the sloped front of Dove's Sherman, throwing up sparks before it flew high into the air.

'Gunner, do you see the spot? Fire when ready.' There was something there. James glanced to the right, past Bell's tank, to see Dove give him a thumbs up. Then he turned back, focusing on the fading smoke by the wall. Something was nagging at him, something half remembered.

The seventeen-pounder fired at that moment, with a flash so sudden, so vast and so vivid that James could not see the hedge in front shake and the leaves ripping from branches with the blast. He felt as if he had been punched in both eyes at once. The drill was for the gunner and commander in a Firefly to close their eyes a second before it fired, but he had forgotten.

'I saw a strike!' That was Bell's voice, so excited that he forgot procedure.

'Maybe,' Dove allowed.

'I did. Look, there's smoke.'

James could see flashing lights and not much else. With a hard thump something landed just in front of the hedge. The gun's flash must have been visible to anyone watching.

He blinked, starting to glimpse his surroundings. Another shot came, this time high, although close enough for him to feel the wash of it as it passed.

'Driver, reverse. Get us back.'

Croucher went straight, and James remembered that he could not see anything behind them, so turned to check that they were not about to run anyone over. The field was empty. He could see that much.

'Baker Three Able to Baker Three. Looks like a hit, sir. Ruddy marvellous.'

'Well done, Greene.' Perhaps they had knocked out a tank or SP, or damaged one. Still, at that distance who could really say. Dark smoke could as easily be exhaust fumes from a tank driving away as one burning.

'Told you all that Mickey would be lucky,' Greene said happily.

'Baker Three to Able and Baker, I'll shift position to the other side of Able. Suspect I'll need to move each time I fire.' Five minutes of careful manoeuvring brought them to another place where the hedge was low enough for the gun to go over it. Once again, for the last part James got out and guided Croucher into position. At that moment mortar bombs started falling. James dived under the hull of the tank until they stopped.

'Thought we'd lost you, skipper,' Greene said when he got back into the turret.

'No such luck, I'm afraid. What do they say about a bad penny?'

'It's Mickey, he'll be lucky.'

James settled back, standing rather than sitting because that made it easier to bob down into the turret. He undid the button on his breast pocket and felt what was inside. He hoped that charms worked.

No more shots came at them for a while. Over the wireless they heard that a 2 Troop tank had been hit and lost a track. No one was hurt. The crew abandoned it until it could be fixed, but although there were a few more shots none had actually hit it. A little later, a solid shot decapitated 2 Troop's sergeant, but in the exchange of fire that followed, they reckoned that they knocked out at least one enemy gun.

Soon afterwards, C Squadron advanced with infantry to take the village of St Pierre, which lay in front of the position. Most of the regiment had moved so that they could offer fire support from the high ground, but 3 Troop was left to watch the other flank, which meant that James could not see any of the action, and instead simply heard snatches of radio traffic, often distorted because they were some way away and other stations were talking.

'Charlie Two to Charlie Two Able and Baker. Brass up that hedge line...'

'... there, red house on the corner. Top window...'

'Enemy hornet. Shit, it's a Tiger!'

'We're hit...'

'Got the bugger! Charlie Three Able, we have brewed an SP!'

They seemed to making progress, but then 3 Troop came under fire again and they were too busy to think of anyone else.

D+4, Saturday 10th June

JAMES WAS IN a new tank, *Hector II* already painted on its hull by the time 3 Troop had pulled back to laager for the night and to restock with ammunition and fuel. Whitefield was his driver again, and Collins his gunner, with two men brought up from the reserves, Blamey to load and Thomson as co-driver. Sergeant Martin had come up to take over the Firefly and James was glad about that, remembering the appalling flash whenever the big gun fired. He had heard that some regiments had put each troop's commander in a Firefly, but did not think that it was the best place to be. He needed to direct all four tanks, not simply their one big gun. Apart from all that, firing the things scared the living daylights out of him.

'Poor buggers,' Collins said. The 75 was traversed to cover the village of St Pierre in the lower ground ahead of them and the Germans were pummelling the whole area with artillery and light and heavy mortars as they prepared to launch a counter attack.

James had his head out in the air, but most of the time watched without the aid of his binoculars as it was hard to see anything, and apart from that the rain kept fogging up the lenses. His eyes were not doing much better, and it would be nice to have a hat with a peak rather than his tanker's beret.

Although they were higher up and could see a long way ahead of them to the heights several miles away, the ground in between dipped and rolled, which would have hidden a lot even without all the immense hedgerows, the trees and the orchards. He could see some of the roofs of St Pierre, occasionally most of a house, and more vaguely sense the village of Tilly, its close neighbour to the west – the right from his viewpoint.

The rain showed no sign of easing. At this morning's O Group, the major had joked that as a Welshman, Taylor seemed to have brought his own weather with him. James did not really think of himself as Welsh. He had been born and grown up there, lived there until he went off to board, and loved the place and still thought of it as home. Yet his father, like so many, had come there for work, and it was the sort of town where you never really heard Welsh spoken, and so many of the names and faces had a very Anglo-Saxon feel to them, with most having roots on the other side of the Bristol Channel. Coal and iron and manufacturing had brought them in their tens of thousands, year after year, changing the very nature of Wales. Many toiled, a few became rich, and rather more prospered. At home there were streets filled with ship owners and investors, less grand ones with ship's masters, and so many others connected to the sea, all living close to Cardiff without actually being in the crowded city. James' father was a doctor, his mother once a nurse, and the practice did well – at least well enough to pay for their only son's education – which had brought him here, in charge of four Sherman tanks. Hopefully it was all worthwhile, although treacherously the line about 'two thousand pounds of education drops to a ten-rupee jezail' came into his mind.

James was British, and perhaps the schools had something to do with that, and his family, and the Church in Wales, and simply growing up in a land where these things were assumed. His father had been at Gallipoli, then in Egypt and Palestine, so did not have many illusions left after all that, and was far from jingoistic. His patriotism was as quiet as it was certain. James had grown up with a sense that being British was a privilege unlike any other in the world, and that all in all a country of pirates and conquerors had done far more good than harm to the world – far more. Old Bill Judd was always questioning everything, at times the perfect sophist switching to opposite viewpoints from one day to the next. Judd doubted everything, with immense energy and determination – God help whoever had him in his platoon. Mark – the ever reliable and predictable Mark – had written to say that they were in the same battalion, but had never mentioned much more about their old friend.

Still, he did not think either of his friends had worried too much about being Welsh, nor had the other chaps, even the ones who really were. Bill Judd had once denounced them all as too bourgeois to admit the truth in one of his more impassioned – and as swiftly forgotten – tirades. Things like that just did not seem to matter much, even though they all suffered prolonged nervous tension whenever Wales played anyone in rugby, let alone for a match against England. That was different, something akin to a sacred duty to will the home side to glorious victory. For James had never really objected when English was used as a synonym, since most of the world lumped everyone together in that way as *les Anglais* or whatever the word they chose. Others felt differently, and good luck to them. After all it was a free country – and wasn't that the important thing about being British or English when you came right down to it?

Well, Bill Judd no doubt had a different view – and might have a different one again by the evening. James smiled as the rain made him blink.

Penny's family were very consciously English, her father genuinely; after twenty years in the area he still could not pronounce the double 'l' in place names. If ever the Shibboleth story was re-enacted in South Wales, then Mr Stevens was in a lot of trouble. Mrs Stevens was a local, and had one of those faces you readily imagined in the black hat, shawl and red cloak of tradition, but in her own mind she was the perfect English lady.

James did not believe that Penny thought much about such matters. Indeed, she never gave the impression of thinking very much about anything, apart from her poetry books and dreams of Arthurian romance. She read little else and had a Victorian sensibility about so many things.

At least that was what James had always thought. Her most recent letters, and that last meeting, suggested something quite different.

'Three Charlie to Baker Three, I see tanks moving. Southwest, range figures one five zero zero yards. Moving to the right on the edge of the village, over.' That was Martin in the Firefly. The fields rolling away from the ridge were larger and more open over there.

'Roger, Three Charlie, it's C Squadron.' James could see them and did not need his glasses to recognise them as Shermans. Apart from that, the radio traffic, partial though it was, was enough to let them know that they were moving to support the DLI[1] better.

'Wilco, Three, out.'

James was not sure what to make of Martin. On the face of it he appeared to come straight out of that mysterious War Department factory that manufactured wonderful NCOs, all as capable, wise, tough, and immaculately turned out as the next. This morning he was talking a lot more over the wireless than seemed necessary. James wondered whether the man was not sure of him as troop commander, so was making sure that he reported absolutely everything. Maybe. Could be nerves, though. It was easy to forget that for all his formidable exterior, Sergeant Martin had never before heard a shot fired in anger. Not everyone coped. Earlier this morning a driver in 4 Troop had smashed one hand when his hatch fell on it. Accidents happened: Sherman tanks were heavy, unforgiving lumps of machinery and there had been a few bad injuries on exercise.

---

1   Durham Light Infantry.

Then again, it might not be chance. Depended on whether someone felt that mangled and broken fingers, perhaps even needing amputation, was a price worth paying to get sent back to England.

The German barrage on St Pierre redoubled in fury for a few minutes and then ceased.

'Hello all stations, this is Sunray.' Colonel Tim's voice was as clear as a BBC announcer. 'Our friends in the village report that enemy hornets and infantry are advancing. Charlie squadron is supporting. The rest keep your eyes open for anyone trying to work around the flanks.'

At the O Group, the colonel had tried to give them some sense of the bigger picture. 'It's fluid, as you would expect,' he had explained. 'The Boche want to fling us back into the sea. The more ground we can grab, the harder it is for them to mass for an attack. Getting 103 has caught them off balance. They have to throw us off. That's why they have pulled back from that attack we saw yesterday going past us to the west. So we hold here and in St Pierre, while the Yeomanry and the infantry will try to give them more to think about by pushing west into Tilly. The Dragoons and another battalion go east to seize Cristot and Point 102.' As usual each point was emphasised by taping the big map with his riding crop.

'The thinking is that the Hun can't be strong everywhere, not at this early stage. We pin him here, draw him towards us and hold him, while the rest of the brigade pushes at the flanks for another weak spot. If we're held, we try somewhere else; if we break through, then Jerry has something else to worry about and sends panzers there instead of gathering them all for his big push.'

James could see the sense in that, although he had always wondered why higher ranks tended to refer to the Hun or Boche singular, as if there was just one of them. That conjured up the image of a single monster, vast in size and strength, wicked in his cunning and wholly malevolent, waiting behind each ridge or hedge. Save that it was so dark, it might have been a dragon from one of Penny's ridiculous stories.

'It's not just us and the Canadians anymore,' the colonel continued, his enthusiasm infectious. 'My old mob, Seventh Armoured Div. have landed. While we are pushing here, they're about to take a big swan to the west. They'll go wide, past the Americans, then south and then sweep round behind the forces in front of us. Again, Fritz will have to rush against them if he isn't to let that happen. Maybe that weakens him here, and we can push on, or maybe it just stops his big attack. If he cannot mount that, then he'll do what he always does and pull back to make another line of defence, twenty, maybe thirty miles back. That gives us more time to get reinforcements ashore.' Colonel Tim used his free hand to flick away an imaginary fly, then gave them a grin. 'So he attacks, and we stop him dead. That's if he hasn't already lost his chance while we were still weak. Or he withdraws to fight again, and we can bring our full numbers against him next time. Either way, Fritz loses in the end.'

James believed that, or at least wanted to. Everyone knew the danger was at the beginning. Just like in 1918 the Germans had to win with their big offensive. This time they had days, perhaps weeks to drive the invasion back into the sea. If not, then the numbers were against them and would never improve, so in the end the Allies would win and Hitler would lose. It was reassuring – as long as you could be sure that you would still be around at the end.

What was the end? Penny kept writing about the end of the war and their life together. James could not really imagine it, being married, having a proper job – proper in the sense that it was mundane and no one's life depended on your decisions anymore – let alone buying a house or having children. Penny obviously thought about these things a lot, and gave the impression of thinking about curtains and carpets, the clothes she would wear for housework and the special dresses to don before 'her hero' returned home. Sometimes he was 'her prince' or 'her lord'. To be honest none of it sounded much like plain old Jimmy Taylor, who was a good cricketer, a decent tennis player and a nice enough fellow in his way.

A crackle in the ear, and again his reverie was interrupted. He really needed to concentrate better.

'Three Charlie to Baker Three, I do not see anything in my forward arc, over.'

Sergeant Martin again. The voice was very assured, very precise, so perhaps the man was simply obsessive.

'Three to Three Charlie, acknowledged.' Should James say more?

'Baker to all stations,' Major Scott began before James could say anything. 'Keep off the air unless you have something vital to say. It's likely to be a busy day, so we need to keep the net clear for the essential stuff, out.'

That was a rebuke, as much to him as to the sergeant, since after all it was his troop. There was no point apologising. Hopefully Martin would settle down.

'Oh, I nearly forgot,' Scott began again. 'Happy birthday, Wallace! Key of the door, eh?' That was typical of the major, who took a deep interest in his men.

'Wallace?' Whitefield asked.

'You know him,' Collins replied. 'Ginger lad, drives the Baker tank in 1 Troop. Skinny kid.'

'Oh 'im. One of the Drivers and Knocking-shop Attendants Union, as well. Good for 'im. Don't look twenty-one though. Just like the skipper.'

'Ah well,' James assured him, 'that's because I lied about my age to join up. I'm really five.'

Collins turned round and grinned up at him. 'That would explain a hell of a lot.'

James heard the whistle and ducked down. Shells landed just behind them, then more, closer, with fragments striking the side of the tank.

'Sunray to Able and Baker stations, this is just to keep our heads down. Infantry report heavy attacks coming in against the village, out.'

After a few minutes the barrage stopped as abruptly as it had started. James poked his head up. Fine rain was falling, and it seemed to distort the sound of fighting wafting up from the village. He caught small arms, the cracks of high velocity guns, mortars and artillery. Then there were whistles, many of them, coming from behind them and some had that distinctive sound of the big naval guns. A huge British barrage fell beyond the village, some of the bursts higher than the trees that sheltered whoever was down there.

Thomson, the new co-driver, whistled. 'Will you look at that.'

'Nothing special,' Collins told him, for long days had passed since his own amazement at the scale of fire on D-Day. 'There's a lot of ruddy Germans down there.'

'Did you hear about the Hitler Youth, skipper?'

'Kids, I heard. Barely out of school.'

Collins cut in. 'Hark who's talking.'

'They're vicious little buggers,' Whitefield went on, his temper boiling up as it so often did. 'Been killing prisoners. Canadians mostly. Tie their hands, bullet in the back of the head. Bang, bang, bang. Wounded too. Fucking bastards. Worse than the fucking Japs.'

'It's a rumour,' Collins said, although he did not sound that confident.

'The Canadians I spoke to believed it. Said that was that, and they wouldn't take no prisoners either, not from the Hitler Youth. Bastards.

'Tell you what, Tommy-boy,' he advised his co-driver, who manned the Browning machine gun in the hull. 'You see any sod with a camouflage jacket, he's SS. If you see one, then you pull the trigger and keep it pulled until you've blown his bloody head off. Hands up or not.'

'We do not shoot prisoners,' James said as firmly as he could. 'We're British,' he added as if that was an incontestable argument in itself. 'If they're no longer a danger, we don't kill them. That's the rule and we stick to it.'

A transmission cut through the talk, as a distorted message suddenly became clear. 'Charlie Four and Charlie Four Able both brewed up.'

'Three Charlie to Baker Three, I can see black smoke. There, near the orchard.' This time Martin had at least seen something.

10.14 hrs, Camp B43, Sussex

The rain was steady, their battledress soaked and drops falling from the rim of each helmet. Since no one could guarantee that they would only fight in good weather, the training went on. Normally, Mark would have ordered his 17 Platoon to sit, but that would be even less comfortable in this weather, so they stood in a rough semicircle.

'There are five section formations,' he said, raising his voice to be heard. 'Each has advantages and disadvantages. The first is of blobs, with everyone in twos or threes and big gaps between them. This offers the best chance of concealment if there is lots of cover.' He felt a cough coming and raised his hand to cover his mouth. The gesture was simply habit.

'The second is single file,' he continued. 'That's one behind the other to you.' There were a few thin smiles, but they were very thin. 'This may be useful to follow a line of cover, such as a hedgerow or wall, but has the disadvantage of being vulnerable to enemy fire and does not allow you to fire back effectively.'

'Third is loose file...' He continued, using the words of the manual as well as he could remember them after reading through a dozen times this morning.

They knew all of this already – at least they had been told this already, again and again and again. Soon they would spread out and practise each formation, moving across a field as open and flat as a bowling green, practising changing from one to another in response to signals given by hand or by Mark blowing on a whistle. The only difference was that today they were carrying newly issued full size spades – or for one in every four men, a pick. The standard entrenching tool folded up neatly to stow in the webbing beneath the large pack on their backs. Clearly, someone believed that they would need to dig deeper and faster when they got to Normandy. If nothing else, at least the drills would help them decide how best to carry the new kit.

'The fourth formation is the arrow head, made irregular to avoid being too visible from the air.' Not that any Hun would be daft enough to fly on a day like this, with the cloud so low. 'This allows rapid deployment to either flank, but is harder to control. Finally, we have the extended line...'

Did repetition mean that the lessons went home? No doubt Judd would have a strong opinion on that. Thinking back to school, Mark knew that much of what the masters had said to him had flowed on by without taking root. To this day, he had not the slightest idea of when to use a semicolon, a handicap which he had not, at least as yet, found to be a significant one. More to the point, there was a good deal of maths and chemistry that made not the slightest sense to him no matter how well and often they were explained.

Mark had never wanted to be a teacher, and did not think that he was a good one. In Basic Training, and then at officer selection and all that followed, he had paid attention because he wanted a commission and was desperate to do well. Half the stuff seemed as useful as semicolons and quadratic equations, but he had studied, remembered and passed. His platoon did not have the same incentive. They had that familiar resigned look, knowing that they had no choice about doing this, so let's just get it over with. Probably summed up their attitude to the war, most of them at least. It was just a nasty job that had to be done. Only a few were keen. Still, it had been like that at school – you got on with it, did your best, but did not make a fuss.

'In all formations, except the blobs, there should be five yards between each man,' Mark assured them. 'Don't make yourself an easy target,' he added. That was not in the manual, although it was implied and was surely the whole point. He hoped he did not sound as if he was pretending to have experience. For a moment he wondered how they saw him, those thirty-five men watching because they had to watch.

At school they knew, and mocked, every quirk and peculiarity of a master's speech, dress and movements. Some of those – the way Old Mr Graham's voice cracked every few sentences and let out a squeak – had been the subject of wagers. In the final months at prep school they had had a new French teacher, Madame de Marbot. Mark had watched her like a hawk. He was just of the age where suddenly girls became a source of endless fascination, and here was a woman, middle aged it was true, but a woman still, and one who wore tight dresses and skirts and clip-clopped in front of the blackboard in her high heeled shoes. Sadly, they'd sent him off to board soon afterwards, where all the staff were men, apart from a matron who might as well have been. After a year, his house master had a kind and moderately attractive wife, but most of the time it seemed an even more male environment than the Army was to prove.

'Orders can be given by gesture. For instance, "Form extended line".' Sergeant Dalton made the gesture, arms extended, one holding out his rifle. 'Arrowhead.' Dalton's arms went back at an angle behind him.

Mark had always been prone to giggle, especially when he was supposed to be serious. The urge grew to say something silly, and perhaps the memory of La Marbot and the mousy Mrs Kennedy in her rather severe dresses at boarding school made him want to say 'silk stockings' or 'frilly knickers'. It would probably get their attention, but it would be something of a challenge to bring the lecture back to the proper theme afterwards. Best not, and instead he tried to think of all the things that he did still remember from school. That was not much help, for first were the readings of Shakespeare with Mr

Thomas, and then the history lessons with Mr Hardwicke. His lessons were good, for he had a lively sense of humour and made them all laugh, even if it was just the inevitable 'let's have a look at the old turnip' when he consulted his pocket watch. Hardwicke had been wounded at Passchendaele and still had a lump out of his neck and, with a bit of artful questioning and prompting from the boys, was always willing to tell them stories of the Last War.

Well, the instruction was complete so it was time to practise. 'Right, let's go through it for real. One section forms on the left, two section on the right, HQ in the middle and three section in reserve.'

They began to move, stiff, probably half asleep and very wet as they shuffled away.

'Come on, get a move on!' Dalton's voice carried easily even though he did not shout. 'You'll move fast enough when it's real.'

That should be soon, Mark thought. At breakfast there had been a rumour of a delay to their move, of perhaps twenty-four hours or even more. By the sound of things, rough weather was slowing down the landing of men, equipment and stores in Normandy.

He hoped the rumour was false because all this waiting and dull routine was not doing anyone's spirit any good. The rain made it all worse. Post had indeed resumed, and there was one from his mother, although still nothing from Anne. A quick glance as the papers arrived revealed that *Jane* was showing a bit of leg today, after a couple of dull days. It was not much, but it was something.

'Right, we will advance across the field and I will call out the orders. Then we will turn around and the section leaders will use signals for each change.' He blew his whistle. 'Extended line!'

Dalton chivvied them. 'Come on, come on! Keep those spacings! Five yards!'

12.45 hrs, near St Pierre, Normandy

C Squadron had lost two-thirds of its remaining tanks and was withdrawn. B Squadron was ordered down to support the DLI, who had lost the centre of the village, but were still clinging stubbornly to its northern edge. As more friendly artillery roared through the air overhead, James and 3 Troop led the squadron along the main road, such as it was. He could not see much, with steep banks topped by hedges and a fair few trees on either side. Sergeant Dove's Sherman blocked a lot of his view ahead. The sergeant's beret was a black blob just above the cupola and James guessed that he would look the same to Corporal Bell following behind. Sergeant Martin and the Firefly were in the rear. Narrow streets would be awkward for the tank to manoeuvre through with its long barrel, and apart from that he wanted his trump card kept in reserve for there was talk of plenty of enemy hornets. The sergeant seemed to have calmed down and was no longer sending message after message.

Dove halted. 'Baker Three Able to Baker Three, the first houses are a hundred yards ahead. I can just about see them around the corner, over.'

'Go in slow, Three Able. The infantry don't think hostiles are this far forward, but cannot be sure. Will do my best to cover you, out.'

'Roger, Baker Three.'

Dove's Sherman rolled forward at a brisk walking pace, easing around the corner. James followed.

'Gunner, are you loaded with HE?'

'Yes, sir.'

'Good. Traverse left. OK, on.' They could not see much of the nearest house through the trees, but even a fraction of a second might help. They reached the corner, Whitefield locking the left track for a moment to turn them.

Three Able was ahead in clear view. They had spent as much time as they could attaching branches to the turret and hull to conceal its shape, at least from a distance. The foliage looked off in this setting, with pale grey houses on either side. They were tall, making even the high Sherman seem small. One had a faded sign advertising Cinzano painted onto its blank wall. There was little more than a yard or two between the tank and the house on either side.

Dove halted for a moment.

'Driver, halt,' James called into the mic. 'No, advance.' Three Able was moving again.

James was between the end houses, swivelling the cupola to peer up at their dark slate roofs, and into the upper rooms. The one on his right had deep green shutters, pinned back and open. There was no sign of life. A machine gun, one of the enemy Spandaus with their insanely fast rate of fire, clattered into life. He could not see it, nor the Bren that replied with its slower beat.

Three Able kept going, more houses on either side of the road, and the tower of the stone church some way up ahead.

Suddenly, the machine guns in Dove's tank opened up. James could not see the target, but the sergeant kept advancing.

'Baker Three Able to Baker Three, infantry in houses up ahead.' The 75mm boomed, the noise echoing back along the narrow street. The shell struck a house on the left, smashing a great hole and throwing up clouds of dust and smoke. Still Dove kept advancing. James was searching the windows on either side. He still could not locate any enemy. There was not the slightest chance of coming alongside the lead Sherman, and none of the gaps between the houses were wide enough to go around.

James saw a streak of flame, coming from low down on the left, presumably someone hiding by the corner of one of the buildings. The rocket from the panzerfaust hit the side of the hull of Three Able, about level with the driver's position.

Smoke was coming from the turret as Dove bailed out, rapidly followed by two more of his crew. They jumped down onto the road, only to be knocked flat as a gout of flame shot up from the open hatch, rushing up higher even than the houses. Fire started to lick out from around the turret ring, where it joined the hull.

'Christ Almighty,' Whitefield said.

James watched in horror. The Sherman was burning so fast. There was no sign of driver or co-driver, but the other men seemed unhurt and scrambled to their feet, half staggering, half walking up to and past his tank.

'Get back to the infantry!' James yelled down.

Dove stared up, eyes blank, but he and the other two jogged away. James glanced ahead again. He still could not see any enemies.

'Driver, prepare to reverse. I'll guide you.' He switched to the external channel. 'Baker Three to Baker. My lead tank has brewed. It's burning and there's no way past. Road is too narrow, out.'

'Understood Baker Three. Pull back and we'll find another way.'

There was still no sign of any Germans, but shells suddenly erupted, shattering the church roof and bringing down part of the tower.

'Driver, reverse. Keep straight. Gently now.' James was watching behind them as they backed up, only now and again glancing towards the raging inferno of Dove's *Halifax* as it burned away, dirty black smoke above the flames that still reached high. 'Gunner, cover us. Shoot anything that moves.' They were making good progress, so thank the Lord for the engineers in Detroit who had built *Hector II* and for Whitefield who had such a delicate touch with the thirty-ton machine even when driving completely blind. 'Corner in ten yards, five, stop right track now, turning, turning, engage track, straight now for a hundred yards.'

14.10 hrs, on the edge of St Pierre, Normandy

Another troop led the next probe into the village, but came under heavy fire from an SP that no one could properly see. They did not lose anyone, but that lane was also blocked. Major Scott brought them through the fields on the north side, hoping to get around and approach the main road from the other direction.

Progress was slow. The fields were small, often only having a gate connecting them to one other field and not leading the way they wanted. Every couple of hundred yards there was steep banked hedge to negotiate. They did not rush. A troop would get into a field, one tank nudging up to the hedgerow, while the others took up position to fire in support. Then it would charge at the hedge and force a way through, climbing the bank. Scott led two troops to the north, while the rest stayed closer to the village, and 3 Troop found themselves at the head of this group.

James took them through an orchard. He was taking turns to go first through each barrier, not wanting Corporal Bell to take all the risks, and keeping Martin and the Firefly back. The sergeant did not seem to mind.

The apple trees were low, the lane between two rows barely wide enough for the tank. Branches tugged at the turret as it passed by, and James held the hatches open because otherwise they would have slammed down shut. Leaves dropped onto him, and so did apples.

'Oi!' Collins yelled in surprise. 'Who's flinging fruit at me?'

'They don't like your act,' Blamey claimed. 'Looks like good apples.'

'You're from the city – what would you know.' They were laughing, almost hysterically, and it was so ridiculous. As long as they did not pile up and jam the traverse or something equally dangerous.

They reached the far side, and a narrow gateway, too narrow for a Sherman.

'Go straight through, Whitefield,' James told him. The wall was dry stone and pretty ramshackle. Whitefield speeded up, the gates folded, most of the wall on either side collapsed and the tracks readily climbed what was left. They were in another field, but he could see buildings to his left. There was only a narrow gap in the far hedge and no other way into the field. A dead cow lay in the middle, belly swelling with gases and its four legs sticking up straight like the barrels of anti-aircraft guns. That and the narrow entrance suggested that it was a pasture, never visited by vehicles. That meant the only way out was through the hedge.

Sharp cracks sounded above the wider noise of battle somewhere up ahead of them. The sound of a tank gun or an anti-tank was unlike anything else on the battlefield.

'Three Baker to Three, I can see smoke ahead of us, two columns. Looks like brewed tanks, over.'

'I see them,' James replied. Like the sound, the narrow, dense pillars of smoke were easy to recognise.

Major Scott came on the air. 'Baker to all stations. Baker One has had two tanks brewed. Looks like AT guns in a wood, but we cannot locate them. Baker Three, what is your situation, over?'

'Baker Three to Baker. Am close to the village, will see if the next field has a way in, over.'

'Let me know. We won't be getting in this way, out.'

Bell led this time, charging the next hedge and surging up the bank and through it.

'Three Baker to Three,' the corporal reported a moment later. 'It's more open this side, and there's a lane ahead. Looks like a farm beyond that.'

James' Sherman followed Three Baker through the gap. Two more dead cows and a few cut logs were the only things in the bigger field, which, as Bell had reported, opened onto a lane. Up ahead were buildings.

'Three Baker, I'll lead. Three Charlie, follow Three Baker.'

Whitefield steered around the dead animals without being ordered, and James was glad. Not that the cows could feel anything anymore, but it would have felt like a desecration. There were the usual high hedges on either side of the lane. It was not paved, and the rain had turned the mud to slush, the tracks churning it up even more. On the left was a timber building, untouched by war, although apparently fairly neglected in peace. It seemed to open onto a yard, with a house beyond and stables or something like that to the sides. James thought he could see roofs behind them.

'Baker Three to Baker and Charlie. I'm going to speed up. You follow up slowly in case of trouble,' James told the rest of the troop. 'Driver, when I say go, give her all she's got. Gunner, shoot anything that moves. Go!'

The Sherman's twin engines roared and it charged along the lane, dirty water spraying up to paint the front and sides of the tank brown, even as the rain washed it away. The farmyard seemed to rush up: half-timbered buildings, rendering cracked and faded and paint on the doors and windows dull. There was the usual detritus of a working farm: an old tractor in an open sided shed, tools, a horse drawn plough looking rusty and dirty.

There were no people, or even animals that he could see. 'Slow down, bring us to the lane on the far side. Baker Three to Baker and Charlie, seems clear. The lane ahead turns towards the village. Join me here and we will push forward, out.'

Perhaps it was Bell's turn, but James felt that he ought to lead the way. This time he took it slowly and Whitefield edged the tank up to where the lane bent around to the left. Once there he could see that it joined a road going straight into the village. About fifty yards ahead there were houses along it and behind them he could see the ravaged tower of the church, most of the tiled roof missing.

James reported where they were to Major Scott and was told to push on.

'Driver, advance. Keep it steady. Gunner, wait for the order to fire. We don't want to stir anything up before we are ready. Co-driver, the same. We don't know what's down here.'

His tank, Baker Three or *Hector II* or whatever you chose to call it, turned the corner and came onto the road, with Corporal Bell following. James had to assume that Sergeant Martin was keeping pace behind them. The road was about as wide as the one they had used earlier and, although the closest houses had tiny front gardens so loomed over him less, there was still no space for another tank to come alongside him. As so often, his scatterbrain sought for a line to describe the situation and Conan Doyle's Gerard stories came to him. What was it? Something like 'the light cavalry were always at the head of the Grand Army, the Hussars of the Conflans were at the head of the light cavalry and I, Etienne Gerard was at the head of the Hussars.'

Something like that. As his mind came up with this foolish thought, his eyes searched the houses, their low walled gardens and the road up ahead. There was a crossroads not far away, probably crossing the main street. There were no Germans.

Yes, the brave, vain and very stupid, but lucky Etienne Gerard and James Robert Alexander Taylor, two peas in a pod.

Oh shit, James thought.

'Baker Three to Baker and Charlie. There's the main road through the village about a hundred yards ahead. No sign of the enemy, out.'

As soon as he said the word a vehicle drove along the main road, coming from his right and going left. It was tracked, with half a dozen little round wheels, big driver wheels at each end and runners along the top. The hull was low, no turret although it was fully enclosed, and there was a long gun with a muzzle brake in front. The whole thing was painted a sandy colour, with swirling patterns of green and brown to give it a mottled appearance. There were boxes, tarpaulins, spare wheels and goodness knows what piled on its rear deck, and on the side was a black cross and the number 324 in red outlined with white. Even in the driving rain it was all clearer than any photograph.

It was also a German assault gun, a Stug III, distinctive because of its wheels, and mounting a 75mm at least as good as the one on the Sherman. A man in a drab green uniform stood in the open hatch and did not seem to notice them, staring ahead and talking into a microphone.

In a moment it had passed, dirty smoke coming from its exhausts.

'My God,' Collins said. 'A bloody Jerry.'

James felt the same shock. It was the first time any of them had seen an enemy AFV so close and so clearly.

An infantryman strolled along behind, the distinctive coal scuttle helmet tipped up on the back of his head, a rifle over his shoulder. He had a camouflaged poncho hanging down past his waist, rain dripping from it. Another man followed, then another and another, with more on the far side of the road, so that they left space for the vehicles to pass.

A second Stug appeared, this one boxy in shape, because on either side it had a large screen as a shield against bazookas. Its commander was also standing tall, and happened to glance to his left. James saw the man's mouth drop open.

'Gunner, target SP, fire!' James closed his eyes, memories of the searing flash from the Firefly still strong.

Collins traversed quickly, stamped the button and the 75mm roared. The shell, an HE loaded some time back, reached the target in a fraction of a second and exploded, ripping up the side skirt on this side and twisting it into a stranger shape. Shrapnel from the shell and the thick metal screen scythed into the infantrymen, and Thomson opened up with his Browning.

'Load AP and fire!'

The Stug had lurched to the side from the explosion, but kept on along the road. Its commander had vanished, whether dead, wounded or simply terrified was impossible to know.

The assault gun had also almost disappeared behind the corner house, but Blamey was quick and must already have put the shell into the breech, closed it, and tapped Collins on the leg to tell him.

The 75mm fired again, and the solid round left a glowing hole as it seared through the thin armour at the rear of the hull, just above the tracks. The Stug stopped.

'Another AP to make sure,' James said. The infantry had vanished, apart from two untidy sacks of old clothes sprawled in the roadway.

Collins fired again. James remembered that he did not have to blink, then wondered why he had not flinched each time the gun was fired and the breech recoiled back with appalling force, only inches away from his loins. He had always flinched in training.

Another neat hole, close to the first, flared bright for a moment. Collins was a good gunner, although admittedly this was desperately close range.

Black smoke came from the Stug, a few flames bright as the fuel in its engine started to burn. It was nothing like the near volcano from Dove's Sherman, but the assault gun was clearly finished.

'Baker Three to Baker. Have approached main street. Two enemy hornets seen, have brewed one, over.'

'Good show, Baker Three… proceed…' The rest of Major Scott's transmission was too garbled to follow. The houses must have blocked the signal.

'Driver, ease us forward gently – better see what we can see. Gunner, watch to the left and ahead. Co-driver, cover the right corner. Don't wait for the order.'

The Stug had settled down to burn with more determination, reminding James of a hexamine tablet in one of the little cookers issued for the invasion.

'Halt.' They were twenty yards from the crossroads. The knocked-out Stug was surely blocking the route to the left, which meant that the first one to pass would have trouble getting to them. There might be others following though, hidden around the corner to the right. James had no intention of going far enough forward to give them a shot. Let them come to him, and if there were more Stugs with their fixed barrels, he should be able to draw a bead on them before they could bring their own gun to bear. Infantrymen were more of a danger for he was well within panzerfaust range.

Thomson's Browning chattered into life, tracer whipping towards the corner house, pockmarking the brickwork and flinging off little fragments. James had not seen anyone, but the machine gun ought to deter all save the bravest.

Something moved directly ahead on the road opposite. It was another vehicle, but much bigger. About a hundred and fifty yards away, a tank appeared along the tree lined road. It had wide tracks – James had a brief glimpse of rows of big round wheels, before it jerkily turned and all he could see was the front. The hull was wide, the flat plate of armour angled back. Above was a squat, squarish turret and a gun, a very long gun traversed slightly to the right, presumably to see around the corner as they had turned. It was a Mark V. A Panther. Apart from the Tiger, the most terrifying beast in the jungle.

'I'll be buggered,' Collins said, with a tone of mild surprise.

'Gunner, traverse right, on.' The 75mm was almost in line with the German tank. 'Range one fifty yards, target hornet, fire!'

The gun boomed, the shell went straight and true, striking plumb in the centre of the hull's front plate.

Then it sparked and flew almost straight up into the air, deflected by the armour.

'Ready,' Collins said, just moments later.

'Fire!'

A boom, James heard or imagined a hiss of the shot racing through the air, then sparks and again it bounced away.

The Panther's turret traversed slowly, inexorably, and the

gun's barrel no longer appeared so long because it was pointing almost straight at them.

'Load HE and fire,' James said. Blamey almost had the black painted tip of an AP shell in the breech, but checked, put it down and grabbed a green topped HE.

The muzzle brake of the Panther seemed dark and immense even at this distance. It vanished for an instant in flame as the gun fired. James felt a savage punch through the air as the round cut past just a yard from the Sherman's turret. Thank God their gunner was not as good as Collins.

Their own 75mm boomed again and the front of the Panther erupted in an explosion.

'Driver, reverse, fast as you can, straight back.'

Whitefield shifted gears and the engines roared as the Sherman jerked into motion. James had forgotten to order Bell to withdraw, but was relieved to see that the corporal was already on his way. The flight of a high velocity shell down the road naturally concentrated the mind.

'Baker Three to Baker, there is another hornet, a Panther, and infantry in the main street. Can't see us getting up it without our own infantry.' James twisted his head round to see behind him. The Panther seemed to have gone, with a just a few wisps of smoke where it had been. There was certainly no wreck, not that he would have expected the HE shell to do much damage against such thick armour. That meant it was still out there, waiting, and maybe there were more.

'Driver, halt.' They were almost at the lane leading back into the farm. 'Take it slow, ready to lock the right track when I say.'

'You mean left, sir, don't you?' Whitefield asked.

James realised that he was thinking as if the tank was driving forward and had confused his left from right.

'Sorry, yes, now... We're round, engage track again.'

18.55 hrs, St Pierre, Normandy

'Gunner, co-ax on the top windows. Keep it high.'

They were behind a hedge and bank, at a spot where it dipped enough for the turret guns to see into the next field. There was a two-storeyed house on the far edge of the field and beyond that a side road leading into the village.

White smoke blossomed in the field as the infantry platoon's mortar plastered it with bombs. It did not spread as readily as on a dry day, but did something to obscure the view.

'Keep firing, just keep at that top floor,' James ordered. If Collins did not alter the angle then the bullets should go well above the attacking infantry. Bren guns added their own fire. James had been struck by the drab, unkempt exteriors of many French houses. He realised that they were not doing much to help.

Dimly, for the smoke was drifting towards them, he saw the shapes of the DLI advancing in rushes towards the house. By chance it was the same platoon he had carried during the advance. It was nice to see that the subaltern was still on his feet.

Grenades exploded around the house. James could not see or hear any return fire, but it was so hard to be sure. There had certainly been Germans inside an hour ago.

'Cease fire.' The infantry were too close to the house now to be safe even when they aimed high. Now was the moment a hidden enemy, pinned down or hiding so far, would bob up and fire with everything they had. He saw the subaltern, his lanky frame and ungainly walk very distinctive, waving his men to follow. More grenades, this time posted through windows, then bursts of Sten gun fire.

The house was clear. The officer appeared in the top window and waved.

Most of St Pierre was controlled by the Germans, and every attempt by the 165th RAC to push into the houses or around them ended in failure, sometimes with the loss of a tank or two. B Squadron was down to twelve fully operational tanks. James did not know how many of the crews were dead or wounded, and how many were safe.

Yet the DLI still held the northern edge of the village, after repulsing attack after attack and enduring heavy bombardments. Their losses were severe, but they were not shifting. Indeed, they were beginning to retake a few houses and fields lost earlier in the day, B Squadron offering fire support. This house was one of them, liberated yesterday, retaken late morning, and now once again in the hands of the Alliance of the United Nations. They had not had to use the 75mm on it, so all in all, apart from the scars of grenades and small arms, it was reasonably intact – at least so long as the Germans did not try to take it back or shell it to oblivion.

21.35 hrs, Camp B43, Sussex

Judd lay on the bed, boots off, and tried to read. Everyone had expected to move tomorrow and now there were rumours of delays. That did not worry him too much. Nobody liked waiting and waiting, but his time in the Army had encouraged a philosophical approach to these big things he could not control. *They* would tell Private Judd when *they* saw fit and do with him as *they* saw fit. No sense in fretting about that.

More disturbing were the two lectures they had all been ordered to attend at the end of the afternoon of wet and muddy football. He had been chosen to play for the Company as usual, and in spite of all experience. Seven one six Williams was on the opposing side, so naturally his legs ached and were bruised.

The first talk had been an AEC special, on the invasion and the justice of the Allied cause. He doubted anyone disagreed with what was said – there just did not seem any need to say it, especially when they could have been drinking tea or watching a picture.

Worse followed, for after celebration of the great cause, with the implication that they were splendid fellows to be leading the way, they were given an hour-long talk on Venereal Disease. Not only that, but it was not by their own MO, a jovial Irishman who was a natural entertainer; even the officers who did not have to be there usually turned up for his talks, which always began with 'Now, I was hoping to show you the film they show the Wrens, but GHQ have nabbed that for themselves...' Instead, they had someone from higher up, a full colonel no less, grey haired and almost as grey faced, who spoke in a flat tone and in appalling detail, illustrating each point with pictures and diagrams. He gave Judd the impression that he expected every man in the room to rape anything with a pulse as soon as they reached France – indeed perhaps to frequent brothels as often as they had a cup of tea.

At first, it was almost amusing, and there were plenty of muttered oaths, and jokes – 'Hey, Jackie boy, he's looking at you.' Gradually, the onslaught of slide after slide of badly diseased genitalia beat down the humour and their spirits. From Crusaders liberating the world, they were now perverts destined for agonising pain and eventual blindness, insanity and death. After half an hour the first man dashed out to vomit on the grass outside the hall. Others soon followed. Judd did not last until the end.

It left a deeply unpleasant taste, literally, and was enough to warn off most of them from even thinking too much about fornication, at least tonight, when the opportunities for such things were nil. There were not many jokes about it afterwards, although plenty of swearing. Mostly they were stunned.

'Dear God, they already put bromide in the tea, what more do they want?' was one of the few lighter comments.

Only later did spirits return to something like normal. The Army was like that, battering you over the head with unpleasantness and discomfort, whether large or small or just straightforward bull. As soon as it stopped, you made the most of whatever time off there was because you never really knew when the next chance would come.

Judd would have loved to be in a room on his own, with a comfortable chair and a good light to read, but since none of that was going to happen, the dim electric light in the hut and the straw-stuffed mattress on this camp bed would have to do. Half the men who lived there were out, mostly at the cinema or NAAFI or on duty, and the rest were not too noisy by army standards. A couple of aspiring tenors at the far end were crooning 'Long Ago and Far Away', from the picture that had been showing. They had most of the words and a fair bit of the tune – and this would not be a Welsh regiment if no one was singing.

Other men talked, and whistled, and tended to kit, read or wrote letters or read books. Jeffreys, a youngster from a village in the Vale of Glamorgan, was focused on a battered copy of *No Orchids for Miss Blandish*, his tongue between his teeth as a mark of concentration. Judd had read it, but could not for the life of him remember whether or not the title character ever got a Christian name in the story. Not a happy tale either, leaving a bit of a sour taste, as you always expected a nicer ending. A few beds along, Franklin, a Newport lad, had a magazine with pin-ups, cartoons and no doubt edifying articles. He was probably better off with that than the thriller. Certainly, every now and again he gave out a whistle or a grating cackle, and then insisted on showing and explaining it to Price on the next bed.

It was not quiet, far from it, but it would do. Everything had become so familiar since that first night more than a year ago, when William Judd had become Private Judd, his short hair had been shaved even shorter and he had stood, everything uncomfortable and awkward from boots to the uniform that seemed designed not to fit anywhere, as a diminutive sergeant, bristling with martial fervour, screamed at them and berated them each time they did not understand something not yet explained to them.

Well, that was not quite true. He had served in the Home Guard at home, so knew a bit of drill and at least knew that issue denims and the rest of it all could be made to fit and to be comfortable. Some of the lads around him had had no preparation at all, which must have made it all even more terrifying. He enlisted in Cardiff, so naturally was given a railway warrant and told to report to a depot in Durham, and there were men from all over the country and every walk of life, shivering in the February cold. Basic Training was cold and wet and deliberately unpleasant throughout the entire six weeks.

Memories had faded and only moments stood out in his mind. The sense of being harassed and exhausted, of doubling everywhere, and runs across bleak hillsides in sleet and snow. Meeting so many men, not simply strangers, but wholly alien in their way of life and speech. There was one Glasgow lad Judd could never understand, and the poor fellow, who liked to talk, could not understand what Judd said either. There were a handful of highly educated men, and next to them illiterates. There was the man who could never swing his right arm when his left leg moved to march, and whose arm and leg seemed as joined together as a teddy bear. There were the would-be bullies, and the snarling and the fights that stopped them.

Judd had decided to pray each night, and to make a show of it, kneeling on the floor, elbows on his bed, eyes closed and hands clasped together. He could not claim that his motive was very Christian. It was more like the gunfighter in a movie twitching back the tail of his coat to show the butt of his Colt. There had been laughs, jokes, and jeers. Fair enough, it was a free country. The man sitting on the bed next to him, a hard-faced Manchester man older than most of them, had gone further. He had blown into his cigarette until the tip heated up, then leaned over and pushed it against Judd's bare foot.

What followed was luck as much as anything else. Judd was quite large, if not as well muscled then as training would make him, and he had done good deal of boxing and he did have a temper. He had twisted round on his knees, turning the spin into a punch and caught the Mancunian under the chin. The angle must have been just right, the force unusual, and Judd knew that he could never do it again, but the punch had lifted the man up, flung him back off the bed. He had landed on the floor, and landed hard and unconscious. Someone had tipped water from the cleaning bucket over him to wake him up.

Much to Judd's surprise, the Mancunian did not bear any ill will. 'Alright, mate, just put in a good word for me next time,' was all he had said. They did not become friends, far from it, and barely exchanged another word except on duty. Such friendships as did develop were more for convenience than anything else, since the odds were against being posted to the same unit as any of the others in the future.

All in all, they got along well enough, insulting each other, and moaning and joking together whenever they had the energy. Day followed day, of PT, instruction on weapons, and cleaning and polishing everything that could be cleaned and polished, whether it really needed it or not, and always there was the parade square. The instructors, let alone the Warrant Officers, strained the English language in many ways, stretching some words and clipping others short. Most had the patter, the jokes that made everything a bit more manageable.

'Mother of God, if brains were gunpowder, he wouldn't have enough to blow his hat off' stuck in the mind as one of the favourite insults he had received.

Judd enjoyed drill, especially as they all became better and knew it. There was such a sense of unity about it, something so rare and appealing for a lonely man, and the clashing of boots and slapping of palms against rifle stocks had a deeply moving, almost dance like, quality for him.

The days were very long, for the Army was not about to give

in to the short winter daylight of Northern England, and they were tired, but the time passed eventually. They learned to do things the Army's way, and the tricks that made it easier, making weights so that their trousers hung properly over their gaiters, or putting a damp towel over the same trousers to put in a sharper crease with a hot iron.

A lot of his memories were of smells, of boot polish, brass polish, of gun oil and a piece of four-by-two coming out grubby and slick on a pull through from a rifle barrel. Most of all the smell of young men cooped up together like chickens. That was the scent of damp wool uniforms, of the mud being cleaned off boots, and the reek of dozens of pairs of soaked thick wool socks as everyone in a hut took off their boots after a long march or a day on the assault course.

A lot of men snored, far more than he had expected and far louder. A few, if more than he would have expected, seemed always to be fumbling under their blankets. Another memory was of someone shaking your shoulder when you had fallen into an exhausted sleep so that they could ask 'Do you want to buy a battleship?' Of waiting until the chap was snoring away before waking him to ask what colour it was. So many of them were so young, which seemed to add a particular pungency to the sweat, and certainly more than a dash of stupidity to their behaviour. Even in the fifth year of war, there was a sense that this was all a game for many of the youngsters. The older men were not like that, for all the older keen ones had long since gone through the system and only the reluctant were left, combed out of previously reserved occupations.

Things were better after Basic Training, posted to a proper regiment, but so much remained the same as they trained and trained and the war passed them by. Different camps, different places, but the same battalion, even after he had been posted a couple of times and then returned to unit. The men were probably much like hundreds of thousands of others in uniform, from all over the country, very much the long and the short and the tall, dressed in the cheapest uniforms of all Allied nations. They were wise and foolish, agile and cack-handed, and could be kind and vicious, and many were a mix of all these things. Judd reckoned that he had learned more about human nature since joining up than he had ever found in his beloved books. They needed a Dickens to bring them to life in all their raucous, sullen, downtrodden and proud glory, but somehow he doubted they would ever get one.

The crooners were struggling, and, somehow, their stumbling confusion over the next verse was more distracting than when they were singing. They stopped, and began to argue over what came next.

That was another surprise, at least at first, for now it felt natural. Whether on screen, on the wireless, or in those performances the Army loved making soldiers stage, they liked their blue jokes and they liked thinking and talking about women – there were pin-ups in all stages of dress and undress decorating the lockers in the hut. Some of the men boasted of their exploits with girls, and some of them were probably not exaggerating by much. They talked of 'doing it' as well as the more direct pieces of Anglo-Saxon. Slogans from the wireless, dumb tunes like the 'Mares eat oats' doing the rounds at the moment, were popular enough. Yet what moved them, what had them cheering for more, was as often a piece of orchestral music, or a song so sentimental that it was almost syrupy. Men who swore as readily as they breathed, got drunk, fought with each other and the redcaps, and were always off limits and visiting brothels, would so often sit, glassy eyed, listening to verses about romance. They liked to hear a woman, even a girl, sing, but a record of Gigli or Tauber touched them deeply, and not just them, but most of the others as well.

Judd adjusted his glasses and angled the book to get a bit more light on the page. His older brother had given it to him when they had both managed to be on leave at the same time a few months earlier. Paul was a Flight Engineer on Halifaxes, eighteen trips into his first tour on ops – well twenty-two now according to his last letter. Judd had wanted to fly, even though his brother had tried to dissuade him.

'You're too tall, and far too fat. There's not much room in an aircraft.' Paul was five foot eight, slim, blond haired and handsome, the image of their late father at the same age. The latter had flown Sopwith Pups and then Camels in the Great War, and caught influenza near the end, which had led to tuberculosis and a slow, increasingly unpleasant death.

Judd had wanted to fly, but the RAF did not like anyone with glasses, even just for reading, and he did not fancy wearing air force blue, but working on the ground in some safe billet. The idea of becoming a military clerk and wearing battledress rather than a suit had horrified him. So did the thought of going to sea, for drowning terrified him and the gentlest swell made him seasick. Judd had decided to go for the Army and was determined to do the real work as an infantryman.

Their father had not talked much about Flanders or flying. Judd filled his imagination by reading everything he could about the aces and aircraft of the Last War.

'Here you are,' Paul had said. 'It cost me a tenner, so take damned good care of it.' The book was V. M. Yeates' *Winged Victory*, and the hardback was battered and stained and had clearly had plenty of owners. 'This is the only good thing written about war flying. The rest is all balls,' Paul assured him.

Judd had already read it through and was well into it a second time, and had to agree. Not that it was encouraging, at least not in a simple way. Here they all were, fighting the Germans once again with weapons even more devastating than last time.

At least no one was using gas. Not yet, anyway.

The crooners had resumed with great enthusiasm and were belting out something about Aladdin.

Judd was not sure what that meant either. Nice tune though.

D+5, Sunday 11ᵗʰ June

L IEUTENANT COLONEL TIM Leyne appeared as fresh as a man who had slept for days in the softest of feather beds. 'Seventh Armoured is finding it slow going. Well, we've all seen what this country was like. Why the farmers of Normandy have not spent the centuries preparing for the arrival of our tanks is anyone's guess! Damned careless of them. It's field after tiny field and while back in the Blue you could see for miles until the desert haze or a sandstorm came in, here you are lucky to see fifty yards. That's why Seventh have not got as far as planned, and our attack to the east on Cristot was a bust in that we did not take the place or Point 102. Those of you who took part know all about that.'

James struggled to stifle a yawn. He had shaved, and that had helped, but these short summer nights were exhausting. In just over half an hour the regiment would stand to, waiting in position in case an attack came up as first light approached. It was something the British Army did, and made a lot of sense, not that that made it any easier day after day.

'All of that sounds disappointing,' the colonel went on, 'until you look at it from Fritz's point of view. He's got some of St Pierre, but cannot take it all. He certainly can't get up here to Point 103.' The regiment had pulled back at last light to positions hidden among the fields on the forward slope of the ridge. 'That means that our gunners can see and his can't.

'Seventh Armoured haven't raced through and have hit some tough opposition, but they can keep pushing on and at the same time swing stuff more to the west. That will stretch Jerry out and there is still a good chance of finding a gap where they don't have men – a very good chance indeed. There is still everything to play for. That was Rommel's genius in the Desert – always found a flank and a way round, so be nice to repay the compliment,' he added with a wolfish grin.

The yawn was fighting for attention, forcing its way up. James raised a fist as if to rub his face. The colonel was staring directly at him. Leyne waited a moment and then winked.

'And, of course, the big picture is that we are keeping them too busy to drive at the beaches. That's still what really matters. We have Panzer Lehr in front of us, Twelfth SS on our left. Both of them are spread out, here and there, plugging gaps in the line, trying to claw back what we have taken. This country isn't easy for them either, whether to attack or defend. Yes, we can't see him, but he can't see us either, and that's a big hindrance for his big guns.

'Well, that's the grand sweep, and my little moment of talking like Napoleon! Our little bit here is what matters to us. Brigade is consolidating to face the attacks that are bound to keep coming in. We're to form Brigade reserve today back on the ridge. A and C Squadrons will go there at zero six thirty hours. B is to go forward again to support the DLI in St Pierre. They will pull back once relieved by the Yeomanry. They're due at ten hundred. Peter,' he nodded at Major Scott, 'I'll want you on the left, just behind where you'll be in the village. I'll show you in detail on the map in a minute. Right, any questions?'

There were a few minor issues, queries about replacement tanks and crew. A Squadron had just nine tanks running, and C Squadron eleven. Recce was at full strength, but there wasn't much role for them at the moment.

'We'll get some, but probably not until tonight,' the colonel told them. 'Everyone has lost tanks, so the shelves are looking a bit bare, but I'm sure the delivery man will come soon enough. Anything else?'

James waited but, when no one had anything practical to arrange, decided to ask. 'There are stories about the Hitler Youth shooting prisoners. I'm not sure what to tell the men.'

'Tell them it's quite true,' the colonel said levelly. 'There have been several incidents that we know about. Don't know whether its official and the whole Twelfth SS Div. is like that or whether it's a few bad eggs. Doesn't matter. Tell the lads to think twice about putting their hands up if those buggers are in the area.' His head turned, staring at each of them in turn. 'What they do doesn't matter because we play the game our way. It's not our job to take prisoners most of the time. Leave it to the infantry who can look after them. But we don't shoot at white flags or men with their hands up – not unless they start it. Clear?'

There were nods, some uncertain, a few dubious, and most simply resigned.

10.00 hrs, Camp B43, Sussex

The move was on, at least so everyone was saying. Kitbags were packed and put in to store, rations and ammunition issued, and all companies to parade in full field service order at 11.00 hrs for departure at 12.00. The camp was a hive of activity, all conducted with an air of excitement. Even the Sun put in a brief appearance, before the clouds closed around it again, but it was dry and there was a simple purpose to everyone's life. Someone had ordered the band to play them off, for they were to follow with the reserve transport, who were sailing from London rather than Newhaven. As the battalion mustered, they played 'Men of Harlech' and all the other marches associated with the regiment. After a while, they switched to some softer Welsh tunes.

At eleven o'clock the battalion came to attention on the drill field in response to the RSM's thunderous voice.

'No move before thirteen hundred hours! Parade, dismiss.'

They were not allowed to go anywhere, but took off their packs and sat on them. A NAAFI wagon arrived to serve tea.

'I hear they've let three seven four Evans out of chokey,' Griffiths said, a cigarette cupped in his hand as he puffed it into life. They were waiting for 9 Platoon's turn to go up for tea.

'Good,' Judd said. Tobacco smoke was another smell of service life, although to be honest that was true of much of the country. Churches and chapels, like museums, were rare havens without it. He was used to it, but still happy not to partake. The rest of the section were in turn glad to have his issue of cigarettes, which meant that everyone was satisfied.

'And Rusty Reade from 10 Platoon has turned up. Said he'd heard we were going and didn't want to miss out.' Reade was one of the battalion's bad characters, a thief, frequently drunk and disorderly, even more often absent without leave. He was a regular from Leeds who had somehow found his way into a Welsh regiment, even if he spent almost as much time in one glasshouse or another as actually with the unit.

'They going to let him come, the daft bugger?' Private 'Sandy' Moore asked. He was one of the Cardiff men.

'He can have my place,' Private Davison offered. He was a Port Talbot boy, with thick curly black hair and the complexion of an Italian.

'Yes. They reckon the colonel's pleased,' Griffiths said. It was never quite clear who the 'they' he so often cited were, but he did get more things right than wrong. He turned slightly, so that he could stretch out, his head resting on his pack.

'Hey, sarge, what's happening?'

'Sounds like there's a war on, Private Griffiths.' Holdworth emphasised the rank. 'Hadn't you heard?'

'Wondered what all the noise was.'

Holdworth seemed about to about to walk on, when he

turned back to face them. 'Now, as you all seem at a loose end, I suppose I could...' He grinned.

'We're busy, sarge, very busy.'

Holdworth snorted. 'Good, that's what a platoon sergeant wants to hear, although really easy to find you something to do. I hear there's a piano needs shifting. Still, not sure you're the musical types. They're not generous with their fags.'

'Mean sod,' Griffiths said, holding up a packet.

'Thanks. Not too long. TCVs will be here at twelve forty-five.'

Judd sighed. A TCV was a Troop Carrying Vehicle or a lorry or a truck to anyone without a military mind. Why did they have to complicate everything and create this language of their own? The Army seemed to live and breathe acronyms.

Griffiths leaned his head back down onto his pack, staring up at the sky. 'God, what a war, ruddy sergeants nicking your snout. I tell you, when the War Department looks at someone's report, they see mean bastard written at the bottom and immediately bump a man up to sergeant.'

'Just because he's scrounging fags don't mean he's a bastard,' 'Sandy' Moore pointed out.

'Yes, but he is a sergeant and they spell that B A S T A R D.'

'I have a legitimate reason,' Judd intoned, reviving a very old joke in the platoon.

'Who's a bastard?' they all bawled out and descended into laughter.

Mr Buchanan passed them, giving a little smile to show that he had heard and then pointedly turning away to show that he had not noticed officially.

The men relaxed, more of them settling down to stretch out their legs and to use their packs as a cushion. Then they waited, as they had done again and again and again since being called up.

'And what did Coop say?' Griffiths whispered.

'Yup!' they all chorused.

17.00 hrs, Point 103, Normandy

A big attack was coming in from the south-west, not that James or the rest of 3 Troop could see it yet. The radio chatter reported a dozen or more tanks and assault guns – some went as high as twenty or thirty, and claimed Tigers and Panthers were among them – and lots of infantry coming with them. That was the most open spot in this country, with a couple of huge wheat fields gradually climbing up towards the end of the ridge. A Squadron and part of B were already lining the hedges on the edge of the high ground overlooking this approach, and were being thoroughly plastered by German artillery. James had just been summoned from his position facing south and ordered to see if he could find cover and a good firing position to the left of the main line of Shermans.

They came into a field, realised that there was no other way in or out, so he took 3 Troop over the banked hedge at the far end, hoping that his memory was accurate and there was at least one more field beyond it. The prospect of bursting into sight in front of all those panzers was not appealing.

Through his headphones, James heard the crackling messages and tried to understand what was happening.

'Sunray to all stations, Shelldrake says that barrage is coming in.' Sunray and Shelldrake, the regimental CO and the senior artillery officer. Whoever had dreamed up the codewords ought to be in Colney Hatch.

James glanced up as he led them towards the gap in the next hedgerow. He thought he saw dark specks of howitzer shells sailing through the air.

'Bloody marvellous! Bloody marvellous,' someone shouted.

'Sunray to all stations, observe correct wireless procedure.'

The noise was appalling, even though he still could not see the impact and even though he had his headphones on and was in a tank noisily racing through a muddy field.

'Driver, halt by the gate.' The timbers of the gate lay crushed on the ground, but Whitefield saw it and came to a smooth stop. James wanted to see ahead, and quickly realised that this opened onto yet another field, one that was wide and stretched away to either side, but narrow and barely thirty yards across. There was a gate – still standing, which was remarkable – over to the left, but that was the wrong direction.

'Baker Three to Baker and Charlie. Wait while I have a dekko, out.' Odd how you picked up that strange doggerel of the Army, a mixture of accents from all over Britain and plenty of mispronounced words from the Empire. 'Driver, turn right, take her up to the far corner.'

By the sound of the chatter, the German infantry were withering under the fire, slaughtered or gone to ground. The panzers kept coming. High velocity shot cracked through the air.

'Got him! No, it bounced off!'

'Able Two to Troop, concentrate on the ones on the right.'

'Christ, Able Four has bought it.'

'Well done, Baker One Able, you've brewed him.'

A couple of plumes of thick black smoke rose from the right, behind a hedge too high to see over. There were other columns from ahead, which suggested both sides were losing tanks.

'They just keep coming!'

'Able to Able Three, calm down and concentrate on your shooting, out.'

'That's it, gunner, on, fire AP!' A voice started to scream across the net instead of the intercom, blotting out every other transmission. 'Fire again. Oh Jesus, it's like a pea shooter. Again! Again! Loader, faster. His turret's pointing at us. Fire, damn you, for God's sake, fire! ... We're hit.' Perhaps it was imagination, but James thought he heard a soft whummph. He certainly saw the flames shoot high, higher than he had seen before. Whoever it was had been close to the hedge bordering this field. A scream came, utterly terrified, agonising, more drawn out and lasting longer than seemed possible. Then it stopped.

'Oh Sweet Jesus,' Blamey muttered. 'Poor devils.'

'Driver, halt.' James snapped out of the nightmare. They were a little short of the hedge and he searched for any spot low enough to see over. There was nothing. 'Thomson, ready with me to clear some of the branches. We'll need the axes. Driver, I'll show you where to come.' He scrambled out, onto the hull and then jumped down, slipping and falling to add more mud to his already grimy trousers. He chose a spot where the hedge seemed thinner and lower and beckoned Whitefield forward. Thomson had his hatch open. He glanced up, like a man wondering whether rain was likely and he ought to carry an umbrella. There were only shells in the air and AP shot out of sight.

James realised that he should have called forward the rest of the troop, but it was too late now, and clearing a firing position was more important. He and Thomson stood on the front glacis and hacked at the branches. They could already glimpse a wide green field beyond them criss-crossed by tracer, ravaged by shells and filled with tanks, some moving, some still and some smoking. Without his headphones, the noise of the battle was appalling. The work was hard and he was sweating, especially down the line of his spine. A poorly judged stroke split a jagged stem and flew back to slash across his forehead. He ignored it and kept slicing away. Thomson worked with more precision and skill.

'That's fine!' Collins was in the cupola, giving them a thumbs up.

'Here, let me take it,' Thomson said, grabbing James' axe.

'Thanks.' James used the barrel of the 75 to help him clamber up onto the turret.

Collins grinned. 'If your poor mother could see you now,' he said, then ducked back into the turret.

Blood dripped down onto one eye. James brushed it away. Back in his seat, plugged in again to the transmitter, he took in the scene. The panzers were edging more to the left, away from him. The closest in front were six or seven hundred yards away. He recognised the angular, predatory shape of Panthers, each with a gun as long as a telegraph pole. There were other tanks, with flat topped, round sided turrets and straight sides. Maybe they were Tigers or Mark IVs with extra side screens like that Stug. To him they seemed smaller than the Panthers, but then that might just be the distance.

'Gunner, traverse right, range five fifty yards, on. Aim at the Panther, but wait for the order. Follow it as it advances.' He flicked the switch to talk to the Troop. 'Baker Three to Three Baker and Charlie. Enemy in sight. Come on to my left along this hedge. You'll need to clear it, but we can see at least ten, figures one zero, hornets in front of us, out.'

His forehead was bleeding profusely, making him blink. He searched for a rag that wasn't filthy with oil and grime. His handkerchief was not much better.

The Panther was advancing with caution, juddering forward a few yards, then stopping and firing several times before moving on. It was a big tank, its sandy coloured paint streaked with brown and green. He could not see much of its side, and memories of his shells bouncing off the front glacis plate at a much shorter range than this made him want to hit it in the side. All tanks had thinner armour on the sides, because the biggest threat was always from the front and there was only so much weight any engine could move.

James wanted to shoot against the side, and really he wanted his other two tanks to fire at the same time. The Germans were not likely to spot them until they opened up. Still, any wait meant that others from the regiment were fighting and dying without them. Bell's Sherman was approaching fast: he glimpsed the Firefly in the gateway, then could not see because the cut kept on bleeding. He unbuttoned the pocket of his tunic, fished inside, got the silk free, wiped vigorously and thrust it back inside. 'Blamey, do we have a field dressing handy?'

The loader turned around, frowning, then noticed the long

cut across James' forehead. Moments later he produced the bandage, by which time James had taken off his beret. He tied the dressing into place, tried to ignore the odd bulge now above his eyes, and put his headphones back on. The battle was still raging, excited commanders almost screeching reports to each other.

Bell's Three Baker was in position twenty yards to his left. As he watched they cleared a gap to shoot through the hedge, completing the job faster than he and Thomson had managed.

James looked for Sergeant Martin's tank and could not see it. 'Baker Three to Baker Three Charlie, where are you, over?'

'Moving into position, Baker Three.'

Other stations yelled out commands and warnings and the net was too busy for more than a minute.

'Three Baker to Three. We are ready to fire, out.'

'Acknowledged, Three Baker. Baker Three Charlie, I cannot see you, over?'

There was a crackle of static, distorted voices, perhaps several people trying to talk at once. James wondered what the hell Martin was playing at. He had wondered all day, getting the sense that in any situation the sergeant was further back than he expected, only a little, but noticeable enough. He seemed at the very least extremely cautious. Now the ruddy man had vanished altogether. Well, he did not have time to find him. The Panthers and other tanks were edging closer, step by step. Another Sherman brewed, although as they were able to report that they were abandoning, it sounded as if the crew was OK.

He could see the side of the Panther, just about read its number through his glasses – 214 in black figures outlined with white.

'Three Baker, aim at the one behind. We'll take the leader, over.'

'Roger, Baker Three.'

James was about to tell Bell to wait until he fired, then to open up and keep on shooting, but the net was a chaos of overlapping reports and he could not wait any longer. Bell would know what to do.

'Gunner, target Panther, f—'

Before James gave the order a streak of bright orange slammed into the hull of the Panther, back behind the turret. He saw the tank shudder like a dog shaking itself dry. Little flames licked up from its engine deck, and figures in dark uniforms were leaping out of the hatches. Collins stamped anyway, whether through surprise, anticipation or thoroughness, and his shell struck the already knocked out tank and ripped off one of the big wheels.

Bell fired, his shell somehow passing between the front hatches and the gun barrel of the second Panther without touching anything. Then there was another savage strike on the side of the hull and the German tank lurched to a halt. Bell hit it with his second shot, only for the AP to skim away without penetrating. Again came the hammer blow on the side, and then a little later a third. The Panther exploded, its turret flipping off and high.

'Baker Three Charlie to Baker Three. Two hornets destroyed, out.'

James sought for other targets, but the Germans were pulling back, reversing where possible to keep their thickest armour facing the enemy. Mortars dropped smoke rounds in front of their own panzers to shield them, adding to the dust and the darker smoke from burning tanks and patches of wheat set on fire.

Once again, the British all tried to speak at the same time and it was a while before the confusion ended.

'Sunray to all stations, well done.' Colonel Tim's voice sounded like someone giving prizes at a school assembly.

19.15 hrs, Point 103, Normandy

'Driver, hard left, that's it, straight, get us by the far gateway.'

Whitefield changed gear, and the Sherman surged forward. They were in a different part of the ridge, in a long, fairly narrow field, the ground undulating, so that the tank bounced as it raced along. They had just entered from an adjacent field. James clung on to the rim of the cupola with one hand and the left hatch with the other to steady himself. Bell's Three Baker was in the corner, shooting through a gap in the hedge at German tanks approaching up a winding lane. James could not see his targets, but wanted to cover the flank in case the enemy had got into fields to their right. Smoke was coming from that direction, the dense, oily black cloud of a burning Sherman.

'Got one!' Bell shouted, voice almost squeaking in excitement.

'Three to Three Baker, well done! Am in position to cover you.' The field on the far side of the gate was larger, dipping down before rising again, so that he could see nothing beyond the far hedge. There were no Germans, just the blazing remains of Two Baker.[1] James struggled to remember the commander's name. Something odd, beginning with H or K. Hanks, that was it. Corporal Hanks. He had been knocked out barely five minutes ago and no one had got out. The turret was lying upside down ten yards from the inferno of the hull. Ammunition and fuel must have gone up almost immediately, the force of the explosion ripping off the turret like the cork from a champagne bottle – and five men were gone. Whoever had done it was probably still there.

James tried to see anything unnatural, any sharp angle or gleam off metal behind the far hedge. It was less than a hundred yards away.

---

1   As new tanks/crews arrived, they took the call sign of those they were replacing.

Solid shot cracked past them.

'There,' Collins shouted over the intercom, and started to traverse the gun before James gave the order. The direction gave him a clue, but even at this close range he could not see anything except for leaves and branches which, with the bank, must have been a good fifteen feet high.

The 75mm thundered, searing into the hedge almost directly opposite them. The bushes quivered. A shot came back, wild this time and further away by a yard, and this time James saw the yellow and orange flash. The German guns did not seem to flare as brightly as their own.

Collins fired again, the shot breaking off a big branch, which dropped down. There was some dirty smoke, not very much, and the German did not fire again.

'Give him a couple more,' James said, forgetting procedure.

Collins obeyed, and the shells savaged the patch of hedgerow, shattering more branches, carving out a scoop in the otherwise fairly regular line. They ought to have been able to see a tank there, perhaps even a low slung assault gun like a Stug. There was no sign of either.

'Reckon he's scarpered,' Collins said.

James nodded to himself. Still, they would stay in position in case that German or another came back.

'Three Baker to Three. One Tiger brewed. He's blocked the lane and the rest have pulled back.'

'Three to Three Baker, good show. Keep your eyes peeled.'

Blamey whistled through his teeth. 'Tiger, eh? That's good. They're supposed to have armour like a battleship.'

A lot of Tiger tanks were being reported today, and maybe they were there or maybe they were not. There was not much time to study the enemy and remember lectures on German armour in the circumstances. Encouraging though, if a Sherman could brew a Tiger. James remembered their shells bouncing off that Panther – and Panthers were only medium tanks, not heavies like Tigers. The important thing was that Bell was in one piece and had knocked out the enemy and stopped that advance.

'Loader, how are we off for shells?'

Without a pause, Blamey gave the answer, the mark of someone very good at his job. 'Twenty-five AP and fourteen HE, sir. We've used about half.' Like most crews, Blamey and Collins had crammed in a few extra on top of the recommended supply.

'Remind me when we get below a third.'

'Will do, skipper.'

This was proving to be a long day, very long, and it was far from over yet with a good three hours or more of daylight still to go. He was so very tired, and even if his crew were a lot stronger and tougher than him – and that was something he believed with all his soul – they had to be tired as well, even if they did not show it.

'Three to Three Baker and Charlie, any sign of trouble, over?'

'Three Baker to Three, nothing at the moment, but there were at least two more hornets out there.'

'Some movement in the wood up on the crest,' Sergeant Martin reported. The Firefly was up the hill behind them, able to see further from a position in the corner of a field. 'But nothing more so far. Three Charlie, out.' Earlier the sergeant had done some pretty fine soldiering, going ahead, guessing that there was another field beyond the one they were in where he could get a better field of fire. No one was about to complain with two Panthers brewed as a result. James really did not know what to make of Martin.

He ducked low as mortar bombs plopped down and exploded in the field just in front. The next salvo came behind him. He closed the hatches as the next three rounds came in. One struck the front hull squarely, rocking the tank and provoking a deluge of swearing. At least, James assumed that all of it was obscene or blasphemous. At moments of great stress both Whitefield and Collins came out with some expressions that he had never heard before the last few days, not even in training. He still was not sure what all it meant, although the gist was clear enough.

'Everyone alright?' he asked, once the initial tirade was over. The MO[2] kept telling them that anyone with the energy to make a big fuss probably was not as badly hurt as all that. Still, the doctor did emphasise the 'probably'.

'Still seeing stars, skipper,' Thomson said. 'Oh and Whitey here needs a minute or two to tidy up his make-up.'

No one was hurt and nothing seemed broken. A mortar bomb, probably an 81mm as that's what the Germans had in greatest number, did not contain all that much explosive, certainly nowhere near enough to penetrate the front armour of a Sherman. At least, that's what all the manuals and instructors said. You never quite knew until you had tried it.

'Laddered a stocking too,' Whitefield added, his voice a little distorted. 'And me with no coupons.' It sounded as if he spat. 'Split me lip. Those fucking...'

James was happy for his driver and the others to let off steam. He was staring through his periscope, watching the far hedge in case the same tank or another came back under cover of the barrage. He saw nothing and nothing happened, so he kept watching, and after a few minutes warily opened the hatches again and peered out. There was the fresh stink of cordite in the air and a dark smear on the drab paint of the front glacis plate on *Hector II*.

He glanced at his watch. It was only 19.50, ten to eight in civilised places. That meant that he had been awake for more than eighteen hours, most of the time in the turret, although now and then dismounted for O Groups or to take a look around and guide the Sherman into a better position. So far he had not had to dismount with a spade to carry out his natural functions. He had used the empty shell case lots of times, like all the rest of them, until now it seemed the most natural thing

---

2   Medical Officer.

in the world to unbutton your trousers and piddle into a brass
tube in front of the others. His bowels did not seem to be taking
any interest in life, and he could not remember going yesterday
either. He had expected fear to have the opposite effect, but so
far that did not seem to be the case and he had certainly been
scared.

Yet everything was fading. The moments, sometimes it
seemed mere fractions of a second, were so overwhelmingly
clear as they happened, and then they were gone, because either
they were followed by waiting and tense calm or by another
moment of violence and terror.

James was beginning to wonder whether journalists or
historians ever gave a true picture of what happened. He had
lived through the day – so far – but could not remember more
than fragments of it all, and he was not sure what order they
came in.

First thing B Squadron had gone down to support the Durhams
in St Pierre. They had spent hours down there, in the fields,
orchards and lanes and sometimes on the fringes of the village
itself, shooting up the Germany infantry when they attacked,
stalking and trying not to be stalked by the tanks and assault
guns. James and his crew had had a couple of near misses, had
added their fire to two other Shermans to knock out a Mark
IV tank that was pushing forward too boldly into their view.
The German tank had burned, but much more slowly than a
Sherman. Only one man had got out and he had been cut down
by the bow gunner on one of the other British tanks. Colonel
Tim was not keen on them shooting men abandoning a vehicle,
for that was not the way of most of the old Desert hands, but
James doubted that anything would be said. C Squadron had
reported that two of their crews had been machine-gunned the
day before. Two, almost three, years on from the war without
hate of Egypt and Libya, things were different.

His thoughts were hazy, and he certainly did not know
how many times heavy shelling had come down on them and

the poor bloody infantry in their slit trenches. At one point a captain from the DLI had asked to come up on top of the rear deck to see better; that is as far as a captain ever could *ask* a second lieutenant, but then they were both British. The man had said he was taking the chance between stonks – the slang the infantry were using for a big barrage. It was a good word.

Otherwise there were hazy memories. The crack of solid shot slicing through the air time and time again. If you heard it, like the snap of a rifle bullet, that probably meant that it had passed and missed you, which did not stop the terror rushing through your body. He remembered infantry helping a wounded tank commander back down a lane until the padre appeared in a jeep and took the casualty back. The padre was turning up everywhere these days, a far larger presence than he had ever been back in England.

One shell had slapped into a wall behind them, showering him with red brick dust. For a while the crew dubbed him Big Chief Black Beret, until the onslaught of fresh excitement and horror made them forget.

In turn they knocked down one house, because the Durhams reckoned a sniper was up in a dormer window. It was quite a pretty house, tidier and better maintained than many, its shutters and door a deep shade of blue. Three 75 HE shells left it a mangled ruin, roofless, and with most of the front wall gone.

The Durhams held on. B Squadron lost a couple of tanks and a couple of commanders who showed too much of themselves out of the turret. One of the tanks was in a field which opened onto a lane and they passed it several times. It did not catch fire as so many did, but the driver was dead or had abandoned it with any other survivors, and he must have left it in low gear with the engine on and the left track locked. Round and round it went in a slow, endless circle, like some giant woodlouse with injured legs. There must have been plenty of fuel because it kept going. There were jokes about ever decreasing circles and its ultimate fate. Thomson offered to go over and see if he could drive it away back up to the rest of the regiment. James was tempted to let him, then they were summoned to help out in another part of the perimeter. They did not see the circling tank after that, and he was glad. There was something uncanny, even eerie, about it.

The Yeomanry arrived around 10.00, and half an hour later, B Squadron, now of ten tanks, pulled back onto Point 103. After that it was a question of periodic bursts of hate from the German guns and mortars. At first the German armour had stayed at a distance, sniping as they had from the start. Gradually they began to push closer and closer. There seemed to be a lot of them, although the ground meant that they had to split up and operate in ones, two and threes, just like the British. Attacks came, and the lower slopes of the ridge on either flank were more or less lost. The Germans kept coming, but so far had not been able to push up to the top and stay there. Both sides lost tanks, especially in that big attack the Germans had made from the south-west.

All day James had felt that the voices on the regiment's net were far more excited and on edge than before, and wondered whether he sounded the same. It was good to hear Colonel Tim's calm words and sardonic humour. He also appeared from time to time in his Sherman, apparently having an instinct for where the next attack would come. One exchange over the wireless was etched into his mind and he could not imagine ever forgetting it.

'Sunray to Able Two stations, am working my way around your left to flank them.' There were four hornets coming across one of the larger fields. 'Hold your fire until I am in position, over.'

'They're bloody close, Sunray, over.'

'Nevertheless, almost there. Now.'

James had been close enough to hear the cracks of the solid

shot, even though this was happening on the far left, well away from his current position.

'Good shooting, Able Two.'

'Got the fucker!'

'Sunray to all stations, observe correct RT procedure. ... But, yes, you got the fucker.'

'Anyone stop that last one – he's running!' The voice sounded like a treble from a cathedral choir in his excitement.

'My bird, I think!' The colonel then forgot to switch his microphone properly. 'Gunner, shoot the bugger. That's the ticket, right on the arse. Again. Beautiful. Reilly, you'll make a wonderful poacher back in civvy street. Or a gunman if you prefer.'

'Long as I get to shoot at the English, sir.'

'Really Reilly – oh that's quite good. Well, I'm sure you know best. What are you pointing at? I've done what? Well I'm buggered...' There was a cough. 'Sunray to all Able stations, bravo. Four Mark Fours out for a duck.'

20.55 hrs, Newhaven

The LSI[3] seemed to tower over them, even though there were far bigger merchant ships waiting to dock and they would dwarf it. At last – at very long last – the Glamorgans were embarking for the Second Front.

Mark waited with his platoon on the quayside. He was tired, which was daft after sitting in the truck's cab for so many hours, but it had been a long day and he wanted to get everyone on board and then sit or better yet sleep. He did not feel hungry, although he probably ought to eat and would go around telling his men to get some food because that was what a good officer should do.

---

3   Landing Ship Infantry.

The journey should not have taken anything like so long. In peacetime they could have covered it in less time on a bicycle. Instead, the TCVs were late, two and a half hours late, and, once they had climbed into the things, they had waited another forty minutes before setting off. They had been a given a strict route, for they were just one of many convoys heading to or from the ports. This was very much the long way round, and plenty of times they stopped and waited, sometimes for a long time, before resuming the trip.

Yet everyone was cheerful. Civilians – and there were still a fair few, even in the areas partly cleared for military use – waved and cheered as they passed. Mark had expected everyone to take the invasion for granted by now, but there was still a strong mood of excitement. The men waved back and shouted out jokes. At one point they stopped in the main street of a village next to a café. It was shut, because it was already evening. Even so an elderly couple, presumably the proprietors, appeared and, aided by their even more elderly neighbours, brought out cups of tea for everyone in the three-tonner. Happily, that delay lasted long enough for them to finish the drink and return the china cups – and for the old folk to refuse all offers of payment.

'Good luck to you all, lads. Very good luck,' the man had said. He looked old enough to have been too old for the Great War, but you never could tell.

'Write home whenever you can,' his wife had told them. 'They'll be praying for you every moment. We all will.'

'Good luck, boys, good luck.' Another old timer had appeared to add his best wishes. This one looked as if he might have been at Waterloo.

The trucks started up again after that. Their driver muttered that it was a pity that they had not stopped next to a pub, but no one else seemed to be complaining. Sergeant Dalton sat with them in the cab, but slept for most of the journey. Mark remained in awe of the veteran, and was never quite sure what to say to him in less formal settings, which meant that this was something of a relief. Still, he would dearly like to learn more from the man.

Folk kept running out into the street or into their gardens to watch them go by. The sight of a woman, any even vaguely attractive woman, attracted the greatest excitement in the back of each truck, men straining to see out of the unfastened covers in the rear. There were civilians, occasionally ATS, some Land Girls in the fields and now and then a traveller. A stout WVS lady, round faced and bespectacled and old enough to be the mother of anyone in the platoon, including Mark himself, waited at one crossroads astride her bike as they went through. She stood, blowing a kiss to each truck, and they yelled and whistled back as if she was Googie Withers or Betty Grable. Some of the servicewomen gave as good as they got – sometimes more – in response to all the wolf whistles and invitations, prompting great roars of laughter from the Glamorgans.

They reached Newhaven in the end, then queued to drive down towards the docks, then waited, disembarked, waited some more, marched onto the quay, waited, and finally started up the gangplank. In the meantime they saw a few Wrens, one a plump, West Country lass who did some remarkable flirting, given that she was on the far side of the dock. Mark's pulse quickened when he saw a Second Officer appear and chivvy the other Wrens away, for the height and figure were there and she did look dashed attractive in her uniform. Then the face turned towards them. It was not Anne, although still a very pretty young woman. Nice legs, too.

'Keep your soldiers in order, lieutenant,' she shouted across to him in a voice filled with petulance. Mark bit his lip not to yell back. Bloody woman, what did she expect? No one was doing any harm. His fists clenched and unclenched. He was angry, angry that the woman was not Anne, angry that Anne did not write, perhaps did not care. No, those kisses must have meant something and all their talks and time together. They certainly had meant a lot to him.

'Making friends, sir?' Dalton said softly.

Mark's frustration deflated. He worried that he might have appeared nervous, even hysterical and that his sergeant and the rest might think that he was frightened. He was nervous, obviously, surely they all were, but it was not something you wanted to parade.

'That Wren officer reminded me of someone.'

'Hope your lass is a bit less angry though! That bint's got some tongue on her. Reminds me of the wife when I come home full. Hell of a lot more frightening that the Jerries!'

That sounded as if he did think Mark was worried. Still, he liked the sound of 'your lass'. Anne would be, he was sure – one day. 'How long have you been married?'

'Dunno. When did they relieve Mafeking?' Dalton gave a deep, very natural laugh. 'She's a good girl, my Sarah. And keeps me a good boy, whether I like it or not!' Nothing was happening so he fished into his pocket and produced a photograph. It was small, the edges crumpled and with a slight tear. There was Dalton, looking severe as folk so often did in snaps, with two children, a girl and boy, in front and a light haired woman with a round face. It was hard to tell, but the mind filled in the rosy cheeks of the country girl she undoubtedly was. Mark would not have said from the picture that she was all that pretty – homely and kind perhaps, but not pretty. Dalton stared at the picture for a long time as if it were an icon.

'Does it worry you,' Mark asked, surprised at himself, 'having to leave them behind to go off to war?'

Dalton shrugged. 'I worry about them, but what can you do? Job's got to be done, hasn't it?'

Mark felt like an infant beside a wise old elder. 'Yes,' he said after a while.

'Glad you've got a girl, sir, but good you're not settled. Gives you something to look forward to. We beat Hitler, then you come back and marry your Wren and have lots of little soldiers – or sailor girls if you prefer.' He grinned. 'Simple as that.'

Mark laughed and suddenly felt very happy.

21.55 hrs, Point 103, Normandy

'Reckon they've finished for today?'

The Reverend Joseph Dobbs was on the back of *Hector II*, and was staring into the next field at the burned out Sherman, its turret beside it. The padre wanted to check on its crew, not because there was any chance for any of the five men, but so that he could see whether the bodies could easily be moved, or at least take their identity discs. The Army had managed to make the discs impervious to fire. Shame it could not do the same for its soldiers.

'Hard to tell,' James said.

'I'll risk it before the light goes,' Dobbs said. He tapped the bag he had slung over his shoulder. It clinked.

'What have you got there?' James asked, unable to help himself.

'Communion set,' Dobbs lied.

'Would you like a hand?' James did not relish the prospect of seeing whatever remnants there were in the destroyed tank, but thought obliged to offer.

'Very kind, but no thank you.' Dobbs had a thin face, prominent teeth, and a stub of a nose which meant that his glasses were always slipping. In appearance and manner he was very much the stage clergyman, the one to be shocked by the slightest thing, mistakenly if the play was a comedy. 'However, I'd be obliged if you would cover me. That is if you don't object to receiving military advice from a mere man of the cloth!'

'Of course not, padre.'

James watched him go, relieved not to be with him, but worried about his safety. Dobbs strode into the field, walking straight for the tank. He did not have a white flag or wear the armband of a medic, which meant that there was no particular reason why any German with a gun should not shoot him.

Nothing happened, so the Germans were not there, or recognised that this was not some martial expedition or any threat to them. Dobbs went to the turret first, but did not spend long there. Then he went to the hull, climbing into the open turret ring, examining everything closely. Most of the time they could not see him, until he popped up. Once, he had a hammer and chisel in hand, no doubt from his Communion set. James shuddered at the thought of what he was doing with it, and was thankful again not to be helping.

After ten minutes Dobbs returned, a little bag in one hand. 'Poor fellows,' was all that he would say for a moment. He refused the offer of a drink from a canteen, and just strode off to continue his work elsewhere, with a simple, 'No rest for the wicked.'

D+6, Monday 12th June

10.30 hrs, off Newhaven

MORE THAN HALF of the battalion were on the LSI, the rest on a similar vessel along with most of Brigade HQ. Their vehicles, carriers, trucks, jeeps, and a handful of anti-tank guns were supposed to be in another ship, setting out from London.

Having got them aboard and crammed below decks, no one appeared to be in a hurry to take them any further. Both ships rocked at anchor near the entrance to the harbour, at the mercy of a considerable swell. Judd lay on a bunk, wishing that the world would end. He had already thrown up several times. Others were seasick, if few as sick as he was.

On the other ship, Mark was coping, helped by that vessel's position, sheltered on one side by a large merchantman. No one seemed to know when they would set out. The captain simply announced that other ships needed to be loaded and their escort prepared. There were barrage balloons over all the ships, anti-aircraft guns on all of them, including the LSIs and more on shore. Not that the Germans put in an appearance. Presumably the main beaches offered better pickings.

11.40 hrs, Point 103, Normandy

So far, the Germans had not put in any more tank attacks. James and 3 Troop, back up to strength again with the return of Sergeant Dove and another Sherman, were overlooking St Pierre. There was still a fair bit of mortar fire, ready to catch the unwary out of their tanks. Artillery stonks came less often and it was easier to hear the shells on their way in.

The Sun put in an appearance and decided to stay. Soon, the inside of *Hector II* was hot enough to make everyone sweat, adding to the mechanical smells and all the staleness of human bodies, urine, and gases from the shells. It stank so much that they all noticed, in spite of living inside the Sherman for the last days.

James' bowels had decided to function again, and to make up for all the lost time. Three times already, he had got Collins to command and brought Thomson up as gunner, so that he could take a shovel and do what needed to be done in one of the rear corners of the field. Once the mortars came in before he could get back and he lay, fingers clawing the earth, as the bombs went off around him. In the end, all it cost was his dignity, and he no longer cared much about that.

Back in the tank, he felt filthy, and not simply because he had run out of the paper that came with their rations and had had to make use of a handkerchief, now discarded, to clean himself. He had managed to shave each day, a simple task since his pale hair was thin and did not grow quickly, let alone show up. It made him feel a little better each time, but the lack of sleep and the days of boredom, frantic activity and fear were catching up. Especially in the heat, everyone came across as sluggish.

Still, they sat and waited, and closed up when the shells were close. James looked at his hands, every line on the skin sharply defined by grease and dirt. Now and then he tapped the pocket of his battledress tunic, but never opened it. He was simply too filthy for that.

Hours passed, and the enemy remained quiet, at least up here on the ridge. There was more shelling down in St Pierre.

14.30 hrs, off Newhaven

Both of the LSIs upped anchor, started engines and moved. Half an hour of delicate manoeuvring later, they stopped and anchored again. Judd did not care, and Mark began to regret having had lunch.

18.45 hrs, in the English Channel

They were off at last, although not heading for France, but for a rendezvous with more ships off the Solent before making the crossing overnight. Judd felt less at death's door, the motion of a moving ship a little easier to manage than when they were moored. Mark went on deck and found it all exhilarating. A destroyer rushed past them, ensign streaming in the wind, and he could not help feeling proud. He was nineteen and this was a remarkable adventure.

21.15 hrs, outside St Pierre, Normandy

B Squadron were sent down to cover the DLI as they withdrew from the village. They were not being replaced, nor were the Germans chasing them out. Division had decided that St Pierre was too far forward and too exposed to hold for the moment, so were pulling back to a line running either side of Point 103. The high ground mattered, and no one asked the Durhams what they thought, so after days and a lot of blood spent seizing and holding the place, they were to give it up.

Colonel Tim had explained it all to the regiment's officers – a smaller band than a few days before – at an O Group early in the afternoon. He dismissed some of the muttering.

'I've fought in the desert, watching tanks burning, men dying and the infantry being shelled and Stuka-ed to bits for stretches of wasteland that could never be worth anything to anyone. Just rocks and sand.

'We've done our job, and so have the DLI and the other battalions. We've wrong-footed Fritz, given as good as we got – better – and now the plan develops. Seventh Armoured haven't found the weak spot yet, so they're pulling out and will do an even wider hook to the west. Don't tell a soul, but there is talk of Brigade pulling us and the other regiments back for a day or two to refit and polish our boots!'

That news had cheered them all up, and no one complained after that. It was a nervous business covering the Durhams, because this was the perfect time for the Germans to attack and create mayhem. James waited, fearing the sound of artillery or worse the whipcrack of AP coming at them as tanks led infantry forward. The Germans did not show up, so must have had other problems or not noticed what was going on. None of the DLI and no tanks were lost in the withdrawal.

Back on the ridge, James just wanted to sleep, and the minutes dragging by until sunset were a torment to him. So was the time doing all the things a tank crew needed to do at the end of a day, and his duties as troop commander. It was midnight before he crawled into newly issued blankets beside *Hector II*. He was asleep in moments.

D+7, Tuesday 13th June

THE WATER JETTED down, not warm, but not stone cold either, and it felt like Heaven. James wallowed in the shower, naked for the first time in nine days and clean for the first time in what felt like a century. This may have been a tent set up by a mobile bath unit, but surely even Louis XIV was never pampered to this degree. This was probably what it was like to be a movie star.

Brigade had pulled them back, along with the two other armoured regiments, although their RA Regiment were left behind the lines to fire in support of other formations. That was the gunner's lot, to stay longer in action, but usually avoiding getting really close. The tankmen came back to recover and to start replacing losses and repairing scarred vehicles.

James did not want to think, although he knew that his turn in the shower was nearly done. He was one of half a dozen subalterns from the three squadrons of the 165th RAC, all that was left of the ones who had come ashore on D-Day or D+1. The rest had already been killed or wounded. That included a couple of replacements. In a week of action they had lost nine troop commanders, more than one a day. Almost as many other tank commanders had gone as well, half of them dead. If they did not stick their head out of the turret they could not see, and more than likely the tank was brewed by an unseen enemy. If they did look out, then they were prey to snipers and shells and anyone else with malice and a weapon. This was not the Desert, and no one was going to stand tall anymore, but you still could not operate tanks properly if you stayed buttoned up. So the commanders died or were wounded, and the odds were that they would go on doing so.

On top of all that, the regiment had suffered another forty casualties, perhaps a dozen of them dead, when tanks were brewed or men were caught outside by shells, and when a truck used by the fitters went over a mine and burned up almost as quickly as a Sherman struck by AP. One week, and already the regimental family, with many men who had been together for years of training, was starting to change.

The other regiments had suffered as much or more, and each had taken heavier losses on D-Day itself when they led the attacks. No one worried too much about the tanks that were lost, because it was the crews that mattered, and if they escaped, then in time they would be supplied with fresh mounts. The Yeomanry had lost two commanding officers and several other HQ men, so were having to deal with all of that. The brigadier had gone as well, badly wounded by shrapnel in the last few days.

No doubt the higher powers would set all this against the losses inflicted on the enemy, on the ground gained and held, and set against that the objectives that had not been reached or had to be abandoned. James did not really care about any of that, although a small part of him wondered whether he should. He suspected that most of the regiment felt the same. The feeling was that the regiment had seen action for the first time and done a decent job, really more than that.

No one mourned, at least not openly. That simply was not the way things were done, but it was proving a lot easier than James expected. Not that he did not care. He had not lost a really close friend yet, partly because he had not made any really close friends inside the regiment. There were plenty of folk he liked, and some had gone. It was more that he struggled to remember what had happened hours, let alone days, before. There was only the present, and in the present he was either too tired or too scared or too busy to think much about anything.

That might change now that they were out of the line, if he started to feel normal again. No, that was not the right word or the sense of the thing. Like a child puzzled when his shoes seemed to keep shrinking and what had once fitted started to pinch, James felt that he was the same and the world kept changing. At the start it had all seemed so unreal, almost dreamlike. Now he was not sure whether or not he was awake.

None of that really mattered, as someone shouted that their time was up. He was free from dirt and grime and about to be given a fresh uniform, everything from underwear upwards. That was happiness enough and contentment for the moment.

16.30 hrs, off GOLD Beach

Nine Platoon had its first casualty before they reached France. Corporal Fuller, Judd's section leader, had been as seasick as anyone throughout the voyage. On the second day, his moaning became stronger and he complained of severe cramps in his stomach and side. By noon, he was in agony, at which point the MO was summoned – himself grey faced and weak – and diagnosed acute appendicitis, perhaps already peritonitis. With the ship's doctor they operated, and there was a good chance that the corporal would recover, but he certainly was not in any shape to invade Occupied Europe in the immediate future.

As a result, Lance Corporal Price was bumped up to Corporal and Griffiths given a stripe in his place as a temporary experiment. Cornelius O'Connor from HQ Company came to them to be Judd's N$^{\circ}$. 2 on the Bren.

'Will you look at the state of you?' O'Connor declared when he appeared to tell Judd the news.

Judd moaned, still unwilling to take a wider interest. If he lay flat and closed his eyes, then the sickness abated. He felt calm, peaceful and nearer to comfortable than at any time since they had climbed onto this floating tin can.

Cold seawater hit him in the face as O'Connor upended a bucket over him. Men nearby shouted in surprise. Some laughed. Judd jumped to his feet, lashed out, slipped and missed. O'Connor grabbed his arm. Judd struggled, and tried to launch a better punch with his free hand. O'Connor dodged, and used the movement to spin the other man around and pin him, using one of the grips they had all learned as part of unarmed combat.

'Are you well now?'

'Bastard!' Judd yelled. That was about as far as he usually went when it came to swearing, at least out loud, and even this was rare.

O'Connor put pressure on Judd's arm, sending a wave of agony through his body. 'Now that's not true, and you should know it. Ma and Pa had been before a priest years before I came along, although Pa didn't hang around long once I did. But if I was an angry man, I might take offence at that insult to my poor old mother.' He tightened his grip again. 'Now calm down, boy.'

No one was interfering and the laughter was growing. This was obviously between the two men and nothing to do with anyone else. Let them sort it out. If Judd could not stand up for himself then that was his problem.

Judd hissed in pain, until he realised that it was not that bad. O'Connor had relaxed his grip. 'Are we calm?' he asked, then without waiting for an answer, he let go, giving Judd a gentle push forward. 'And are we still down with the old mal de mere – or did you not know I was educated?'

O'Connor had a slim face and an easy smile, the very picture of a black haired Irishman from film or story, save that his accent was pure Grangetown – a real Cardiff lad through and through. He had charm and a lot of experience, having served with another battalion in France back in 1940 and later in

Tunisia. Rumour said that he had also fought in Spain, although in a Nationalist battalion of Catholic volunteers serving Franco, so not on the side Judd was accustomed to see as the path of righteousness. He had not been with this battalion of the Glamorgans long, but had readily been accepted. He was liked, respected, and no one had been inclined to mess with him.

Judd took a deep breath, spat out some seawater, then breathed again and realised that the seasickness had gone. Perhaps he had already been better, or the shock and sudden anger had driven out lesser concerns.

O'Connor stared at him for a moment, as if reading his thoughts, and then nodded. Judd guessed that the man was about thirty, but did not know much more about him than the bare rumours, so had no idea whether or not he was married and had family, or why he was still a private in spite of his record.

'Now then, boy, we're muckers from now on, and I can't have you lounging around. I plan on coming through this in one piece, which means I'm not about to let any daft sod get me killed. Especially you.' He jabbed forward with a finger to prod Judd in the chest. 'Understand?'

Judd nodded, just as O'Connor had done. The audience, denied a fight or shouting match to break the monotony, lost interest and went back to chatting, playing cards, smoking and simply feeling ill.

'Good.'

D+8, Wednesday 14th June

MARK LEANED ON the rail and marvelled. To their right, perhaps a mile away, was a port. Not the little harbour of a French fishing village, but a complex of concrete and metal built in the last week. There were old ships sunk or anchored as an outer breakwater and then rows of vast grey blocks, sunk presumably, since surely they could not float, joined by metal roadways. He could see ships moored alongside, men and cargoes disembarking, and trucks driving along the roads over the great blocks and onto the beach.

'They call it Mulberry,' a petty officer had told them, 'and it's a bloody miracle, begging your pardon. The Yanks have one as well, further up the coast. Best thing we have until we take Cherbourg or Le Havre.'

The portable harbour was only part of the wonder of the scene, for the sea was full, ship after ship, landing craft after landing craft, row upon row of them, some anchored, some moving and presumably all conforming to a vast, complex pattern beyond his understanding. Over it were the barrage balloons. He'd seen them before, of course, for since the War began the great grey balloons had been as familiar as rationing and shortages and articles telling folk how to push tiny bits of old soap together to make a fresh cake. Just something you accepted and barely noticed. He had seen them over ships as well, in Cardiff docks and the other harbours, but had never seen so many. It was as if a small town had settled down off the Normandy coast, and above it, even at this early hour, were the first Allied planes, flying this way and that, the black and white stripes showing whenever they banked. Not many came down low, wary of the barrage balloons and quite probably of trigger happy gunners on the ships. There had been an air raid alert during the night and the noise as the fleet's ack-ack guns flamed into life had been staggering. No one seemed to have hit anything, but then none of the ships had been bombed either, so it was a fair exchange.

'Next party ready!' A young snotty was in charge of embarking D Company, and Mark's 17 Platoon were to go next. He did not relish the prospect, not because he was not eager for action, but because this was a landing ship and they would have to climb down rope netting into the little LCA bobbing up and down in the water beside them. The wonderful Mulberry Harbour was for others, for vehicles and crates of stores and perhaps more favoured humans. The Glamorgans were going in by assault craft, and almost two days later than scheduled, because everything had taken longer than expected. After another look around at the fleet, Mark could readily understand why. It was remarkable that things were going as smoothly as they were.

Evans was beside him, his skin pale, his many pimples brighter and more livid than ever. The lad had been quiet since his release, and was doing his job with great efficiency, like a small child given a warning and making a show of being good.

'Right, first men onto the nets!'

Mark made sure he moved before any of the others. That was his job, to go first and show the way and prove that it was safe. It was awkward, laden down with all his kit, his Sten gun determined to slip off his shoulder, but he managed it and his feet found the ropes easily. His trousers were a little tight, which made it awkward. Given that there was a good chance they would be landed in the surf and wade ashore, they had all been issued with denim trousers to wear in place of their battledress. The material was coarser – and that was saying something – and usually reserved for fatigues.

The climb was easier than he expected, although he glanced round a few times to judge how far he had got. Beneath them, the LCA was bucking like a wild horse as the swell took it. Evans was beside him, insisting on staying close to his officer. The boy's face was locked in a rictus of sheer terror, and several of the other men were much the same. Mark thought of the poor devils who had done this back on D-Day itself, all the time knowing that after this peril there were still the Germans waiting for them on the shore, fingers ready to curl around triggers.

'Right, lads, wait, wait.' The Able Seaman guiding them into the landing craft was from Sunderland, and dragged out the vowel sound. 'Wait, wait. Now jump!'

Mark landed well; Evans skidded for a moment as he came down, so he grabbed him to steady him. There was a flash of irritation in the boy's eyes. He clearly did not want to be helped, but was not about to complain to an officer, let alone his officer.

The rest of the platoon followed. Private Jenkins – it was bound to be 562 Jenkins – lost his balance and somehow ended up dangling upside down, knees over the netting holding him in place. His rifle slipped from his shoulder – he must have been the only man not to put it round his neck and across his back – and fell with a splash into the water. Jenkins did not yell or scream. He never really did when his clumsiness caused yet another mishap. He simply dangled there, swinging a little so that he banged against the hull, and waiting for someone to solve the insoluble mystery that had caused all this to happen. Men helped him, and only then did he start to speak, berating anyone who grabbed him too hard.

'Keep still, you daft sod!'

'Watch where you're shoving!'

'Come on, Jenks, I've got you, swing your leg out.'

'Mind out, my pack is slipping.'

'Oh shit.'

The pack joined the rifle in its watery grave. The clips attaching it to the webbing were strong, and ought not to have broken, but that was true of so much of the King's property mangled or destroyed by Private Jenkins. For such a short, slightly built youth, he had a remarkable strength when employed in just the wrong place at the wrong time.

Mark saw Major Jackson peering down from the landing ship and sighed inwardly. Up until then, 17 Platoon had been doing everything well. The major did not say anything, having the sense to realise that an extra voice was unlikely to help matters, at least until the delay became too long. Jackson would also understand that this sort of thing happened around Jenkins with appalling regularity. Not that the man was stupid, for 562 could turn into a fluent barrack room lawyer when he chose. Like any platoon, Mark's was a mixed bunch, with some frighteningly clever and well-read men, often far more politically savvy than he was, if from a particular slant. There were also a couple of men who on a good day might just qualify as halfwits, but they generally caused less trouble than Jenkins, as long as you avoided leaving them on their own with any complicated task.

'That was your fault,' Jenkins complained, once they had freed him and brought him down to the LCA. There was a great tear in his left trouser leg. At least these were only the denims so would soon be replaced.

The rest of the platoon came down, the LCA was full, and at a signal, the coxswain started the engine and steered the craft away so that the next one could take its place at the bottom of the net.

'If you'd only let me come at own speed,' Jenkins explained to an uninterested audience. They were used to him, and indulgent. As far as 562 was concerned, no misfortune was ever his responsibility, but something caused by the mistakes of others.

'Pipe down!' Sergeant Dalton snarled, in a rare moment of anger. 'Now,' he added, raising his voice, 'check your kit.'

07.20 *hrs, GOLD Beach*

Judd found the rapid, bouncing motion of the LCA did not cause him any real discomfort. They surged in, slapping into the high waves of the turning tide, which sent spray all over them. The smell of the salt water and hints of seaweed reminded him of home, and all those long summer days exploring cliffs and paths, going crabbing and swimming in the grimy water of the busy Bristol Channel. A hint of oil amid the smell of the sea seemed natural to him, and there was plenty of it in this busy stretch of water off the landing beach. For them it was like taking a trolley bus, but everyone was bound to think about the men who had led the way for the actual assault.

There were several wrecks, one a big LST, its sides scorched black, which must have been caught on beach obstacles and then shelled. It lay, side on to the shore, so that craft had to steer past it on either side. There were other wrecks, mostly smaller LCAs like this one, and on the shingle ahead of them burned out tanks, one or two tipped over on their side. Pieces of equipment, lifebelts, broken crates, shattered rifles and other things impossible to recognise bobbed about in the waves. There was something else, something in khaki, floating alongside them for a while. The shape did not look human, nor did the strange pale mass protruding from what might once have been a jacket. Judd wanted to look away and could not, until eventually the remnant was caught on a different current and was left behind.

The LCA ground onto the beach, the ramp dropped, Mr Buchanan waved his arm and led the way into three inches of foaming water. The platoon followed, muttering that it was typical of the bloody Army to tell you that you have to wade and then land you dry. As usual, the openly expressed opinion was not that this was a piece of good fortune on their part, but contempt for the fools higher up who never knew what they were doing. Judd had been surprised at how much time many of the adults in the office had spent complaining and criticising the authorities. Yet even that had not prepared him for the energy soldiers put into bitching. He might have been wrong, because there were many regiments in the Army, but did suspect that the Welsh had turned this into a fine art. As they tramped ashore with no more than slightly damp boots, they cursed the generals and Churchill and the King. Someone even had a go at Vera Lynn and Tommy Handley.

The beach was bustling, a few areas still taped off because they were not yet clear. Men in helmets with white bands around them shouted instructions, voices overlapping as one called to one unit and another to the next. There were also signs, with unit symbols and acronym after acronym.

'A Company, this way,' the major shouted.

'Nine Platoon, follow me,' Buchanan called, not seeming to raise his voice, but clear enough for everyone to hear.

They marched off the beach and inland, the number of unit signs proliferating as they went. An hour later they were directed into a field, the last of the battalion to arrive.

'Bugger me, what's going on?' 'Sandy' Moore asked. The battalion was undressing, taking off packs and webbing, then tunics, so that they could slip off braces and dispense with the denims. There were hundreds of men in their shirt tails, some with underwear and some without, as they prepared to don battledress trousers.

'It's a new order, boy. Go into battle bollock naked to scare the frightful 'un. Orders straight from Monty.'

'Could be tradition,' Judd suggested. 'The ancient Celts used to go into battle naked and they're our ancestors. They reckoned it scared the Romans. Polybius says it stopped their clothes snagging when they ran through thorn bushes.'

'Who was 'e?'

'A famous Greek historian.'

'Silly man, by damn – who runs starkers into thorns?'

'I said he was Greek.'

'Now then, get a move on.' Sergeant Holdworth was unimpressed by such historical speculation. 'Over there and get those trousers off.'

'I'll bet that's what he said to those Land Girls,' Moore whispered.

Davison agreed. 'And it bleedin' well scared them as much as the ruddy Romans.'

'Move, you idle shower!' Holdworth had quite a voice on him and the Platoon knew that there was a limit to his patience. 'At the double, left, right, left, right, trousers down!' The sergeant was clearly enjoying himself. 'When are you going to get another order like this? Be something to tell your grandchildren.'

They went and did as they were told. 'Bloody Army,' Moore muttered.

'The things we do for King and Country,' Judd declared, and got a few smiles, but Holdworth was at them to get on with it and they were too busy to think much of anything else.

12.30 hrs, near Bayeux

James had slept well for another night in spite of the noise. There was a regiment of field artillery with their twenty-five-pounders set up in an adjacent meadow, and twice during the night they had had fire missions, blazing away for a good twenty minutes each time. He had not woken. Nor had the stick of bombs dropped onto the artillery by a wandering German bomber interrupted his rest, even when it set off a ready magazine. James slept on, as did his crew, and all were amazed when the next morning someone told them about the air raid. They decided that from now on they would dig a shallow trench then drive the Sherman over it and all sleep underneath for protection.

Rest and a break from making decisions that might cost his life, or that of others, had done much to restore him. He felt well, had plenty of energy, and when the Sun came out again, there was an air of a summer camping about the regiment's laager.

Yet feeling better and fresher also allowed his brain to start thinking again of more than the immediate, vital decisions. There were duties to perform, and the hardest was writing letters to the next of kin of the men he had lost from 3 Troop. There were three dead, one from his tank and two from Sergeant Dove's. If he was not careful, the image of Miller's shattered, headless torso readily came to mind. At least with Albright's mother he could say that the prospects were good, and her lad ought to recover.

He could not say anything like that to Miller's aunt, who had raised him, or the next of kin of the other two. They wanted words of comfort, not the grim truth, that their nice, cheerful, shining boys were gone in the blink of an eye. At least he could say with all honesty that the end had been quick and that they had not suffered. Was that last bit true? Miller's mutilation was so awful. A line of poetry came to mind – 'the monstrous anger of the guns'. It was monstrous, flesh and bone ripped and savaged, bits of a man sprayed around. James feared that there was agony, awful, all-encompassing pain for an instant which might not have seemed like an instant to poor Miller.

Dear Mrs Miller

It is with great sadness that I write these lines. ... Your boy was a wonderful fellow, liked by all. He served in my own tank, as assistant driver, so that I got to know him very well. ... I know it is only slight consolation, but I can assure you that the end was instant and that your Jack cannot have known any pain. One moment he was making us laugh and encouraging us and the next, he was gone. ... We will miss Jack, but are proud to have known and served with him. ... If there is anything else you would like to know, or anything I can do...

James stared at the letters. Each one was much the same for he could not think of other ways of expressing what needed to be said. He was sincere, hid only what might upset, and still it came across as a schoolboy exercise for an essay – 'write a letter imagining that you wish to console someone for a loss'. This felt like that, unreal, written by someone far too immature to understand such deep things. Another line came to him, this time from a picture, *The Dawn Patrol* – one of Bill Judd's favourites. He remembered Basil Rathbone beginning to crack, and talking to the adjutant about the letters of condolence; something like, 'Write what you like, it will break her heart just the same.' At least Rathbone was a grown-up, experienced; the actor had surely been in the Great War so knew something about it all for real and not just on the silver screen. James Taylor had been in battle, fought and killed – or at least given the orders that led to killing – and got some of his own men killed and wounded. He knew that he could function, give orders and not panic, and did not doubt that he could do it again. He was less sure that he was doing it well, that his mistakes had not caused the deaths. It all seemed too serious and important, and he felt like a little boy donning his father's suit and pretending to be an adult.

James picked up the four letters one by one. Even his handwriting seemed boyish and inadequate. He sighed, sealed the letters and put them aside to hand in later. Then he picked up another letter, with even more childlike writing than his own.

My dearest, dearest darling, my knight in shining Sherman tank!!!

Forgive my little joke, but the papers say this is a great Crusade, and so my squire has girded on his sword and taken solemn parting, his lady's favour ever close to his heart as token of undying, pure love. I do hope so deeply that this is so, that my poor adoration may help you with this stern task, that

*the token stays as unblemished as you remain whole
and safe through all the maelstrom.*

James sometimes wondered whether Penny actually knew
what half the words she used really meant. Yet no one could
doubt her enthusiasm.

*My prince, my Roland, my Hector, my purehearted
Sir Galahad, do not worry if you have no time to
think of a silly girl sitting at home, spinning her
weaves like a more famous Penelope, although not
to ward off suitors.*

James imagined her sucking the end of her pencil, wondering
whether she should assure him that plenty of others adored her
for her beauty, but that she was devout in her worship of him
alone, or feared that he might become jealous.

*That is my silly joke, of course, for how could any
other not pale into invisibility beside my beloved.*

Oh well, no doubt that was a disappointment to Errol Flynn.

*The Americans whistle, of course, and make
inappropriate suggestions, but they are harmless,
little more than children really,* – a word was
crossed out heavily – *children, and I pay no heed,
although several come to tea on Sundays. I show
them your picture and tell them about you.*

James gave a wry smile. Bet they love that.

*And there are the Airmen of course, especially
as they near the end of their training and get
more passes.*

That last word was unfortunate, although most likely she would not understand why. The Stevens kept open house to servicemen, as so many families did, as far as they were able.

They are nice boys, but do seem mere boys compared to you, and I do not take their jokes seriously.

Good God, if they were younger than him, they must still be in nappies. Should he be jealous about the 'jokes'? Perhaps, if he had the energy, or understood how he really felt about Penny, he might. Still, it was surely harmless, although he could not quite be sure, for the surprise of how she had been on that last day's leave remained strong.

He finished the letter, then began to pen a reply.

My dearest
 I do not know what more to say, for that simple word sums up all my feelings.

If only that were true. He did not know what his feelings towards her really were, and the thought of marriage was as unreal as pretending to command men in battle. James wrote the sort of letter he felt an ardent lover ought to write to his affianced, although he reined back a little on some of the passion – censoring his men's letters having significantly expanded his range in this respect. Like the condolences, this felt like an exercise, the sentences constructed rather than natural.

At least this was easier that the other letters. 'After the War' was too vague and unreal a concept to make much difference. For the moment, it was nice to feel that his fate mattered to an attractive young woman back home. Even the thought that she would weep for him and be heartbroken if he was killed offered a strange and selfish comfort, for it meant that he mattered. Someone cared, apart from his parents, who did not have much choice in the matter because he was their child.

Penny did not have to love him, indeed it baffled him why she should. She wanted to marry him, she wanted him to take her to the marriage bed and make love to her – with an enthusiasm bordering on impatience to judge from her letters and other things. That any pretty girl – and a nice girl at that – was willing to let him was a very nice thought. Plenty of the other officers had their affairs, including some of the married ones, and at least a few more or less openly took advantage of the places where women did such things commercially. The thought of that revolted James. When he was with a woman, he wanted to matter to her, wanted to be loved. Well, Penny was promising him that in abundance, and now that he was here her admiration felt less of a burden, whether or not he would later try to live up to her expectations.

James wrote the letter, avoiding talk of battle. He was half tempted to say that he had taken a wound after being attacked by a hostile stick. Penny would like the thought of a cosmetically pleasing scar, so there was no sense raising her expectations for a mere scratch, already nearly healed. Apart from that, she probably did not want to hear that he had used his lady's favour to wipe away the blood – or maybe she would find that desperately romantic. Cleaning was a problem, so for the moment the clotted blood would stay.

He finished what he hoped was an amusing and adoring love letter, even if the words and the shape of the letters still struck him as rather naïve. It would do. It would have to do, because he had duties to perform. James sealed this last letter and addressed it, and the billet-doux to please a whimsical young woman would go off with the notes offering thin comfort to the sorrow in other homes.

Beside them, the field artillery roared into life. He did not pay any attention. It was simply one of the sounds of Normandy.

D+9, Thursday 15th June

U P CLOSE THE Panther was huge. The name was apt, for this was a beast in every sense of the word, designed to hunt and kill. The briefing said that it was half as heavy again as a Sherman and James could easily believe that. It was wider and longer, hull and turret alike flat, and that immense gun barrel reaching forward for prey. Yet for all that it was not quite as high as a Sherman, and for all its size, it would be easy for a Panther to hide among the woods and hedges of Normandy. That was in the close country. In the open fields more common the nearer you got to Caen, that long gun could kill you from a couple of miles away.

Even knocked out and abandoned by its crew, this Panther exuded menace. Most of B Squadron's tank commanders had driven over to see the vehicle, put out of action in the early days by the Canadians and since used as a target. Panthers could be knocked out. The 165th RAC knew that from experience as well as the evidence of this and other wrecks peppered around the beachhead. Yet James also remembered watching the 75mm rounds ricocheting off one of them in that first encounter. Looking at this one, he could understand why.

The front of the hull, the glacis, was sloped on a Sherman, but nothing compared to the angle on this, and that was frightening. If an armoured plate was sloped, it increased the chances of a shell being deflected away. More than that, a shell coming flat and level had to drive through a greater depth of steel than against a flat plate. To all intents and purposes, it made the armour thicker than it really was, and the Panther's was thick enough in the first place.

Sergeant Dove looked thoughtful as he poked a finger into a gouge on the Panther's glacis. It was not deep, little more than a dent in the armoured plate. Around it was a circle of red paint to show that this had been done by a 75mm gun on a Sherman at point blank range. There were almost a dozen strikes with the same marking. None had penetrated the armour, and it was unlikely that any would have done much to upset the crew inside. Strikes from six-pounder anti-tank guns, circled in green, were no better. The conclusion was simple. At the closest of ranges the standard weapon in a Sherman, Churchill or Cromwell could not get through the front of a Panther's hull, even when the panzer was obligingly parked and not fighting back like this target. The six-pounders had some new ammunition that did better, not that that was much compensation for a tankman.

'Well, I guess we don't shoot at the hull,' Dove concluded, but the front of the turret was only a little more encouraging. The mantlet mounting the Panther's long 75 was curved, like half a drum pointing outwards. It was made from thicker steel than any part of a Sherman's armour, but one or two of the strikes here had gone deep, perhaps deep enough to fling red hot debris off the inside wall of the turret.

'They reckon the trick is to hit the lower half,' Dove went on, doing his best to sound confident. 'Look here.' He pointed at a mark very low down. 'This one bounced off, but went down, into the plate by the driver's hatch.' The armour there had cracked open.

'Got to get close to do that,' Bell said dubiously.

'We're always bloody close in the bocage,' Dove pointed out. 'But that's the spot if you get one head on.'

'Better yet, creep around the side.' James felt that he ought to try to encourage. That was the point of this excursion in a truck borrowed from A echelon, the close support section of the regiment who did the simpler repairs and resupplied them.

James led them around the tank. 'Look at that!' The left-hand side of the Panther was against a wall, but the right was exposed to the open field and it was riddled with holes, many marked in red and green.

'I hear they store their ammo in the side,' Dove told them.

'And that's the engine and fuel as well,' James added. 'Hit 'em there or in the rear and they're in trouble.'

'Won't burn as fast as a Ronson though.' Sergeant McDonald had the Charlie tank in 2 Troop and had all the dourness of a true Highlander. The nickname Ronson was used a lot now by the crews. The advert for Ronson lighters proclaimed that they lit first time, and plenty of tankmen were willing to believe the same of the Sherman. 'Still,' McDonald added as if weighing a great question, 'the devils will burn. We've seen that.'

'And you've got a ruddy great seventeen-pounder, you gloomy old sod,' Dove pointed out.

'Aye, but it's still a Sherman.'

They spent a long while crawling over the enemy tank and getting inside. James was pleased to see that there was no trace of its former crew apart from a stale smell and a lot of pin-ups of scantily clad girls. They must have been fixed with some powerful adhesive, because one or two were torn, but none had pulled off.

Dove sniffed. 'Thought you said these were Hitler Youth? Expected them to have only pictures of Adolf to warm their little hearts.'

'Bloody hell, that's a nasty thought,' Bell said. 'Photos of Der Fuehrer in a swimsuit! Christ!'

'Or with stockings and garters!'

'Thank you for the nightmares,' James said and climbed out of the turret hatch so that others could take a turn. He paused for a moment in the cupola, trying to imagine what it was like to command one of these things. He wondered whether there was some weakness, like a limited view in one direction. James shook his head and got out. As far as he could tell, the tank was well designed – not as comfortable as a Sherman perhaps, but good enough. The intelligence reports said that the engines were temperamental and the whole thing very hard to keep running and repair. Well, that was fine in its way, but unlikely to help much when you did run into one or more of the ruddy things. On top of that the Tiger was even bigger and nastier than the Panther.

An engine roared as a truck drove down the nearby lane at breakneck speed, sending up great clouds of dust. The noise was not loud enough to mask the deluge of angry protests from the men camped in the field beyond. This lasted long after the lorry and its noise and dust had vanished. As it died down, he heard the faint sound of singing as a column of infantry approached. Goodness knows how the truck had got past them for the lane was narrow.

James climbed down and noticed that Sergeant Martin was at the front, staring at the marks left by the shot. Seventeen-pounder hits were painted with yellow circles, and a good deal more encouraging.

'Sometimes on the hull and just about always on the turret,' James pointed out. 'That must make you feel a bit better.'

'Still got to hit first and fast,' Martin said. He was rubbing his chin like a mechanic about to give bad news to the owner of a car in for repairs. 'Doesn't matter about the range for him. Hit us anywhere – front, side, up the dock – we're brewed.'

The marching infantry were alongside them, invisible behind the hedge, although their voices carried, the determined, none too musical chant so familiar from all the exercises over all the long years. There was something different though, not that he was paying much attention.

'You've got two of them,' James pointed out to the sergeant.

Martin nodded slowly, then went back to smoothing his chin. 'I saw them before they could see me, sir. Reckon that's what really mattered. We saw them first and shot first. And from the side.'

'It was a great bit of work,' James said, then wondered whether that came across as arrogant, suggesting he picked off these big tanks all the time.

'Maybe yes, maybe no. I'm here, which is the main thing. But it's as much about seeing as shooting – more really. And when they're attacking, we've got a better chance. See one from the side and you can get him. See one from the front and it might be better to clear off and wait until you see him from the side – especially if he's bringing his mates along. But when we attack, they're the ones waiting, watching...' Martin was staring straight at the tank, but his eyes seemed to be focused on some far distance.

'That's why we work as a team,' James said. The others were all inside the tank or round at the back, and this was the first real chance he had had to speak to Martin alone. In the laager there was always someone in earshot. 'We need to be a team and rely on each other. That's true when we're defending and doubly true in the attack. You need to trust me to make the right decisions and I need to trust you to follow orders – and we all need to trust each other to know that the rest will always back us up.'

There, it was said, although as so often words felt inadequate, almost meagre. The bit about relying on each other was true enough. James was less sure that they all ought to trust him to make the right call in every situation.

At first Martin did not seem to have heard, for he kept staring, until at long last he sighed. 'You're not married, are you, sir?'

'Recently engaged,' James said.

Martin nodded. 'Yes, I heard that. They say she's a stunner.'

Did they? James wondered how anyone knew. He had a picture, but could not remember showing it to anyone, even in the Mess. 'I think so,' he said at last.

'Good for you, sir, good for you.' At long last Martin turned to face him and stared straight at him. The intensity of the gaze was unnerving. 'I'm married. ... Seven years now. Two nippers and a third on the way.' He smiled. 'That was my last leave.'

'You are very lucky,' James said, and rather surprised himself because he really meant it.

'Perhaps. But it gives a man responsibilities. They depend on me – Ethel and the kids. Life's hard, and would be a hell of a lot harder for a widow with little ones, or a wife with a husband still living but missing his legs or his arms or his eyes. Do you understand me? No offence, sir, but I doubt it. Give it some years and maybe you'll be a husband and father and then you'll know.'

James made no reply, feeling even more of a child than usual compared to these grown-ups. Martin was something like twenty-eight.

'I'll do my bit,' the sergeant told him. 'Hitler needs stopping, everyone knows that.'

It was rare to hear anyone discussing the War unless made to by the Army Educational Corps. Instead, most of the Army accepted it as they accepted the rest of life. Nearly all were conscripts, so had not had much choice. Martin was right though – pretty much everyone understood that the Nazis needed sorting out. They just did not want to make a song and dance about it or say that it was so great to be part of the cause. Get the dirty job done and go home was the attitude for most, and these days James was starting to share it. The glamour of service had worn off, although there was still the sense that fighting a war was simpler than starting out in normal life.

'So, I'll do my bit,' Martin went on. 'But I'm not doing more, sir. And I'm not taking risks that don't have to be taken. Understand, sir? I plan to go home, and get my crew back to their homes as well.'

'Hey, it works!' Corporal Bell came slithering out from underneath the Panther. 'There's a hatch down below, just like ours.'

The others were emerging, chattering, which spared James from answering the sergeant. There was not much that he could say, and he certainly could not order Martin to be a hero and expect to be obeyed. James felt that he understood the man better now, and could give his orders accordingly. The fear of any subaltern was telling a man to do something and being told to go to Hell – in practice if not in so many words. Martin would not be bold, but it sounded as if he would continue to fight and fight well in the right circumstances. That at least was something.

'Jerusalem,' James said, not meaning to speak aloud. The column of infantry had gone past, the singing faint, but at long last he had recognised the tune. His mind assured him that the words had been pretty close to the official version as well. 'Sorry, just realised what they were singing. Sounded like a hymn. Usually something nearer the knuckle, isn't it.'

Martin shrugged. 'We all need all the luck we can get.'

Soon they were driving back through the crowded beachhead. They had to wait for a good ten minutes at a crossroads while a seemingly endless column of trucks and guns passed by on the main route. An immaculately uniformed MP directed them. It was not the same man who had been there when they came through earlier on. By the side of the road was a crater, and next to it a shapeless mass under a blanket. Only the protruding boot showed that the remains had once been a man.

Waiting was hard, with the 'Dust brings death' sign right beside them. The convoy was flinging up a great cloud of dust and the shell hole suggested that the Germans had the range worked out very neatly.

'Thank God,' the driver said when they were at long last called forward.

D+10, Thursday, 15th June

THE REGIMENT WAS back close to where the earlier fighting had been, helping the infantry who had stayed behind to claw their way forward and hold on to what they had already taken. This was a lull for the high command, and a series of life and death struggles for the men involved, even if none of the nasty little actions would change the course of the campaign in itself. Seventh Armoured Division's attempted right hook had met Germans coming the other way.

'I heard a Tiger got behind the leading regiment,' Blamey, the loader, told the crew. 'Drove along a road, took them all by surprise – bang, bang, bang and twenty-five tanks brewed, by the one soddin' Tiger. Then more turned up and knocked out the rest of the regiment. Their shells just bounced off like tennis balls. Desert Rats too, so they weren't any pushover.'

'It weren't twenty-five tanks,' Whitefield chipped in. 'There were half-tracks as well and carriers. How could they stop any tank, let alone a Tiger?'

James waited before contributing. Colonel Tim had been very clear about it all the night before, sensing that wild stories were circulating. 'Whitey is right. They were caught strung out, bad luck as much as anything, but that one Tiger knocked out a load of transport – and most of the tanks were from the Recce Troop.'

'Poor bastards,' Whitefield interrupted. 'Going up against an eighty-eight with just a piddling little thirty-seven mil. Shit, I mean...'

'Again, quite right. The proper tanks he knocked out were HQ ones, some of them RA with wooden guns. And no one was ready and half the crews dismounted. And afterwards that Tiger and a couple of others were brewed up by our lads. And a lot more Germans came up. It was a big fight over two days and the Desert Rats gave as good as they got.'

The colonel had rammed that point home. Losses were heavy on both sides. Yes, the attack had been blocked, but so had any German offensive in that area. So that meant strengthening the front line and preparing for a bigger attack as more divisions came ashore. The colonel did not want anyone getting into a panic about Tigers. They could be beaten like any other tank.

James wanted to believe that that was true.

This morning B Squadron was attached to an infantry battalion tasked with occupying a village. It was good to have Sergeant Dove back with them in a fresh Sherman, named *Haymarket*, a diesel this time, which some said were less inclined to catch fire than the petrol versions. However, there were not enough tanks available in the vehicle parks to bring the regiment up to full strength. For the moment, B Squadron was operating with three instead of four troops, and James' was the only one with its full complement.

Each day they were attached to a different infantry unit, which meant that it was difficult to get used to each other and work well together. This battalion was better than most, and did not expect the tanks to do the impossible. James was in support of their left flank company, commanded by a captain since the major had been wounded by a mortar bomb a few days ago. Preparations were thorough and the artillery barrage pounding the suspected enemy positions most impressive.

The Shermans kept to the flank, letting the infantry go ahead through the wheatfields. Spandaus opened up, tracer flicking the corn aside as it passed. Their own infantry vanished, diving down into the high crop. James remembered how difficult it was to see the panzer grenadiers back in that early fight. Now it was just as hard to see their own infantry.

'Baker Three to Three Able and Baker, shoot up the edge of the wood ahead of us. Three Charlie, watch our flank in case of hornets.'

James not could see the muzzle flashes of the Spandaus, but the tracer's direction gave a fair idea of where they would be, and apart from that the treeline was the obvious cover. 'Gunner. Let's work in from the left. Fire co-ax. That's it. Give them an HE.'

Their own tracer, red rather than yellow-green like the enemy's, snaked towards the woodland. Sometimes the lines crossed, and the explosions from the shells were close together. James still could not see any infantry and since their radios were on a different wavelength he could not speak to them. He could hear the rest of the squadron and they seemed to be making steady progress over on the right. He could not see them, because hedgerows separated this field from the rest.

'Gunner, cease fire. Three Able and Baker, cease fire.' Little figures had appeared on the edge of the wood, throwing bombs and dashing forward. He could not see any return fire from the enemy.

A thick column of black smoke suddenly sprang up on the far side of the hedge.

'Baker Two Able has bought it!'

'Enemy hornet on the right. And another. He's...' With a sharp click that station went off the air. Another plume of smoke appeared, close to the first.

They listened to a fight they could not see, all the while watching for dangers to their own front. After a few minutes, the enemy had been destroyed or withdrawn at the cost of a third Sherman brewed up. Yet the infantry had occupied the village, and the surrounding woods and orchards. Major Scott moved the remaining tanks forward to help defend against counter attack.

14.35 hrs, a field in Normandy

The Glamorgans were a couple of miles inland from the beach and a few miles back from the fighting. As they had waited for so long in Sussex, and less comfortably on board the LSIs, now they waited in Normandy until someone decided to commit them. They were the first battalion of their brigade to arrive, and the other two had only just joined them. The vehicles for each unit were still off shore, waiting their turn, and the other two brigades of their division, along with all the supporting units, were still in England.

There was no space to train, for there was barely space for them to bivouac. Every other field was crowded with supplies and men, with units preparing or pulled back to rest and refit. Then there were the batteries, mediums and heavies, self-propelled and towed, with gun lines and command posts all ready to spring into life day or night. It was like living in the middle of a firing range, and apart from the guns on land, the ships often added their shells to the hate sent towards the enemy. So far, the Glamorgans had not been hit by any return fire, although during the night some of the lone bombers came close, throbbing overhead with that strange, unsynchronised whine that was distinctively German.

Barrages were fired, in the daytime their own aircraft buzzed around overhead, the rain showers came, some of them heavy, and occasionally the Sun decided to show up. The Glamorgans waited. They were pretty good at it by now, for it was one thing the Army trained men to do better than anything else. Some of them watched the engineers who were clearing the ground to make an airstrip close beside their camp.

There was brief excitement at the thrill of being in a foreign country, and for most of the battalion, including Mark Crawford and Bill Judd, this was for the first time in their lives. So far it did not look or feel very different. They had left a southern county jam-packed with men and stores and tanks and guns and everything else wanted for the invasion and now they were in Normandy, surrounded by a good deal of all those things and people transported to the other side. The only village close enough to reach easily had been smashed to pieces and had only a few inhabitants still in residence. If they had welcomed the Allies at the start, they were now too busy trying to salvage what they could of their lives and tending to their surviving animals to pay much heed to the soldiers. So many animals were dead, and they had had to clear a dozen or more dead cows to prepare their own camp. Dead cattle, dead horses, dead sheep and pigs were everywhere. There were probably dead people as well, but all they had seen were burials, usually with a rifle and helmet marking the spot. Normandy smelled different to home, and it was the heavy, sweet and very sickly smell of death and decay.

Rumours spread quicker than usual, because there was so much time to waste and a lot of nervous people. They were being held back to make a last ditch stand when the panzers attacked. This story was popular because it was so gloomy, even though it was clear the Germans were still miles away. They were being held back to lead the next big push, one where the slaughter would make the Somme seem like a picnic. Again, the depressing nature gave this a special appeal. The wilder ones seldom enjoyed a long life, even if what they got was more than they were due. One was that they would all be issued with GI uniforms and were to be sneaked into the American sector by night, so that the enemy would not realise that the big build-up was over there.

The French remained a puzzle.

'All collaborators,' some claimed. 'Welcomed the Germans and did well selling them food.'

'Nah, there's so few because the rest have killed all the collaborators. Pretended to be friendly then crept up on them at night. Used knives. Gutted them one by one, they did. Sent the women to the brothels.'

The last statement tended to raise a few heads in interest. So far they had not seen a woman younger than seventy and most looked older.

'Some was shagging the Jerries. In love too. They've had a dozen women snipers and had to kill them all.'

'I heard that on D-Day, some Canadians found a woman collaborator and dragged her around behind a jeep, holding her by the hair.'

O'Connor was unimpressed. 'Everyone talks bollocks most of the time during a war.'

'What about in peacetime?' Judd asked.

'Then they don't stop at all. … Now stand up and let's have a dekko.'

'Not a pretty sight, is he?' Moore said. He was lying down next to them, happily smoking.

'Oh, I dunno, boy,' Davison chipped in. He was in charge of their little stove and just getting the tea ready. It came ready mixed, milk substitute, sugar and all, and the water tasted of the chlorine used to purify it, but it was still just recognisable as tea. 'No, fair play, his beauty is of a rare type – like a Picasso, you know, big nose and funny eyes all in the wrong place.'

As so often, Judd was surprised at the knowledge of some of his comrades, if never by their sense of humour. He raised two fingers on his left hand.

Davison shook his head in disappointment. 'Oh, shocking it is.'

'He's been mixing with rough soldiers,' Moore added. 'And him a good chapel boy as well. Terrible.'

'He doesn't have to look pretty, just help us all keep alive,' O'Connor said. 'And you sods can learn from this as well, so pay attention. That's your webbing. See mine – and see the difference.'

'Do we win a prize?' Davison asked. O'Connor ignored him.

'The pouches?' Judd ventured. O'Connor had special webbing as N° 2 on the Bren, with the standard two long ammunition pouches at his waist and two more higher up. The ones on his belt were pushed back so that the gap between them was wider.

'Good. You've got to crawl, haven't you? You want to be low as you can, but also comfortable because you might have to keep your head down for a long time. Ease them back – not too far or they'll get in the way of your arms. I can't do much with these upper ones, but I have shifted them a little higher and got my shoulder straps a little looser.

'Now, tip out your pouches.'

Judd obeyed. He had a couple of magazines in his right, and another in his left along with a couple of bars of chocolate, some boiled sweets and a smoke grenade.

'No fags? Well, please yourself. ... I'm right-handed, so I need all the important stuff in my right pouch. That's ammo – first and always ammo. Get as many mags in there as you can. And in the left. Chocolate is nice and sweets, but they're not essential, so put 'em elsewhere. Understand?'

Judd nodded. He could not help thinking that this was the sort of instruction he would have liked back in Britain.

'I'm left-handed,' Davison announced.

'Doesn't surprise me,' O'Connor answered. 'Thought there was something cack-handed about you. So, what does that mean?'

'I put the ammo on the left.'

'Well done, you win a banana.'

'In wartime, you'll be lucky,' Moore said. 'After all, bananas don't grow on trees.'

'Ha bleeding ha,' Davison said, but they were all paying attention.

O'Connor went back to his instruction. 'You've got your

smoke, but you need a couple of 38 grenades. See where I have mine.' He turned, a bit like a girl showing off a new dress. A pair of grenades were clipped onto his belt near his right buttock. He had widened the pins very far to make sure that they would not catch on something and go off on their own.

'You'll want a dressing quick if you do need one.' He patted his tunic. 'Best place is here, inside your blouse. What about Bren mags? I'm guessing everyone in the section has one or two.'

They nodded.

'Thought so, that's the drill book way. Problem is, it's the Bren that needs them, and when we really need them, there's going to be so much shit in the air that the last thing you'll want to do is come running over to give 'em to us. That's where this comes in.' He pulled a haversack from his shoulder. Inside was a tin box with a lid. 'This is where they go. On the march you can share the weight, but in action, they're here with me and with the gun. *Mallum?*'

They nodded, familiar enough with the Army to know a Hindustani word for 'understand'. At least, that's what the old regulars meant by it. God alone knew what an Indian would have made of the pronunciation or the sense.

'And the Corporal's happy with this?' Moore asked. Corporal Price was coming over to them.

'Who do you think asked me to talk to you?' O'Connor told them. 'Ain't that right?'

'It is, at least as long as there's a cup of char and smoke in it for me,' Price said.

D+12, Sunday 18th June

14.35 hrs, a field in Normandy

'YOU TAKE THE legs this time,' Judd said to O'Connor. 'I'll get his shoulders.' There was no head, simply a stump of a neck above the field grey collar.

The battalion had moved forward, closer to the line, and there were rumours of being sent into action tomorrow or the next day. For the moment, they had dug some shallow shell scrapes in case of bombardment, and once that was done set about tidying up their new position. The smell of decay was as strong as anywhere, and apart from the dead cows there was a score of dead Germans among the scarred trees of a copse. They seemed to have been caught in an artillery stonk, mediums by the size of the craters, and either everyone had been killed or the rest had run away from the deluge and not returned. Nor had any of the British units who must have passed the spot been inclined to or had the time to deal with the corpses.

Judd and O'Connor were with the fifty volunteers sent to clear up – all of them volunteers picked by the sergeant major who informed them of their decision. Most men were digging, and digging well and deeply, both through a sense that a man of any army deserved a proper burial and also the thought that rumour might be wrong and the Glamorgans could be in this position for some time.

The Sun was out, a rare enough thing in these last few days, and its warmth had invigorated the hungry flies buzzing in the air and crawling over the dead. All the volunteers had tied a camouflage scarf or a plain handkerchief over their mouth as some protection against the stench and the insects. It was not enough, and Judd wished he had worn his gas mask, stifling though that would have been. They were some of the men chosen to bring the corpses to their graves, where the chaplain waited to say a few words.

O'Connor crouched and took hold of the dead soldier's legs. He did not wear the jackboots of the films, but short boots and gaiters much like their own. Judd bent his legs and sought a hold under the man's armpits. The flesh beneath the rough wool jacket moved under his fingers in a way that was deeply unpleasant, but as his hands gripped, the hold seemed steady enough.

'Ready then,' O'Connor said. 'On three – one, two, three.' They lifted the corpse, and like the others he felt heavier than Judd had expected, especially as this one was minus his head. Judd went backwards, taking little steps. 'Left a bit, boy, that's right, take it steady,' O'Connor said to guide him.

'Room for one more on top,' one of the grave diggers said, 'or should I say on the bottom. Blimey,' he added noticing the state of German. 'And you can't get your penny back if the top's missing.'

O'Connor shook his head. 'Bloody comedians. Ready, lad?' They laid the man down carefully alongside the hole, and went back for another. The grave diggers pushed with their feet, rolling the corpse in. The first time this had happened Judd had wanted to say something, but he did not have the heart. This was a nasty job, and everyone wanted it done as soon as possible.

The next one was more complete, but the flies crawling in the open mouth and where the eyes had been made this a mixed blessing. As usual they changed around, with Judd taking the legs this time.

'On three – one, two, three.' They lifted, holding the limbs firmly, and the corpse fell to pieces, the legs coming away in Judd's hands, the stomach bursting open when the torso hit the ground. Judd vomited into his scarf and swallowed some of it again because there was nowhere for it to go. He ripped the sodden cloth away and doubled over, vomiting again and again.

D+14, Tuesday 20th June

MARK TRIED HIS best not to shiver. He thought back to his Basic Training and a warrant officer assuring all the recruits that being cold was a state of mind. He had not believed it then and still did not. Above him, the powerful gusting wind shook the trees, making it hard to hear very much. There was no sign of the gale relenting. It had blown most of yesterday and throughout the night, the lulls rare and short-lived. Clouds raced south across the sky, which at least meant that the savage rain storms never lasted too long.

That had still been enough to soak them all as they crouched in the back of the carrier on the way up to these forward positions. That had been a bumpy ride, avoiding the roads as much as possible because they were busy and because the Germans had zeroed in their guns and mortars on them, and especially on the crossroads and junctions. There were signs everywhere – 'Dust brings death' and 'Dust means death'. The rain had dampened things down a little, but all vehicles, and especially anything with tracks, tended to announce their presence by their noise, exhaust fumes and all the muck and dust they threw up behind them. A carrier looked like a little open topped tank, but the armour was as thin as paper, and might at best stop a bullet – on a good day that is.

The Glamorgans were due to relieve this battalion in the Forward Area in twenty-four hours. There were no front lines in this war it seemed, not like the trenches and no man's land of Flanders. Instead, there was the Forward Area, where a unit knew that ahead of them somewhere was the enemy. Both sides were taking great care not to be seen, because being seen invited the enemy to pound the spot to dust and ashes. This battalion, a unit from the North of England, held positions among a patchwork of little hedged fields, orchards and woods, with the 'high' ground little more than gentle folds in the landscape. There was no continuous trench, and the men were scattered in little two or three man slits, covered and camouflaged if possible. The Germans were somewhere out there, half a mile or more away.

'Panzer grenadiers mostly,' a captain from the other battalion explained, raising his voice enough to be heard over the wind. At least the noise should not carry much further. 'Some plain old infantry on the left.'

'Armour?' Major Jackson asked. His D Company, including Mark's platoon, were due to take over these positions. He had brought forward the CSM[1] and Mark as a platoon commander, and together with Lt. Col. Davis and representatives from the rest of the battalion, they had driven up in carriers to take a look at the ground they were to hold.

'Now and then, but I reckon they think the same as us,' the captain said. He was acting CO of the company they were to relieve. 'If a tank turns up, it fires at the enemy and feels very good about itself. But the enemy see it and get on the blower to the guns. By this time the tank has buggered off back for tea and cakes, and the poor sods of the infantry are left to get all the hate from the artillery. So, we prefer it when the tanks stay away, and the Jerries seem to think the same way.'

The battalion was stood-to, waiting, watching. Mark could not see them because it was still dark, although he had a rough idea of everything from the map. He would get a clearer idea

---

1   Company Sergeant Major.

when the Sun came up. D Company would take over these positions, although the captain warned them that they would need to do a bit of digging.

'We'd lost a quarter of our strength before we got here.'

'And since?' Jackson asked.

'About a dozen from the Company. Probably much the same from the others. Mortars mostly, and the damned snipers. Not wise to move about in the open, not in daylight.'

'And the known positions are all on the map?'

'Yes, I'll point out what I can when it's light. They do move about a bit though. Not much patrolling. ... I reckon they're as tired as we are.'

Mark could sense Jackson bridling in the darkness. The major was a vocal advocate of aggressive patrolling.

If the captain noticed, it did not provoke any reaction. He had the familiar, mock casual drawl of so many British officers. He also sounded very tired. 'Still, it's hard to know anything in this country. A week ago we were further west. Had a listening post out in the corner of a field. It was three days before we realised that the Germans had one of their own on the other side of the hedge in the corner of that field.' He chuckled.

'What happened?'

'Oh, you know, grenades and gunfire and all that stuff, and both sides legged it back to the main positions. Brown trouser job all round I should think. ... But your sense of direction goes in the hedgerows. Have to be on your guard all the time. Yesterday morning a couple of Huns strolled into the farmyard where the cooks had set up. Must be half a mile back, and down in a little valley. Thankfully they only wanted to surrender to someone, but somehow they got all the way through the brigade's positions without seeing anyone or being seen.' He laughed more deeply. 'By the sound of it the senior Gyppo wants a medal.'

'Well, he did save the soup,' Jackson acknowledged. 'Must

count for something. And as Napoleon said, an army marches on its stomach.'

'True, and never more true here,' the captain said briskly, suddenly serious once again. 'The snipers are murder. Don't move at all in daylight, unless you have to. When you have to, crawl on your stomach – or run if it's a short distance. Oh, and word to the wise, best not to be too King's regulations up here. I mean I know we're all trusty and well beloved of HM, but there's nothing the Hun likes better than a juicy officer. They'll see you from a mile away or more through their little Zeiss lenses, spot a crown or some pips on your shoulder, spot a map case, binoculars or revolver and – well, that's it, another lonely grave in the hills.'

'Isn't it important that the men can see us – and we need maps to do the job.' Jackson was in all respects a man and soldier of the old school.

'Please yourself. Just do it discreetly if you want to last.'

The day had started, from grey twilight to the reds and pinks and then the great circle of the Sun rising. Stand down was ordered, and men relaxed. Even though it was daylight, all Mark could see was the odd movement of a helmeted head above a slit trench. The captain pointed out their own positions and then what was known of the enemy. Mark tried to concentrate, but he felt numb after the cold, and the sunshine was not yet warm enough to restore his limbs to life. He wanted to stand up and stamp about, hoping to get his circulation going again. From all the captain had said, that did not sound like a good idea, even among the trees.

'Anything else?' the captain asked them. He had rushed through his briefing and appeared to be in a hurry.

Major Jackson asked about registered targets for the artillery.

'On the map, but to be precise,' the captain started to point, 'there, there, there and there. Our mortars cover the same spots and a few others.' Again, the finger jabbed in succession at a series of landmarks. 'But your fellows will no doubt want to sort all that out yourselves.' He grinned. 'Now you can stay longer if you like, but I want to get moving. It's nearly zero six hundred and for the last two days Jerry has mortared this wood spot on six. He's a methodical chap, so odds on that he'll do it again.'

To Mark's great relief, Jackson was content, so they followed the captain, crawling back along the path they had followed to get here. Only once they were on the far side of the wood did they stand. The captain suddenly looked alarmed.

'Run!' he shouted and started to sprint away down the slope.

'What the hell...' Jackson began, until the first bomb exploded in the woods behind them. Half a dozen more followed almost instantly. They ran, haring after the captain, but before they could reach him Jackson shoved Mark hard in the back and he fell. Two bombs exploded close behind them, showering them with dirt. The rest fell in the wood. For two more minutes the bombs landed, bigger and louder than the 3″ used by the Glamorgans. Then it stopped. The captain appeared and beckoned to them.

'His watch must be fast. Methodical and creatures of habit, but not one hundred percent reliable,' he said, then glanced up. There were whistles in the air as shells sailed past high over their heads. 'And that's our lot responding. They're almost as predictable as the bloody Germans.'

D+15, Wednesday 21ˢᵗ June

'STAND DOWN.' THE order was hissed around the A Company position. Judd relaxed. He left the Bren gun on its bipod, pointing down the slope into the shallow and wide valley, then sat down. O'Connor did the same. They were on the right of the Section's row of slit trenches, and 9 Platoon was on the right of the Company's position. There was a space of a few hundred yards to the outlying dugouts of the neighbouring battalion, but behind them, set back a quarter of a mile or so, there was a pair of the Glamorgans' six-pounder anti-tank guns. Judd could not see them, but then surely that was the point.

'Want a fag?' O'Connor held out an open packet. 'No? Please yourself.' Now that the Sun was up it was safe to strike a match with its betraying light. The Cardiff Irishman had taken to offering Judd a cigarette at any opportunity. It seemed to amuse him, unless it was simply habit. Most of the battalion – most of the Army – smoked, and Judd had sometimes been tempted to take it up simply to fit in. So far, he had resisted.

O'Connor cursed softly when the match refused to light. Even in their trench with its sheltering sides, the wind remained strong. At last, he succeeded, and puffed to get it going, his face adopting that relieved expression every smoker wore as he sucked in the first few puffs. Judd always felt that they had the happy, almost ecstatic look of a man reaching the lavatory just in time.

Judd jumped when the crump of a detonation rolled towards

them. He jerked up, staring out over the parapet, and saw a series of explosions in a wood higher up and over to their left. He had seen mortar barrages and artillery fire during exercises, and this was not so very different, except that it was on the Battalion's positions. Other men had their heads up, watching in fascination.

'Get your bloody heads down!' Holdworth bellowed.

Judd shrank back into the trench. O'Connor had not moved, and was squatting there, happily puffing away. His head tilted a little to one side and he stared at Judd, saying nothing.

A shell exploded above them and a little behind, the noise appallingly sudden and loud. A little piece of twisted shrapnel whizzed through the air into the trench and stuck in the side wall. There was another crack as a second airburst went off, this time just in front of them. Nothing followed. Judd waited for the onslaught, already smelling the sour chemical stench of explosives in the air. There was silence.

'Got us bracketed now,' O'Connor said, as if talking about the weather. 'They know they can hit us when they want. Guess they don't want to at the moment.' He drew heavily on the cigarette. 'That was an eighty-eight by the way. They use them a lot, as artillery as well as against planes and tanks. Had 'em in Spain and they're still good.'

'Should we move?'

O'Connor sniffed in contempt. 'Where to? We're here to hold this spot. Hopefully they just want to hold that spot over there,' he explained, jabbing the almost finished cigarette in the general direction of the enemy. 'They hold there, we hold here, we shell each other on and off, and after a day or two, we're off somewhere else and no harm done.'

'Seems a bit pointless.'

'Take it up with Churchill. What we have learned is that they can see us if we move, so what, in the opinion of your majestic intellect, do we do?'

Judd shrugged. 'We don't move.'

'That's right, and hope their observers get distracted somewhere else and try to blow the shit out of some other poor bastards. Now, let's get that stove going and brew up.'

12.30 hrs, west of Point 103, Normandy

James found his attention wandering. Thomson was singing softly to himself. This time it was 'Java Jive'.

No one was talking much. The Sun was out, and although draughts from the wind came through the open hatches, it did little to freshen or cool the stifling, rank atmosphere inside *Hector II*. B Squadron, down to a dozen tanks again after losses in the last few days, was lined up behind a long hedgerow, overlooking a pretty little village. Nothing much was happening, and there was no obvious sign of the enemy believed to be occupying the houses. On the other hand, there might very well be a line of panzers or SPs hiding over there, just as the B Squadron was waiting over here.

Major Scott had been caught by a mortar bomb on his way back to his tank after an O Group. Shrapnel had peppered his face, neck and back, so he had been evacuated and SSM Egan was in charge in the meantime, until Captain Morbey came back from regiment. James' 3 Troop was the only one still at its full strength of four tanks. Corporal Bell had gone over a mine a couple of days ago, breaking the track and one of the sprockets, but Three Baker was now repaired and back with them and otherwise they had been lucky. Tony Lightfoot had three Shermans left in an improvised 1 Troop, and Sergeant Rawson was in command of 2 Troop with three more, one of them loaned from HQ.

Today was the quietest day for a while, once plans for a battalion attack on the village ahead of them were abandoned. The operation had been intended to prepare the way for the next big show, but that had also been postponed. The colonel told them that the bad weather was wreaking havoc with the landing schedule, with nothing and no one coming ashore for the last few days. That was bad news, very bad, because the Germans were coming by train and road, not by boat, and there was a real danger that they could get ahead in the rush to move reinforcements to Normandy. The RAF and the American flyers were doing what they could, but this weather severely restricted them as well. Because of all this, Corps and Army were content to slow the pace of everything for a while, and were hoping that the enemy would not spoil this plan.

James was glad. It would have been a shame to shoot up the pretty little village.

Thomson ended his serenade by drawing out the last word for ages.

'Making me thirsty. Speaking of which, how about a brew, skipper?' Whitefield asked.

'Okay.'

23.55 hrs, somewhere in front of map reference 859620, Normandy

Mark Crawford was lost, and was trying desperately hard to keep calm. They had only left the Company positions thirty minutes ago, just the four of them, and at first the thick cloud had seemed a blessing, blocking out the moonlight and shielding them from unfriendly eyes. Now it was a curse, like the wind whipping through the tall crops.

He had studied the route on the map and through his binoculars, noted the waypoints, plotting a path that should keep them sheltered as much as possible, weaving among the little fields.

Now they had come to a stream. It was not very wide, in a gully snug against the bank of a high hedge, and even after the rainfall of the last days it was no more than knee deep. The problem was that it should not be there. The only water marked on his map was miles away, and his luminous watch confirmed that they could not have travelled that far, not even if they had run all the way. So presumably this was too insignificant a bit of water to be marked on the map, and the trees looming high over the hedge out in front of them reminded him of the copse about two hundred yards east of the farmyard they were supposed to explore. The question was, should he press on under that assumption, or should he try to retrace their steps and get back to a definite landmark?

Mark wished that he had brought Dalton, instead of one of his corporals and two soldiers, one of them the eager Evans. All of them carried Stens and had pouches full of grenades, even though the intention was to avoid any unpleasantness with the enemy. This was a reconnaissance patrol, and a fighting patrol sent out to make mischief would only follow if they found something worth attacking.

He glanced behind him. Evans and Private Goodhall were crouched in the ditch, each staring off to cover one arc, just as they had been trained. Corporal Finch was in front.

There was a sputtering sound, and ahead of them an orange flare wobbled as it went up from somewhere close to the trees. It burst, the light dazzling in its brightness, casting long shadows around them, the shapes quivering as the wind blew.

All four of them pressed flat against the side of the little gully without the need for any order. Mark's heart was pounding. A machine gun opened up, the bullets coming so fast that the sound was like tearing thick cloth. They could not see the flash of tracer, so presumably it was beyond the hedge to their side. The Glamorgans had sent out other patrols, one of which must have bumped into the enemy.

Another flare popped, just as the light from the first was fading. A second machine gun joined in, and then both went silent.

Mark and his men crouched as low as they could and waited.

D+16, Thursday 22nd June

00.20 hrs, a field in Normandy

MARK TROD AS softly as he could, the branches of the hedge brushing against him because he pressed as close to it as he could. He had left the others in the ditch, signalling to them to wait. A good fifteen minutes had passed since the last flare had faded, and the machine guns had been silent even longer. He had decided that it would be unwise to press on, but wanted to take a look through the gap in the hedge at the far end of this field. One could see as well as four, and that one might as well be him, so he left the others and his Sten gun behind. That was one less thing to snag on something, and the guns had a reputation for going off when you did not want them to.

He was tempted to hurry, and with all the noise of the wind in the hedges and branches the risk was low. The thought that his men might see him, and might judge him windy, was all that stopped him and made him go steadily. Mark knew he was windy. He did not want to do this; he wanted to sneak home as quietly as he could, but did not want to have to tell Major Jackson that the patrol had achieved nothing. Competing fears pushed him this way and that, the strongest fear winning, so he edged towards the gap.

The wind dropped a little, although there was still enough to hiss through the crops and the bushes. The gap opened into a lane and on the far side was another high hedge and another gap, just a little to his right, with the shape of the trees just behind it. There was no sign of the enemy.

Mark drew his revolver. The heaviness in his hand reassured him, and he had done no better and no worse with it on the range than with anything else. Like a child playing, he raised it to aim at the gap in the other hedge. He wanted to go back, but he still had so little to say and a glance at his watch showed him that he had left the others a bare four minutes ago. He had whispered to Corporal Smith to wait for him for fifteen minutes and to go back if he did not return in that time.

Rain started to fall, pattering onto the leaves. Mark crouched and walked into the lane, the mud soft, deep, and rutted by big wheels or tracks. At the next step his boot sank so deeply into the mire that it was hard to free it and he almost overbalanced in his Quasimodo-like stance. He jumped to clear the rest, landing with a loud splash and then freezing in case someone had heard.

The rain was getting heavier and the wind picked up again, driving it against his back. Mark reached the opening in the hedge and peered around it. The wood was a bit further back than he expected, the trees so tall that he had judged them closer. There was a darker, straighter shape to one side, which he guessed was one of the farm buildings.

His watch said that it had taken him three minutes to cross the little lane and he could not understand that. It meant that he ought to head back soon, in case it took him as long to go back as to get here. He just needed an excuse, some salve to his conscience to prove that he was not a coward and failure.

There was movement among the trees. It might be the wind or some farm animal still alive in spite of all the shellfire. Mark edged back as slowly as he could to get behind the hedge.

With a sudden spurt of flame a machine gun opened up, perhaps three hundred yards away, spitting a quick burst of tracer into the night and then going silent. He guessed that it was in front of the farm and to its left, perhaps dug in because it seemed near the ground. He wondered why the enemy had fired, although given the chance he would have thanked them, for it gave something definite for him to report.

He blinked, little flashes still in his eyes, and by chance the rain stopped as if a tap was switched off. He heard footsteps.

Gulping, Mark took a slow step backwards, keeping next to the hedge. Once again his boot sank deep into the mud. His hearing was not playing tricks, for the noise came closer and closer. He gulped, raising the revolver to cover the gap in the hedge. He wanted to run, but could not, and his arm was quivering no matter what he did to control it. The steps were very close now. They stopped, and for what might have been seconds or might have been days, there was silence apart from the sighing of the wind.

Then the steps came close, and a shape appeared in front of him, eyes glinting softly. Mark pulled the trigger and nothing happened, and he remembered that he still had the safety catch on, and all the while a long face stared at him.

It was a cow. He let his breath out, panting to recover, and leaning against the bank. His heart continued to pound away like a bass drum. A second animal appeared behind the first, squeezing out into the lane. Goodness knows where they had come from and how they had managed to escape being killed in the fighting or by some hungry soldiers.

After a while, Mark felt well enough to move, and made his way back. This time he wanted to hurry, and realised that this was not through a desire to get things over with, but from a strange elation. He had not died, and his mind seemed to be telling him that this was because obviously he could not die. With an effort, he slowed down.

The rest of the patrol had gone. He had been away more than twenty minutes, so that was fair enough, but did mean that he was now on his own, unless the others had stopped at the emergency rendezvous point he had signalled during the approach. It also assumed that Mark could find his way there. Still, the first stretch was easy, following the little gully with the bank and hedge on one side, then to the corner, scramble under the bushes where there was a bit of room, down the bank into the next field, then straight across to a single tree, turn right, follow a track between two wide patches of standing corn to a sunken lane.

Mark made good progress, but there was no one at the ERV,[1] and no sense in waiting since they would surely have got back here before him. The rain had returned, heavier by far, and he was soon drenched. He was still clutching his pistol, finding it oddly reassuring, and only now checked that the safety was still on and put it back in the holster.

The night was split by a flash and a dull explosion, close by, at the far end of the next field. It was not far ahead. A man started to scream and then stopped abruptly.

Mark scrambled over the bank and went through an opening cut in the hedge, the very one they had come through earlier. After that he went slowly, crouching again. Instead of the revolver, he fished out a 38 grenade, ready to throw and then flee if there was trouble.

Voices were talking, and something about them was familiar and friendly even before he could make out the words. He went closer.

Someone was sobbing.

'Sorry, corp.'

'It's alright, boy, alright, we'll get you back.' That was Evans, although his voice was steady and kind, and more confident than he had ever sounded before.

'Quatre,' he called out.

'What the 'ell?'

'No, it's bra, bra,' Evans said. 'That's Mr Crawford.'

Mark smiled. Major Jackson had come up with the password, inspired by one of the regiment's battle honours, which, along with Waterloo, would have been celebrated in June in normal

---

1   Emergency rendezvous point.

times. It had the virtue of being unusual, not something an
enemy was likely to guess, and did not much matter if the men
did not pronounce Quatre Bras properly.

He went over to them. One man was on the ground.

'It's Corporal Smith, sir,' Evans explained. 'A mine. He can't
walk, sir.' From serious, he managed to make his voice almost
jovial. 'But it's fine, Smitty, we'll carry you, boyo.' Even in the
dark, Evans' small frame seemed to swell.

'What about the other mines?' Goodhall whispered.

'Follow me,' Mark said. 'I'll lead, so try to stay right behind.
We'll go through the crops, there won't be mines there, only
out in the open bits.' He had a vague memory of someone
saying something like that in a lecture, or maybe he had read
it somewhere, but true or not it was something positive and he
could not think of anything else to do. 'Come on.'

The two soldiers managed to lift Smith, who in spite of
his pain was able to put his arms over their shoulders. Mark
checked that they were ready, realised that the corporal had
a stump where his right boot should be. 'Have you put on a
torniquet?' he asked softly.

'Yes, sir,' Evans said.

They set off, the first few steps nervous for all of them and
especially Mark. He shouldered his way into the wheat, forcing
a path through. The ground did not explode under him. Poor
Smith moaned, and now and then hissed or cursed in agony,
and as swiftly apologised and thanked them.

Another flare rose high into the sky, but it was far away to
their left, as was the gunfire it provoked, so they did not stop.
The ground was rising, which was a good sign, and after half an
hour they were back with the Company.

16.30 hrs, A Company positions, near map
reference 859620, Normandy

'Coop' had a plan, and Judd was one of those chosen to take part in the little scheme, which meant that before it was fully light a dozen men from 9 Platoon had left their slit trenches and gone back to other positions in the rear, away from the prying eyes of German snipers and spotters. A couple of times a flurry of mortar bombs came down in the sector, aimed by map and good judgement rather than zeroed in by eye. None of the 9 Platoon men were hit, although a signalman from Battalion HQ was badly wounded, both legs torn apart by the whirling fragments of metal.

He joined the slow trickle of casualties suffered by the Glamorgans. A lieutenant in C Company was shot by a sniper, the only time the man fired in the whole day. His victim was dead before he hit the ground, and no one saw any flash or could work out where the invisible enemy lurked. He would soon have changed position after the success, so any slight chance was missed. Smith had gone back, first to the regimental aid post and then to a field hospital. His war was over, and the same was true of the man shot through the body when the other patrol had been caught by the German machine guns. Shrapnel from mortars injured half a dozen more here and there in the battalion's positions. Unless it was really bad, the men bandaged themselves or were helped by their mates, and waited until darkness to get back to the aid station. A little after noon, a single bomb was lobbed high and dropped down in A Company's positions. Mortars were not precise instruments, but chance is fickle, and the 120mm bomb plopped neatly into a slit trench. Little was left of the two men sitting inside.

In return, the Glamorgans' sniper section claimed two kills during the course of the day, and the battalion's mortars had fired off over a hundred bombs, which may – or may not – have hurt anyone. Mr Buchanan had an idea to do rather more, for on a recce patrol during the night he had come close to a German patrol returning home. 'Coop' was sure that the enemy had not seen him, and his air of confidence was infectious. He had also discovered traces showing that the enemy had gone some way forward, exploiting the gap between the Glamorgans and the neighbouring battalion, and reckoned that this was something they were doing most nights. It might explain why Brigade HQ, almost a mile back from their positions, kept getting mortared with uncanny accuracy.

Judd sensed that most of the men were excited as they were briefed and then rehearsed the fighting patrol Buchanan was going to lead out tonight. It was real Davy Crockett or Hawkeye stuff. Added to that, it gave them time in a quiet area to relax and sleep, as it was going to be a busy night. The wind had dropped, the Sun came out, and lying at the bottom of a slim trench Judd felt good about the world. Even O'Connor's snoring did not stop him from falling fast asleep.

D+17, Friday 23rd June

THE STARS WERE fading. The night had been clear and the slim crescent Moon had done little to diminish the brightness of the little dots of light. Judd lay on the grass, the Bren gun ahead of him and enough of the grass pulled aside or pushed down to let him see clearly. O'Connor lay beside him on the left, and beyond him was another machine gun team from another of the sections. Sergeant Holdworth was on the other side, and all of them watched the path Buchanan was sure that the Germans would take. That is if he was right, and if the Germans had come back overnight. Up to now, they had seen nothing, and day was not far off. Judd realised that it had been midsummer a couple of days ago. He had not had the time to notice on the day.

They had been in position for four hours, as presumably had the lieutenant and the cut-off group making up the other part of the ambush. Buchanan reckoned that the Germans would have come past by midnight, and suspected that were more likely to be careless on the way home than on the way in, so he had waited and then led them to their positions, leaving Holdworth in charge of this group. Mortar fire was arranged in case they needed help, and both the officer and the sergeant had a flare pistol to give the signal.

So, they waited, like hoodlums in an alleyway intent on murder. Apart from the task, it was a nice night, warmer than recent days. At the start Judd's mind had raced, wondering whether he would kill someone – whether he could kill someone. He certainly did not want to die, and the Army had trained him to shoot and to shoot well. He was not eager, and had no feelings of the sort he imagined the keen hunter must feel. For a man who dissected every aspect of his life, it almost bothered him that he did not feel stronger emotion and conflict about so great a matter. As the hours passed, he found that he thought and felt even less about it. The great struggle was to stay awake, with only an empty meadow to stare at, but having to keep still. They had eaten heartily that evening, with stew hot and fairly fresh brought up by the cooks, and some tinned rations since then. Yet he felt ravenously hungry, as well as tired. He could not make up his mind whether he craved more a good NAAFI meal or bed and undisturbed sleep.

Once, he had almost dropped off, but O'Connor seemed to sense it and nudged him. He grinned in thanks. The other men were probably desperate for a smoke, so at least that was one torment he was spared. They carried the basic kit, had their faces daubed in green and brown camouflage cream, which in Judd's case seemed to attract insects like honey. There was grass and leaves in the nettings on their helmets, and they had to keep still and not draw attention to themselves. On a night as calm as this, any noise, let alone any spark of light, would announce their presence in an instant. It was all about silence, and waiting, and being still, and they had practised these things many times during training.

That was not the same as doing them, and only O'Connor had done it all before, although Buchanan may have come close during his time as a Mountie. The whole platoon fervently believed that 'Coop' could do anything.

O'Connor shifted ever so slightly, and Holdworth a moment later. Without needing to see, Judd could tell that both men were alert. Then he heard the faintest of clinks – something metal touching something else that was metal. That was sloppy.

Before the patrol went out Buchanan and Holdworth had made every man jump up and down in front of them to make sure that none of their equipment made the slightest noise.

The ground dipped gently ahead of them for forty yards and then more steeply away down into a little valley. A shape appeared, bobbing slightly from side to side – a man's head, turning to search the darkness. The rest of his form rose up as he walked slowly forward and came up into the open ground. His shape was clear, silhouetted against what was left of the night sky. The helmet was rounder, less flat than their own, the trousers gathered to tuck into high boots. Another man followed, a few paces behind and just slightly to the side, then another. They did not hesitate, and kept to their steady progress. After that earlier clink they were now almost soundless.

O'Connor reached back with great slowness, and unclipped one of the grenades from his belt. Carefully, he adjusted the bent pin to make sure that he could slide it out. The closest German was barely thirty yards away now, four more men in the open behind him and a sixth just coming up over the lip. O'Connor nudged Judd, pointed at the enemy, and gave a nod. Bill Judd glanced to the other side, and Holdworth waved his hand palm down, telling him to wait. The sergeant also had a grenade in his other hand.

'Hande hoch!' Holdworth shouted. 'Hande hoch!'

The leading German dived forward. The others hesitated, then began to scatter. O'Connor slipped out the pin from the grenade, then held it for a moment. Holdworth was struggling to arm his own bomb, and without conscious thought Judd squeezed the trigger and the Bren fired, the muzzle flash dazzling him with its brightness. He still saw one of the dark figures stagger, lurching to one side, and realised that the next two rounds went high. The leading German shot back with a sub machine gun, a clattering ripple of bullets over their heads.

The other Bren opened up with its reassuring thump-thump-thump. O'Connor's grenade landed and exploded almost immediately, and there was a scream of pain. Holdworth threw his, but it must have had an eight-second fuse because it did not go off straight away. Judd sought for targets for another burst, thought he saw movement and loosed off five rounds in that direction, but could not see whether or not he had hit anything. The German sprayed again, lower this time, for Judd could feel a round punching the air just above his head. Someone grunted, like a man being tackled hard in a rugby match. The second grenade exploded, followed almost immediately by another bomb thrown by O'Connor. The German on the ground stopped shooting, but Judd fired a couple of bursts at where he thought he was just in case. He squeezed the trigger again and the gun just clicked. 'Gun fires a few more rounds and then stops' – the words came into his mind out of habit. O'Connor already had the old magazine off and was clipping a fresh one into place. Judd could not believe that he had emptied the first one, but it had all happened so fast.

'Cease fire,' Holdworth called. Someone out in the meadow was moaning.

A grenade exploded, off to the left, and then there came that distinctively tinny clatter of Sten guns. The Germans must have fled and run into Buchanan and the cut-off group placed there for that very reason. More grenades exploded, and there was more gunfire, some of it German. After a while there was silence.

A whistle blew two distinct blasts. Buchanan liked to use it for signalling, which in the past had prompted plenty of 'Typical bloody copper' comments.

'Bairns?' The other Bren gunner was shaking his N° 2. 'Oh Sweet Jesus.'

'What's wrong?' Holdworth whispered. There still might be more enemy out there.

'He's dead, sir. Jimmy's dead. Got him in the head.'

Judd heard Holdworth sigh. 'Keep your heads down while I take a look.' The sergeant rose to his feet and went forward. The moaning was softer now. Holdworth kicked at something on the ground where the German leader had gone down. The body did not move. A little further on Holdworth crouched down over something.

'Water,' came a cry from the darkness.

'Loo,' Holdworth responded. The Glamorgans were sticking with their battle honours as passwords for the moment.

'Coop' brought in his party, all of them striding up and standing tall, and with them another two shapes, hands on their heads. Holdworth did not rise and seemed to be doing something, and the officer did not stop him and instead crouched down to help.

Judd sat up. Bairns was rolled over on his back, helmet almost flat on the ground, as his face stared up at the skies. Judd saw, or thought he saw, a neat dark spot in the centre of his forehead. One bullet, not properly aimed, but sprayed to keep their heads down, had found its mark as neatly as any sniper could do with his telescopic sights.

O'Connor nudged him, holding out a loaded magazine. Judd took it and slid it into his pouch. The gunner was always to carry as many magazines ready to fire as possible. O'Connor had already put the empty one away in his own pouch to be refilled later.

'Judd, see what you can find on that one,' Buchanan called softly, pointing at the corpse of the German leader. Judd got up, leaving the Bren, which O'Connor took and turned around to cover the ground behind them. A flare popped up, then another, both some distance away. The ambush site had been chosen because it was not visible from the German positions. Machine guns opened up, British and German, as nervous and tired men started at shadows – unless someone else was abroad and up to mischief.

The light was growing, although still too little for Judd to make out the dead German's face with any clarity. The man's smock was ripped and torn, his chest wet with blood. Judd could smell the strong scent of it in his nose. He had read that the smell was metallic, but it did not seem that way to him. Trying to remember his training he felt for the shoulders, and with some difficulty took off the man's epaulettes. The pockets were empty, which meant that at least someone was doing things by the book and carrying nothing that could be useful to the enemy – no maps or orders, not even the poignant photograph of sweetheart or wife and children so beloved of cinema. His left sleeve had something around it. Judd fished for his clasp knife. As a Bren gunner he did not carry a bayonet, and apart from that the pig sticker was no more than a spike without a cutting edge so would not have been much use. It was good for punching a bullet sized hole in a target on a range if you wanted to help a mate out with his score.

With a bit of effort, he pulled off the man's cuff title. There were badges or medals on his chest. Judd left them, and instead fished inside the man's smock and the tunic underneath to find his identity disc. The German ones were big and metal, and he snapped off one half to carry away. That ought to give them information about the man. The other piece could stay with him, so that the corpse could be identified when someone got around to burying it.

Dawn was almost upon them. At the moment they were sheltered from view, but there was a short stretch not covered by ground, trees or hedges on the way back and they needed to move. Four men carried Bairns, so that he could be buried properly. The two prisoners were told to help the wounded German bandaged up by Holdworth. The sergeant, along with Judd and O'Connor, brought up the rear as the patrol made its way back to the battalion positions.

10.30 hrs, within the battalion lines, Normandy

Judd was tired, but could not sleep, and not simply because every twenty minutes or so the Germans sent in a dozen mortar bombs, most likely in retaliation for the failure of their patrol to return. Of the six men they had ambushed, one was a spotter and another his radio operator.

Battalion was pleased with the night's work, as was Buchanan.

'Well done, boys. Got 'em all – and Brigade will sleep sounder at night once they have moved their positions from the ones the Jerries had pegged down. They're Hitler Youth – the ones we've heard so much about. And that cuff insignia was *Leibstandarte Adolf Hitler*. Get that – the Fuehrer's own bodyguard. That means he was a veteran of Russia sent to teach these Hitler Youth kids how to fight.' By 'Coop' Buchanan's standards, that was a Shakespearean oration, and afterwards he added his usual comments: things they had done well and things they needed to improve.

That night, Company had asked him to take out a recce patrol. It only needed a few men, but to Judd's surprise the lieutenant asked him 'if he'd mind' coming along. It was a compliment, he supposed, a mark of faith and he could not see how he had earned it. O'Connor was not going, but 'Coop' Buchanan wanted the extra heft of a Bren just in case.

'Of course, sir.' Well, what else could he say? After all, he could not really ask for a night off or say that the prospect of creeping about in the enemy infested darkness scared him silly. 'What time do we go?'

'You can rest for the morning, son. We'll do a rehearsal at fifteen hundred and study the maps. Quiet day until then, so see if you can get some sleep.'

Judd tried, but could not. He had seen the wounded German close up because by the time they were back the Sun was up on what promised to be a bright day. The man was shot through the lungs, each breath a wheezing struggle and the dressings tied to his chest already drenched. Judd reckoned that he was the man he had hit and seen stagger, so that was surely his bullet in there. Yet he did not really feel anything; not satisfaction, certainly not guilt or regret or any notion of justice for the dead Bairns, a man he had known for months and liked well enough. Novels tended to have heroes who slaughtered at will without the slightest thought or those who agonised. Didn't Remarque's Paul spend pages where his mood swung back and forth like a pendulum after stabbing a Frenchman and watching him die? Had Remarque done just that and experienced all that exultation and angst rolled into one – or had he made it all up? Judd had always read a lot about the aces of the Last War, and some like McCudden had expressed surprise when he realised that there were men inside the aircraft he was shooting to pieces. Mannock was keen on killing the enemy and suffered nightmares about it. Richthofen had had his hunting trophies – and men like Judd's father rarely said anything about it at all.

The German prisoners had seemed rather ordinary. They had SS runes on their collars, symbol of all that Judd hated, all that he saw as evil, and the men came from a division rumoured to have murdered a lot of prisoners. The men of 9 Platoon were not gentle, except with the wounded man, the signaller from the party, but nor were they angry or brutal for the sake of it. Someone soon offered cigarettes to the unwounded pair. One of the Germans refused brusquely, and was called a daft bugger for his pains, while the other accepted with puppy-like enthusiasm and then coughed his guts out. That one was seventeen from his identity disc and looked about twelve, with his round face, snub nose and pale, almost white hair.

Judd tried out his schoolboy German and thought that the other one said that the German army did not give them tobacco because they were young, and issued them with sweets instead. He fished out a bar of chocolate he had taken with him and then forgotten to eat in spite of his hunger. The lad's face showed an inner battle between pride and contempt for the decadent British enemy, and most likely lust for the treat. In the end the prisoner took it, although he did not seem too happy about it and scowled at them in between munches. It was more comic than irritating.

Judd did not really care. He was always able to swap the cigarettes in his ration for something more appealing. For a while his father had worked as a sales representative – the proverbial commercial traveller – for a chocolate manufacturer and always brought home plenty of samples. At nineteen Judd still had a child's carving for all things sweet, and a set of false teeth, courtesy of the Army, who had removed his real ones as ruined beyond repair.

The Germans seemed young, even if they were only a little younger than he was. Language aside, for there was only so far his rudimentary knowledge took him, he felt no strong desire to get to know the prisoners before they were hustled off to Battalion HQ. That was the surprising thing about this. He really did not care much about them one way or another, and shooting a man, perhaps fatally, as the wound was bad, did not really bother him at all. Judd worried that there was something deeply wrong with him, with his character or even his soul for want of a better word. He did not care all that much about anything at the moment, apart from whether there was the chance of getting comfortable, and whether or not anyone was making him do something. The danger had faded for the moment, and would surely fade again as long as he survived each threat. So far, so good. He was alive, Buchanan seemed happy with the platoon and Company seemed happy with Buchanan. Things could be worse – and they might be before long – and worrying about all that felt like too much effort. This was not what he had expected.

Then again, no one else seemed any more animated or hostile to the enemy, or for that matter openly saddened by Bairns' death. Still, they were British, and that was the way of things, although the Welsh did tend to enjoy gloom. Yet none of the others talked about any of it, and they just chatted and smoked and loafed about and ate just as usual. Most dozed off after a while, the sawmill sound of O'Connor's deep sleep beginning very quickly. Judd lay there, wondering whether smoking really did help to pass the time.

Revelation came suddenly. He could not believe that he had done anything special on the patrol, or really at all, certainly anything sufficient to warrant Buchanan's praise. However, with Bairns dead and the other well-practised gunner from 9 Platoon still in the forward trenches, he was the only and obvious choice to take. Not being seen as special was a comfort.

Within a few minutes, Judd was soundly asleep.

Two hours later he woke, to be told that the Glamorgans were being relieved and the patrol had been cancelled.

'They've got something much nastier than that reserved for us, bach, you'll see,' Davison assured him. 'Much worse.'

19.15 hrs, near Putot, Normandy

The 165th RAC was concentrated once more, and replacement tanks and crews had arrived to bring them up to three-quarters of their full strength. B Squadron would continue to operate with three troops rather than four, but all had four Shermans. They were spread around this wide field, for they were back in the more open country, as the crews tended to them, aided by the men from A echelon, the forward support element of the regiment. Wheels, suspension and tracks were checked, altered when necessary, Browning machine guns stripped, cleaned and oiled, the big guns brushed through and the sights checked to align with the gun. Then there were belts of ammunition to fill, shells to restack inside the tanks, small arms to check, fuel to replenish, rations to be issued. There was a lot of work involved to keep tanks operating properly, and everyone was busy and everyone was cheerful, because this was the quietest day they had had for some time.

James helped as much as he could with the maintenance of *Hector II*, because it was good to muck in, although he was called away for O Groups and briefings where they studied maps and aerial photographs. A big attack was due in the next few days, and they were given some idea of their role in it with more to follow later tonight or tomorrow. There would probably be a recce of the route, and James had been warned that he would most likely go along as one of the most experienced subalterns. God, that was a thought, after less than three weeks on campaign. His promotion to full lieutenant had even been confirmed.

The weather helped the happy mood, for it was a mix of sunshine and cloud and pleasantly warm. Most of the men were in shirtsleeves or vests and a fair few bare chested. There was nothing as fancy as a bath unit nearby, but plenty of water from the stream and they all felt better and moderately clean. Around them all was busy, with artillery batteries setting up shop, and other tank regiments preparing for battle. A whole new tank division, 11th Armoured, was nearby, getting ready for its first proper battle. Everything had been delayed by the appalling weather, but now they were just about ready.

Well, as far as James was concerned, just about was fine by him. He was in no hurry. A fairly good friend, Keith Turner, had appeared to take over the troop commanded by the sergeant, and it was pleasant chatting to him for a little while before both were called away. He suspected that a few weeks ago he had had the same eager impatience to be off that now radiated from Keith, who had been very disappointed to be LoB for the invasion. There seemed little point trying to warn him, and in the few moments of serious conversation, instead he tried to pass on the most useful tips. Keep your head down, but only close up when you must. Take it slow. Get out and find the best path instead of just blundering about. Guide the tank forward. Watch out for the bazookas and the AT guns as much as the tanks. James had to stop himself because he was on the verge of recounting every loss they had suffered.

Keith was polite, but seemed too excited to pay full attention. There was something different about him, some extra swagger on top of the keenness to see action after so much training.

Turner was like so many of them, happy to let loose in the Mess, brimming with confidence on the various schemes, and naïve and shy in so many other respects when it came to real life.

When the summons came to break up their little tête-à-tête, Keith had dropped his voice and given a conspiratorial and immensely proud grin. 'You know that woman I told you about? Charlotte?'

James nodded. In the past Keith had rarely talked about girls, but now and then had started off with an enthusiasm that suggested they were always much on his mind. The lady in question was older than them by a few years, married, but with a husband serving in Italy.

'Yes.' For a moment Keith was like a child too excited to find the words. 'Charlotte. ... I managed to get out of camp and see her.'

James tried to lighten the mood. 'Oh dear, espionage and careless talk and all that. Are the MPs after you?'

Keith did not seem to listen. 'I saw her. Twice.' He was breathing quickly. 'We did it! ... She let me! And she says, if I can get leave, we can do it again!'

James guessed that Keith had to tell someone or burst with excitement. 'Congratulations,' was all that he could think to say. Questions about what it was like felt both foolish and sordid, and Turner was unlikely to wish to discuss the morals of adultery. He was radiantly happy, in love with life as well as sex and excited to be going into battle. Given the risks that he would soon face – that they all faced – James did not begrudge him any of it. He just hoped that it would not make his friend careless, as if nothing bad could ever happen after so wonderful a discovery. 'Sorry, old lad, I had better go,' he said instead, and hurried off, leaving Turner with a rather dopily happy expression on his face.

D+19, Sunday 25th June

MARK CRAWFORD HAD another look around to check on his platoon. Two sections were in front, dim shapes in the chest-high wheat, each of nine or ten men spread out in a blunt arrowhead formation, four or five yards between every soldier. If they had knelt down then all would have vanished. Instead, they waited, some still, some nervously shuffling or fiddling with equipment.

Around him was his little HQ, a pair of men with the 2″ mortar, another couple with a PIAT,[1] the cumbersome gun on one man's shoulder and the other with two cases of bombs. Evans waited, dog-like in his devotion, and Sergeant Dalton to one side, his old pattern rifle slung on his shoulder. The third section was behind them, to act as reserve, and they were little more than darker shapes in the night.

Cradling his Sten gun under one arm, Mark checked his watch. One more minute to go. He coughed to clear his throat.

'Fix bayonets!'

Major Jackson had told each platoon commander to give the order just before H-Hour, reckoning that it would give the men a boost. There was something predatory about the scraping of metal on metal as men twisted the bayonets into place, even if

---

1   Projector Infantry Anti-Tank – the British version of the bazooka.

they were little more than stubby spikes. Dalton's old-fashioned blade was a good deal more intimidating.

Mark licked his lips because they were so dry.

Right on time, at 04.00 hours precisely, the sky behind them lit up as hundreds of guns opened fire. Whistling shells were soon overhead, soaring towards the unseen enemy. Flashes sprang up ahead of them, explosion after explosion, brief but terrible in their sheer violence even at this distance of three hundred yards. It felt as if the whole land was being torn apart.

Mark raised his hand into the air. His 17 Platoon was on the far left, the rest of D Company to their right or behind them, and B Company further to the right. The rest of the battalion was in support, another battalion from their brigade a short distance to their left. This was part of Operation Martlet, not that such grand affairs mattered very much to a lowly second lieutenant. The rest of the division had not arrived, delayed by the stormy weather and changes of priorities, so their lone, orphaned brigade had been attached to another division for this offensive. What mattered to 17 Platoon, and D Company more generally, was advancing first to clear a walled orchard and then one arm of a tiny village ahead of them. Once that was done, C Company was to pass through them and lead the assault on a second, somewhat larger village half a mile further on. There were Churchill tanks and other armour in support, not that he could see any of them at the moment. During the briefing he had hoped to hear that they would get the 165th RAC to aid them. It would be nice to see James Taylor and hear how he was getting on.

Mark turned slightly to stare behind him, then glanced down at his watch. It was nearly five past, their start time. Something fluttered out of the darkness and he instinctively raised his left hand to brush it away, even as he realised that it was just a moth. His right hand twitched, and whether it was sweat on his palm or just plain luck Mark would never know, but the Sten gun dropped to the ground.

A Sten gun was not an elegant, sophisticated weapon. It was cheaply made, designed and manufactured when a desperate Britain needed guns, any guns, as fast as it could get them. To make it safe the bolt was drawn back and pressed into a depression in the metal. As Mark's one fell onto the earth, the steel butt struck the hard ground and the bolt bounced out and immediately slammed forward. The first 9mm bullet went up at an angle and smashed into Dalton's mouth, the next went into his neck and then four more drove into his chest, almost ripping it open and destroying his heart and lungs. Then the gun stopped, because Stens were never predictable, and the weapon plopped onto the ground.

The burst of fire had been appallingly loud even over the artillery barrage. No one said anything, no one swore, they simply stared as the sergeant seemed to fold downwards on himself.

'Oh Christ,' someone gasped at last. Mark took a moment to realise that it was him. Dalton was dead, killed in an instant by an accident.

'What's happening?' Major Jackson came rushing out of the shadows. 'Get moving! Get moving! Don't lose the barrage!'

Mark could not speak.

'What the hell's the matter with you?' Jackson snarled as he ran up. 'Get going.'

Mark stared at him.

Jackson glanced at the corpse, then at the men around him. 'Seventeen Platoon, prepare to advance!' He lowered his voice. 'Get going, Crawford, now!'

'I killed him,' Mark stammered. 'I dropped my Sten and...'

'And you can't bring him back,' Jackson said brutally. 'Advance!' he shouted to 17 Platoon. 'Follow the barrage! Stay close.'

The men started to move, jerkily like puppets, but they moved.

Jackson put his hand on Mark's shoulder. 'Lead them. If you don't, I'll find someone who will, but they need a leader now.'

Mark managed to nod. 'I'll go,' he gasped. His rear section was almost level with him.

'Good.' Jackson patted him and then took his hand away. 'What matters is what happens now. The past has gone. Don't lose the barrage!'

Mark nodded. He spotted Corporal Thomas, a section commander. 'Thomas, you're acting sergeant. Reece, you're in charge of the section. Pick someone as lance jack.' It was easier to do than to think. Mark ran forward to rejoin his HQ. Thomas jogged with him. The Sten gun lay where it had fallen. Mark wanted nothing to do with it.

In the flickering light of the explosions, he could see the platoon on his right a little ahead of his own men.

'Watch things here,' he told Thomas, then ran to urge his leading sections to speed up. This was what they called a creeping barrage, and every few minutes the gunners would adjust the inclination of their gun barrel and the size of the charge, so that the aiming point shifted forward by one or two hundred yards. A well prepared and dug in enemy was hard to kill, no matter how much explosive was thrown onto a patch of land. Most would survive, stunned and bludgeoned, but they would survive. The trick was to keep them wary and with their heads down until the attacking infantry were on top of them. That meant that the leading men had to keep close behind the bursting shells, so close that the odd bit of shrapnel was bound to land among them and the blast would feel like being punched hard in the head and chest. If anything landed short – because the settings were wrong, the gun barrel too worn or the charge not as reliable as usual – then it was bound to fall right on top of them. The theory was that the casualties risked in this way ought to be lighter than those bound to occur if the infantry hung back, and gave the defenders time to man their machine guns.

Up with his leading sections, Mark did not want to go forward. Even this short distance closer, the exploding shells seemed far louder, the flashes far brighter. Every wave of blast coming back over them was like the gust of a storm.

'Keep up!' he shouted. 'Keep going.'

A man in the section to his right stumbled and fell.

'Leave him!' Mark screamed. His voice was getting higher pitched with every moment and he must sound positively boyish. 'Leave him for the stretcher bearers.'

'I'm alright. Go on, boy,' the man said to his mate who was hovering over him. Friendship was one thing, but the instinct to help combined with the excuse to go back could mean that for every man hit, two, three or four were out of action helping him away.

'Keep going!' Mark jogged a little closer to the fallen man, whose thigh had been badly slashed by a piece of shrapnel.

'I'm alright, sir, I'm alright.' The soldier was fumbling with his dressing, but although he wanted to do it for him, Mark knew that he could not stop. Already his HQ was getting close. He saw Jackson, and wondered whether the major was checking on him.

Mark went back to the forward line. 'Come on, keep going!' he called. His voice was hoarse, the rank stench of the explosives chokingly heavy in the air, but he made himself shout. 'Keep going! Keep going!' Don't think, don't stop, just keep moving.

A shell burst behind him, behind even his rear section. No one seemed to fall.

Evans appeared beside him, face taut and very pale.

'You don't need to be up here, Evans,' Mark shouted because that was the only way to be heard.

'I'm your runner, sir. It's my job.'

'Then stay with me.' Mark checked his watch. 'Stop! Stop!' There was a minute before the next shift forward for the barrage. Without orders men crouched or knelt down, waiting.

There was a pause, a strange, uneasy silence. More shells

landed, again behind him. He heard Major Jackson shouting something, turned, saw him, then there was a blast of flame and earth flung high. The major was not there when it cleared.

Shells started to pound the hedgerow and trees two hundred yards ahead.

'Right, get up, get moving!' Some obeyed straight away, some after hesitation.

'Move, move! Get going!' Mark yelled. The rest stood and started to walk forward again.

05.55 hrs

A Company were in reserve, and only began to follow up as the leading troops pushed forward. Some men had already come back through them, limping or carried by the stretcher bearers. Other than that, they had little idea of how things were going. Then almost twenty men came running back in a group, looking confused. Buchanan yelled at them to stop. So did Holdworth, and then the great voice of A Company's CSM joined in. They stopped, and the CSM led them forward again. None of them had seemed to have much idea of what was happening, nor really known why they had fled, except that everyone else was doing the same thing.

Judd did not feel much wiser even when they started to advance. The cloud had returned, thick and brooding, so that it was not a bright day. Ahead of them the concentrated barrage of the initial phase had long ceased. There were plenty of guns still firing, both ours and theirs, but there was less of an obvious pattern and the symphony of the shells soared and dipped to a theme he did not know or understand.

Smoke shells had been fired at some point, giving off clouds of thick, dirty white mist, all of which added to the fumes and dust thrown up by so many thousand explosions in such a small area. Nine Platoon walked forward into a fog thicker and more noxious than any pea souper at home, and the still air did little to shift it.

Judd could see O'Connor beside him, one or two others from the section on the other side, and that was about it. He followed them, hoping that they could in turn see others and that somehow everyone was keeping together and going in the right direction. Now and then he heard Buchanan or Holdworth telling them to keep on.

07.45 hrs

Mark's men were pinned down by Spandaus with their insanely fast bursts of fire. They lay, pressing as close to the earth as they could, while the bullets snapped overhead, cutting through the heads of corn and showering them with bits of the plants. Mark lay with them. He had twice tried to get them moving, standing up lobbing a smoke grenade forward and urging them on. Evans always sprang up behind him, and so did one or two others, but then the German gunners adjusted their aim and the stream of bullets hissed through the field, and they all dived back down again. He was not even sure where the machine guns were. There were two, perhaps more, but staying up to spot them would surely have been suicide.

There was a clatter of tracks and the roar of an engine, all coming from behind them and hopefully friendly. The tank stopped and another, further away, began to advance. Machine guns fired, the slow, steady beat of an Allied gun, then a cannon boomed.

Mark got onto his knees, then straightened and tried to see out. The orchard wall was smashed in a couple of places, with tracer dancing overhead to throw up more dust as it struck. Behind him were a couple of Churchills, rather old-fashioned looking tanks, lower than a Sherman with longer hulls like something out of the Great War, and a boxy turret on top.

Mark stood. 'Come on!' he bellowed as loud as his parched voice would allow. It was only a few hours into the attack and he had already drained his canteen. 'Come on Seventeen Platoon!'

Evans, reliable Evans, was next to him, his head seeming smaller than ever under his tin hat, but his face determined and his rifle ready. Other men started to appear and the Spandaus were no longer firing.

Mark ran towards the orchard, trusting that the tankmen would see him and not shoot him down. He had his revolver in one hand and was waving it in the air. 'Come on, Seventeen! Come on! Follow me!' He tripped in the corn, staggered, regained his balance, and kept going, and was out into the open scrubby grass just in front of the wall.

'Sir!' Evans shouted a warning. He had a grenade in his hand and lobbed it over the wall. More and more men were joining them, and by the time it went off with a dull boom, almost half the platoon was there. They scrambled over a great gash in the stonework made by one of the Churchills' shells.

Yards away a German lay sprawled in a strange, ungainly posture, as if all his joints had gone. He was covered in dust, eyes staring sightlessly at the sky. There was an odd smell to add to the reek of cordite and death, something Mark had never smelled before. Apart from the one corpse there were piles of empty cartridge cases, a helmet upended on the ground and a rifle with a broken stock.

Thomas appeared, grinning, giving him the thumbs up. There were about twenty men from the platoon, all clustered together, relieved to be alive and to have got this far.

Mark turned to wave back at the tank commanders. As he did so something streaked across the field from the left and struck the hull of the nearest tank. Smoke started to curl up from it, and men were scrambling to get out. The other Churchill reversed, firing off smoke bombs from its discharger to hide from the unseen enemy gun.

'Take cover!' Thomas was screaming at them, and Mark

heard the whistle of shells. Four big explosions ripped through the lines of apple trees, snapping off branches, and shattering a few of the trunks. Jagged pieces of wood as well as metal flailed through the air. Moments later another four shells came in. Mark and his platoon were lucky because most of the shells landed near the centre of the orchard and they were on the edge, but the luck only went so far. The third salvo was wilder than the others and one shell landed almost on top of them. A soldier was cut in two, his innards spilling out onto the earth. Beside him a lance corporal lay dead, without a scratch on him, but killed by the blast. Three more men were wounded, bleeding from splinters driven into them.

After a minute or so, Mark got to his feet, surveying the destruction. He spat because his mouth was full of dirt, and it was hard to speak.

'We have to go. Get to the other side!' He gestured at the far wall. 'Get moving! Get moving!'

'Come on, you heard the officer. Get on your bloody feet!' Thomas was sounding more and more like a sergeant.

Evans offered Mark a canteen. 'Charlie won't need it anymore,' he explained and Mark realised that he must have got it from one of the dead. Such things no longer seemed to matter and he took a long swig. That was better.

'Come on,' he said. 'They've got this place zeroed in so we're not staying here. Arnold,' he looked at the least hurt of the wounded, a man with splinters in his leg, but still able to stand up, 'do what you can and wait to be picked up.'

Arnold nodded, his face a little blank.

'Come on!' Mark felt a surge in energy, as if the water from the canteen had been something stronger. He ran towards the far side of the orchard, jumping over tree roots in his path and waving his right arm to beckon the others on.

There was an iron gate in the far wall, and it stood open. Beyond was a road, and then the low walls of the gardens of a pair of stone houses. Mark leaned out to take a better look. There was a shed in each garden, and perhaps ten yards of vegetable plots. The houses had two storeys, and dormer windows in their high tiled roofs.

A bullet drove into the wall just by his head, throwing off a puff of dust. Mark ducked back down. His men were coming up around him, Evans in the lead.

'Keep your heads down!' Thomas was yelling as a burst of fire came from the top windows of one of the houses. A man fell, but had just skidded and slipped in the mud. Wild eyed, he crawled to join them.

'Anyone got smoke bombs?' Mark asked.

Thomas produced one, and a corporal had another.

'Good. When I say, chuck them over the wall.' Mark counted and saw that he had thirteen men, wondered whether that was unlucky and then remembered that he was there to make fourteen. He had little idea where the rest of the platoon had gone. He certainly had not seen so many get hit.

There were two Bren teams. 'That corner,' he said, pointing at one of them, then turned and sent the other one to the opposite side of the gate. 'When we're ready, open up and hit the windows. Get their heads down as much as you can. Understood? Good.'

Another cluster of shells came over and burst at the far end of the orchard. Mark thought of his wounded men, worried, but could do nothing for them.

They lobbed the smoke grenades, waited, heard the fizzing as the white cloud started to blossom.

'Now, fire!' he yelled at the Bren gun teams and they started their steady thumping rhythm. A Spandau answered, chipping shards along the top of the wall. One team ducked back, swearing, but the other was still firing.

'Follow me!' Mark yelled as loud as he could and pelted through the open gateway heading straight for the garden wall. The white smoke was all around him and he coughed as he ran.

He did not look behind and just hoped that they would

follow. There was the sound of boots splashing through the big puddles in the muddy track, and the Bren and Spandau firing, the crack of rifles. Mark was almost there. A bullet snapped the air as it went by, someone grunted, a heavy weight fell, and he was at the wall, breathing hard as if he had sprinted a mile. He crouched behind the bricks. Evans squatted beside him, eyes bright, and the boy had a Sten gun in his hands instead of his rifle. Thomas came in on the other side, with a fervent 'Oh Christ!' of relief. There was no one else. Mark stared back at the drifting smoke. There was a dark shape stretched out in the mud, but no sign of anyone else. Both Brens were firing again, and there were rifles and the Germans answering.

Mark realised that his hands were empty. He shook his head in baffled wonder, and reached for a Mills bomb. There was no sense in staying where they were, and maybe the Germans would have trouble firing down at them now that they were close.

'Ready?'

Evans gulped and managed to nod. Thomas breathed out. He mouthed something that was probably 'oh bugger', but the Spandau was clattering like a mad thing and the words were lost.

'Come on!' Mark yelled, trusting that they would understand if they did not hear and jumped to his feet, rolling to get over the garden wall. Bullets flew around him, so many that he could not count, but none hit and he ran, caught his foot on some chicken wire netting, freed it, and sprinted for the door, hurdling over rows of cabbages.

Somehow, he was alive. He flattened himself against the wall between the back door of the house and a window missing almost all its glass. He pulled the pin out of the grenade, tried to remember the length of its fuse, counted to two and then panicked and backhanded it through the window. Moments later it went off with a dull boom, flinging what was left of the glass outwards. He fished out his only other grenade.

Mark was alive and alone. He could see the tops of the others' helmets by the wall. The smoke had almost cleared and the rest of his men were still in the orchard, although the fire seemed to have slackened. He sent his second grenade through the same window, and fished out his revolver. After the second boom, he jumped forward and kicked at the door, which slammed back, obviously already ajar.

'Come on!' he screamed as much to feel better as anything else, and ran into the room. It was a kitchen, the table and chairs scarred and tipped over by the grenades. He crossed it. The door into the hallway was open.

A German appeared, his camouflage smock and helmet cover white with plaster dust, a sub machine gun in his hands. Mark had his pistol at waist height. He pulled the trigger, without aiming, without thinking. To his amazement it went off, the noise echoingly loud in the narrow hallway. To his utter astonishment, the German doubled up, dropping his own gun. Mark fired a second shot, again without conscious thought, and the falling German's face vanished in a smear of blood.

Thomas came in with Evans behind him. Mark had stepped over the dying German. There was no one in the front and side rooms of the house. He gestured at the stairs.

Thomas pushed past him, and Mark was tempted not to let him. He felt invulnerable because this was all so unreal, like being in a film. There was a loud click as the acting sergeant cocked his Sten.

The stairs were enclosed and narrow, and Thomas went slowly, lowering his weight with great care at each step. He turned a corner and fired a burst as bullets pecked into the plastered wall behind him. With a roar like an animal Thomas pounded up the remaining stairs. The gun chattered again and there was a scream that was cut short. Then came the boom of a grenade, and dust and plaster cascaded down onto them as the ceiling rocked.

Mark reached him as Thomas calmly reloaded, carefully putting the empty magazine away and clipping a new one on.

'House cleared, sir,' he said in a flat tone, habit taking over, for that was what they were all taught to say in training.

Thomas stood in the doorway of the back room. One German was dead, to add to the one he had killed at the top of the stairs. Two more were scorched and peppered with metal fragments from the grenade. Their machine gun lay between them, one of the newer Spandaus, an MG 42. There were scores of empty casings on the floor, but plenty of full belts left.

'Thank you, sergeant,' Mark said, the words feeling as if they were spoken by someone else and came straight from a script determined to show the phlegmatic British as ever stiff and formal.

'Watch yourself, you daft bugger!' Thomas called to Evans, who had walked across to the window. Instead of replying, the boy opened up with his Sten. Mark went to the other window and saw that Evans was shooting at half a dozen Germans retreating from the house next door into the street in front. There were no houses opposite, only a wide pond with fields and trees beyond it. The rest of the village was up the road to the right.

One of the Germans stumbled and was lifted by a comrade, but most of Evans' bullets were far too high as the Sten pulled up. The boy kept his finger on the trigger until the bolt clicked because the clip was empty. Mark fired once, twice with his pistol, and if this had really been a movie rather than real life, no doubt the cowboy or gangster would have plugged two of them. Instead, they ran on and disappeared into the fields.

'I had better go back and fetch the lads, sir.'

Mark had no idea how long he had been standing at the window before Thomas had prompted him. He stepped back quickly and gestured to Evans to do the same.

'Yes, thank you,' Mark managed to gasp at last.

Thomas nodded, and went off.

'I'll check that next door's clear, sir,' Evans declared.

'Fine.' Mark was struggling to think. He only just caught the acting sergeant's muttered 'More fucking heroes.'

10.37 hrs, on the western edge of the village

B Company was supposed to clear the right-hand sector of the hamlet, then go firm, prepared to defend it, while A Company went through them to spearhead the attack on the next village. D and C Companies were supposed to do the same on the left.

That had not happened. Almost everyone had got lost in the smoke and the dust, had got well behind the creeping barrage, and instead of a coordinated onslaught with tanks supporting the infantry, everything had gone in piecemeal. As D Company went forward shells landed on its leading platoon, killing the subaltern and his sergeant in the blink of an eye. A man, spattered with their blood, sat down with his hands over his eyes, howling like a child. Another one turned and fled, followed by another and another. In a moment most of the platoon was running, the rest cowering on the ground. Half of each of the supporting platoons joined in the flight.

Lt. Col. Davis was watching, and ran forward, waving his revolver and threatening to shoot anyone who did not stop. His anger was all the greater because the brigadier was watching and saying nothing.

Nearly everyone stopped, and after twenty minutes of shouting and cajoling the advance was resumed. Yet the attack failed, not least because the Germans defended with great skill and determination. Machine guns scythed through the cornfields, mortars and artillery flayed the men lying down for cover, and now and then tanks and SPs emerged, fired a few rounds and then withdrew to cover. All three Churchills in direct support were knocked out, one them still burning hours later. B Company had only one officer left on his feet, a subaltern, who with his men was pinned down in a little field short of the village. Their CSM led the company, as far as he could, for the other platoons could barely move without bringing down overwhelming enemy fire onto themselves. Half the strength of the company had gone, and it had achieved nothing.

Lt. Col. Davis had moved to the other flank and now ordered A Company forward to restore momentum to the attack, but the combination of dust and drifting smoke from burning houses created much the same confusion. One platoon reached B Company and was soon just as pinned down as the rest. Another found a minefield in its path, and had to double back and edge more to the right. By luck, by judgement, or by some mysterious instinct of a frontiersman, Buchanan's 9 Platoon went much further to the right, weaving its way along gulleys, behind hedgerows, through woods. Fate was with them, for whenever they had to cross open ground it was more than half covered by dirty smoke. They reached the road leading out from the village and found a garage with a walled yard and empty petrol pumps, little more than fifty yards from the end house of the main street.

Buchanan sent a runner back to Company, who reported by wireless to Battalion, and Davis altered his plan. The company commander came to join them, bringing with him an artillery captain as forward observer. More support was on the way, from the other platoon, the Glamorgans' carrier platoon, anti-tank guns and tanks.

Judd's section went to protect the FOO and his operators as they climbed to a wooded rise behind the garage. They did not meet any enemy, and the simple fact that they had infiltrated this far suggested that there were rather fewer Germans in and around the village than everyone seemed to assume.

'Fire mission battery...' The observer began to call the guns down on likely targets in the village. Judd and O'Connor lay in the grass, gun ready, with a couple of fresh magazines laid side by side to be handy.

Shells began to explode among the houses.

12.20 hrs, the left side of the village

Mark and what was left of his platoon were back in the orchard. Ten men had joined him in the houses and started to prepare for defence, piling furniture into barricades in the middle of the upper rooms, so that they could stay in cover and still see and shoot out. Any remaining glass was smashed from the windows, for no one wanted that flying around whenever the Germans shot at or shelled the place. For a while it was quiet, apart from the snap of shots when anyone showed too much of themselves to someone watching the windows. The sniper must have been up in one of the trees judging from the angle. There were near misses, but no hits, and after firing a few magazines from the Brens at the wood they gave up. The sniper appeared untroubled, and Mark was worried that they would use up too much ammunition. There had been no contact with anyone else for hours.

The first high velocity shot punched a hole through the corner of one of the houses, filling the upstairs with thick dust. When it cleared, they could see the low slung shape of an SP hugging the side of the wood. It was at least a hundred and fifty yards away, far too far for the PIAT they had lugged around all day. There was no way of calling for artillery, still less for one of the fighter bombers that might be circling overhead above the clouds.

The SP juddered as it shifted target, one track frozen so that the other turned the whole vehicle and allowed the Stug to aim.

At the second shot Mark realised that it was hopeless. 'Get out the back!' he shouted. No one needed any more urging, and boots pounded down the stairs and out. Thomas was bringing the men out of the other house at the same time. There was no sort of position in the little gardens, so they dashed back to the orchard wall.

Six more shells followed, bringing down most of the house Mark had been in and tearing great holes in the other. That seemed to satisfy the enemy assault gun, for it did not fire again.

The houses were ruined, but Mark did not think that the Germans had come forward to occupy what was left. Nor was he willing to go forward in case the SP resumed its work. For the moment, neither side could see each other. He told his men to dig in behind the wall, taking a turn himself with the spade. Thomas used a pickaxe to smash out some of the stones and make loopholes low down on the wall.

There they waited, not knowing what was happening anywhere else, although the heavy shellfire and bursts of small arms made it clear that there was plenty of fighting.

15.25 hrs, in the village

The new attack had taken a long time to plan and organise and for everyone to get in place. Eventually, they were ready. Already weakened by a succession of bombardments, much of the village fell quickly, the defenders retreating rather than fighting. A few were stubborn, or trapped, and defended a house until they were blasted out by tanks, or the infantry got close enough to bomb their way inside.

Judd's section was left behind in the line of fir trees at the start, and only called forward when things were slowing down. The main street of the village was in British hands, but at the end of a second road heading off at a right angle, the enemy was still holding out, especially in the solidly built schoolhouse at the far end. At least two Spandaus shot at anything visible in the street, and mortars were coming down with uncanny accuracy.

Attempts to outflank the school had failed. The only approaches were too open to German machine guns and tanks on the edge of the other village, some three-quarters of a mile away. Nine Platoon was given the task of clearing the building. They were crouched by the T junction, hiding from view behind the walls and waiting as a Churchill approached, driving carefully because the already narrow road was pitted by shell fire and blocked in places by piles of rubble. The tank was like some cumbersome leviathan as it approached and turned jerkily to face the far end of the road. Spandaus opened up, the bullets pinging off the tank's thick armour.

This was not an ordinary Churchill, for it towed a wheeled trailer, with a thick pipe running from it into the tank. They called it a Crocodile, although this particular one had the rather innocuous name of *Littlehampton* painted on either side of its hull. Judd had heard that the tanks mounted a flamethrower, but had never seen one work.

Once the tank and trailer were fully in the street, Buchanan gestured at Judd's section. 'Come on. Stay behind it.' The Canadian officer dashed across the yard or so of open country until he was sheltered by the tank. Griffiths led Judd and O'Connor after him. A bullet bounced up off the tarmac between them, but they all reach cover. The rest of the section followed, so that they were all huddled behind the trailer. Judd could not help thinking that if a shell came now and landed on them then they probably would never know. The trailer was surely full of all sorts of volatile chemicals.

The Churchill Crocodile trundled along the road, noisy on its tracks. They were a hundred and fifty yards from the school, a hundred and thirty, a hundred and ten, a hundred. The tank jerked to a stop. Buchanan held up his hand for the men to wait.

From ahead, a hissing rocket rushed down the road, but it was already losing speed long before it got to the tank and simply struck the side of a house, throwing up sparks.

There was a liquid cough, another, then an almost gentle sound like a cross between thick paper tearing and a soda syphon as a jet of fire streamed out from the flame gun in the hull towards the school. Thick, oily black smoke rose in a dense cloud above it. The stench was appalling, like swimming in petrol.

Even at this distance they heard the screams. The Crocodile gave another long squirt of fire, then the engine roared and the tank juddered into life again, driving forward. Judd and the others followed, warily. The German guns were all silent.

When they were closer Buchanan pointed at Judd. They were about to pass a driveway between two of the houses and he pointed at the wall of the next one along. Judd dashed, O'Connor following, and they set up with the Bren resting on the top of the wall. It was too narrow for the bipod to stay balanced, so Judd would have to keep a firm grip when he fired. There was no need.

The tank stopped, less than fifty yards from the burning school. Judd watched, ready to cover them, as Buchanan in person led the rest of the section forward. A figure appeared from the front door, man shaped, but wholly on fire, and it was hard to believe that anyone could live so long in such agony. Judd wanted to shoot, but found he could not pull the trigger even though this would surely be a mercy. The German sank to his knees. Griffiths took careful aim and fired one shot with his Sten into the man's head.

Buchanan sent the men to either side of the blazing school, and turned to beckon the Bren team to join them. They formed a line on the edge of the yard, waiting for a response from the enemy. The stench was appalling, chemicals mingling with scorched meat. Judd remembered the reek of the fire bombs during the Blitz, but this was far worse. It took all his will not to shake with revulsion and horror. He prayed that the Germans had nothing like this.

The Crocodile nosed its way forward, until an AP shot came from some far distance and bounced off the road just in front of the tank's hull. It began to reverse, no easy thing with the trailer behind. The turret hatches opened and the commander's head bobbed up, watching behind to guide the driver. Another shell skidded past and knocked a hole clean through one wall of a house and out the other side. By fits and starts the tank withdrew and then was gone.

Judd wished that he had no sense of smell, and tried to think of dragons in stories. What he had just seen brought a whole new horror to those ancient fears.

17.03 hrs, in the left sector of the village

Mark and his men were gradually joined by other Glamorgans, including some stragglers from his own platoon. Later, men came down the main road to secure this part of the village. The day was far from over, but it was obvious to everyone that the battalion was spent, at least for today, and that there was not the remotest chance of pushing on to the objective of the other village. What mattered now was not to lose anything that they had gained, so the key was to dig in and hold fast.

Major Jackson was dead, killed by the shell burst early on in the advance. Mark realised that he must have seen it happen when the major vanished. Captain Price was in charge of what was left of D Company, and he wanted Mark and 17 Platoon to stay where they were and help anchor the position here on the flank. That was good because it meant that they would not need to move and start digging afresh, but bad because they were still in the orchard, with all its risk of splinters. Thomas chivvied the tired men to dig deeper.

Mark struggled to keep still. He ought to be tired, and instead felt that he wanted to run and jump. He did not want to rest and think, for that meant remembering Dalton and facing what he had done. How could be possibly write to the man's widow – *Dear Mrs Dalton, I am very afraid that I clumsily dropped my gun and chopped your husband in two...* It was still hard to believe that it had happened, that the self-assured, seemingly indestructible veteran was dead, killed in a stupid accident – and killed my him.

A runner appeared, summoning him to a Company O Group, and it was a blessed relief. Mark hurried to get there, Evans doing his best to keep up.

20.05 hrs, on the edge of the village

'Mike Target, reference oh seven eight...'

Judd and O'Connor were behind a tipped up bed in the back room of one of the terraced houses, the only house still with most of its roof left. There was another window, through which the FOO watched the enemy and called in fire missions.

'Mike Target means we want all the guns of our regiment.' The RA Captain was accompanied by his batman, who seemed to have little to do and liked to chat.

Judd tried to remember. 'What's that, twenty-four?'

'Yes. If we call for Uncle that means all the guns of the Division – three or four regiments. Victor means everything from Corps. Only seen that once before.' The gunner obviously took a lot of pride in the destructive power his officer might summon.

'What's up from Victor?' O'Connor asked.

'Buggered if I know. Bomber Command, I guess.'

The Germans had attacked twice, but only once had Judd been able to see heads bobbing up in the corn about half a mile away. He had fired the Bren and been cursed by O'Connor because he had not adjusted the sights and was firing short. That was a daft mistake to make. He had never done anything like that in training. Everyone else had been shooting as well, Brens, rifles, the Vickers guns brought up to help in the defence. Judd had no idea whether or not he had hit anyone, but once he moved the sights his rounds were certainly going into the right

area. Either way the attack petered out. Judging from the sound
and what he could overhear from the gunner's radio, the other
attack was similarly tentative.

Later, the Germans made a bigger effort, at least two
companies of infantry and half a dozen tanks pushing in from
the right front. The RA Captain called in an Uncle Target. The
response was awesome in every sense of the word. Shell after
shell pulverised the fields the Germans were using. The attack
withered before it reached the village.

Half an hour later a summer storm rolled in with lightning
and thunder that put to shame the petty might of mankind. It
rained for hours, drenching everyone. Judd was glad that he
was inside the house, for they were mostly dry. Otherwise, it
was a mixed blessing being in one of the few more or less intact
buildings with a view of the enemy. The superstitious might
say that the place was lucky; the statisticians would no doubt
counter that eventually someone would score a direct hit.

D+20, Monday 26th June

'DRIVER, HALT.' JAMES breathed a sigh of relief. Driving anywhere in a tank in the dark was a nervous business, and most of all when so many units were shifting position. Whitefield was good, but even the best could do little about the risk of sliding into a ditch or crater, each equally hard to spot in the shadows.

The 165th RAC had been sent to reinforce the neighbouring Corps for some big show. Oddly enough it had brought them to the same area further east where they had been in the days immediately after the invasion. At least that helped, for he had a sense of the route to add to what he could see on the map.

'Operation Epsom,' Colonel Tim announced at the O Group summoned as soon as they halted. 'The overall aim of Army is to thrust south and surround the city of Caen rather than taking the bull by the horns and going in head on. The eastern attack doesn't concern us, but will come to the east of the River Orne. We're part of the western thrust. The infantry go in first, the Jocks of Fifteenth Div. due to start at oh six hundred. You'll all know when you hear the barrage as they say it will be something special. Once they have broken through, then Eleventh Armoured Div. will go through them and swing round to the south-east. We're attached to them to give them a bit more punch if they need it.

'This is the intended axis of advance, but we won't get

timings until Corps gets more sense of initial progress. In the meantime, tidy up, check everything, and be ready to move on four hours' notice.'

James stepped out of the farmhouse whose main room they had used for the O Group. Drizzle pattered onto his face. They had heard the storm last night and seen the flashes, but it was some way away and had done nothing to clear the air over here. It remained heavy and close. In the past, James tended to get throbbing headaches on days and nights like this. Now, there somehow did not seem the time for such trivial inconveniences.

'Thrilling stuff, isn't it?' Keith said, coming alongside. 'Stirring deeds to win the empire and all that.'

'By the sound of it not for a day or two as far as we are concerned.' James stretched out to yawn. Much as he liked Keith, he was not really in the mood for conversation. All he wanted was to pass on the orders, do anything else that needed to be done, and then sleep. Still, a friend was a friend, and you had to make an effort. 'How are you finding your troop?'

'Marvellous! Reckon they're the best around, if you'll forgive me. The old hands are trying to teach us new boys the ropes.' As far as James could see, Keith's whole world was wonderful. It was truly amazing what the fulfilment of his adolescent dreams had achieved. There was no sense of fear or worry at all and that still seemed uncanny and dangerous.

'Sergeant Finch is one of the best,' James said. 'He'll keep an eye on you – just as Dove does with me.' He surprised himself by managing those syllables without mistake. He was so tired, so very tired – and they had not even started this new operation yet.

'I had a letter from her,' Keith said, barely able to contain his excitement. He guffawed with laughter. 'If it wasn't so much fun over here, I'd probably swim the Channel and run all the way to her house.'

'Burma,' James said without really thinking.

'Hey?'

'B U R M A.' James spelled it out. 'You'll see it on some of the men's letters, like SWALK.'

'I know that one – Sealed With A Loving Kiss.'

'It's like that, only it stands for Be Upstairs Ready My Angel. Or some say it's for Undressed instead of Upstairs.'

Keith threw his head back and roared. 'I like it,' he said, when he had recovered himself at last. 'Yes, I like it. Although the undressing...' He stopped himself, suddenly realising that he was speaking aloud.

'Get some sleep,' James told him. 'It's precious. That's one thing you'll learn quickly.' Or get a cold shower, he added to himself. Penny had written to him again, but he had not yet had the chance to read it. Lacking Keith's ardour, James was happy to save it for a better moment. Sleep was all he craved now.

06.05 hrs, north of Rauray

A Company had suffered less than the rest of the Glamorgans, so was pulled together and given a job. The Brigade's reserve battalion had passed through the village and was to advance on Rauray, the bigger village up ahead. To help them, A Company and a troop of three Churchills were to take a walled farmyard on the left.

To the east, there was a rolling thunder of artillery. Buchanan had told them that there was a big attack there as well, and the RA captain's batman had warned Judd that a lot of the big stuff was shifting away from them to support that operation. 'Good luck, mate,' he had added as they departed.

Like yesterday morning, they knelt in a wheatfield, waiting. One of the tanks was just to their left.

Buchanan blew his whistle and waved them on.

Judd stood, the others rising around him. The rain had stopped, but there was still that scent of damp earth in the air. The main barrage on Rauray was not due for another twenty minutes or so, when that attack began. There was nothing to cover them, although the RA captain and his team were with Company HQ some way behind them.

Not that anyone could see very much. This morning it was not smoke, but mist, thick and milky, that made it hard to see much beyond twenty yards. Even the Churchill was no more than a dark, noisy shape. A hedge was on the right, and if they followed it, then they would come to the farm they could not see. Word was that a patrol had been there and reckoned that the Germans had no more than an observation post in position.

Judd had the Bren cradled in his arms, ready to swing up and shoot from the hip if need be. A man had to brace himself to do that and not fall over, but there was a knack to it and it was another thing he liked so much about the gun. Bessie would see him alright.

He was wet, uniform soaked by the rain and his back slick with sweat. The air was humid and sticky, but it was more than that. Judd was more afraid that he had ever been before in his life. They were walking into the unknown, almost into nothingness. There might be no one there, or dozens of machine guns ready to fire on fixed lines and cut them to ribbons, visible or not. Judd prayed, in silence to himself, and more devoutly and desperately than he had ever done before in his entire life – except when he had begged God not to let his father die.

Judd took another step forward. Poetry came to him again – 'like a man in irons, which isn't glad to go, they moves 'em off by companies, uncommon stiff and slow.' Kipling again. That man wrote some rubbish, but he wrote a lot more that seared to the heart. Dear God, he wasn't glad to go and his legs did not want to work.

The high stalks of wheat resisted and had to be forced down, and they were another two steps nearer. He glanced to either side. O'Connor was slightly back, rifle slung and haversack with the ammo box ready. Moore was on the other side and like the rest had his rifle at high port, bayonet fixed. He could not read their faces or tell their thoughts. Surely they must be scared, and even the least religious chancing a prayer or two. Still, why should God listen to anyone, including him? What made William Judd worth preserving?

Dear God, if it must happen make it quick. A snap of the fingers and gone, not bleeding out, body torn to shreds or burning like that poor devil yesterday. And not the eyes, Lord, please. I couldn't live without seeing.

The outline of the farm loomed out of the mist. They were close, very close, and still the world was silent, since the distant rumble of guns felt like it belonged to another world altogether.

A green blur rushed at him and there was the sound of a hatchet sinking into something heavy but soft. Moore gasped and dropped forward. Everyone else was diving as the bullets cracked in the air. Through a hole made in the farmyard wall flashes came from the muzzle of a Spandau.

Judd hesitated, bringing up the gun ready, and was about to fire when the idiotic folly of it sank home. He dived forward, down between the corn stooks. A moment later bits of the head showered down on him as it was shredded by bullets.

He could not see anything, could not shoot from down here. He made himself crawl forward. Someone was shouting – Buchanan – and a grenade went off. Men were cheering, the savage ripping of the German MG sounded again, but nothing passed over his head. Someone screamed.

Judd hauled himself up, saw that one of the other sections had charged and gained half the distance before dropping down again. The Spandau was pointing that way, sending more green tracer through the wheat. Judd spread his feet and fired five rounds at the loophole. Private Franklin was up, yelling something, lobbing a grenade over the wall. A single shot, and Franklin fell, rifle falling, hands clutching at his chest. Judd fired again, another short burst. Dust plumed from the rendered wall around the loophole.

'Come on, boys!' Buchanan was up again, men rising around

him, and they surged towards the wall. Holdworth appeared, waving his Sten gun over his head, and men were at the wall, out of arc of the German gun, which was still firing. One of the men bringing up the rear was hit, so many rounds striking his body that he spun around before falling.

The tank fired, over their heads, bringing down part of the farmhouse to their left. Its tracer laced across the wall. A German fell from a window. Shots were coming from up there, and the Churchill sent another HE round into the building, bits of debris clattering down into the yard.

Judd ran forward, dodging to the side, and others were with him. The Germans were shifting their aim, but the British were so close that they got out of their arc of fire. Griffiths was next to him and grinned. There was a gate next to them. Griffiths nodded, and Judd stepped up, kicked hard, breaking one of the almost rotten planks. The gate door did not open. Judd managed to free himself and kicked again and this time the thing came off its hinges.

Griffiths bounded through, swinging his Sten to the left. Judd followed. Two Germans were stretched on the ground, dead or wounded. Two more were with the Spandau, but they immediately let go and raised their hands.

'Kamerad!' The voice wavered and the German repeated it, trying to sound more confident. 'Kamerad!'

Judd sighed and relaxed.

Griffiths stared at the Germans, then glanced back the way they had come, not that he could see anything with the wall in the way. Perhaps he was thinking of Moore and Franklin. Perhaps not. He turned back to the Germans.

The Sten stuttered into life and the two surrendering men writhed as the bullets smashed into them. Griffiths emptied the magazine, then unclipped it, and put in a fresh one. 'Too late, chum,' he muttered.

Buchanan and the rest surged around through the gateway.

'Well done, corporal.' He searched around the farmyard. The

big house was smashed and silent, but there was a stable, a barn and several other outbuildings. 'Holdworth, take this section and clear the barn. Griffiths, Judd, Morgan, follow me. Three section, spread out to the right! Go!'

They went, or, in the case of Judd and the others, followed their officer. The stables were ahead of them, a row of boxes with split doors. Before Buchanan could send a grenade into one of them, a white flag appeared, followed by a nervous Feldwebel, who looked to be about fifty. Four more men came behind him, all equally timid.

'Check 'em for weapons, any papers or anything else of use. I'll cover.'

'No need, I am Polish,' the Feldwebel said in accented but clear English. 'We all are. We don't want to fight.'

'Polish or not, you're prisoners now,' 'Coop' told them.

O'Connor appeared. Judd saw him relieve the Feldwebel of his pistol.

The Poles were happy to talk. They were conscripts, unwilling ones, but they had no say in the matter. They hated the Germans and did not want to fight the Allies. They were also from an artillery unit, so until today had been happy enough directing shellfire onto those same Allies.

'Take 'em back,' 'Coop' told Griffiths. Judd watched him go and wondered whether or not the prisoners would reach Battalion. He remembered his friend coldly mowing down the two surrendering soldiers with no more emotion than someone squashing a fly. Still, wrong though it was by all they had been taught, Judd struggled to condemn. After all, the Germans had killed until the last minute and then expected to live. He did not think that he would have done the same as Griffiths, but could not be sure.

The bombardment opened up on Rauray. It was not as heavy as the one before yesterday's attack, but not by much. Hopefully that would keep the Germans too busy to shell or counter attack this farm.

17.00 hrs, near Bretteville-L'Orgueilleuse, Normandy

The 165th had not moved, and after checking all the tanks yet again, there was little to do. To James' astonishment, some men had the energy to kick a football around. He noticed that Keith joined them at one stage, which was less surprising. The fellow surely had to do something or burst.

James read Penny's letter and wondered whether she was of a kind. Not in style of course, for she was waiflike where Keith was big and brimming with muscular energy. She did not talk about the proverbial, mystical 'it' of course, at least not directly.

My most beloved sweetheart, my knight, my hero
I miss you every moment of every day, selfish child that I am. I want to be with you, to hear your voice, and feel your touch.

The last words were a little smudged – from sweat or tears, he was not sure.

I lock all your letters away, to keep them safe, in that little jewellery box you gave me for my birthday. All that is, save one, whichever is the most recent, for I know that you have touched it

– as have a fair few grubby soldiers and postmen by the time it gets to you, lass –

To hold it, so as to be as near to you as I can. I keep it with me wherever I go, and keep it close. Shall I tell you where? Perhaps I should not, for I blush

– and giggle, I'll be bound.

> *Let us just say that it is as close to me as it is possible to be. It could not be any closer!!! My only wish is that you were as near. One day, my darling, one day.*
>
> *On that note, Mama has managed to find some white silk – probably best not to ask from where it has come.*

Before settling down to the mundane there was one more burst of enthusiasm.

> *Silk, these days, would you believe it? I do so love silk, for its sheen and its softness. So like to skin, so very like. There is plenty for the dress and for – well, the groom must find out what else in good time!*

After that it was a catalogue of local news, the raging passion almost wholly switched off. That was probably just as well. The state he was in, having a letter like this within half a mile of Keith was likely to make the man explode.

Yes, passion came in all forms, but there was a good deal alike between Penny and his friend. His own desires seemed modest, prudish almost, by comparison.

In the background, Whitefield had started one of his lewder tales, urged on by the rest of the crew and a few visitors.

'You'd never believe it,' the Londoner explained to his rapt audience. 'There I was on me ladder…' Ah, it was one from his days as a window cleaner in Mayfair back before the War. James had seen enough of those grand houses not to fancy climbing up the side of them, but from Whitefield's stories it had all been a marvellous, bawdy romp with enough material to fill a dozen more verses for George Formby. That's assuming any of it could get past the censors.

'Oh Gawd, it terrified me. There was this big fat bloke, bollock naked apart from his shoes and socks and waving a feather duster. And he was chasing his wife, even fatter than he was, and she had nothing on apart from her hat! Gawd Almighty, it was a sight. Then they saw me and wanted me to join them!'

The audience howled with laughter that was almost hysterical. James guessed it was simple release. Blamey was lying on the grass, face red.

'What did you do, Whitey?' someone asked.

'Do? I were down that fuckin' ladder faster than a fireman on his pole! Never got paid, neither, but I weren't going back there!'

'Tell us about the rich young widow,' Thomas asked.

'Which one?'

'The blonde.'

'Which blonde?'

They roared with laughter again.

James never knew how much or little to believe when he heard stories like this. Whitefield was a pretty nondescript little bloke, scarcely the sort you would expect to be a Casanova. Still, you never knew, and James could not help suspecting that a fair chunk of the world lived far more interesting lives that his own.

Well, they could have it, at least for the moment. Having most of the German army trying to kill him was interesting enough as far as he was concerned. The rest of life could wait, assuming he lived, that is.

James folded the letter away and put it with the others, wondering whether to send them all back with his kit stored by the rear echelon or keep them in the tank. He decided to keep them. Several had burned with *Hector* nearly a fortnight ago. Better than him burning. Perhaps her token – his lady's favour if she insisted – was lucky. James did not think that he really believed in charms of any sort or that luck could be controlled somehow. Could not do any harm though, and if desire and worship counted for anything then Penny was giving her all on his behalf.

He put the letters away and reached into his pocket. She was right, silk was so soft, almost like skin.

It was also cold, like the dead, and the dried blood was still there.

21.01 *hrs, the Odon Valley*

Judd was tired, and it seemed as if the day itself was feeling much the same, for the clouds had rolled in and it was getting dark much sooner than usual. O'Connor was asleep in the bottom of the trench – the man seemed to have the enviable knack of sleeping anywhere and anytime, even for just a few minutes. Judd wished that he would not snore so loudly though.

A Company was in a field bounded by big hedges, although to his right front these merged with an untidy patch of woodland. This was supposed to be a quiet sector, and they had only been mortared a couple of times during the day. Only one man per section was on guard, in each case manning the section's Bren. When he had taken over, Judd had checked with great care to ensure that no damned fool had fiddled about with his, but to his relief, Bessie was as he had handed her over. The gun was in front of him, resting on its bipod, aiming at the trees.

There was movement. Judd leaned forward and brought the gun up to his shoulder. He thought that he heard another sentry moving.

A head appeared from behind a tree, the body still hidden by bushes. The head wore a helmet, covered in netting and decorated with leaves, but still unmistakeably a German helmet. A hand was high beside it, perhaps with a grenade. Another German came behind.

One of the other Brens opened up with its reliable thump, thump, thump, and Judd squeezed the trigger. The first German shook with the impact and fell. The second dived down.

'Goddammit! Stop shooting my goddamned prisoners!' The voice was American and very familiar.

'That you, Paul?' Buchanan called.

'Sure to Christ is!'

'Then what's the Goddamned password?'

'Shit! I mean Ink, no Inker!'

Buchanan chuckled. 'Reply is man, so come on in.'

Lieutenant Kowalski was one of the CANLOAN officers. Hailing from New Jersey, he had crossed the border and enlisted with the Canadians in 1940. No one was quite sure whether this was from a sense of adventure or a fear of the authorities at home, but he had proved an excellent soldier and was a sergeant by the time of Dieppe. He did well there and was sent home – or at least to Canada – for commissioning. Like Buchanan, he was often sent on patrols.

Now, he was angry, with one of his three prisoners badly wounded and the other two terrified. A son of New Jersey was proficient at expressing his anger. Even O'Connor, roused by the shooting, was impressed, but Buchanan had little sympathy. 'Next time, get them to take off their helmets. And hands in the air, not behind their heads.'

The argument was still raging when the Glamorgans were relieved by another battalion and allowed to pull back.

D+21, Tuesday 27th June

09.45 hrs, a field in Normandy

JUDD LAY AGAINST the bank, the Bren ready, muzzle pointing through a handy space between the lowest branches of the hedge. He was watching the cluster of trees near the corner of the field. Buchanan reckoned that the Germans were there – two or perhaps three of them. 'Coop' was out in the long grass, doing his *Last of the Mohicans* stuff, along with Griffiths, who was presumably doing whatever it was men from the Rhondda did when they tried to move with stealth.

The Glamorgans had been pulled back almost a mile from the front lines overnight, relieved by another battalion now that Rauray was captured. They were to get a respite of a day or perhaps two, allowing them to sort themselves out and bring up replacements. Rumour said that Brigade – and especially the Brigadier – was none too pleased with them. He was an austere Ulsterman, without fear himself, so unable to understand it in others. By all accounts he had enjoyed the First World War immensely, and eked out the bitter years of peace by getting posted to the North-West Frontier and anywhere else with a good chance that someone would shoot at him. The Glamorgans had got the impression that he had never liked them. One story was that when someone had assured him that the Welsh made excellent soldiers, he had countered by saying that that was true, but only if they served under white officers. Judd had no

idea whether or not that tale was true, although he could sense
that the higher ranks of the battalion felt hard done by.

'Sod him' was the politest comment Judd had heard about
this when anyone in the ranks had bothered to take notice at all.
The battalion had lost twenty-six dead and three times as many
wounded in their first action – and shouldn't that be enough
for the most bloodthirsty of commanders? Apparently, it was
not, and HQ was talking about the Glamorgans as windy, even
unreliable. He sensed that the officers and senior NCOs were
unhappy.

Perhaps that was why Buchanan had got so angry when a
couple of riflemen started to fire into the straggle of houses
and farm buildings where the battalion was settling down for
its quiet day. The cry of snipers went up immediately, even
though no one had been hit. 'Coop' was unimpressed by the
enemy marksmanship, as well as restless and determined to do
something about it. He asked for volunteers to go hunting, and
to his own surprise, Judd stepped forward. O'Connor stared
at him as if he was mad, glared for a while, and finally went
forward as well.

'You're a bloody fool, what are you?' the old soldier had said
at every opportunity since then. There were not many, because
soon they were stalking the intruders. Another Bren team with
Holdworth and some riflemen were in the next field, waiting to
cut the Germans off if they tried to retreat.

A helmet showed in the grass, round-rimmed and very British
in spite of the covering of foliage.

A rifle cracked and the helmet dropped. Judd thought that
he saw a tiny flash from the greenery of the nearest tree. He
let his breath half out. Before he fired, there was another sharp
snap, this time from the long grass and this time definitely a
.303. A shape fell from another tree, arms and legs flailing, and
then stopped abruptly, suspended on a rope. It was not the tree
Judd was aiming at, and another German fired, so he squeezed
the trigger and put four rounds into the spot where he thought

he had seen a flash. He nudged the side of the breech slightly with his hand to shift aim and fired another short burst. A man in a camouflage smock dropped down and slammed into the ground. Judd was so surprised that his finger stayed on the trigger. He shifted aim and pummelled the body, emptying the magazine. It was so close he could see the corpse twitch with each strike.

There was silence, broken only by O'Connor snapping in a full magazine. Empty cases that had come out of the bottom of the gun rolled down the bank and Judd shifted because they were hot.

'Careful, he might not be dead!' Griffiths shouted from the field.

The Lee Enfield fired again, three shots in rapid succession the way someone good with the old SMLE could do it. A third German was pitched out of one of the other trees.

'That's three!' Buchanan called out. 'But keep down.' The Canadian appeared out of the grass. He knelt, watching, and only after a while got to his feet and went over to the trees. He prodded the three German corpses, then beckoned to the rest of the patrol.

10.38 hrs, returning to the Glamorgans' position

Mr Buchanan was obviously pleased with himself and with them as he led them back to the battalion area. The Sun had come out from behind the clouds, the air was alive with birds and insects, and higher up the fighter bombers and further away a distant barrage. Judd was not thinking of anything very much, the danger was over, and he was warm and prepared to clean up, eat and perhaps read or write a letter, or simply doze if he got the chance. He was tired, as he had not been earlier in the day.

Groups of Glamorgans were dotted around the fields, yards and by the buildings. There were also a lot of vehicles, trucks and carriers of their own battalion, the little six-pounders of the battalion's own AT platoon, and beyond them on the main road, most of an RA battery equipped with towed seventeen-pounders, which were far bigger, longer and heavier. There was that sense of a lull in an exercise, everyone quite happy to take a break because they knew that eventually someone would start hounding them to rush. There was not much activity or much noise and those who were chatting did so quietly.

Going back to the rest of the battalion Judd had the same comfortable sense as returning home after a long day at the office. That would have set him thinking just days ago. Now, all he really wanted was to sit or lie down and to have a cup of tea. O'Connor had that furtive look that meant he wanted to slip away and do some foraging. So far, Judd had refused to accompany him, more through lack of energy than anything else.

Some tanks came roaring along the road. It was not much of a road, little more than a lane, but it served this little community which did not even warrant a name on the map.

Judd was glad that they were trudging through the wet grass of a field rather than on the road, as the tanks' tracks threw up great plumes of muddy water. One of the AT platoon gave a half-hearted yell of anger when each tank in turn sprayed his carrier with muck.

There was something reassuring about the size and power of the tanks, half a dozen of them, big, but low, with angled front and sides to the hull and turret and immensely long gun barrels, every bit as big as the seventeen-pounders. Probably that's what they were. They certainly weren't Churchills and he remembered Shermans as having rounder, more dome-like turrets.

Four tanks were already well ahead, the lead one nearly at the house used by Battalion HQ; the fifth was passing them, the sixth following, and its commander was standing tall, more than half out of the cupola, his dark, almost black uniform sensible enough for anyone spending a lot of time in vehicles. He had a low cap with a peak, rather than a beret.

Buchanan stopped dead at the head of the file of men.

The sixth tank was level, no more than twenty yards away in the lane. It was an odd colour, sandy with spreading stripes of deep green and rusty brown all over it – and a neat black cross outlined with white near the front of the hull.

'Shit!' Buchanan yelled.

10.41 hrs, a few hundred yards away

Mark had a short break, and was trying to write a letter home, sitting on an empty box that had once contained 2″ mortar bombs. He felt he owed the family one, if simply to reassure them that he was still alive. Yet after the conventional banalities and assurances not to worry, he did not know what to say. Some mention of the fighting ought to go in, he supposed. His father had always revelled in descriptions of shrapnel, shellfire and heroism and no doubt considered himself cast in the heroic mould, although robbed of his chance of glory because pressing duties had kept him at home throughout the Last War. Maybe some modest talk of blood and guts would make the old fart show him a little respect? Thinking back, Mark shuddered at the memories. There was horror and guilt at killing Dalton, and then wonder at what he had done, charging around like a madman. It had not felt like courage then and it did not now. Just things that had happened.

Mark was afraid that he would not be able to cope next time. Dropping the Sten and having the ruddy thing go off and kill had left him empty. If Major Jackson had not appeared and yelled at him to get on, Mark suspected that he would have given up, perhaps gone mad and howled at the sky. After that he did not think or feel very much of anything. He just did things mechanically. There was guilt certainly, how could there not be, but Mark did not think that he had tried to make amends by getting himself killed. He had not wanted to die, and certainly did not now.

The Officers' Mess truck had turned off the main lane and was coming into the field, heading for HQ. Whether any of its bounty would reach mere subalterns like himself was harder to say, and for a moment it bogged down in the mud, rear wheels churning and sending up spray. After a struggle, some ribald encouragement from men not about to volunteer to push, the tyres came free. Then the truck exploded, the petrol tank igniting in a great boom. Even at this distance the heat of the flames was savage.

Mark dived to the ground, waiting for more shells to come in. He could not hear any, but there was the sound of big engines close by. Beside the lane was the RA battery, its men suddenly stirred to life like a prodded ants' nest. They ran to the big guns attached to the tow trucks. Bullets threw up fountains of mud and water and tore into bodies, spinning them round and pitching them over.

The muzzle of a gun appeared from behind the blazing Mess lorry. It flashed, flames shooting forward and sideways from the muzzle brake, giving off an astounding crack, and one of the artillery trucks was flung on its side, crumpled, smoking. The machine guns chattered again, yellow-green tracers flaying the gunners. After the long, long barrel came a big tank, its front hull plate at a steep angle. It halted, methodically slaughtering the artillerymen. Another tank, as big and predatory as the first, pulled into the field on the other one's right.

Mark was bareheaded and his hands clasped his skull as if they could protect it. The leading tank fired its main gun, then the second did the same and the range was so short that the crack of discharge and explosion of the shells was almost instant. Four gunners had lifted the trails of a seventeen-pounder off the tow hook and were struggling to drag it round to face the enemy when the high explosive flung them in the air, bodies torn to shreds. Others were fetching ammunition from a truck when it was hit and the shells went off an instant later, flames shooting up.

Yet the gunners did not give in. They tried to take their guns into action even though it was a race that they could not win. Mark watched, too terrified to move, as the tanks flayed the battery with fire, then advanced to finish them off. One tank ran over one of the big anti-tank guns, and a wounded man screamed for a moment as the great tracks rolled over his legs as well. The gunners were cut down, dead or wounded, and did not fire a shot.

There was chaos everywhere, other big tanks marauding around the position. Carriers, trucks, jeeps were blasted, crushed flat or riddled with bullets. The heat and stink of burning petrol and rubber was everywhere. Only a few of the ones in plain view had escaped, driven away by the quick witted or hidden from view by trees or wrecks.

Mark pressed himself against the earth and tried to be as small as possible.

10.50 hrs, near the lane

In ten minutes the six Panther tanks had spread ruin, destruction and death along the lane and in the fields either side. Yet this was not a proper attack, or if it was, then the Germans had blundered, for it was not properly prepared and there were no infantry to follow the panzers and mop up resistance.

Anything big enough to be visible through the vision slits of one of the tanks was immediately engaged with high explosive and machine gun bullets. The same was true of anyone bold enough to be seen. The six tanks had spread out, causing mayhem, but without a clear focus beyond destruction. The RA battery was gone, guns and vehicles destroyed and the surviving gunners hiding out of sight. The Glamorgans were also hiding, but as minutes passed the shock of the sudden onslaught was starting to fade.

'Now!' Buchanan yelled to Judd and O'Connor.

Judd hefted the Bren and laid it on top of the low wall. There was a Panther no more than fifty yards away, at an angle to them, the turret slowly revolving, searching for fresh prey.

The Bren gun thumped back into his shoulder as he pulled the tigger, and he had not quite balanced it properly. Shots flew high over the turret. Its hatch was open, but they could not see the commander's head and wanted to keep it that way. Judd crouched, pulling the butt of the gun back so that it was properly into his shoulder. His next burst threw off a few sparks on the cupola. He kept firing, the rounds landing within inches of each other.

Buchanan was further along, behind a tractor half covered with a tarpaulin. He used his rifle, aiming at the same place as Judd. Griffith crawled out beside him, clear of the tractor, a PIAT cradled in his arms. He put its single leg down and flicked up the sight. There was a dull, almost soft crump as the bomb sailed wobbling through the air. It clipped the front of the Panther and flew on past to explode harmlessly.

'Mother of God!' O'Connor hissed as he changed magazines.

The tank's turret had come round, and the Bren team dived down just before the co-axial machine gun raked along the top of the wall. Judd was frantically crawling ahead. He hoped O'Connor was following or going the other way, but then with a great roar the world exploded around them, lumps of stone and earth flying everywhere, half burying them.

10.59 hrs, on the other side of the lane

Mark rose a little so that he could see out of the ditch, then immediately ducked back down, fingers clawing at the earth in case this could bring him any closer. There was a Panther just twenty yards ahead of them, side on, but with its gun facing in their direction. No retaliation followed.

Thomas scrambled along the ditch towards him, carrying a box of PIAT bombs. Without a PIAT to shoot them, they were so much lumber.

'I've got grenades, sir,' Evans said eagerly.

'They're not close enough,' Mark told him. 'Not yet.' He tried to sound more confident than he felt. Most of the battalion must be hiding just as they were, dotted around the buildings and fields. Some were fighting back, because there was shooting and now and then the crump of a PIAT. As yet, it did not seem to be making any difference, and the German tanks clattered around, shooting at will, but they were like elephants clumsily trying to catch dozens of cats.

Mark had half a dozen men from his Platoon and a few other strays and they kept low in this ditch bordering one of the main fields. It led to the deeper ditches either side of the main lane. It was also muddy, the bottom filled with a foot of water, but it was enough to hide them.

'That way!' Mark said, pointing towards the lane. More of the Glamorgans' vehicles had been parked over there. They might be able to find more men, more gear, and perhaps someone who knew what the hell was going on.

They went as fast as they could, slipping and falling into the muddy water. A new sound came, the crack of high velocity shot less loud than the big tank guns, and adding a fresh note to the machine gun fire and the detonations of ammunition in burning vehicles.

The lighter gun fired again, then another similar one, and Mark saw one round as a dark blur whipping down the lane. A hail of machine gun bullets answered the challenge, the tracer bright green in the air. They were near the road now, and the tracks and great round wheels of a Panther filled Mark's view as it surged by, going surprisingly fast. Above it, the tank itself seemed toweringly vast. The panzer fired, the noise appalling, then it seemed to rock back on its haunches. A round hatch at the back of the turret opened and a man in black uniform half fell onto the rear deck of the tank. Another man came from the main hatch with a third behind. Their clothes were smouldering.

Mark raised his pistol and flicked off the safety catch. Before he could shoot, a Sten chattered right by his ear, almost deafening him. Thomas was halfway up the bank. His first rounds knocked the man off the back. From somewhere a Bren opened up on the others.

'Come on!' Mark shouted, although his ears were still ringing and he could not really tell whether he was loud or quiet. The ditch joined the one beside the lane. In front of the smouldering Panther was a six-pounder gun, with four men lying dead or wounded around it. There was no carrier, which meant they must have pushed it there to take on the tanks. Further back, about seventy yards or so, was another anti-tank gun, this time partly behind a brick wall on the far side of the lane. It fired, the round slamming through the air as it went by. There was the rumble and clatter of another panzer, which fired, the shell too high and splitting a tree in two, some way behind the gun.

Mark led them to the left, on the opposite side of the road, but closer to the gun. He glanced over his shoulder. The other Panther had stopped. A six-pounder shell struck the front glacis of the hull, scarring the paint before it flew off to the side. Machine gun fire threw up dust off the brick wall. A gunner reeled away, face bloody.

They were almost level with the gun when the Panther fired its long 75mm. Again the shot was long, but closer, and this time it had fired AP and the solid shot struck a gunner at waist height, ripping him in two and flinging his torso high.

The German tank started forward; the driver slowed, edging to the right, perhaps wanting to make them a harder target. The machine guns in the hull and turret were still firing, the rounds striking all around the gun, so that plumes of red brick dust hovered over it. Another crack, and the six-pounder fired, giving a high pitched squeal as it struck the hull front and ricocheted away.

'That's the stuff!' someone was shouting. 'Let me help!'

Mark recognised the Colonel's voice and had never before heard him so animated.

With a growl the Panther started forward again, and Mark thought it was veering right until he realised that the edge of the lane was giving way and the big tank was sliding sideways into the ditch. The engine revved and screamed in protest, but the panzer kept going, tipping almost onto its side, the right track going round and round in thin air.

'Ha ha!' Lt. Col. Davis was yelling like a schoolboy whose team was winning. From this side, Mark and his men could only see the underside of the tank, and left the crew to someone else.

Mark pulled himself up the bank and sprinted across the road to the gun. Only one of the proper crew was there, the gun layer who sat in his chair on the left, and Davis had a shell in his hand, ready to load.

'Can we help, sir?' Mark asked.

'Any gunners with you?'

'I used to be, sir,' Thomas snapped before Mark could ask.

'Then give us a hand, and we'll bag another of the bastards! But we need shells.' He gave Mark a smile. 'I'd be obliged if you could fetch me some. No use there.' He jerked his head towards a row of blazing carriers parked a hundred yards away.

'There should be readies in the tows,' the lance corporal gun layer said. 'Back there somewhere.'

'Traverse right! Traverse right!' Thomas yelled, pointing. Another Panther was nosing around in the fields where they had come from, making a juddering turn in their direction.

Mark grabbed a trail, Evans with him. Other men took the other one and lifted, turning the gun around to face this new threat.

'Bloody marvellous. Now go, boys, go! We can't pot the bugger without ammo! So run!' Davis shouted at them to be heard over all the noise.

'Come on, sir!' It was Evans who urged him on, lightly tapping Mark on the shoulder.

They ran, and as they did heard the six-pounder crack like a whip as it fired.

'Damn! Bloody shame!' the colonel yelled in encouragement. 'Never mind, next one.'

The field was thick with black smoke from wrecked and burning vehicles. Small arms rounds went off from inside the back of one truck, pinging around, unpredictable and alarmingly close. Mark went away from it, but the slim figure of Evans bounded past.

'Here, sir! A carrier!'

Something made Mark turn before he followed the lad. The six-pounder fired again, grazing along the side of the panzer's turret. Moments later, machine-gun bullets flayed the gun's crew. He saw Davis staggering, Thomas with his hands clutching his throat, and the gun layer slumped forward, one arm over the gun's low shield. An HE round exploded on top of the gun itself, the blast flinging the men aside like ragdolls.

'Oh my God,' Mark gasped.

11.05 hrs, back in the field

Griffiths did not miss this time. The bomb from the PIAT flew, deceptively slow in the air, and struck the rear of the tank's hull just below one of the storage boxes. It left a glowing hole in the metal.

'Hit him again,' 'Coop' told him, putting the bomb in the tray itself.

'Bastard hasn't cocked,' Griffiths snarled. The big spring that lobbed the bomb was supposed to use the pressure from a shot to coil back and hold ready to fire again. It did not always work. Griffiths rolled onto his back, pushing the pipe-like contraption down so that he could use his feet to press, as the spring was powerful. The PIAT looked as if it had been designed and made in someone's back garage out of bathroom fittings. Yet it worked, if you could get close enough, and proof of this came as orange flames surged out of the vents on the back of the Panther, as the tank that had killed Davis began to burn.

Crewmen spilled out, their clothes smoking, but hands in the air as soon as they could.

'Shoot the bastards,' O'Connor hissed, but Judd ignored him.

Mr Buchanan was up, rifle aimed, but shouting to them to come down. 'Watch 'em, boys.'

'They're fucking SS, sir,' someone said.

'They're our prisoners,' the lieutenant said without any emotion.

'Drop it, Frankie-boy,' Griffiths said, giving up on trying to cock the PIAT. Five of the Panthers were knocked out, one by the gun, one from driving into the ditch, and the rest worn down by hit after hit from PIATs. Hundreds of yards away, the sixth sped up the lane and away from them. No one on foot was going to catch it anytime soon.

'Guard these,' Buchanan told Griffiths. He smiled. 'You've earned a breather. Come on the rest of you, let's round up the rest of the buggers.'

Judd breathed deep, hefted the Bren and followed. He wondered about Griffiths. His old mucker had escorted the prisoners back without harm the day before, in spite of his fears and in spite of shooting down the pair trying to surrender.

15.45 hrs, the village of Cheux

Cheux had surely been a pretty little place until just a few days ago, but as the 165th RAC tried to pass through it they looked on a ruin. Hardly any of the houses had any tiles left and most did not even have roofs at all. They were shells, some still with traces of having been a home, pictures on the scarred walls, furniture tipped over, beds covered in dust in rooms that had no more than half a floor.

Whitefield and Thomson had their hatches open, and for a change Collins had come up from his gunner's little cell and was standing behind the turret. Suddenly he laughed loud enough to be heard over the engine.

James turned, puzzled. Collins could not speak, only pointed at one of the ruined buildings. One whole side was gone so that it looked like a child's dollhouse, albeit one designed by a madman.

Eventually, Collins recovered. He leaned forward to make sure James could hear him. 'Reminds me of when the Jerries first bombed Bristol. My ma was down there, working, and the house she was staying in was flattened. We went down to help her with what little stuff she had saved. You remember the bombing, don't you, sir?'

James nodded.

'Ar well, it was like this, only new then. One house flattened, the rest fine, or one street gone and the next untouched. Anyway, we walked with Ma all the way to the station, and halfway there she stops and stares for a long, long time. A house like that, cracked open on one side. "What is it, Ma?" we asked. "Did you know the people?" And still she says nothing, before shaking her head. "No," she says. "Didn't know 'em. Never been here before. But I don't like those curtains." That was it. Whole house blown into a pile of shit, streets on fire, and she notices the ruddy curtains!'

'Women, eh,' James said, unable to think of anything else.

'What's that?' Whitefield piped up on the intercom. 'I didn't see any. What've I missed?'

James retold the story, not too well, but Collins did not want to come back inside yet, in spite of the jets of water spraying back over the tank. Rubble had clogged whatever drains Cheux had had in the first place; tanks, half-tracks and heavily loaded trucks had churned up the roads, and the rain of last night had left great pools almost everywhere. More often than not they were halted, waiting for the column ahead of them to move on. As far as anyone could tell, it was not the Germans holding things up, but the traffic.

Still, at least they were going forward. Colonel Tim had told them that morning that the brass hats were encouraged. They had not been pleased with progress yesterday, but today they had their breakthrough, or at least scented one, so the tanks were going forward to exploit it. Break through, cross the River Odon, then swing south-east, well behind Caen, and get across the Orne to the city's east, surrounding it altogether. That was the big plan. The immediate plan, the one that really mattered, was to get forward ready to go once the infantry had made a gap.

That was easier said than done. Roads in this part of Normandy ran between Caen and the big towns, especially Bayeux, or smaller ones like Villers-Bocage. They did not go the way the British wanted to go, south, then south-east. After all the rain, there was even less chance of wheeled transport getting anywhere off a road, and it was not much easier for tanks because of all the little fields and hedgerows. Everyone had to use the roads and no one could go straight to where they wanted to go. On top of that the artillery preparation for yesterday's and today's attacks had clobbered the villages and roads. In the country that meant a fair few big craters in the roads and lanes, and trees down, which all needed to be moved. In the villages, like Cheux, it meant rubble and flooding and more craters.

They turned a corner and the Sherman ahead of them dipped suddenly down, water surging over it like a destroyer in a newsreel racing through the Atlantic. It must have gone down a good five feet before it started to climb again, out of huge hole left by a shell, quite probably fired by the RN. It went slowly, tracks struggling to grip the side of the crater because the water and the passage of so many tanks had turned it into a slide.

'Fucky Nell,' Whitefield yelled, diving down into the tank and closing the hatch after him. 'Don't forget the driver, sir, don't forget the driver.' Thomson similarly vanished.

'Do you want to come in?' James asked Collins.

'Might be wise, sir.'

James told Whitefield to wait while he got out, let Collins in, and then got back in himself.

The other Sherman, Bell's Three Baker, was up and out and they followed. James presumed that they must only be sending tanks by this route and the rest must be using a side street, assuming there was one. Nothing else would make it, and even a carrier would be swamped.

They were just through the flooded crater, the hatches all closed, when Three Baker ahead of them suddenly fired its 75mm, the HE shell skimming past another tank in front and tearing into a building.

'Sorry… I mean, this is Baker Three Baker. We had an accident.'

The airwaves became blue with unrestrained anger. Eventually Bell explained that a loose shell on the floor of the turret had rolled onto the firing button with enough force to push it down.

'Give 'em a fucking Iron Cross,' someone suggested. The station did not identify himself, but James suspected it was Sergeant Rawson.

The tank in front of Bell was also a Firefly.

'Baker Two Charlie to Baker Three Baker. If this road was wider I'd traverse and brew you up myself.'

'Sorry,' Bell apologised again.

'You know, this war is getting bloody dangerous,' Blamey said.

18.25 hrs, the Odon Valley

Recce Troop had not had a good day. They had got off well, early in the morning, and near noon stopped to rest and eat – and brew tea. A German tank, some said a Tiger, although no one saw it clearly, spotted them from half a mile away, where some high ground was still in German hands. It sent a shell, if not an 88mm then something almost as fast and lethal, at them. Two of the Stuarts were parked side by side and the shell punched straight through one and into the other, setting both on fire. A sergeant, dosing in his seat, was the only person on board and must have died instantly. The German, no doubt satisfied, did not shoot again.

A couple of hours later they were on the move once more, and going well until a tank or an anti-tank gun – again no one saw it – sent a shell smashing through the thin armour of the lead tank. One of the crew was killed, two more wounded, and the tank did not burn, and was still there, on a stretch of road where the going was in plain view for two hundred yards. The Germans were a couple of miles away, which meant that with speed and luck other vehicles could get past the spot unscathed. The rest of Recce had done it, as had almost half the regiment. Now it was B Squadron's turn, and, so far, it was going well. The Germans had fired a few shots and missed every time. Thankfully the road was wide enough to get by the wreck without having to slow down. Still, the Germans were getting plenty of practice, and the law of averages was on their side.

They did it one by one, in case someone stalled or was hit, trapping more tanks. Bell was still leading 3 Troop and as he was approaching the abandoned Stuart an AP round slammed into the wreck, making it shake. It still did not catch fire, even though a gaping hole was ripped about the engine. The puny 37mm gun pointed to the sky.

'Ready?' James asked.

'Aye. Now I know what a duck feels like in a shooting gallery,' Blamey said.

'Don't know about a duck,' Whitefield began as he set the tank rolling, 'but I could do with a...' He trailed away, intent on his driving. He had the hatch open again, in spite of the risk. 'Hail Mary, full of grace,' he added through gritted teeth. The Sherman was racing, and James with his head out could feel the wind and worried that they were too fast to get past the wreck without colliding.

Whitefield clipped it, making the Sherman judder and sparking a chorus of oaths and protests. The two hulls ground together, but *Hector II* did not slow down. The Germans fired again, but once more struck the Stuart and the Sherman was racing into the cover of the trees up ahead.

James breathed out. 'I think I've aged five years,' he said.

Collins chuckled. 'Another ten then, and you'll need to shave, skipper.'

'Aye,' Blamey agreed. 'Stick with the Cockney and we'll all be old before our time.'

Sergeant Martin came on the air. 'Baker Three Charlie to Baker Three. I think there is a way around. Should keep us out of sight, over.'

'Negative, Three Charlie. There isn't time and the ground is too soft in the fields. Wait for Three Able to come through and then follow, over.'

'Sorry, Baker Three, am already in the field.'

James turned his head and glimpsed the shape of a long-barrelled Sherman to the left of the road, before it vanished behind the crest. In the meantime, Sergeant Dove roared across the gap and the leading tank of 4 Troop was approaching. James could not hang around and create a traffic jam.

'Baker Three Charlie to Baker Three. Sorry, but we've bogged down, over.'

Bloody man, James thought. 'Baker Three to Baker, permission to leave road and try to tow Three Charlie out.'

'Negative Baker Three. Leave him for REME.' Major Scott sounded resigned, and James could imagine his expression, a mix of frustration and impatience. 'Baker Three Charlie, wait in position and catch up as soon as you can. We'll need you, out.' Scott was back, face covered in plasters as if he had shaved in the dark, but determined to return to duty. Plenty of others would have stayed in hospital for weeks, but the major had not.

'Baker Three Charlie to Baker. Understood, out.'

And sod you too, James wanted to stay. Instead, he got on with things. 'Driver, advance.'

19.45 hrs, by the River Odon

The Argylls had taken a bridge.

'Well, the ruddy Campbells will steal anything,' Captain Fraser of A Squadron said when the colonel told them the news.

'No doubt,' Leyne said, grinning, but impatient. His driver had managed to botch the crossing of a culvert over a stream, so that the CO's Sherman was now half in the river bed, and also waiting for a tow. Colonel Tim was back in a Stuart, just like in his Desert days, and was impatient. 'What it means is that we are over the river. With luck they'll find another bridge or two, but even if they don't, we are on our way. If you look at your maps you will see that it soon gets more open to the south. Splendid tank country. So that's where we are going. First, south-east.' He traced the line of the roads, inevitably a jagged route against the grain of the country. 'Next key waypoint is here, the high ground at Point 112, then around Caen and to the Orne. So let's get moving.'

They did, as fast as traffic and the roads allowed, and from now on only occasional bouts of shelling reminded them that the Germans were out there. Sergeant Martin did not reappear. The man could fight, as he'd shown back at Point 103. He just

did not want to take any risks, and that put the rest of the troop
in danger. In a way, it was one less worry, not to have him with
them. Yet James suspected that they would need that seventeen-
pounder in the Charlie tank.

D+22, Wednesday 28th June

JAMES WAS TIRED and knew that this was only the beginning. He had seen Keith briefly at the morning's O Group and even he had been struggling not to yawn. So close to midsummer the nights remained very short. They had waited until dark before pulling back a little and concentrating the regiment to laager, because otherwise that was asking to be spotted and shelled by the enemy. James and 3 Troop were some of the last to get there, guided by the railway tracks which ran in front of the position chosen. It was gone 23.00 hours and in pouring rain before everyone was settled and almost midnight before the A echelon came up in their lorries and brought fuel, ammunition and food.

'They told me to keep the church on my left as I went through Chou,' Corporal Wilkins explained to his old friend Collins. James guessed that the Somerset man meant Cheux. 'Only there was no ruddy church anywhere to be seen. Nearly ran over an MP in the dark.'

'He was too fast for you, was he?' Whitefield asked. 'Never mind, next time... Now where's that sodding petrol?'

The luckiest may have got two hours' sleep by the time all the work had been done. James managed barely an hour and had to be shaken awake when the officer's conference was called. Just as they could not risk being spotted concentrating for the night, so they needed to spread out before the Sun came up if they did not want to be pasted by the German guns. Two squadrons were to push forward, with the village of Baron on their right, to where the ground started to slope up to the high ground of Point 112. The hill itself was given the codename COUNTESS.

B Squadron moved out in the dark, forming a rough line next to Baron in the best cover they could find. Reports suggested that the place had been almost as badly smashed up as Cheux, but the infantry were there, watching the flank and rear. Things were not so good on the left flank, which was up in the air and likely to be bristling with angry Germans, and up ahead there were only Germans – although how many was yet to be seen. Colonel Tim had warned them that the enemy was bound to see the threat and would be rushing reinforcements to the spot. To add to the three crack panzer divisions they had already encountered, Corps thought that at least five more were on their way. It was not a comforting thought.

The rain slackened and then faded away to nothing as James and his crew waited in position. Soon the sky became grey rather than black.

Thomson was crooning again, this time about swallows coming back to a place called Capistrano, wherever the hell that was. Perhaps it helped him stay awake.

05.30 hrs, in front of Hill 112

'Baker to all Baker stations, prepare to advance behind Item tanks.' Three of the remaining Stuarts from Recce were to lead them as they approached the hill. 'Baker Three to lead, then Two, HQ, then Four, then One. Charlie Squadron in position to cover us.'

'Here we bloody go,' Blamey muttered. 'Sorry, skipper, I meant let's be at those beastly Huns!'

'Thank you, loader, nice to see enthusiasm. Here, have a medal.'

'Ta.'

There were groans from the rest.

'Capitalist corruption,' Whitefield told them.

They were led to the right, weaving through the shattered streets of Baron, seeking cover from the ruins. There were some trees outside the village, which offered a little more protection from view, then the open ground on either side of the railway, before they swung left, dipping down into a hollow and following the slope around. James could not see much, even though the day promised to be a bright one, but at least that should mean than no one should see them.

The colonel had been right: this was much more open country, with broad fields of ripening wheat and barley. That change seemed to have come almost overnight, for instead of green the crops were distinctly yellow. James reckoned that in another day or so they would be seas of gold.

Ahead of them, the high ground did not seem very impressive, just a gentle rise a hiker or even a cyclist would barely notice. It was a long rise though, so would mean that their legs would get tired before they reached the top. The road running up it was almost perfectly straight, making James wonder whether it had first been made by the Romans. That would not have surprised him. Normandy felt old, like so much of Britain.

The squadron spread out into a rough line before the ground began to climb. They waited and watched, and a little later started to move forward. James had Sergeant Dove on the left and Corporal Bell on the right, a good fifty yards between them. His own tank was in the gap, back about the same distance. Martin had not yet reappeared, so they were stuck with just three tanks. One troop would move at a time, while the others gave close support.

07.05 hrs, Hill 112

'Baker to Sunray, we have reached Countess,' Major Scott reported.

'Did you ever reach a countess, Whitey?' Thomson asked.

'Dunno about a countess,' Whitefield said, 'but there was a duchess and a couple of ladies who weren't too ladylike. I could tell some stories...'

James was tempted to shut them up, but suspected silence would be worse. They were pushing forward slowly and with care. So far there had been a few shots from a far distance. Tony Lightfoot's 1 Troop had had a tank put out of action with a broken track. They'd also claimed a hornet destroyed, although at this range it was surely very hard to know. The fire had come from the south-west, not the hill itself, and everything up there was still. That could mean that there was hardly anyone up there or simply that the gun layers were waiting until the Shermans came closer.

The methodical advance continued. A few shells soared over and landed among the tanks to their left. No one reported any damage. James and 3 Troop rushed forward two hundred yards then halted, ready to cover the others. The German gunners switched their attention to the supports, back down the slope.

The airwaves crackled, someone tried to speak, could not get out the words. It went silent for a moment. 'Sugar One, I need a robber immediately.' That was a regimental HQ call sign.

'What's a "robber"?' Blamey asked.

'Dear oh bloody dear,' Thomson told him. 'Don't you know that? It's the RAMC[1] – means they want a red cross half-track to help some poor bugger.'

'R for robber, R for RAMC,' Whitefield explained. 'As in Rob All My Comrades.'

'All stations, Sunray is wounded.'

---

1   Royal Army Medical Corps.

'Oh Christ, not the colonel,' Whitefield said with surprising bitterness.

'Hope it's not bad,' Collins added.

James guessed that the shellfire had dropped around HQ, perhaps when Colonel Tim and others were out of their tanks, planning. His crew went silent, a rare thing for them, and no one seemed in the mood to joke.

'So, driver, tell us about this duchess,' James said after a while. 'Is there a feather duster involved?'

'No,' Whitefield said slowly.

'You know, I reckon we're corrupting the poor lad,' Collins told them. 'He was pure as the driven snow before he met us – especially you, Cockney.'

'Boy's got to learn, hasn't he? Don't want him disappointing his missus when they marry.'

James could not remember telling them about his engagement; soldiers, and especially tank crew, just had a knack of finding out about everything.

'Well, I'm not going to take a feather duster on my honeymoon, I'll tell you that.'

'Hark at him. Decadent, that's what he is,' Thomson told them.

'Typical public school boy,' Blamey added.

'If I can get a word in edgeways,' Whitefield cut in, 'and tell my story like the good officer asked – no, it weren't a feather duster for the duchess. The duchess liked a riding crop – like the ones half the officers carry.'

'Always need a good swisher,' James assured them. 'Show the old tank who is boss.'

'You calling your lass an old tank?' Collins asked.

'Will you let me bloody well finish...' Whitefield said in mock anger. 'Lot of kids, you are. Now the duchess says to me, "My man..."'

'Baker to Baker Three, I repeat, advance, over.'

James had not been paying proper attention. 'Apologies

Baker. Baker Three to Three Able and Baker, advance level with the road sign.'

09.00 hrs, on the slope of Hill 112

Keith Turner's 2 Troop had lost its first tank, which was burning away merrily on their right. Tony Lightfoot's 1 Troop had lost two, only one of which had burned although thankfully only after the crew had all escaped. The fire was coming from somewhere on the top of the hill. James' map showed an orchard with a distinctive diamond shape. From here it simply appeared to be the largest of several clusters of trees. There were also some walls, low in themselves but enough to help conceal a dug in AT gun or tank.

James could not locate the enemy, nor could anyone else in B Squadron, and the advance had halted because any tank going forward immediately became a target. The radio told him that C Squadron was engaging targets at ranges between two and three miles, with neither side doing that much damage.

Regiment sent up an RA Troop with seventeen-pounders mounted in open topped turrets. There were known as M10s or Achilles for something a little more catchy than the American designation, and based on the hull of a Sherman, but with lighter armour to keep the weight down. The gunners tried to find targets and shot a good few rounds at where they guessed the enemy might be. James watched the great flashes as the guns fired and was reminded of his time in the Firefly, which in turn reminded him of the continued absence of Sergeant Martin.

The German fire did not slacken, and with rounds coming close, the RA reversed down the slope into cover. James could not blame them. The Achilles was not designed to lead the advance, and for all its frailty, the Sherman was better suited to that role.

Not to be defeated, the field artillery took over, and a FOO began calling in a series of strikes on the orchard and other targets. While the shells were landing the Germans stopped firing. As soon as the gunners finished, the fire resumed and a tank from 1 Troop had its track ripped apart by solid shot and was left stranded until the crew could repair it or someone came to tow it away.

Overhead, fighter bombers of the RAF were circling like birds of prey hovering on the thermals. No one could speak to them directly, but they were waiting to attack as soon as they found a target. The RA officer had field guns load with red smoke shells and hit the suspected enemy positions. One round was short, plopping down and fizzing away in the middle of B Squadron HQ.

'Oh shit!' Scott's voice came over the air. 'I mean Baker to all stations Baker, put up some yellow smoke, out.'

'Got the grenade?' James asked Blamey. He took the smoke bomb, pulled the pin and raised his hand to toss it to the side, so that it would not obscure their view too much. It started to flare, burning his fingers, and he dropped it down into the turret. Yellow smoke engulfed him, followed by a deluge of complaints and violent oaths. Coughing, he crouched down, unable to see properly.

'Where is the bloody thing?' he gasped.

'Buggered if I know,' a voice replied, probably Blamey's.

Bright yellow smoke was everywhere, surging around them, out of the turret hatch and from the two front hatches, because Whitefield and Thomson had bailed out, fearing that the tank had been hit and was about to explode. Someone thrust the cannister into James' hands; he stood up again and hurled the thing away.

Whitefield and Thomson stared up at him, and then doubled up in laughter. 'High Mandarin in charge.' Both of them bowed, 'Honourable soldiers Little Stepney and Big Bottom send honourable greetings to chief of Chinese army.'

There was a foul chemical taste in James' mouth and it only got worse when he licked his lips.

'Oh Gawd!' Blamey pushed his head up, gasping for breath. His beret, skin and tunic were yellow, and James realised that he must be as bad or worse. It took a while to dissipate. No Germans fired at them, which meant that they were out of sight, that the clouds of smoke confused the enemy – or that, contrary to all the stories, the Germans really did have a sense of humour.

James and his crew heard rather than saw a couple of Typhoons come down in screaming dives and fire volleys of rockets at the red smoke in the orchard, but the pilots still could not see any clear targets, so soon gave up. A few minutes later a half-track further down the slope was struck by AP. It stopped, engine smashed.

'Baker to Baker Three, if you've quite finished larking around, advance to the crossroads, out.'

'Well, at least he didn't say chop-chop,' Whitefield conceded.

They went forward, the straight Roman road on their left. Ahead another smaller road crossed it and beside it there was a little shrine, a calvary carefully carved and brightly painted. It reminded James that he was not in Britain anymore, although presumably such things had once been common back in the Middle Ages.

As they went forward, his view improved dramatically. The high ground had a fairly flat top, and although it had not seemed much from a distance, it was a wonder how far he could see in every direction. There was a low hedge and a straggle of poplars lining the side road. He had 3 Troop halt behind them. Gradually the rest of the Squadron came up alongside. C Squadron was also moving up and the motor company of infantry was getting out of their half-tracks and carriers and preparing to assault the orchard.

Hector II shook as something slammed into their right side, low down, and the engine stalled. James' heart pounded, and he was about to leap out before the fire erupted, then he stopped himself. There was no fire. They had been hit, but the shell had not penetrated. He raised himself a little.

'They've hit a wheel. Cracked it by the look of things.'

'I'll take a look, boss,' Whitefield said, and had his hatch open and was out before James could respond.

'Gunner, traverse right.' James could not see anything, but reckoned that was where the shot had come from. Sergeant Dove fired, the big 75mm booming, but whether that was based on a sighting or mere optimism was hard to say.

'Reckon she'll go,' Whitefield shouted up. 'Back far enough to make it easier to get her to the workshop anyway.'

'Baker Three to Baker, am pulling my tank back for repairs.' James wanted to get them under better cover before he took over another tank. Then out of the corner of his eye he saw a Firefly heading up the slope towards them. The prodigal had returned.

'Baker Three to Three Charlie. Halt in position.'

Whitefield reversed, and apart from a few more squeaks and an uneven ride, the Sherman went willingly enough. He brought them alongside the Firefly.

James told Martin to take over his tank and get it back to safety. The sergeant stared at him, face resentful. James was surprised: he had thought the man would want any excuse to get out of the way.

'Rather stay with my crew, sir.'

'I need you to get mine to safety – and get the thing repaired as soon as you can.'

'Sir.' Stiffly, Martin climbed out of the turret and jumped across to the other tank. 'Jerries a bit lively, are they?'

'A bit. Good luck,' James said and jumped onto the Firefly. As he went back to Dove and Bell, the injured Sherman turned and went its unsteady way down the hill.

10.50 hrs, on Hill 112

Infantry from the Rifle Brigade had taken the orchard, helped by a barrage from the field artillery and supporting fire from the 165th. B Squadron was sent forward on their right to help them hold it.

'Driver, take it gently,' James said. 'Easy, easy. Halt.' The Firefly lurched to a stop. From the open hatch he had a grand view across the top of the wide hill and far beyond. The training manuals taught that the best position for a tank was to be hull down, which meant that to the front, only the turret should be visible. Then the tank could engage the enemy with its main armament, while offering the smallest possible target to return fire. Hull down meant that the hull was hidden behind the crest, which was straightforward when there was an easily defined crest, or the bank of a bocage hedge or a wall of suitable size. The high ground around Point 112 curved only gently, which meant that it was very hard to know what a distant enemy gunner would be able to see and what he would not. Dove and Bell brought their Shermans to a stop on either side of him, roughly level, which suggested that their judgement was the same as his.

'Three Baker to Baker Three, I see dust trails, ten o'clock, about five or six hundred yards, over.'

'I see them, Three Baker.' James licked his lips. The chemicals from the smoke bomb had made them even drier than usual. 'Gunner, traverse left, on. Something moving there. Load AP.'

'Already have, sir.'

Ahead of the dust trails three tanks came rolling through the high grass. They had flat plates around their turrets, and two had big square side plates on either side of the hull. The other must have lost them, for its hull was visible. They were Mark IVs and trying to come at the orchard from the flank.

'Gunner, target closest tank, range five fifty yards. Fire when ready.' James blinked before the savage flash shot out of the muzzle and the tank rocked back with the recoil. Both Dove and Bell were shooting, as was Keith's 2 Troop to their right. For the moment, the rest of the squadron could not see the enemy.

The leading panzer seemed almost to stagger, lurching to one side as several shots slammed home. Its turret began to turn towards them, until another shot struck it. Black smoke poured from the engine covers as the crew jumped down. The next tank was hit, a big chunk of the turret plate ripped off and flung into the air. It started to reverse. The third one had already gone, perhaps hit, but still driving and vanishing behind the fold from which it had appeared. The other one, the one hit in the turret, also vanished, but it was trailing a lot of smoke.

To James' right, one of 2 Troop's Shermans exploded, turret flying high into the air before it dropped. Another shuddered as it was hit and began to burn, the crew spilling out to hide in the long grass.

'Baker Two to all stations, have lost rest of Troop. Think the so and so is over there, at one o'clock, range two zero zero zero yards. Am engaging.'

James scanned the direction with his binoculars. He thought he saw a flash. 'Gunner, traverse right. Range two thousand yards, halfway along that line of trees. That's it, on. Baker Three Able and Baker, watch my shot.'

'Good God, I'm hit,' Keith announced with what sounded like mild surprise. 'Am bailing out.'

'Fire!' James called, realised that he was shouting and closed his eyes just in time. The big gun thundered, the shot slicing through the air. Seventeen-pounders were powerful, but he had heard that their accuracy trailed off at such long ranges. Still, if it did hit, it was still a big shell going damned fast, so would spoil anyone's day.

A solid shot punched through the air between his tank and Bell's.

'Driver, reverse. Three Able and Baker, reverse thirty yards.'

Corporal Bell's Sherman was struck so hard that it shook and James expected it to brew. There was smoke and dust everywhere, and when it cleared the tank was still going. By some freakish chance the shell had landed on the gun barrel, ripping it in two and leaving jagged shards at the end of a sawn off stump.

'Are you alright, Three Baker?'

'Hell of a headache,' Bell replied. 'And Pearson's out cold.' That was his gunner. 'Everything else is still working.'

'Get back, Three Baker, you're no more use up here.'

14.00 hrs, on Hill 112

More than half of B Squadron was gone, disabled or so damaged that they had to abandon or retreat. A and C Squadrons were not much better. The open ground Colonel Tim had anticipated was good for tanks, but that included the German tanks with their bigger guns. It was hard to tell how many there were out there, but the number seemed to have grown through the course of the day, and there were also 88mm guns somewhere. The top of the hill was a trap. Anyone on either side who nosed forward too far became visible, and was soon knocked out or – if they were lucky – streaking back with their tails between their legs. The trick was to creep forward as far as one could in a tank, then peek over the hard-to-distinguish crest, pot the enemy and then clear off before his friends saw you. They spent hours doing this, hiding in the smoke, cowering behind wrecks, scoring a few clear successes and far more that required the eye of faith.

All the while the British artillery sought out the hidden German positions, and the German guns tried to scour the hill clean of their enemy. The Rifle Brigade in the orchard got the worst of it, pounded again and again. Some of the shells were big and some were huge, from the multi-barrelled mortars, whose rocket-powered shells moaned, almost sobbed, as they came in. Time and again James felt the Firefly rocked by the blasts. Somehow, he and Sergeant Dove in his Sherman were still in one piece, in spite of a fair few near misses. It was like Point 103 in some ways, but much worse, for nowhere seemed to be truly safe for any length of time.

A third of the regiment was out of action and everyone left was low on ammunition for the big guns. Machine guns were not much use, even for aiming at these sorts of ranges.

'Sunray to all stations. We're being relieved. The RTR are coming up to take over.'

'Thank Christ,' someone said without realising that they were broadcasting.

'Amen,' came another voice.

'Sunray to all. Observe correct wireless procedure.' Major Scott was now in command of the regiment, for the second in command had been killed by the same shell burst that wounded the colonel. It was nice to hear his voice, although it reminded James that he was the only officer in B Squadron still in a tank. Tony Lightfoot had been wounded when his tank was brewed, and he was not sure what had happened to Keith after he had bailed, or that new fellow in 4 Troop whose name he could not remember. All of 4 Troop had been made up of replacements, which seemed foolish. Better to have some leaven of experience.

'Baker Three to all stations Baker. Not long now. Stay sharp.' Dear God, it sounded trite. All the other commanders were NCOs older than him in years and far older in wisdom.

'Baker One Able to Baker Three, I can see a couple of hornets to my right front. Could do with a hand, over.'

'On our way, One Able. Baker Three to Three Able, you come in on One Able's right and I'll come in on his left. Make it fast, nip in and then come back, over.'

'Acknowledged, out.'

'Loader, how many rounds do we have left?'

'Fifteen AP and a couple of HE.' James could barely remember shooting off so many in the last few hours.

'AP up the spout?'

'Yes, sir.'

The Firefly roared into life, churning up a spray of mud as it turned. It was a risk going so fast, because movement drew attention, but One Able was lower down and the slope might just screen them.

They came alongside the Sherman from 1 Troop.

'Driver, halt. Gunner, traverse right, range six hundred yards, that's it, on.' There were three panzers, Mark IVs, one behind the other and probably thinking they had found a covered route around the British flank. He could not see their tracks, only the side screens and turrets, but they seemed to be climbing very slowly. 'Baker Three to One Able, you take the one in the middle. Three Baker, you take the one in the lead. I'll get the one at the rear. Fire on my order.'

They both acknowledged. 'Gunner, follow him as he moves.' Wait, James told himself, wait. The leading panzer was easier to see now, so he had been right about the shape of the ground.

'Fire!' It was not neat, not three shots as one, but they came in quick succession.

'Shit! The Firefly had missed and the gunner was not happy. The leading Mark IV slewed to the left. The second was going too fast and barely missed ramming into the back of the leader. Then the second one exploded, hatches flying open and flames gouting from them. The third one halted, its turret beginning to turn. James reckoned that the German turrets were all much slower to traverse than the Shermans' and it was nice to have something up on the bastards.

'Yes!' His gunner yelled in triumph as he drove a shell straight through the flimsy side screen around the turret and into the turret itself.

'One more for good measure,' James said. 'Driver, prepare to get us out of here. Do a full turn when I say and then foot to the floor.'

The remaining German tank, the one that had been in the lead, tried to drive out of the ambush. The other two Shermans hit it almost in the same spot low down, and it stopped. A camouflaged crewman bounded out of the turret. The Firefly finished off the rearmost tank, setting it on fire.

'Right, driver, go, go!' James realised that he was excited and yelling. 'Baker Three to Three Able and One Able, well done. Pull back before they catch on.'

The three Shermans locked one track to spin around as fast as they could. The manual said that you should keep your front armour, the thickest and best, towards the enemy so that it was better to reverse away when there was a threat. German guns did not worry too much where they hit a Sherman and James reckoned speed was a better option. A solid shot carved a groove in the ground to his left, but a miss was still a miss. They all got away.

Half an hour later, the remnants of B Squadron pulled back as the new regiment took over.

D+23, Thursday 29th June

T HE GLAMORGANS WERE going back to a forward position. Major Probert had briefly held command after the death of Davis, but a new colonel had arrived, a very tall and rather thin Guardsman named Dorking-Jones. No one was quite sure what to make of him, although the Welshmen said that a fellow countryman could not be all bad.

'Unless he's from North Wales, of course.' Mark recognised Evans' voice and the approving laughter from a group of nearby Valleys' boys.

'I tell you, he'll get us all killed.' The voice was Peterson's, who had just been made up to lance corporal. He was from West Wales, so was inevitably considered strange. 'He will, you know. Guards are too brave for their own good. My dad was in the Scots Guards in the last lot.'

'Scotties?'

'Yes, well he had a bike.'

'And he must have lived long enough to have you, so he didn't get killed.'

'Yeah, old Mr Peterson's snug in Carmarthen or pigshit or whatever you call the place, getting his end off with your mam.'

Mark wondered whether he would need to intervene. Sometimes things could get out of hand. Fortunately, the essentially charitable spirit of the British soldier put in an appearance.

'Probably spent his war outside the palace presenting arms.'

'He got the DCM.'

'What, for guarding the palace? Bloody outrageous.'

'So, he was brave as well as ugly. Pity he didn't play with himself more or we might have been spared listening to you.'

'Up your pipe!' Peterson told them, bringing the debate to an end.

The Glamorgans were not to move before 22.00 hours for the initial march, and then to relieve the other battalion under cover of darkness. It gave them time to get ready, to absorb the other replacements left out of battle at the start, and for the Support and HQ Companies to sort out all their replacement vehicles.

The Brigadier was happy, which was a rare enough thing, and had even deigned to praise the Glamorgans. Everyone seemed very impressed by the story of the sudden appearance of the Panthers in their midst and how they had not panicked and eventually knocked out five of the six. Mark was none too sure about the not panicking. The sudden chaos had certainly terrified him and it had been a while before he was capable of doing anything. Still, it seemed for the moment that their august leader no longer considered them shaky. There was talk of a posthumous gong for Davis, which was no less than he deserved. Mark hoped that the rumour was true because he needed some good news.

Letters had arrived, with two from his mother. Silence from Anne was no longer surprising or even too disturbing. In the first letter – his mother's habit of putting a number on the envelope was very useful – there was a lot of small news from home. He read the pages, not really paying very much attention. Little of it seemed immediate, even real, to him as he sat in a field in Normandy. It was like trying to read Dickens when you were too tired to pay real attention or care all that much. The second letter had news of Anne.

Anne Saunders was home on leave for the weekend and brought her fiancé so that she could show him off. He seems a nice boy, and not at all brash as you tend to expect with Americans. His name is Charles Montagu the Third and he is a captain in their Air Force. They seem very happy together, so I passed on your very best wishes. I know you have always adored Anne and she was good with you when you were younger, taking you on excursions when I was busy.

Mark sighed. Bloody Yanks. Overpaid, overfed, oversexed and over here. Bastards. Rich, swanking bastards. He had heard the jokes – she wears the new Utility knickers. One Yank and they're off!

He crushed the pages of the letter into a ball and threw it away like a petulant child. How could she do this to him? He knew he was younger by a bit, but she could not ask for anyone more devoted. And he wasn't so bad looking. It was back to poor old Mark Crawford, quite good, but never good enough for the prize. Bet the so and so wasn't even a flyer. Just some desk wallah with all the time in the world to sweep innocent girls off their feet, bribing them with chocolate and nylons. Bastard.

Not that Anne was that innocent, not now anyway. She had always been smart, probably the cleverest person he knew, and that included the likes of Jimmy Taylor and Bill Judd. She always seemed to have read everything, and if you mentioned a book or idea she had opinions, and usually far better reasoned ones than your own. Even Judd only held his own with her sometimes when it came to debates. Anne had always had the amused expression of someone who had seen through the world and understood the joke behind it. Going into the Wrens had broadened her outlook even more. The story of her first leave had raced around the chapel and half the town. All very prim and proper in a dress rather than her uniform, and the whole family in their Sunday best for lunch, she had failed to

attract her father's attention, so had followed up with 'I said
pass the effing salt, you daft bugger!' She had not known what
the words meant, just having picked them up from the other
girls. At least that was what everyone said. Mark reckoned that
you could never be sure with Anne.

He sighed and began to laugh. He had not been there, but
the scene was so vivid in his mind. The shock, the outrage, the
younger sisters asking what 'bugger' meant. Anne had glided
through it all with her usual grace. Perhaps she was too much
for him. It would be like hoping to wed a film star. Well, good
luck to you Charlie Montagu, because you'll have your hands
full with that one. Doesn't mean I like you, you bastard.

Having nothing vital to do and not being in the mood to
write a reply, Mark wandered over to the temporary Mess. One
gift from the new colonel was a replacement for the Mess truck.
As an Army vehicle had not been available, Dorking-Jones
had somehow acquired a captured German bus – presumably
conscripted from home or requisitioned in France. It was
painted in the usual Hun sand, green and brown, but now had
a big red, white and blue roundel on the roof in the hope of
dissuading our own pilots from shooting at it.

Inside there were plenty of seats, albeit arranged in rows.
A few officers were chatting, others reading papers amid the
haze of tobacco smoke. Mark lit up and had a search through
the ones already discarded. The newest was from a couple of
days ago and there was a lot about what was happening in
Normandy, far more than they knew, assuming that the press
actually knew what they were talking about. The Yanks were
doing well and had taken Cherbourg. Good for them, even
if they had brought bastards like Montagu over with them.
However, by the sound of it, some MPs and newspapers were
criticising Montgomery for dragging his heels. Mark could not
be bothered to read on. Let the buggers come over and have a
go themselves if they were impatient.

After a while he found a few copies of the *Daily Mirror*.

There was a flash of stocking top in one when *Jane* fell over trying to crank the engine of a van, but otherwise the blonde was in full control of her clothing. Bloody women, you just couldn't rely on them.

16.55 hrs, to the north-west of Hill 112

B Squadron was back up to a strength of nine tanks, and remarkably, James was still acting commander. He had organised two troops of four, with SSM Egan in charge of one and Keith Turner leading the other, while he was back in a repaired *Hector II*, as Major Scott had taken his own tank with him.

The morning had been quiet, undisturbed by shelling not because they were out of range, but because the enemy had so many other folk to bombard. From what they were saying it was pretty hellish for the tanks and especially the Rifle Brigade up on the hill itself. Another regiment of tanks had gone forward on the right, trying to ease the pressure by the ridge around Point 113. The crump of shells and the distant cracks of tank guns was almost constant throughout the morning. James found that he barely noticed it. They were not involved, were fairly safe, and he found it surprisingly easy to relax.

There was a poignant half hour when the Rifle Brigade's padre held a burial service for five men killed when their half-track had been hit. No one said anything, let alone gave an order, but nearly all the 165th who were not required to do anything went over, forming ranks in silence. They sang 'Abide with me' and listened to the words of the service and the prayers, and a bugler sounding the Last Post. It was very English, very quiet, and deeply moving. Before coming into the army, James had often thought deeply about life and death and God. All that earnest discussion seemed irrelevant now. What he felt was a deep emotion and he did not need to define it, indeed trying to do so would be unnatural, almost offensive.

Three hours later they moved back into action, going through the rubble of Baron and beyond it to deploy outside Gavrus, another little place left in ruins by the war. There were infantry dug in in the gardens and amid the wrecked houses, but they had been coming under more and more pressure from Germans supported by tanks.

Major Scott had outlined the situation in a hasty O Group. The advance had reached Hill 112, but resistance had thickened so much that he could not see them going any further. No one could hold the top of the hill, because to be there was to make yourself a target to every gun in range. That was true for the Germans as much as it was for them. Every sign was that the new panzer divisions reported by intelligence were coming into the line. Most likely enough to stop them and maybe enough for a big counter offensive aimed at the sea. That was if the Hun was given the chance to organise. At the moment the 165th with the other regiments was at the front of a long corridor reaching into German lines. They were threatened from the front and from both flanks. They were holding and would keep on holding, and the more they could fix the Germans' attention on stopping this advance, then the less chance old Jerry would have to line up his panzers and charge for the coast.

That was the big picture, or probably part of the big picture, and it was all very well, but as far as James was concerned his war came down to the fields, hedgerows and woods south of Gavrus. The fields were smaller and less open to unfriendly eyes than the land on and around Hill 112, if not as small as the real bocage they had seen. All that really meant was that the threat was different, and there was more chance of an enemy getting close before you spotted him.

'Baker to Baker One, push up to the hedgerow on the right. We'll cover you, over.'

'Baker One to Baker, acknowledged, out.' SSM Egan never wasted words. James watched as the ad hoc troop manoeuvred, going carefully, two tanks stationary and ready to shoot while the other two moved, leapfrogging the four hundred or so yards to the hedge line. Once they were all in position, guns pointing over the low hedge, he sent Keith's Troop, which included Dove and Martin, over to the right, where there was a straggle of farm buildings and a few clusters of trees to offer cover. Then he moved up to be between the two units.

'Baker One to Baker, think they're up to something. There's movement in the woods to my front, over.'

'Roger, Baker One, am coming up beside you to take a look.'

James hunched down as mortar bombs began to explode all around them. These were light ones, not the big rockets, and no real risk to a tank. Even so, he realised that he was hunching his shoulders, as if he could make his body smaller and somehow that would mean that the one in a thousand bomb straight into the hatch would not happen.

'Baker One to Baker, I count five, repeat five hornets, with infantry.'

'Driver, halt.' Whitefield had brought them next to a sunken lane heading towards the enemy. They were at the end of the hedge held by SSM Egan's tanks. 'I see them, Baker One. Hold your fire until they get closer.'

There was a chance that the Germans did not know that they were waiting. The hedge put them hull down, and each Sherman had its turret covered with branches, camouflage netting and, for the luckiest and best scroungers, green silk taken from parachutes, to conceal its shape.

He saw the boxy shapes coming through the high corn. They were Stugs, low slung and with fixed guns. Around them were little blobs of helmeted heads as the panzer grenadiers came with them.

'Gunner, target right-hand SP, range four hundred yards.'

'On,' Collins reported, boot poised over the firing button.

'Baker to Sunray, hornets and infantry advancing across the field.' James had the map in front of him on the turret top and hastily read the map reference. 'Request fire mission, over.'

'Sunray to Baker, will see what we can do.'

'Baker to Baker One. Fire when I do, over.' James switched back to the intercom. 'Gunner, fire!'

The big 75mm roared at the same moment as a mortar bomb landed beside the Sherman, making James cower down into the turret as little fragments of metal whizzed past his head. One of the hatches fell with a clang. Blamey had already reloaded and Collins fired again, without waiting for the orders.

'Baker Two to Baker,' Keith's voice came through the head-phones, as puppy-like and enthusiastic as ever. 'I reckon I can go up the lane and get on their flank. Permission to try, over?'

James struggled to think. The other Shermans were firing. One Stug was burning, another had been hit and was going round and round in little circles like an injured insect. The one Collins was shooting at had stopped and had not yet fired back.

The Sherman to his left – to his shame he could not remember who was in it – erupted in flame, black smoke rising high in just a moment.

'Go ahead, Baker Two. Baker One, watch out for friendly station coming up on our right, out.'

A shell landed, a big one, in the middle of the field, flinging up muck and dust.

'Baker to Sunray. On target, fire for effect.'

The Stug that had stopped suddenly fired, the shell narrowly missing Hector II's turret.

'Cheeky bastard!' Collins said mechanically, almost as a reflex. He fired back, but it was hard to see whether or not he had hit. Swathes of the crops were on fire, adding to the smoke and making it hard to make out anything very clearly.

James had a thought. 'Baker to Baker Two, stay well back from the field – a stonk is coming in, over.'

'Baker Two to Baker, understood, out.'

He waited, but the shells did not come. There was bound to be a delay, as James told HQ and they told the FOO who called the battery. Even so, this seemed unduly long.

The Stug juddered as it was struck from the side. It immediately started to reverse, and then another AP shell slammed into it and thick black smoke started to pour out, adding to the haze.

'Got the bugger! Got the bugger!' Keith was shouting like an excited schoolboy, unaware that he was transmitting and blocking the wavelength. 'There! Machine gun those men. Ha! Ha! That's it, pour it in. There's more. I mean, traverse right, two hundred and fifty yards. Come on, Two Troop, soak them good.' James tried to transmit and tell the fool to get off the air, but Keith was too excited to notice. 'Go on, kill 'em, kill 'em all! Dear God, look in front. Range thirty yards, no closer! Oh Sweet Jesus, they've got a bazooka... Oh my God....' There was a harsh click and then silence apart from the hissing static.

Thick black smoke appeared above the trees lining the lane.

'Baker to Baker Two stations, what is happening, over?'

'Two Able to Baker... gunner, hose the hedgerow... Sorry, Two Able reporting. Baker Two is burning. Oh Shit. Two Baker has brewed.' James saw a gout of flames close to the black smoke.

'Pull back, Baker Two, get out of there, over.'

'Doing my best, Baker.'

Shells erupted in the wheatfield, half a dozen or more, and heavy calibre by the sound of it. The three Shermans to his left kept firing, so James decided to check on 2 Troop, and guided Whitefield back from the hedge and then around to the farm yard. Sergeant Martin was already there, hull down behind a pigsty, the long barrel of the seventeen-pounder pointing towards the mouth of the lane. Dove appeared moments later, head back so that he could guide his driver as the Sherman reversed. There were several men on the back behind the turret.

Dove came onto the wireless. 'Two Able to Baker, there are a lot of infantry up there with bazookas. They got the others. Two Baker brewed straight away. Two wounded and one other from Baker Two.' The sergeant's normally calm voice was quivering.

James saw that Keith was on the back of the Sherman. His right leg ended in a stump just above the knee and was pouring blood even as they tried to tie it off. His face was a smear of blood and his tunic was ripped. Another man's left arm hung uselessly.

What he could see of Keith's face was very pale, and his eyes stared without seeing.

'Baker to Sunray. Please send robber urgently.'

20.00 hrs, north of Hill 112

The 165th RAC were pulling out, along with everyone else. Four armoured regiments and supporting infantry had gained Hill 112, but if they stayed there, they would only be ground to powder for no gain. The losses were already heavy. No one was thinking anymore of swinging around behind Caen and reaching the Orne. Instead, Division and Corps and probably Army were concentrating on the seven or so panzer divisions trying to mass against them.

'There's a whole SS Panzer Corps of two divisions that were fighting in Russia on D-Day and now they're here, or damned well will be soon,' Major Scott explained. 'Now, Colonel Tim' – who was doing well and being a damned awkward patient by all accounts – 'and any of the other Desert hands will tell you that ground itself isn't worth anything. The Hill is no good unless it's useful to us and at the moment it isn't, so we're pulling back. Eleventh Armoured Div. and the Scots and the rest will set up a solid defensive line in the Odon valley. Let the buggers try and dig them out. Frankly the best thing that could happen is for the Hun to attack here, where he's still in range of the Navy let alone all the batteries to come ashore.'

'What about us, sir?'

'Back to Brigade. They're still supporting infantry on the western side of the breakthrough. Jerry is as likely to strike there as anywhere else, so it looks like we'll be busy.

'We pull back during the night, A echelon leading, then C

Squadron, HQ, A Squadron and B bringing up the rear. That should keep you busy, Frank.'

Captain Frank Harding, newly arrived with replacement tanks and crews, had assumed command of B Squadron.

There was a lot to do, but there was time to bury Keith, who had bled to death before the half-track could arrive. They put him next to the graves of the riflemen, but there was no bugler to sound. Staring at the faces, James realised that he was the only Troop commander to have landed on D-Day or D+1 who was still with the regiment. As the padre spoke, and spoke well, James could not concentrate on the words. Keith, excitable, enthusiastic Keith, was dead. He had got his wish and done 'it' and now was gone.

James blamed himself. He should not have sent the troop forward when the artillery was on the way to break up the attack. Tanks in a narrow lane could not manoeuvre, and certainly could not see infantry until they were already well within range of the deadly panzerfausts. His mind sought refuge in trivialities. What would the right plural be – panzerfausten? Tank fists. Bloody silly name. Bloody silly Keith too for leading and for getting so excited, revelling in the carnage he was causing. Should have been more careful. Should have been luckier. Never get to do 'it' again. I never have. Should I care? Would Penny have let me if I'd tried? Innocent, whimsical, romantic Penny. Was she just like one of Whitefield's conquests – panting for it, as the Cockney was inclined to say? Did he want her to be like that? Was that what was behind his silent disdain for her flights of fancy? Did he really want the other Penny, the one he had glimpsed?

The padre put his hand on James' shoulder and he flinched.

'Sorry, old lad. But it's done, and no sense wallowing.' The others had already broken up to get about their business.

James shrugged. 'I wasn't really thinking about him,' he confessed.

'We all have a lot on our minds. I don't think old Keith would begrudge us that. He was a good lad.'

'One of the best,' James said. As so often, he felt that he had to play along and say the words everyone expected. Keith had been pretty ordinary really, just like James or Mark Crawford or Bill for all his pretensions of deep thinking. There was nothing that special about any of them, nothing at all.

James knew that his eyes were becoming glassy and it was not for poor Keith.

'Maybe you could do with a rest?' the padre said softly. 'You've been on the go longer than anyone. Perhaps a day or two with B echelon? Get some proper sleep. I could say a word or two if you like.'

'No,' James snarled. He was angry and did not understand why. It was an effort not to punch the chaplain. He remembered back in Basic Training when he had taken a fall and sprained his ankle so that each step was painful. Someone had seen him struggling, had offered to carry his rifle for him, and the sense of humiliation had turned to rage, a rage that had carried him to the end of the march and then to a week in sickbay.

'Sorry, padre.' James tried his best to smile. 'I really am sorry. But no, please do not say anything. I can do more good here.'

The chaplain watched him for a while. James' eyes were clear again, at least of tears. A tank commander's job meant keeping his head out of the tank exposed to wind, rain and the clouds of dust and muck. The whites of his eyes were reddened and sore, the rings around them a deep, deep red. On top of all that, his skin was still decidedly yellow from the smoke cannister.

'Alright, my boy, have it your way. But remember, this war isn't going to be over quickly. You can't sprint through it. No one has the strength and stamina for that. We all need to stop from time to time, just to catch our breath.'

James smiled. 'Ready for the next innings.'

'Now what would a southerner like you know about cricket?' the padre said and they talked for quite a while about matches against touring sides and Roses rivalry and the best balance for an eleven.

D+24, Friday 30th June

A T LONG LAST, they were underway. James felt a lot better after his stroll and talk with the padre, but then there had been a long wait. Before they could pull back, the two tank regiments ahead of them had to come back from Hills 112 and 113. They had both lost heavily, as had the Rifle Brigade who came with them. Everyone was tired, more than a little numb, and the columns had to be careful because drivers and commanders were falling asleep and there was a risk of collisions. There were near misses, but somehow serious accidents were avoided, even though it was a dark night and everyone drove in a fog of dust from the other vehicles.

The Germans did nothing, so did not know or were too tired to care. Once the other units were through, the 165th began their own withdrawal. Even that seemed to take an age.

'Baker to Baker Three, you can lead off, over.' Enough replacements had come up to reform 3 Troop, although it only consisted of James, Dove and Martin. Bell and his crew were still waiting for their tank to be repaired or a replacement issued.

'Roger, Baker.' James led the others, not because he was in a hurry to go, but because he felt that he ought to be the one to set an example by staying awake and not losing the tank ahead of them.

It was a struggle, and a long night, and once he almost guided Whitefield into a ditch, seeing it at the very last moment.

His eyes hurt from the dust and the strain of peering into the darkness. They went through Cheux in the early morning, and it looked no less forlorn and broken in the pale sunshine. Time and again they halted and waited, as army columns always halted and waited, before moving on without ever finding out what had caused the delay.

19.15 hrs, half a mile in front of Rauray

Buchanan held up his hand to halt them. The patrol immediately knelt down. This was pasture land, but the half dozen cows still in the field were dead and bloated and the grass had grown quickly and was now up to the men's waists. They were close to the hedge, in its shadow, and that was pleasant because the day had grown hot. Judd rested the Bren on his knee and waited, while Buchanan went up to join Griffiths, who was scouting for the patrol.

A few minutes later, Buchanan pointed at each man in turn and showed them where he wanted them. Judd and O'Connor were sent left and the other Bren team to the right, next to Griffiths. All of them lay down, for this hedge was not one of the big bocage hedges mounted on a bank. It was just a thick hedge, the sort you could see almost anywhere in Britain. There was a foot or so of twisting branches underneath the leaves and plenty of gaps. From the other side, the grass would almost meet the bottom of the hedge and make it hard for anyone to spot them.

'Coop' came to lie beside Judd and the Bren. The Canadian gave him a wolfish grin and pointed. In the field on the other side, he could see a faint path beaten through the grass. It was not deep enough to have been made by cows, and apart from that the animals were all dead or long gone. The field was a small one, almost a wide road connecting some of the bigger ones, but twisting and turning. Following it north would lead to a low rise just in front of the British positions. They were on part of the hedge where it curved around, so that they were looking down an open stretch.

They waited. The Glamorgans had been supposed to take over positions from another battalion last night, but the Army being the Army, nothing was straightforward and there had been delays. In the end, only A Company had come up and taken over slit trenches on the flank of the position. The rest of the Glamorgans were on their way, and might even be occupying the less visible dugouts at the moment. The Germans were not close here, although the troops they were relieving were convinced that they were massing a mile or so back, and in big numbers. The major had sent Buchanan out with a patrol to try and get a prisoner or at least information. The Canadian seemed to get chosen rather a lot, and Buchanan tended to take the same men with him. That again was the Army mindset. If you showed talent, they used you again and again until you seemed less good or were killed. 'Coop' was good, very good, but maybe his nationality and his frontiersman look had made too much impression on those higher up.

Judd shifted his legs slightly. The right one was itching, just behind the knee, and he tried his best to ignore it. He had a boil on his neck, which the coarse battledress collar rubbed mercilessly if he turned his head too suddenly. At least they did not have problems with lice. Whenever he had seen German prisoners up close, they all seemed to be crawling with vermin. Someone said that the first thing they did when they got to the POW cages was to de-louse them.

The itch refused to go away, and he leaned back and tried to scratch it. He could not reach, and did not want to get up. Buchanan noticed, raised an eyebrow and smiled. Then the lieutenant's nose twitched. Judd smelled it as well, a stale scent, like mildew, but not mildew, but it was there, carried on the wind. German prisoners smelled that way, and anywhere the enemy had been for any time carried a hint of it for days after they had gone. It was the smell of Hun or Jerry or Fritz – and if it was absurd that in the middle of the twentieth century and its great industrial war that something so primeval as smell warned you when the enemy was near, that did not mean that it was not true.

The wind was blowing towards them, carrying the trace of the enemy, and up until now Judd had not really noticed it. He wondered whether Buchanan had put them here to make sure that they were downwind. He probably had.

The officer produced a grenade and showed it to the men alongside him. They nodded, and each man got one out of his pouch. 'Coop' laid his in the grass beside him, so that it was handy, and then brought his rifle up into the firing position. The others nodded again and did the same.

A German soldier appeared, his MP40 sub machine gun held low. The man's manner was casual, but his eyes searched the path ahead of him. His boots were invisible in the grass, but when he stepped, Judd could see that they were the short ones with gaiters. The man had camouflaged trousers and smock, and instead of a helmet wore a peaked cap, the sort Judd always associated with newsreels showing the Germans in Africa. It had an eagle sewn onto the side, rather than the front, and that and the collar tabs showed that the man was SS. Another man appeared a couple of yards behind him, similarly dressed, save that he was wearing a cloth covered helmet.

The first German held up his hand and stopped. Behind him, the second one sank down just as the British patrol had done not long before in response to Buchanan's signal. The patrol leader scanned the hedge where they were hiding, and Judd felt the man's eyes were right on him. He held his breath, knowing it was silly, but unable to help himself.

A hand gesture beckoned the patrol forward again. There were five of them, all in camouflage. None had dark cream smeared on their faces, something that the Glamorgans also no longer bothered to do.

Buchanan had told them to wait until they could not miss. The Canadian had his left index finger raised and pointing up. Flicking down was the signal for Judd to fire and everyone else to open up. He had not known what the patrol would find, or whether it would find anything, but his instructions had been clear.

Judd dared to breathe out. The patrol leader was close now, so that he could see dark stubble on the man's chin. That seemed wrong, and he expected the Germans to be smarter – especially Hitler's elite. Still the man's skin was swarthy, more Italian than the classic Aryan and he may simply have been one of those unlucky fellows for whom no shave lasted very long. The Bren was pointing right at the man, his face neatly in the sight.

Buchanan's finger flicked forward and at the same instant the German hesitated.

Judd squeezed the trigger and the German's head exploded like an overripe pumpkin, bloody fragments flying in every direction. Judd's second round smacked into the mess that was left, and the third went past before the body began to drop and went under the helmet and into the forehead of the panzer grenadier behind. Two more rounds followed and smashed the rest of the man's face.

The other Glamorgans were firing. Buchanan's Lee Enfield gave its solid bang beside him and Stens were chattering, as was the other Bren. It was over in moments, a thin skein of smoke drifting across the meadow. All the Germans were down and lying still. Someone was moaning.

'Stay and cover us,' Buchanan whispered to Judd and O'Connor. 'Come on,' he said to the men on his other side and they all pushed their way through the hedge.

A German near the back sat up, dazed, but with an egg-shaped grenade in one hand. Judd shifted the Bren and fired and the other team must have done the same because the man twitched as two streams of bullets struck his torso and tore holes in his mottled smock and his flesh.

No one else moved, but the moaning continued. Griffiths was first to the man, and kicked something out of his hand, then stooped to take a look. This was the only one still alive, and he had been hit twice in the chest. They tore open his smock and tunic and fixed on dressings. No longer moaning, the German stared at them, eyes filled with hatred and contempt.

They moved quickly, searching the bodies, pulling off the cuff titles which read *Hohenstaufen*, and breaking off part of the identity disc of each man. Then they went back, still cautious and following a different path to the one they had taken on the way in.

21.45 hrs, Rauray

Mark's platoon and the rest of D Company was in battalion reserve, on the rear slope of the low ridge around the village. They were near HQ and saw the scout car drive up. A captain and a lieutenant got out, their black berets marking them out clearly as tankmen. The lieutenant was conspicuous form a tunic stained in faded yellow and a face that was almost the same shade.

Mark laughed with sheer joy. He ran over.

'James!'

James Taylor blinked as some infantry subaltern dashed at him, waving his arms like a maniac.

'James!'

'Oh, it's you,' James said and smiled, his fatigue unable to withstand the onslaught of his friend's enthusiasm. 'I'd forgotten you were with this lot.'

'By this lot, I take it that you mean the finest regiment in the British Army.'

James shrugged. 'I heard they were a load of Welsh thieves.'

'The two are not incompatible, old boy,' Captain Harding pointed out.

James made introductions. 'I was at school with this fellow,' he explained in an apologetic tone.

'Accidents do happen,' Harding said with quiet reason. 'But we had better be about our duties and meet the exalted ones of HQ. You can chat afterwards.'

'I was wondering if I'd run into you at some point,' Mark said when James came back, as if discussing a trip to London.

'Is Bill Judd okay?'

'Gloomy as ever, so yes. "He thinks too much, such men are dangerous". Remember doing that back in school?' James nodded. 'He's in A Company,' Mark went on. 'They're up front and on the left, next to the Scottish Borderers.'

'I remember,' James said softly. The O Group had gone through all the Glamorgans' positions, and made the usual extravagant demands infantry battalions made on armour. Reports suggested that there could be a lot of Germans out there and plenty of panzers. Patrols had identified elements of the 2nd SS Panzer Division and the 9th SS. It was not an encouraging picture, especially after the ordeal down at Hill 112. The 165th RAC was still understrength, and the men were either pretty new and raw, or old and tired like James. Harding was waiting by the scout car. 'I'd better go,' he said. They shook hands, the gesture slightly artificial, but less so than saluting.

'Wonderful to see you, really wonderful,' Mark said and he was wholly sincere.

'Yes, they should stage a war more often,' James said. Mark found that very funny.

D+25, Saturday 1st July

00.11 hrs, D Company positions near Rauray

MARK WAS JERKED out of his slumber by the crump of mortar rounds landing a couple of hundred yards away near the northern edge of the village. That was very close to HQ Company, and everyone there sprang to life, gathering up kit and dashing or driving away. Seventeen Platoon, far enough away not to be at risk and for the moment unable to sleep, watched with some amusement as the flashes split the darkness.

After a while, and some impressive shouting by the new colonel, whose voice was far more powerful than his spare frame suggested, HQ moved across behind D Company and settled back down.

On the opposite side, invisible because of the rising ground, forward positions shot Very lights into the air to make it easier to spot any Germans trying to slip into or through the Glamorgans' positions.

04.55 hrs, A Company

Judd was stiff and cold and tired. They had done two-hour stags throughout the night, he, O'Connor and Griffiths all taking turns, but it had started late because they had spent some time improving the slit trench before any of them slept. There were plenty of craters dotted around the company position to argue in favour of a deeper hole, and it was surprising that the previous occupants had not gone down further – at least until you thought about all the craters and realised that any movement or activity in daylight had likely drawn down a lot of fire.

Several six-pounder anti-tank guns, new ones issued to replace the ones crushed or smashed by the Panthers, were dug in within the company perimeter. The gunners had used charges to blast holes in the hard earth as quickly as they could, then improved on them with picks and shovels. All in all, it was a good position, and everyone was snug and protected as well as time had allowed.

The battalion was on stand-to, everyone awake and ready, staring out into the darkness as it began to fade. Buchanan came round a few times and warned them that they might well be in for a big fight today.

'Panzers again, boys. They have to get through us if they're to drive to the sea, only the fools don't know that they're not getting through us. There's tanks of our own back there,' he added, waving his arm at the rise behind them. 'And these here six-pounders. And enough field and mediums within range to sink the Grand Fleet. We'll show 'em.'

Buchanan's 9 Platoon still had three sections, but each was down to just six men, and HQ consisted of a mere four, with Buchanan, Holdworth and a PIAT team. Their 2″ mortar had managed to get run over by one of the Panthers and a new one was yet to arrive.

Most of the Glamorgans were in a similar state, platoons at about two-thirds strength. A couple were commanded by sergeants, but Buchanan explained that they tried to avoid doing that. 'Makes us officers look bad by comparison.'

The Sun was rising, and the day would have been clear were it not for mist coming off the ground, thickened by smoke shells fired by the Germans. With a series of distant crumps and crashes, mortar rounds started to fall to the right, probably among C Company. German machine guns began their manic rhythm.

A little later, bombs began to fall around A Company. At the same time British artillery was coming down on suspected enemy positions. 'Coop' was back in his own slit and no longer inclined to wander. Judd ducked as the hot shockwave of an explosion reached him and bits of earth pattered down around them.

07.00 hrs, D Company

Mark listened to a battle he could not see. His platoon was close to Company HQ, so he was able to hear some of the messages coming through and try to make sense of the thunder of artillery, the lighter crashes of mortars and grenades, the chatter of machine guns and small arms and the sharp cracks of tanks. The Germans had laid down a smoke screen and were bombarding the Glamorgans' forward positions as panzers and infantry came at them. C Company was hit first, and now B was under pressure. By the sound of it there were far more tanks than the half dozen that had caught the battalion by surprise.

Sergeant Jenkins, known by his friends as 'Taffy' even in such a Welsh regiment, had arrived to take Thomas' place. Mark hoped that his third platoon sergeant would have better luck than the others, and he certainly seemed to know what he was doing. A small man, he was immaculate, even in a slit trench, exuding authority and competence. He had a small moustache, the black mottled grey like his hair. It was square-ish in shape, which had earned him the nickname 'Adolf', only used behind his back. One of the original territorials, he had been left out of battle until now. Mark felt lucky to have him. If this was the first time Jenkins had heard shots fired in anger – and it was – no one would have guessed.

'I'll just check on the boys, sir,' the sergeant announced.

'Of course.'

Jenkins hauled himself out of the trench with surprising ease for a man of his height, and left Mark and Evans to their thoughts.

A weird sound like a giant sobbing great tears suddenly grew louder and louder. Mark couched down, hands pressing his helmet tight to his head. Evans was on the floor of the trench, eyes wild. Half a dozen booming explosions burst out in HQ's position behind them. More came, the strange moaning building and building until the bombs went off and the whole ground shook, even at this distance.

By the time it stopped, Mark was panting like an asthmatic. There was plenty of shooting still going on at a distance, but it still felt like silence.

07.40 hrs, A Company

With a howling whow, whow, whow the big rocket-propelled mortar bombs straddled the field in a row of appalling detonations. The very ground shook, and bits of earth tumbled down from the edges of their trench. Judd felt like he had been punched in the chest or struck by a cricket ball. He struggled to breathe, crouching and hugging his knees to make himself as small as possible. O'Connor, the veteran of many wars before this one, was on his side, shaking as if with a fever, hands over his eyes. Griffiths, hard as nails Griffiths, had his hands shielding his crotch.

The awful sobbing began again and there were more explosions. Screams came from one of the trenches. Buchanan was shouting, and Judd realised that the lieutenant was running about, and could not understand how anyone could force their limbs to move in this storm of fire and steel.

The bombardment relented, distant gunners shifting their aim to another target. Instead, there was the roaring of tank engines from in front. German tanks always sounded louder and more angry than the British ones.

Buchanan had assured them that there were tanks behind them, ready to help when the time came. There were also three Shermans in this big field held by A Company. They were dead Shermans, armour holed and burned out a week or so ago in the earlier fighting. 'Coop' had got them to camouflage the tanks almost as well as if they were still in action. Judd had helped, and smelled the foul stench inside one, with its hint of charred and rotting meat. He and the others had done a good job, and were surprised when the officer came and told them off. 'We don't want them hidden, we want them almost hidden.'

It seemed to have worked, because the closest one gave off a great echoing clang as a German AP round slammed into its turret. It did not burn, for there was nothing left in the Sherman to burn or explode. Another round came in and another, and the German aim was good for they scored hit after hit as they tried to kill a tank that was already dead.

Judd could not see very much. They were all in a broad field, with an oddly irregular shape because it had five sides. The ground sloped up very gently in the direction of the enemy and the front of the field was marked by a steep banked hedge, and in front of that was a sunken road. The panzers were somewhere beyond that, able to see the high turret of the Sherman, but not the men in the trenches.

Over to his left, one of the six-pounder anti-tank guns lay smashed, one tyre punctured and flat, the barrel almost drooping because the mounting was broken. The crew, frail human beings rather than solid metal, were in worse shape. One was dead and all save one other wounded. Buchanan was pointing, sending them to the rear. By the look of things, one of the forward sections was in a similar state.

Another six-pounder was at the right-hand corner of the field, and as Judd watched, the loader slammed a shell into the breech and snapped it shut. The detachment commander was pointing out over the hedge a couple of yards in front of the gun pit. They fired, a sharp, almost high pitched whip crack sound, only for the round to bury itself in the earth bank and tear a lump out of the hedge. Judd realised that although the crew could see over the hedge, the gun itself was just inches too low for a clear shot. The gunners grabbed the split trails, pushing them together, hauled the long gun back out of the pit, then steered it around and ran it up to the hedge, so that the barrel was over it. Trails were spread again, the gun numbers[1] went to their places, a fresh AP round was rammed into the breech. They were shouting, as gunners always did, and then there was another crack as they fired.

08.15 hrs, in support of the Glamorgans

'Gunner, traverse right, right, on,' James said into the intercom. 'Target tank, range eight fifty yards.' The panzer was a distant squat shape, half concealed behind a fold in the ground and only intermittently visible in the haze of dust and smoke. 'Fire!' The 75mm boomed, the heavy breech slammed back, ejecting the empty brass case and adding to the noxious fumes inside the tank. Even with his binoculars, James could not see whether or not they had hit. There were at least half a dozen panzers out there, mostly Panthers, and that was only on 3 Troop's front. The rest of B Squadron was spread out and were reporting twenty or thirty tanks approaching.

James had brought his three Shermans up and had them in a row, hull down behind a thick bank with only a straggling hedge on top. It was a good position, the field of fire decent and only their turrets on show to the distant enemy. For the

---

1 Artillery practice is to designate crew members of a gun by numbers, e.g. Number One in charge, Number Two loading, Number Three working the sights, etc.

moment, there was not really anything he could do to direct the others; he was simply in command of his own tank.

'New target. Traverse left.' The first panzer had gone, perhaps damaged or simply deciding that his current position was unhealthy. James directed Collins on to another. Rounds were coming back at them, several driving into the front of the bank, but for the moment the panzers were busy with nearer targets.

Something smacked the top of his head, twisting his headphones off. James made himself small with all the instincts of a frightened animal, ducking down inside the turret. A second bullet pinged off one of the open hatches.

James pulled the headset completely free, taking his beret with it, and felt his scalp. It was sore and there was a faint trace of blood on his fingers. Blamey looked over the breech at him, face concerned. Collins turned back as well.

'Well I'm buggered,' he said, as he saw James put his index finger through a hole in his beret, shaking his head in disbelief. 'Reckon you were born to hang, sir!'

James breathed out. He shoved the beret into his trouser pocket. The arch of the headphones was bent, so that he could really only hold one earpiece in place at a time.

'Baker to all stations Baker. Infantry report that unfriendlies are infiltrating between their positions. B and C Companies virtually surrounded. A Company under heavy attack. Watch out for snipers and machine guns.'

'He ain't ruddy kiddin', is he,' Collins said, with even more of a West Country burr than usual.

James did his best to see through a vision port in the cupola, turning it to scan the ground ahead of them. 'Gunner, traverse left. Range two hundred and fifty. See the two trees close together?'

'Yes, skipper.'

'Give that hedge a belt of co-ax.'

The Browning chattered, red tracer stitching a row along the hedge.

09.20 *hrs, D Company*

Someone laid a smoke screen on top of D Company just after a couple of carriers from the carrier platoon rattled past taking ammunition up to the guns. Others were hauling .303 to the forward companies, assuming that they could reach them.

Lieutenant Colonel Dorking-Jones ordered D Company to send out a platoon to deal with infiltrators near Rauray. Mark's 17 Platoon were in reserve, so were the obvious choice. When the orders came, he felt his heart sink for a moment. There were still enough shells coming down to make his narrow trench feel like the snuggest little home in the world. Once he was out, it was actually a relief to be doing something.

They moved through the haze of smoke. Rather than go for three small sections, D Company had reorganised their platoons to have two sections, each with nine or ten men. Sergeant Jenkins took one and the PIAT team through the fields to the left of the road, while Mark and the others went along the shallow ditches on either side of it.

Gradually the smoke thinned out, although it remained hard to see much further than a hundred yards. They went steadily, and since he could not see him, he had to rely on Jenkins to keep pace. The road curved gently as it led into the village. One cottage was isolated, a dark shape up ahead.

Something flashed from low down, an MG 42 shooting over the garden wall. Plumes of dust sprouted up all across the road. Mark dived flat along with everyone else.

'Bennett, drop smoke, drop smoke!' Bennett was number one on the 2″ mortar, a squat, long armed and exceptionally hairy man from Cardiff's docklands. Mark had left him at the rear with the stubby little mortar. It did not have supporting legs like the bigger ones, and was just a broad baseplate and a simple tube a couple of feet long. It did mean that it was easy to set up and fire, but it was far from accurate. Smoke would give them a chance to pull back and outflank the position.

The Germans kept firing, rounds clipping by not too far above them.

The mortar banged. The sound always reminded Mark of a starting pistol on a school sports day. He had expected the muffled sound of a smoke bomb, but instead there was a boom, like a grenade. The Spandau went silent. Mark risked a quick look, just as a second HE bomb plopped squarely on the garden wall and exploded.

'Come on!' someone shouted from the other ditch, bounding along the road, charging and firing his Sten as he went. Men were moving out from behind Mark, and he gave in and followed. A grenade was thrown into the garden, and shots came from the flank against the upstairs of the house. Mark heard the PIAT shoot and send a bomb through a window.

It was over in seconds, as four camouflaged Germans appeared, hands in the air. Two more were dead and another wounded, peppered with fragments from the grenade.

'Je suis français,' one of the prisoners insisted. 'Alsace, Alsace.'

Cuff titles proclaimed that they were from the *der Führer* Regiment, would-be Frenchman or not. They all were young, boys even to someone like Mark, and they seemed helpless and scared.

'Glamorgans?' A voice shouted from cover ahead of them. The accent sounded distinctly Geordie, but you never knew.

'Yes, who are you?'

'DLI.'

'What's the password?'

'How the fook should I know?' The neighbouring regiment was from a different brigade.

'Reckon you'll do, lads,' Jenkins called, beckoning to them.

The sergeant and his men had come over from the field, obviously pleased with themselves, as were all the others. By now the prisoners were smoking British cigarettes or drinking from British canteens. All were very eager to please. The wounded man was patched up and a crude stretcher made from their rifles, bolts removed, and their camouflaged ponchos. A quick discussion with the Durhams' sergeant confirmed that they had swept through the area and dealt with the few Germans to get this far. That seemed good enough for Mark to take 17 Platoon back to the Company.

10.05 hrs, in reserve near Battalion HQ

'B Company are pinned down,' Captain Price explained. 'The Durhams are trying to get at the MGs that are doing it, but it isn't easy. Still, they're holding, but they need more men and most of all they need ammunition. Seventeen Platoon will help them out.' The captain had to shout over the 3″ mortars firing from their weapons' pits beside them. 'The CSM is bringing up ammo now. If you can get through, we'll send a carrier with more.'

Mark nodded. After all the Army would not want to lose an expensive carrier when he and his men were there to act like canaries in a coal mine. There was a long, rolling field that rose to a low crest, just high enough to hide a man, then dipped before rising again towards B Company's slit trenches. Mark was not sure how much of it was visible to the enemy. The CSM arrived, and along with him came men with tea as well as the ammunition.

'Get this down you.' CSM Samson was a larger than life character, jovial and ferocious in turn. Mark sipped from a mug and coughed. There was a large dose of rum in the tea. He could see his men perking up, starting to grin as they took the bandoliers and boxes of rounds. 'You might want these.' Samson was not tall, but built like a brick oven. He had a Bren gun in each hand.

'Lovely,' Jenkins said, slinging his Sten gun. 'You know how to use one of these, lad?' he asked Evans.

'Yes, sarge.'

'Sarge? Hark at him, and barely out of nappies. Take it then, boyo.' He tossed one Bren gun to Evans, who staggered back as he caught it, and then took the other himself. 'Let's have some mags.' The sergeant turned expectantly to Mark, who recognised the expression. This was the NCO's 'Sir, I am wording this as a suggestion, but we both know that it isn't and that I'm right, and you'd be a bloody fool if you say no.' 'Reckon we might send one section up each hedge. We hang back and follow in the middle, with the two inch, these Brens and the PIAT. That way if they hit any group, the other two can cover them.'

'Good idea.' It was. 'Just what I was thinking of doing.'

Within ten minutes they were ready to go. Five minutes later everyone hugged the dirt as mortar rounds went off in the field. When the smoke cleared, they began to go forward again, until machine guns started to scythe through the long grass. It was not closely aimed, but sweeping fire that meant that getting hit or being safe was largely a matter of chance. From then on, they crawled, inch by inch, and clung to the earth for dear life whenever the bullets came close.

A carrier appeared, racing towards them from where they thought B Company was. Mark stuck his head up and saw the little vehicle flung onto its side by a hit. It began to burn. None of the men inside were moving. Then a burst of machine gun fire flicked aside the grass just ahead of him and he pressed his face to the ground.

10.50 hrs, A Company

British shells sailed overhead and burst out of sight, behind the spur in front of their position. Over to the left, a couple of panzers stood amid the corn and sprayed what was left of A Company with machine gun fire, adding a shell whenever the mood took them. There were more panzers beyond them, part of the hammer blow that had pushed some of the Scottish

Borderers back. Others were surrounded, clinging on somehow or other. On the other side a single Panther now and then drove up over the crest, shot for a bit and then reversed out of sight. British tanks fired at it each time, which was why it did not stay, but so far had failed to persuade it not to come back.

There was no contact with B Company and the line back to HQ had been cut so that the field telephone was useless, while the wireless set was riddled with shrapnel so also US.[2] The only link was the RA captain's set, so messages to Battalion had to be relayed and took time to get there and back. Not that anyone minded, for only the barrages had stopped the Germans – so far at least. There were plenty of Germans behind the forward hedge and the crest, just out of sight, and no doubt plotting mischief.

Judd had yet to fire, but found himself nervously emptying a magazine and then reloading the bullets one by one. They had seen scarcely any Germans, but had been pounded again and again by mortars, by shells, by the Moaning Minnies, and skimmed over by bullets. Both the six-pounders had been destroyed. Seven Platoon had been on the front left of the position, until the Germans overwhelmed them. They were now back in the rear; at least a lance corporal and five men called 7 Platoon were digging desperately at the far end of the field. Eight Platoon had vanished – killed, captured or managed to escape, no one really knew.

A salvo from medium artillery burst in the air, the big jagged lumps of the shells raining down. O'Connor grunted and was staring at his left arm, because the hand had been cut off and was dangling by a thin strip of skin.

'I'm hit,' he said. Judd had noticed that men nearly always said that when they were wounded. It did not sound real, was not what he had expected, but that was what they did. He tied off the wound.

---

2   Unserviceable.

'Better get back, mate,' Griffiths said, and they helped O'Connor out of the trench and watched as he half jogged, half staggered back past Company HQ. Judd held his breath, fearing another batch of shells, but they did not come and O'Connor disappeared from sight.

A moment later, Spandaus began to rake their position, two from the right and another from the left, with the panzers adding their fire. Judd cowered against the side of the trench, hearing the rounds snap by above him. Men were shouting, a strange unrecognisable cry and the machine guns at last relented. Grenades went off, one close to them, but somehow Judd forced himself to crouch and took hold of the Bren. There were a dozen or more men rushing at them from the front, firing sub machine guns or throwing stick grenades.

The Bren hammered out. Judd stopped, shifted aim, squeezed the trigger again. Griffiths' Sten gave its high pitched clatter and others were shooting. The men in their camouflaged smocks and helmets began to tumble and fall.

'Look out, Judd. Watch the left!' Buchanan's voice carried over the confusion and shooting. Judd glanced left, saw five men coming from that side. He hefted the Bren, brought it to his shoulder rather than steadying the bipod, put three bullets into the leader, who fell, but the man behind was shooting, the bullets flying wide. Someone grunted, and the German was heading straight for him, only a few yards away, his mouth open as he screamed. He seemed to be ten foot tall and built like Goliath.

The Bren had pulled up because he had struggled to hold it when it fired. Judd took just an instant, which seemed to him like an age, and steadied himself, and aimed before he shot again. Bullets were going past. A bright red mushroom sprouted on the SS man's smock, then another and another. The man's arms waved as if in spasm, but he kept running and screaming. More bullets struck, tearing at the man's body, but still he came on.

Judd saw the man come at him, flying through the air, landing on top and knocking him down onto the floor of the trench.

There was the bang of a grenade, very close, and Judd's ears were ringing. His face was covered in blood, his tunic wet and stinking.

The German did not move.

'Help me!' Judd called out to Griffiths. There was no answer.

He struggled to push the German off, but the man's dead weight pressed down and he could not shift the body. The firing slackened and then died away. No one was shouting anymore.

'Come on, mate, get him off me,' Judd begged. No one replied and he lay there, unable to move.

After a while, someone began to lift the dead SS man. Judd pushed, felt the body moving, so rolled it to the side so that he could just squeeze out, his back pressed against the side of the trench.

'My, he's a big son of bitch,' Buchanan said. Once Judd had got his breath back and could move more easily, they somehow managed to lift the corpse and tip him out onto the grass.

Griffiths sat at the far end of the slit trench. A hole that seemed tiny and unimpressive was in the centre of his forehead and his eyes stared at whatever the dead stared at. There was not much blood, whereas Judd was bathed in it, like a butcher in a slaughterhouse.

'Well, we held them,' Buchanan said.

11.55 hrs, in support of D Company

James felt naked out in the open. None of the shells were landing close at the moment, but there were enough craters to show that this could easily change. He beckoned to Whitefield and walked backwards, guiding him. There was just a narrow patch of field where they ought to be out of sight of any of the German tanks. Behind Whitefield came Martin, with Dove bringing up the rear. James had not wanted the Firefly to hang back so had put it in the middle.

This was it. He held up his hands, and once the Sherman stopped, he clambered up the front and got into the turret.

'Baker Three to Three Able and Charlie. We're in dead ground here, but once we're past that tree they can see us. The Jerries are putting in another attack. There are twelve to fifteen hornets at seven hundred yards on our left, but they don't know we're here. So, we go fast. When I stop and turn left, you do the same. We'll be right on their flank. Give 'em five rounds of AP, and then clear off as fast as we can. Understood?'

The two sergeants acknowledged.

'Driver, advance, fast as you can.'

'Right, boss.'

'For what we are about to receive,' Thomson intoned.

The Sherman bumped as it raced at a good thirty miles an hour across the field. Whitefield always seemed able to coax the engines to give just a little more.

'Now, hard left!' *Hector II* slewed around.

'Shit,' Collins whispered, even though he had been told what to expect. At least a squadron's worth of Panthers were rolling forward to attack the Glamorgans. Yet for all his shock, he went mechanically about his task, training the gun even before James gave the fire orders. He stamped on the co-ax button and tracer winged its way towards one of the closest German tanks. It fell short, so he adjusted and once it was on the panzer he stamped the other button and the 75mm crashed out. Martin and the Charlie tank fired at the same moment, Dove slightly later.

James was counting in his head, and each shot felt like it took an age. The Germans were reacting, spreading out, some stopping, some turning the whole tank or just the turret towards the new threat. One was quicker off the mark than the rest and James watched as the high wheat parted in the wake of the speeding shell, which drove into the earth and sent up a spray of dirt about twenty yards in front of them.

Collins fired the fifth shot.

'Driver, hard left and get us out of here!'

Another AP round came at them, its glowing tip passing in between Martin's Firefly and James' Sherman. Then they were back out of sight.

'Skipper,' Whitefield began. 'I may have to warn you that that sort of thing is against the rules of the Drivers, Co-Drivers and Associated Workers' Union.'

'Thanks, I'll bear it in mind.'

Sergeant Dove interrupted negotiations. 'Three Able to Baker Three, permission to stay here. I think I can do some good, over.'

James hesitated before replying. Officers were supposed to be decisive and have all the answers, but he needed a moment.

'Baker Three to Three Able, please repeat request, over.'

'Three Able to Three Baker. Request permission to stay here. I can nip forward now and then and make life hard for them, over.'

'Permission granted, Three Able. But come when I call, we may need you. ... And watch out. Not sure they'll fall for it again, out.'

12.15 hrs, A Company's position in the five sided field

'Now that is an Uncle Target,' Buchanan said, his voice full of admiration. There was smoke rising in the distance, a sign of the deluge of big shells from the entire artillery of an Army Corps all coming down at once. They were hammering the German assembly areas and that was good, but not likely to give a quick result.

'Do you miss being a Gunner, sir?' Judd asked. His Platoon commander had stayed with him in the slit trench, because he 'might as well be here as anywhere else'. They had lifted Griffiths out, with considerably more respect than the German, but they had done it to give themselves space.

'That's an odd question, son. … No, no, it's not out of place. Just odd. Like, shouldn't you be an officer?'

'The Commissioning Board didn't think so, sir. RTU.' Judd chuckled at the memory – Returned to Unit did not seem to matter much now. 'They didn't like me saying no when they asked me whether I would always obey an order without question.'

'Really, they feared you were a mutinous dog out to spread revolution!'

'I said that it depended on the order. If someone told me to cover a doorway and shoot anyone who came out, and then a woman holding a baby appeared, of course I wouldn't obey!'

'Huh, Selection Boards.'

'Are they better in Canada, sir?'

'Coop' Buchanan gave a slow smile. 'Nope,' he said.

'Oh, you know about the nickname?'

'Yup.'

'And don't mind?'

'Some of the things officers get called are a lot worse. I served under a major known as Dickhead Dickens. 'Sides, I like Gary Cooper.' The lieutenant fished out a packet of cigarettes and offered one to Judd, who shook his head. 'No? Good for you. … You got a girl, Judd? Know you don't write to one.'

'No, not really.' Judd thought of Anne, of the handful of nights out, the few eager fumblings, where her eagerness wore off a lot faster than his and she made things very clear. Beautiful woman though – and maybe the smartest person he had ever met. 'No. One day, I hope. If we…' There was no point finishing the sentence.

'Yup.' Buchanan was silent for a while, enjoying his smoke. His eyes never stopped moving, although it did not take long to take in the tiny position held by 9 Platoon. 'You should have a family. Kids are just… well, they make everything have a point to it. Work, even the War, I guess.' He fished inside his tunic and produced a photograph of his wife and three children, one a babe in arms.

'Lovely children,' Judd said after looking for a moment. Most children looked alike to him, and these glared at the camera. 'And your wife is very beautiful.' That was not a lie, for she had dark eyes and a lively expression rare in photographs.

'Hey, you find your own girl!' Buchanan accepted the picture back, stared with fond reverence for a moment, and then stored it with great care. 'We want more kids one day. Maybe six or seven, even ten.' He sniffed. 'I guess Rosie does all the work, but she's as keen as I am.' He noticed Judd's expression. 'Yes, my wife's name is Rosemary and, yes, I used to be a Mountie. Will go back too – afterwards. But no, neither of us can sing worth a damn and her family is Irish not Indian.'

'You're very lucky, sir.'

'Coop' smiled. 'Yup,' he said.

A surge of mortar bombs made them hunch down. It was followed by tank engines, getting closer every moment. There were five Panthers driving past to their left, turret tops just visible over the hedge, dust spuming up from their wide tracks.

Then the Panthers turned and came at them. Up close their long guns reached over the hedge.

The PIAT team set up, launched a bomb which went off in the hedge without reaching the tank's thick armour. A moment later machine gun bullets smashed the gunner's face and spun his loader around. With a great flash a 75mm shell followed, the explosion ripping the men apart.

Another tank halted at the hedge, the gun depressed and it fired at such close range that the sounds merged into one. Three men from the forward section died in a moment as the HE went off inside their slit trench.

Buchanan had a smoke grenade and threw it. Holdworth was shouting, had another grenade in his hand, until he vanished as the shell scoured out their trench, pulverising the sergeant and the runner who was beside him. One moment they were there and the next they were gone.

'Get back!' Buchanan yelled at what was left of 9 Platoon. 'Back to the trees!'

Judd hesitated, not sure whether he was supposed to stay with the officer or let him go first.

'Goddammit, run!' 'Coop' shouted and pulled himself out of the trench.

Judd did not have his pack and did not stop to retrieve it. He grabbed Bessie the Bren, hauled the gun round and threw it out of the back of the trench. Then he climbed out and ran, grabbing the gun by its handle as he went, and ran on, the gun's butt bouncing against the grass. A shell exploded to his left, showering him with earth, the blast making him lurch sideways, and he dropped the Bren. Machine gun bullets, led by green tracer, flew towards him and he yelped like a child and ducked down, almost falling back into a trench again.

Judd ran. He did not look back, he certainly did not go back, and not enough of his mind was working to zigzag. Men he knew were running with him, in front, alongside and behind and no one even glanced at each other. They all sprinted, eyes wild, mouths open to gulp for air, aware of nothing save their terror and the drive to flee. Few still had weapons, none their small packs, and a fair few undid their belts and tried to pull off their webbing and pouches.

They swerved to the left, only because that way the trees were closest and they longed to hide.

'Stop! Form here!'

None of them heeded the voice, they just ran and ran, hearts pounding.

'Stop or I'll shoot!'

They still ran, and whoever was shouting at them did not open fire.

12.45 hrs, near B Company positions

Mark and his men had inched their way through the long field. They fired whenever they could. Bennett shot off all the HE rounds for the 2″ mortar and then started dropping the smoke rounds onto the enemy. Some of the German guns went silent. They began to move forward again, not the clear tactical bounds of training, but a crawl, some shooting, cowering in the dirt while hopefully someone else did some shooting, crawling again, and so on. Eventually they were no more than twenty-five yards from the enemy held hedge.

Sergeant Jenkins lobbed a couple of grenades with great precision – the man would be quite something in the outfield, Mark thought, then he could only wonder. For Jenkins stood up, Bren on a shoulder strap and held in both hands. He began to walk forward, firing short bursts as he went. Bullets zipped past him, over his head and into the ground at his feet. The sergeant kept walking, pumping rounds into the base of the hedgerow.

'Remember Albuera!' he shouted. 'Come on the Glams!'

Bennett was near to Mark and turned to stare at the officer. 'What the bloody hell is he doing?'

'Come on, boys!'

None of the boys got up, but they marvelled, and all who could fired as fast as they were able.

Jenkins was halfway to the hedge, still shouting, until the bolt simply clicked forward. The sergeant unclipped the empty magazine, dropped it and put another on, even giving it that little shake to make sure that it was properly in place. A stick grenade sailed over the hedge, but whoever had thrown it could not see or did not judge well for it went over the sergeant's head and came down well behind him, detonating with a soft boom.

The sergeant cocked the Bren gun and opened fire again, resuming his walk forward.

'Give me the gun,' Mark told Evans. He still refused to carry a Sten and his revolver was not likely to be much use.

'Sir?'

Mark grabbed it from him and felt his skin scorch because the barrel was hot. The boy's face showed annoyance and resentment, but none of this was real any longer.

Mark Crawford stood up. 'Come on!' he screamed at his men. Without looking to see if they obeyed, he jogged after the sergeant.

Jenkins was pushing his way through the hedge. He vanished, but Mark heard a few more shots from the Bren. He ran closer, tripping on a root so that he shoulder-charged the hedge. Battering it down with the gun and pushing with all his might, he managed to get through, at the cost of tears in his trousers. The sergeant was kneeling, covering the right, for this was a narrow field with another high hedge in front of them.

Jenkins glanced at him, then saw something. 'Behind you, sir!'

Mark turned. The panzer grenadiers had appeared from around a corner to the left. They were as surprised as he was, although he doubted that they could be as scared. He lowered the Bren, tucking the butt under his arm, and pulled the trigger. The gun hammered out a long burst, the muzzle leaping high so that he sprayed the air above the Germans' helmets. They turned and ran.

Jenkins bounded to his feet and ran after them. When he reached the corner he let off five rounds, breathed in, and gave them another two bursts. Then he strolled back.

'Got 'em,' he said in a matter of fact tone, but his face was gleaming with sheer joy. Mark found it unnerving.

'Better get the lads up,' the sergeant went on. 'Oh, and grab that empty mag I left in the field. We might need it.'

13.30 hrs, near B Company positions

Sergeant Dove was doing well, reporting over the net that he had knocked out a Mark IV and an SP. As far as James could tell, the sergeant and his Sherman were still unscathed, lurking in the dead ground, then sneaking forward to make hit and run attacks on the enemy.

Three Able was doing a grand job, but was still out on his own, so when the order came for 3 Troop to help out B and D Companies of the Glamorgans, there were just the two tanks to answer the call. The problem was a few German machine guns, ensconced in the hedges at the corner of the field and keeping everyone's heads down. All the attempts to suppress them had failed, for they were a small target for mortars and the guns must have been so dug in to the bank beneath the hedge that they were not much troubled by small arms.

Of all people, Mark was the one sent to show James the target, not that there was time to say much. The infantry subaltern led him, crawling to keep below a fold in the ground, until they could just peek over the edge and James could see the target. The crawl back seemed to take an age, and all the muscles in James' legs, arms and belly ached in protest. After that he had to work out the best route for his tanks to take. There were a lot of panzers out there, and even if the range was long, one hit from a German gun was usually all it took to brew a Sherman. B Squadron had been able to make good use of a decent position and plenty of cover to snipe at the panzers and hold them back. Even so, two Shermans had been brewed, one burning so quickly that no one had got out.

It all took time, and meant cowering from the mortar bombs plopping down every now and again, but eventually James came up with a plan. Mark waved him goodbye and crawled back towards his men, who were frantically digging in next to B Company.

James led, and not simply because he did not altogether trust

Sergeant Martin to go forward with the necessary boldness. The Firefly carried HE, but no one thought much of the shell. This really was a job for an ordinary Sherman, and *Hector II* was the only one he had. Whitefield raced them forward. At the start they had shelter from a fold in the ground, then a high hedge, a gap, a cluster of trees, another longer gap, before turning and coming up three hundred yards from the machine gun nest. Collins hosed the hedge and then sent three HE shells into it.

Martin had not joined them.

'Three Charlie to Baker, there is a hornet nine zero zero yards to your flank. Am engaging, out.' James heard the crash of the big gun, and as they belted back the way they had come noticed that the Firefly had barely advanced into the open at all.

14.45 *hrs, B and D Company positions*

Mark had the benefit of a deep trench, dug by B Company. One of the previous occupants was still there, a corporal with half his head missing, the flies crawling over his exposed brains and blood no matter what Mark did. Evans shared the trench, but the boy had gone forward, taking a bandolier of .303 ammunition over to men from B Company. Mark was busy filling a Bren magazine, clipping in one bullet after another. When a couple were ready, he would wait for a quiet moment and then dash across to his forward section to hand them over. He had given them the Bren that he and Evans had used to bolster their firepower. Jenkins seemed inclined to keep the one he had.

The magazine was full and he slid it into a haversack, so that it would be easier to carry. All of D Company was now forward in support of the remnants of B. C Company had taken a pounding and been forced back, but was still holding on just in front of the village. A Company was gone. Now and then he spared a moment to hope that Judd was alright, but he really did not have much time for thought.

Mark sat with his back to the rear of the trench and then straightened up, easing his head above the lip. He had found that this was better than peering out at the front. Less of his head was exposed and he could see more. A figure, the slight figure of Evans, dashed from one trench and dived into another. He was on his way back and would be here soon. There were a lot of panzers half a mile in front of them, dotted around the wheatfields in a seemingly haphazard manner. More, a dozen more at least, were swinging around their left flank at a similar distance and others were on their right. They fired when the mood took them, machine guns and HE. More Spandaus joined in, shot by infantry sneaking around in the hedges and fields. The Glamorgans fired back when they could, not that it seemed to matter much.

The Royal Artillery was saving them. Hour after hour, hundreds of guns answered the call and savaged the fields ahead of them. A few times they came in right in front and once on top of the position when a wave of grenadiers had been on the point of overrunning them. It had felt like the end of the world, the violence and heat of the explosions so appalling that Mark was left numb, struggling to breathe, let alone think.

Yet they were still here. No doubt the Germans would keep coming, but as long as the guns kept slaughtering them then the Glamorgans might just hold on. If any of them were left. The Germans had guns of their own and mortars too, and if they lacked the numbers and the inexhaustible supply of shells of the Allies, they were still deadly.

Mark watched as Evans sprang out of the trench and raced over to dive into this one.

'Well done, lad,' he told him. A few second later a shell went smartly into the slit trench the boy had just left and erupted in flame and thick black smoke. The two men in it had no chance. Mark wondered whether there had been time for fear or for pain before they were turned into so much offal. The corpses he had seen in the last weeks, the men with stomachs turned inside out, bodies torn, crushed by shells or flattened by tanks, were not like the paintings or even the photographs you saw. To be frank they looked filthy, untidy, even vile desecrations of life. He struggled to believe that such piles of dung could ever contain a soul.

16.55 hrs, near Battalion HQ

The survivors of 9 Platoon and the rest of A Company were gathered at Battalion and told to rest in the holes vacated by D Company. There were not many left, although rumour said that some had made it over to the Scottish Borderers. By some grim chance, there were nine men left from 9 Platoon. There had been ten, but one man, a grim faced, tough as old boots Newport man, had collapsed into tears. He had huddled up on the floor, sobbing and sobbing, until eventually they had led him away for the MO to give him a shot of something. Judd was glad, not for the man himself, but because he was worried that if he heard him for much longer then he would join in.

'He might be alright in a day or two,' Buchanan told the others, before heading off to find them weapons and equipment to replace what had been lost.

Judd wondered whether the man would ever be alright again.

Some of the Quartermaster's minions appeared with a caddy and poured out mug after steaming mug. Judd drank greedily, almost choked, but managed to keep it down. There must have been some tea with the rum, but not very much. He drained it to the last dregs and felt warmer inside. His throat was burning.

On the wind came the smell of flames and burning, lots of it, with the chemical odour he remembered all too well. A troop of Churchill Crocodiles had come up to support the Glamorgans. Somehow or other, the Germans had been held, and now the battalion was counter attacking to retake the lost ground. The colonel appeared, did a quick scan of the remnants of A Company, and went on his way.

A little later, someone else came up asking for volunteers to help the stretcher bearers. Judd's mind desperately wanted to say yes, but his mouth would not speak any sound and his legs refused to move. He stared at nothing, and the man went away without any help.

After a while, Judd fell asleep.

D+28, Tuesday 4th July

THE GLAMORGANS WERE going forward and once again Mark was with a party sent to familiarise themselves with the positions they would occupy. This battalion had an air of competence about them, helped because most of their positions were on the reverse slope of a ridge and not under direct observation of the enemy. It really was a pleasant sensation to be able to walk about in daylight without fear of snipers or shells.

That changed as they went forward to the advance positions and listening posts on the forward slope. Most were hidden by groups of trees, but at one point they all had to crawl for a good way. The grass was wet from the rain, so they ended up damp and muddy. Still, this all gave the impression of being a better spot than many, and that would make a nice change.

Mark was tired, but still found it easier to concentrate than he had in the early days. He had a better sense of what mattered and what did not, so saved his energy for the former. All in all, he reckoned that he had a good sense of the position. The occupying battalion were dismissive of the infantry regiment facing them, and that impression was reinforced when a few prisoners were brought in, wearing ill-fitting uniforms and defeated expressions. One was wounded in the leg and lying in a wheelbarrow pushed by the other three. After a brief interrogation, a corporal herded them back to Brigade, setting out a little before the advance party of the Glamorgans went back along the main path through the woods.

A Sten gun gave its distinctive tinny clatter somewhere fairly, but not too close, by. As Mark and the others reached the carriers, the corporal came back towards them, pushing the empty wheelbarrow. His helmet was tilted right back on his head and he was smoking a cigarette with an expression of deep contentment on his face. A Sten gun was slung from his shoulder.

No one said anything, and Mark did not break ranks. Other battalions were strangers, families who might bicker with each other, but closed ranks against outsiders. Apart from that, he had not seen anything. There was a chance that the corporal had found someone else to take the prisoners all the way back, and a chance that the burst of fire had had nothing to do with him. Mark's conscience insisted that neither was very likely. He did not listen to it, and was more worried about getting something to eat before they brought the Glamorgans up to this position.

19.30 hrs, near Bayeux

James sat in the farmhouse being used as a Mess and refilled his glass of wine. He was drinking a lot, far more than ever before, although he resisted the ferocious Calvados, the stuff the Normans laughingly called cider. A thimbleful of that would have him on his back, snoring away. The wine tasted better and was gentler in the oblivion it offered.

The 165th RAC were back from the front, but no one seemed to know for how long. There was certainly no sign of the Germans packing it in any time soon. It was good to be out of the turret, and it was good to be clean and dry for as long as it lasted.

James drank deeply and soon the glass was empty again.

D+30, Thursday 6th July

JUDD SIPPED AT his coffee. It was pretty good, better than he had expected after all the tales of rationing in Occupied France. Perhaps the 21st Army Group had brought it with them, or, if they were really sensible, had swapped something with the Americans to get a supply, and then someone had done a deal with the café owner. The sheer scale and surely the cost of the War often astounded him. So did the amount of waste and corruption.

Months and months ago in another life, he had been sent to a depot after failing the Commissioning Board. It was full of the sort of characters drawn to those places, and while all he was expected to do was fetch and carry, he had found that he was involved in something. One night, he was sent out with an old sweat and a three-tonner packed to the gills with boxes. They'd gone well out of camp, to a garage in a village, where another pair of soldiers were waiting. Most of the cargo went into a couple of sheds, some into a civilian van. Money changed hands, bundles of big white five-pound notes. He was offered his share. He declined. The mood turned ugly, and one of the men picked up the handle of a pickaxe. They wanted to know if he was going to report them.

The thought had never crossed his mind. School life had drummed into him that sneaking was a hideous crime, never to be contemplated or forgiven. He said he was not a grass, since sneak did not seem the right word for this company. He would say nothing and wanted nothing. Told them it would bring bad luck, and with the Invasion coming he needed all the luck he could get. They believed him, at least for the moment, and fortunately his posting came and he was out of the camp by the next afternoon. The rogues had probably whipped a dozen more lorryloads since then or were doing time in the glasshouse. Either way he did not care.

Judd leaned back on his chair, another great sin at prep school, at least as far as the masters were concerned. The Sun on this glorious day was hot and it felt good on his face. He noticed the silence after a while, for he had not really being paying any attention. Mark Crawford was doing most of the work, chattering away, anxious to please, and sharing all the news he could.

'Thinking profound thoughts, William?' James Taylor asked. 'Of the sort only those of exalted rank dare even to contemplate, while we mere mortals slink about in the shadows.'

Lance Corporal Judd smiled. 'No, I was just thinking that it was a lovely day and this coffee is good.'

'Wisdom, Mark, do you hear it? Only the deepest thinkers understand the simple things with such clarity.'

'Aristotle and me,' Judd said, crossing his fingers. 'We're like that, only I'm the smart one.'

'Modest too,' Mark said. 'I shall have to guard my laurels. Today a mere lance jack, but surely with a marshal's baton in his backpack!'

Bill Judd smiled with them. He was still not used to the change. A few days ago he had run away and been scared out of his wits and the response was to promote him. Well, not really promote, as lance corporal was an appointment not a formal rank, bringing a little extra responsibility, very little authority and absolutely no increase in pay. Now he was 'Corp' to a section, most of whom were complete strangers.

An immaculately uniformed captain glared at them as

he walked past, no doubt on some vital and dangerous duty known only to the service corps. Bayeux was full of them, mostly British, a few Canadian, some American and goodness knows what. The supporting arms, the British Liberation Army's administrators and lawyers and trick cyclists. There were also the soldiers, a different breed altogether, whether the many still waiting to go into action, but knowing that it was coming, or the rest, who had seen action and survived so far.

This particular example evidently disapproved of two officers sharing a table with an Other Rank and treating him as an equal. No doubt it was prejudicial to good discipline.

James stood up and raised his glass of wine. 'My dear fellow, will you join us? This is Mark Mignon of the Free French Women, and this is my twin brother, Augustus Dobbin, who is with the Secret Service and very hush, hush. He has just been decorated for cleaning windows under fire. He is really my identical twin, but he's in disguise.'

The captain stood there, blinking.

'And I,' James added, flourishing his glass and spilling half the contents over the others, 'am the Count of Monte Cristo, at your service.' He bowed and lost most of the rest.

'You're mad,' the captain said at last. 'But good luck to you. Good luck to you all.' He strode away.

'Jolly good, cheeri-jolly-o!' James called after him. He was only on his third glass, but was acting like some of Judd's men when they had been given Calvados by a farmer – or at least, how they acted before they passed out.

'Don't think he meant any harm,' Mark said, his face concerned.

James' expression was belligerent. 'Well bugger him. Why couldn't he have the courtesy to be a proper Blimp rather than a decent enough fellow in his way. ... Prick,' he added, after a moment.

This was not the old friend, captain of the cricket team and aspiring writer that Bill Judd remembered. He had bumped into the other two in the street, and they had pressed him to join them. Up until this moment the mood had been light, filled with laughter and far from the War.

'Garcon!' Mark called to the waiter. 'Two more glasses... I mean deux tas, no not tas, what's glass, oh hell...' He held up his own glass and raised two fingers of the other hand. 'Do you want another coffee, Bill? No. You sure?'

Judd beckoned to the waiter and explained that a demi-bouteille would be fine.

'Oh well, if you're going to remember your vocab,' Mark said airily. 'You know that's just showing off.'

James was clenching and unclenching his left hand, but his face was less tense. He had definitely changed, even more than Mark and – Judd guessed – himself. A line from the book *Winged Victory* came to mind, about seeing a young battalion commander out with his officers. Something like, 'he had worked in a bank before the war, and looked like he would be robbing them afterwards.' James had always seemed a gentle, generous soul, competitive as the next man on the pitch, and as kind as summer the rest of the time. As far as he could remember, James Taylor never had a scrap at school, because his charm and good nature meant that he had never needed to fight.

Now, there was no doubt that he could fight. He had been at it longer than the others, not that time really seemed to matter anymore.

'Sorry,' James said at last, as if noticing them for the first time. 'Shockingly bad form. I think I've just got used to sorting out all my problems with a few rounds of HE or a belt from the Browning.' He shrugged. 'Come on, Mark, there must be news from home. Someone's cat had kittens, that sort of thing... tell us all the sordid details, whether the tabby or the black tomcat is the seducer.'

'Afraid not, the doings of the feline population have escaped my correspondents. Oh, I hear that some blackguard called Jim

Taylor has got engaged to Miss Penelope Stevens, spinster of this parish.'

James touched his nose with a finger. 'Yes, man's a scoundrel and no mistake. Probably *had* to pop the question. ... No, that's in poor taste. Scrub that.'

'Many congratulations,' Judd said, reaching over to shake his hand. 'That really is wonderful.'

'Doesn't seem real, to be honest.'

'Well,' Mark went on, sensing that James did not wish to say more, 'the other set of banns is rather more disappointing to Messrs Crawford and Judd – have you heard that Anne Saunders is engaged to a Yank?'

'No. Ah well.' Judd was not really surprised. He had known that his prospects there were not good. Even a year or two in age was a big gap when the girl was the older one. That was hard to bridge, and it was not as if he had had much to offer. 'Bravo the Yank. He'll have his hands full.'

'Dear, dear, my boy, you're getting vulgar!' James said. He had filled his glass and was already close to doing so again. His words were starting to slur. 'She's a big girl, and no mistake. She's in the Wrens, of course, and this joke is about the ATS, but I am sure it applies. Do you know what sizes ATS brassieres come in?'

'I fear such information has escaped me,' Bill Judd replied.

James beamed at them. He was performing and no mistake. Judd guessed that they all were in different ways. They pretended not to be frightened so that everyone else thought that they were the only one and somehow you all kept going. This was James pretending to be the brash young cavalry officer.

'Do you give up? What about you, Mark?'

'No idea.'

'Well, it seems they have five sizes, and the QM takes a look at the girl and chooses – Small, Medium, Large, Great Scott and Good God!'

They laughed politely, not that James seemed to notice. He stood up. 'I need to commune with nature,' he announced. 'Dear God, this stuff goes through you.'

After he had gone, Judd leaned over to Mark. 'Think you had better get him home.' They had talked of all going to an ENSA concert, but their friend was unlikely to be in any sort of state for that.

Mark nodded. 'His regiment is in a rest camp, like us, but I think they have been trying to give him a longer break. Said there was a chance he might be sent back to England on a course.'

'Good.'

'You'd think so, but he says he can't leave. Not so soon, and not when others have to stay.' Mark lowered his voice. 'If you ask me, I think he desperately wants to, and that's why he can't go. From some of what he said before we ran into you, he feels so responsible for his troop. Guess it's the decisions you make. Tell a man to go there and he walks right into a shell – or right away from one. It's... Well, I don't know.'

Mark had changed too, more than Judd had realised. The old Mark would not even have thought like that, let alone said it.

'Sorry about Anne,' Judd said to change the subject. There was not much to be gained by talking about such things. 'If it's any consolation, whenever I took her out, she spent half the time asking about you.'

'Ah well, if only it had been three-quarters of the time, I might have been in with a chance. Still, if I'd got the news back in England, I think I would have been heartbroken. Out here... well, out here it doesn't seem to matter so much, not really. It doesn't seem real... Not that I think I'll go back and sweep her up in my arms, not that. It's just all of it – home, pretty girls, all that. It's not real anymore. Maybe one day.'

Judd smiled and raised his almost empty cup. 'Here's to maybe!'

'Carousing, I see!' James declared as he came back. 'Rough

and licentious soldiery in the very flesh. ... And it's so good to see you both!'

Judd had got used to drunks since joining the Army, but was happy to let Mark manage their friend. He bade them farewell and wandered off around the streets. Soldiers and vehicles were everywhere, and there were a few military lasses among them, nurses and clerks. Like the civilian females, they were always the centre of attention in the great crowds of men. Bayeux was bustling, a sea of khaki with the shoulder flashes, headgear and cap badges of dozens of regiments and corps. It was strange how even men desperate for a rest took the trouble to tart themselves up before actually taking it. Maybe their units insisted, but Judd had taken great care with his appearance, sewing all the badges onto his newly issued battledress tunic. No one had told him to do it, although he suspected that they probably would if he had not got on with it. He did not need to be told, just did it, out of habit. It showed how much the Army had got its claws into him – into all of them really.

He bumped into Davison, the Port Talbot lad, and just afterwards they met Douglas, late of the International Brigade, as he came back past a long queue heading for a house showing a red light.

'Might need to see the MO when I get back,' he told them. 'Got a light?' Davison obliged, and lit another for himself. Judd declined. 'Times like that I miss old Cornelius, the miserable git.' In spite of fighting on opposing sides, there had been a bond between the two veterans of Spain, and now and again they had gone off together on a long debauch.

They explained that they were going to the show and Douglas fell in with them. Off duty, on the closest thing to leave likely during the campaign, the three men walked in step without even noticing. So did almost all the other groups that went by.

The show was the usual, with the inevitable bawdy comedian, the old dear playing an accordion, some magic tricks, and a couple of big-thighed dancing girls, who did a lot of high kicks and not a lot else. It did not matter, for the audience was happy to ogle their legs.

Apart from the accordion there was a piano, played by a gap-toothed man who looked like a defrocked vicar. Not that the quality mattered. It never did. The Army loved its concerts, and most of the time found willing volunteers or men who could be volunteered. Bill Judd had committed grievous bodily harm to several Rob Wilton monologues in his time, and fluffed his lines in a performance of *The Ghost Train*.

There were three singers, none of them familiar names, although rumour said that George Formby was coming in a week or so. A tenor was first, immensely fat in spite of years of rationing, and with a decent, if overstrained voice. He kept it all sentimental and the rows of soldiers loved that. A little later there was a torch singer in a slinky red dress slit high at the sides, and she put on an American accent and flirted with them as she belted out 'Begin the Beguine' and 'Over the Rainbow' and the like. She even did 'Long Ago and Far Away' to be up to date. They loved it and whistled and waved their caps in the air.

Just before the whole cast assembled for the finale, a young lass came out. She must have been old enough to be allowed to join ENSA, but looked sixteen or even less. The audience went quiet. She sang simple songs so full of sentiment as to be saccharine, some very English and some the Deanna Durbin stuff. They were rapt, unmoving, absolutely quiet. When she finished with 'Beneath the Lights of Home', Douglas was sobbing into his hands and he was not the only one. This was a taste of something different, something hard to define and something many, even most, had never really known, except that it was not the War or anything to do with it. As the last note faded away from the girl's rather thin voice, they cheered and stamped for more. She seemed almost embarrassed as she did a little curtsey, her face reddening, eyes modestly down, like everyone's favourite little sister.

Afterwards, with half an hour still to go before the lorries came to take them back to camp, Douglas declared that he was off to dip his wick again and asked if they wanted to come. Davison checked his watch and said no. So did Judd, although he wondered whether the temptation would have been stronger were it not for the concert.

'Please yourselves,' Douglas told them, 'but it might be your last chance.'

He ran up just as the trucks were ready to depart about half an hour later, with a cheerful, 'Anyone got a fag?'

They drove back to where the Glamorgans were camped. It was not far, only a couple of miles, but everywhere was so crowded that it took an hour. Even compared to when they had come ashore, the Normandy countryside overflowed with lorries and tanks, and guns and carriers, and half-tracks and jeeps, and ammunition dumps and fuel dumps and supply dumps, and everywhere soldiers. The front had not advanced to keep pace with the flow coming off the ships.

'Bastards will have us at it again soon,' Davison said with all the gloom so relished by the South Walian.

D+34, Monday 10th July

05.00 hrs, the Odon Valley, north of Hill 112

THE SUN WAS a red ball in the east, setting the sky and clouds afire in reds and pinks so wonderful that to see it was to feel all the joy and sadness of the world. It was a sunrise so perfect that if any painter had possessed the genius to capture every aspect of it, then the eye would not accept it and dismiss it all as false and exaggerated.

On the dot, over one thousand British guns boomed out onto preregistered targets on the south side of the valley. There were twenty-five-pounders of the field artillery, hundreds of them and by far the majority of the shells flying against the enemy. Then there were the 4.5″ mediums, which threw a round more than twice the weight, and the 5.5″ guns whose shell was four times as heavy. Yet the sea was still not so very far away, so that HMS *Rodney* added 16″ shells weighing some two thousand pounds to the avalanche falling onto where the Allies believed the Germans were hiding.

'Christ,' Private Kennedy said, staring open mouthed, and shading his eyes with his hand.

The ground shook, the air seemed to throb and the senses were dulled by the sheer noise of so many missiles being hurled over their heads.

Davison drew in on his cigarette, his back against a low wall, and made it clear that he was unimpressed.

'How can anything live under that?' 'Nobby' Clarke asked.

Davison indulged himself with a derisive sniff. 'Just be glad we're in reserve, boyo.'

Along a wide stretch of the Odon, a new offensive was starting, but for the moment, the other two battalions of the brigade were to lead and they were to support. The word was that they were unlikely to go in that morning, and perhaps not until tomorrow.

'Is that smoke?' Kennedy asked. They were on the edge of the concentration area for the Glamorgans, on the lip of a hill, and able to see across to where the barrage was landing.

'No, it's bloody snow!' Davison snapped. 'Where the 'ell did they find you lot? Course it's bloody smoke. The poor sods will be going in soon. Sit down, bach, for God's sake. You too, Nobby, you're noisier than the ruddy guns!'

The two men sat, and tried to appear as disinterested as Judd, Davison and the other old hands, who were doing their best to make it seem that they had seen all this before. In truth, Judd was almost as much in awe as the youngsters. The barrage before their first attack had been big, but this was much bigger. If the smoke and dust drifted this far, it would probably blot out the Sun and make it feel cold. He'd heard men say that when the RAF had bombed Caen a few days ago that it had felt like winter in the gloom when the dust cloud hid the Sun. The north of the city was finally in British hands, more than a month after D-Day and after pulverising half the streets.

Since Rauray, the Glamorgans had reorganised. All the remaining LoB men had been brought up as replacements, along with dozens from other regiments, who were hastily issued with a new cap badge. Even so, there simply were not enough riflemen to replace the losses because every other unit committed was losing men at a similar rate. Rather than have very small companies, Dorking-Jones decided to go down from four to three, A Company ceasing to exist for the moment and the men reinforcing the others. Buchanan's 9 Platoon was now in D Company, although sticking resolutely to its former number. Judd was in charge of 3 Section, with Davison as the only other experienced man. In addition, he had Clarke and Protheroe with the Bren, and Kennedy and Button as riflemen. All were new and seemed so very young.

Judd wondered whether he should try to teach them as much as he could, even at this late stage, but decided against it. It would probably worry more than it could help, and the main thing he had learned was that luck meant more than anything else. Buchanan was a good officer, and they were fortunate to have him. The other two sections were similar in size and composition. They still did not have a 2″ mortar, nor a PIAT of their own, although 'Coop' said that a team was bringing one from HQ Company. There were twenty men in 9 Platoon, the last being newly promoted Sergeant Reade, the 'Rusty' Reade of long charge sheets and frequent desertion, who had turned up before they embarked and proved himself a superb soldier ever since.

'Get some breakfast, lads,' Reade told them, going round the platoon. 'Be a long day, like as not, and best to be fed. Eat all you can, and when you're not hungry, eat some more. You'll need it.' His skin, sallow to begin with, and lined by a hard and angry life, never really seemed clean, and his teeth were yellow. Reade was not an easy man to like, and Judd wondered whether he had been sent to Buchanan because they thought the Canadian was tough enough to keep him in hand.

'Corporal Judd.'

'Yes, sarn't.'

'Take two men and collect some more grenades. Shift your arse and get going.'

'Yes, sarn't.' Judd turned and looked around him. 'Protheroe, Button, come with me.'

It was odd to give an order, or even pass a simple one like this.

They went, the two newcomers chattering excitedly. They walked past Mark Crawford's 17 Platoon and 18 Platoon commanded by CSM Wentworth. Before they could get back a single shot rang out. Someone from C Company had shot themselves in the left hand.

17.00 hrs, in an Observation Post half a mile north of Hill 112

The attack had stalled. All along the line battalions had gone forward at H-Hour, hugging the barrage as closely as they could, with Churchill tanks in support. They walked into a devastated land of craters and fallen trees. Direct hits on German trenches left corpses and pieces of corpses scattered around. Yet not all the Germans were dead or wounded or driven insane by the deluge of shells. They had roofed their dugouts with timber and several feet of earth, and for all the horror, a good few were still there when the barrage lifted. Spandaus were raised back into place, the belts checked, the bolts drawn back and then driven forward again, and as soon as the dark shadows appeared in the smoke, the machine guns began to scythe them down. Rifles cracked, mortars soon added their bombs, the artillery was called down and reinforcements went forward to meet the attack.

The British plodded on. In the smoke, men got lost, and more often went past German dugouts without realising. Suddenly, groups of men found themselves being shot at from the rear as well as the front. Nearly all of one platoon was killed or wounded when a salvo from a battery of 5.5s dropped short and fell directly on them.

There was progress, but it was slow. Every field, every ravaged wood and orchard, every little house of every little village had to be fought for, then fought for again as the inevitable counter attacks came in. They were taken, lost, taken again, perhaps lost again, as the battered houses were reduced to ruin and units of both sides withered in the storm.

'That's it, gentlemen, Hill 112,' Dorking-Jones told the O Group of his Company commanders, the indispensable gunners, and tankmen from B Squadron of the 165ᵗʰ RAC. James was one of the latter, as was Colonel Tim, and everyone felt better with him back in charge. All of them had come forward to an OP close to the HQ of one of the leading battalions. Two units had been sent to seize the hill, and the closest either had managed to get was some five hundred yards before the sheer weight of German fire pinned them down.

'They've had the lot thrown at them,' Dorking-Jones explained. 'Moaning Minnies, mediums, mortars, SPs, tanks – a lot of Tigers, the absolute lot. Mostly Tenth SS Panzer Div., but some of those blighters from the Twelfth SS as well.

'Well, don't matter who they are. They're tough little swine, we all know that, and you have to dig them out one by one or blow them to pieces or bury them.

'However, Div. reckons that the attacks today have drawn in all the reinforcements in this neck of the wood. Give them a night and there'll be more, because you can bet your life the devils will be rushing everything to the spot as we speak. But that means that we have a chance, a moment where we can go in and grab the high ground. That's where we come in. The Glamorgans are to advance and take Hill 112 and then hold it.'

The sound of fighting was constant in the background and some came from not very far away, but even so James felt that the group had gone quiet. This was the first day of Operation Jubilee – and why did they come up with such strange names? There was not much to celebrate so far. Codenames for all the places were towns and cities this time, and there was even a Cardiff among them, although he was not sure anyone would get that far.

Hill 112 had not changed very much in a couple of weeks. There were still the same open fields sloping gently up, the Roman road running through the middle. James focused his glasses on the crossroads and could see that the little shrine was still there. Yet the fields were pockmarked with a few craters, and there were lines through the high wheat where it had been flattened by tank tracks. The tanks were still up there as well, burned out hulks of Shermans, Churchills and panzers. He could not quite work out which one had been Keith's – things did not look quite the same from down here, but the ground had not changed, and there was still the orchard and the smaller groups of trees.

'H-Hour is twenty-thirty hundred hours,' Dorking-Jones continued, starting to go into details.

'Sorry, but my lads are unlikely to get here in time,' Tim Leyne said. 'Sorry to cut in, but when I say unlikely, I mean that it is impossible. Not through all the traffic.' The colonel lifted the bandage over his eye and adjusted it. James had noticed that he did it quite often. Only B Squadron was attached to the Glamorgans, so strictly speaking there was no reason for Leyne to be here. However, they all knew that since a tank troop was usually attached to an infantry company and a squadron to a battalion, the senior officer of the tanks was bound to be junior to his infantry counterpart. Infantrymen often did not understand, and wanted foolish, unreasonable things, so James guessed that the colonel had come up to put their case more forcefully.

Dorking-Jones rubbed his chin. 'Can't be helped.' He turned to his adjutant. 'John, get on to Brigade and see if the RTR can spare us a few Churchills in the meantime. I'll speak to the brig once you get him.' He sighed. 'When do you think your lads can get here, Tim?'

Leyne considered for a moment. 'At best twenty-one hundred, more certainly twenty-one thirty.'

James felt a chill. This whole plan seemed foolhardy, flinging one battalion at the key piece of high ground in the area and expecting the Germans to let them take it – and then to let them hold on to it. This was getting close to Charge of the Light Brigade stuff, especially for the Glamorgans. Poor Mark and

Bill were in for it in no uncertain terms. At least B squadron would not be going with them in the first charge. Still, arriving late was only a little better. James did not relish being stranded on those open slopes in the dark, with the panzer grenadiers creeping around. Dear God, it was not much better in the day, with the long guns picking you off one by one.

He should have gone home. They'd given him the chance – an honourable chance, if so archaic a word was not absurd. He knew that it wasn't, not to him, or not to the man he had thought he was. There was a posting to a training unit, and he could have gone back and been with Penny and her devoted attention. They could marry and he could follow Keith's example and do 'it' – often and with great enthusiasm judging from her letters. Plenty of men would be happy with less.

He could not go. He knew his nerve was going. It was alright in action, but afterwards there was the soul searching, the dissection of every mistake, and the dreams, the constant, terrifying dreams in which he saw again every death and lived his own, time and time again, trapped in a burning tank, smashed by AP, cut down my mortars or machine guns.

The padre had seen it all that time ago. It must be obvious to everyone by now. Sweet Jesus, he had got drunk three times in as many days. He had never been drunk in his entire life before those couple of days back with the B echelon to help with the reorganisation. He was falling apart, moment by moment, and it could not go on forever. Mark had told him that the Glamorgans had just received a brace of second lieutenants who had been told that their life expectancy was two weeks. That sounded optimistic, for a tankman as much as an infantryman.

James knew that he was going to die or he was going to crack up – and soon. Perhaps today, perhaps tomorrow. If he stayed alive then the mental collapse was all the more assured. What would Penny think of him if he came home a gibbering failure, terrified of loud noises? What would he think of himself?

He should have swallowed his pride and gone. He should.

Except, he could not. Then Colonel Tim had reappeared and casually asked whether he would do him a personal favour and turn down the posting to stay with the regiment. They were short of good officers, desperately short. You could not really say no to a man who had discharged himself from hospital and wangled his way back to France to resume command of the regiment before someone was sufficiently organised to replace him. On top of that there was Dove, and Whitefield and Collins, and all the rest. He had to go on for their sakes and because they had no choice. No one was offering them a cushy billet back home.

James had come back to B Squadron, and the officer's seat and the cupola of *Hector II* felt like home – and the stinking depths of a death house.

Eventually, after detailed discussion with the gunners, the O Group came to an end. Dorking-Jones had secured the assistance of a troop of Churchills from the RTR if they were available. The gunners were more definite, and, if it would lack the awful splendour of the morning, were still able to promise a heavy weight of fire on the objective and in support afterwards.

'Well, there is a lot to do. May God grant us the victory.' Dorking-Jones did not notice, or at least pay any attention to, the raised eyebrows of a few of the others. Presumably he was a religious man. James reckoned that they could do with all the help they could get. The Divisional commander had said that they must go, so goeth they would.

'Gentlemen, I know this won't be easy,' Dorking-Jones concluded, head turning around the group to stare each one straight in the eyes. 'But we're going to do it anyway, and ruddy well win!'

20.30 hrs, start line at the foot of Hill 112

The guns began to pummel the treelines just visible at the top of the slope. There was no sign of the Churchills, but there was a battery of Bofors anti-aircraft guns lobbing 40mm rounds at the treeline with a steady thump, thump, thump. There were also Vickers machine guns, shooting high so that their bullets would fall as rain on the far side of the hill, and add an extra risk to anyone moving around there.

The Glamorgans waited behind a hedge and down in a gully close to the front line reached by the other battalions earlier in the day. Then they went through the gaps or forced their way through the hedge if they could not, crossed the road running east to Caen, and began the long walk. C Company led on the left, B Company on the right, with D in reserve, and HQ in the middle.

Mark had been close enough to hear Dorking-Jones as he called Brigade to say 'Bacon', which indicated that they were ready, and then receive the reply 'Eggs' to begin. Then the artillery and mortars drowned out everything. He saw officers open their mouths to shout and saw the hand signals that actually got everyone moving. Then he waited for them all to move off, counting in his head before turning to watch Major Fletcher, OC of D Company. HQ was already on the move.

Fletcher brought his arm down, several times, signalling for them to go.

'Come on!' Mark shouted, and 17 Platoon were close enough to hear. They stood up and began to walk forward, the hedge easy to cross because so many men had pushed through it.

Ahead of them was nothing, just wide, wide fields of golden wheat with not a shred of cover, and dotted around it the figures of the Glamorgans trudging forward, step by step. They hugged close to the barrage, rounds exploding so close that clods of earth and little bits of shrapnel fell among them. Sometimes men were knocked over onto their backs, only to rise and start plodding on up the slope. There was smoke and dust in the air, so that it was gloomy even though the Sun was still up, and away from all this would be casting long shadows.

Mark and 17 Platoon were on the left, with the CSM's 18

Platoon on the right, and Buchanan – and Bill Judd – supporting, so that the company mirrored the battalion's deployment, if on a smaller scale. Mark had acquired a rifle, still refusing to carry a Sten gun, but wanting to have something a bit more useful than a revolver. He carried thirty loose rounds, because it was not really his job to shoot.

The wheat was high, and where it had not been trampled it came up to his chest and sometimes made it hard to see very far. Smoke blanketed the top of the hill, so with the explosions of the main barrage, there was not a great deal to see apart from the Glamorgans plodding step by step up the slope. Unless you looked closely, it could easily have been a scene from the Great War. From what he understood of the plan, it was not a great deal more hopeful, save that the skill of the gunners was great, and the science at their disposal made them a good deal more powerful than their predecessors.

Odd how a slow walk could make you tired. This was hardly a steep slope, not like some they had gone up in training or the hills they used to climb after taking the train up to the Brecon Beacons when they were young. Funny having Judd here, just like the old days, and since the 165th were supposed to support them later he might see James as well. Poor James, he had clearly been having a rough time of it.

The leading companies were halfway there now. Hard to think of James getting married – and to Penelope Stevens. Pretty enough, beautiful maybe, but so insipid. Mark liked poetry as much as the next man, but, well, good poetry. He did not believe it was all true either.

Another step and another. The men were going steadily. More than half were new, strangers really, since so few came from the regiment. Seemed good though. No need to encourage them, they were coming on like the rest; maybe even quicker than the men who did know what was to come.

Smoke erupted from the ground where B Company was advancing. A man dropped his rifle, raised his arm theatrically and slowly spun around before falling into the wheat. Just like something out of an old movie – not quite real, and at this distance lacking any sense of violence about it. Mortar bomb though. Bound to be more soon.

Another step, pushing the high crop aside and almost tripping as it caught around his foot. On again, another step. God this was hard work. Like climbing a ruddy mountain.

A row of mortar bombs went diagonally through B Company – one, two, three, four. Men dropped – dead, maimed, sheltering. Machine guns spat yellow-green tracer across the slope. More men fell. The rest went to ground, vanishing from sight amid the crops.

A Churchill tank rattled past on the right. Mark had not noticed the armour arrive. It fired a couple of times and then moved on, stopped and fired again. Bullets snapped past, the glowing balls of the tracer rounds suddenly very fast as they came at him.

'Down! Down!' he shouted, gesturing to his Platoon to take cover. One of the new ones hesitated, then was hit in the chest and dropped like a puppet with its strings cut.

'Stretcher bearers!' Mark shouted, not that they would get much chance to come up until the Company got moving again. He crouched, trying to see out. The fire was not well aimed, simply passing across the field from side to side. A carrier rushed forward through the crops and then lurched to a halt, the way they did when they stopped suddenly. In a few minutes there was the distinctive sound of heavy mortars coming down on the ridgeline.

Mark could see the main orchard straight ahead. To the left was the line of the much smaller one closer to them. He saw a rush of men from B Company go at it. Grenades went off, some German, some British, and they were in. C Company was moving again, veering right, going for another cluster of trees, marked as Quarry Wood on his map.

Major Fletcher ran up. 'Where's Mr Crawford?'

'Here, sir.'

'We're going to pass through B Company while they go for the quarry. For God's sake just keep them going. Don't stop whatever happens. We must keep going!'

'Seventeen Platoon, advance! Come on, get moving.'

'You heard the officer!' That was Douglas, newly posted to him from A Company. The veteran of Spain and God only knew what stood and waved at the others to go. 'Get moving, get moving. They can't see us, so you're as safe going on as staying. Come on!' The man ought to be a sergeant at least, but refused all promotion.

'Follow me!' Mark yelled, holding his rifle in both hands over his head, so that they could see him.

The advance resumed.

'Don't run, keep it steady.' He turned to walk backwards and promptly tripped over and fell down. He managed to pull himself up. 'Don't follow that bit!' Dear God, some of them were smiling. Fixed, more than a little manic smiles, but somehow they were smiling.

'Keep going!'

Tracer whisked across, slicing off heads of corn a few yards in front of them. They hesitated.

'Keep going, it's stopping, it's stopping!' Dear God, I hope I am right. They were moving again and no one was hit. A mortar bomb landed behind them, and one of the men in the rear section fell forward on his face. They started to jog, fleeing from the explosion even though it was over.

'Not too fast, keep it steady.'

'I can see them on the left,' a Bren N° 1 called out. 'Permission to engage.'

'No, keep going, keep going, don't stop!'

Even with all the noise, Mark heard a dull slap and one of the riflemen sank down onto his knees and then fell forward.

'Mark the spot, then keep going! Keep going!'

Taking the wounded man's rifle, a corporal drove it bayonet

first into the soil. It was supposed to make things easier for the stretcher bearers, although in the high wheat it might not make much difference.

Already yards ahead, Mark glanced back to make sure that the corporal kept moving. The man nodded and gave him a thumbs up. Hopefully that meant the casualty was not too bad, but there was no time to think.

The wheat ended in a neat line and there was mud and thin patches of grass and weed for ten yards or so up to the bank topped by trees that marked the edge of the orchard.

Something glinted dully as it came through the air at them. It was a stick grenade. Two more followed.

'Throw 'em back,' Douglas yelled. 'Throw 'em back!'

Mark let go of his rifle with his right hand and plucked one of the bombs out of the air as neatly as any slip catch. Hoping the bloody man was right, and German fuses were long, he twisted it to get a better grip and threw it back before diving for the earth. Other men did the same, and all three grenades exploded in the trees.

'Come on, charge!' Mark yelled, pushing himself up. 'Charge!' He turned the cry into a scream of mixed terror and rage. Others were yelling, surging forward. On the right CSM Wentworth's platoon were howling like Furies as they raced ahead, past the edge of the orchard and after a group of fleeing Germans.

Mark scrambled up the bank and between two trees, and only then realised that he had not fixed a bayonet onto his rifle. He reversed it, ready to use as a club, but there was no one there. His men were bursting in, blood up, ready to take revenge on those who had bombed and shot at them, but the Germans had gone, leaving only a couple of dead men behind them. On the inside of the bank there were holes dug into the side, and beneath it, empty cases, bits of equipment and weapons – and that musty smell the enemy always left behind him.

'Come on,' Mark shouted and went forward between the

trees. A fair few had scarred trunks and branches snapped and hanging down from the shelling.

A man appeared from behind a tree, coal scuttle helmet on his head, and fired his rifle. It missed, and a fusillade of shots went back, which also seemed to miss, although they pock-marked the tree trunk. The German ducked down as one of the Bren teams set up. Mark and the others were on the ground, finding the best cover they could.

The German appeared again, flinging a grenade this time. It went high, bounced off a tree, flew away from everybody and then finally exploded without doing any harm. The Bren team fired, and the panzer grenadier shook with the impact and fell.

A moment later he appeared again with another grenade. His movements were feeble and awkward, but still he drew his arm back to throw. Mark took a shot. Rifles, Stens and the Bren all hammered the man, who slumped back. His own grenade was just next to him when it went off.

Slowly, warily, they stood and went forward again.

21.20 hrs, the Orchard, Hill 112

Judd lay against the bank at the far, southern side of the Orchard. Most of D Company and reinforcements from B Company were further back, for in the middle of the orchard there was a track wide enough for a tractor and cart, and on either side of this there was a bank and hedge. That was the main line of defence, and only a few men, like his section, were sent to the edge to watch what the Germans were doing.

At the moment they were doing plenty. The Sun was setting, the light fading, but the smoke of the battle had cleared enough to see a row of tanks, very large tanks, forming on the slope below them. The infantry were harder to see, taking cover behind a wall and hedge and hiding in the crops. They were there though, for now and then groups broke into the open, dashed somewhere and vanished again.

Buchanan ran up and threw himself down beside Judd. A man followed with a radio set on his back.

'They're getting telephone cables up to the main position,' Buchanan explained, 'but this will have to do.' He produced a map and unfolded it, keeping it flat with one hand and using the other to hold his binoculars and study the slope below through them. He grunted. 'About five minutes, I reckon.' He turned to the wireless operator. 'Can you get Company?'

The man switched on and called in. With a small 18 set like this, you could never be sure of the range. This was short, very short, but trees in the way never helped.

'Goddamned useless,' 'Coop' Buchanan muttered as he compared his map to the actual ground. 'They haven't even marked that wood down there at all. Oh well, we'll do it the old way.'

'I'm through, sir,' the operator told him.

Buchanan began calling in grid references and requests for fire. Company would have to pass it on, and that would take time, but hopefully there was enough. A proper FOO was supposed to be on his way up.

'Well, let's hope that works,' the Canadian said at the end.

They heard the whistle of shells, and not their own.

'Everybody down!' Buchanan shouted, not that they needed an order. The first explosions were at treetop level, twenty yards or so behind them, as trunks were cracked and branches shattered. Jagged splinters added to the hail of shrapnel. Mortars were landing as well, going off when they hit the ground rather than as airbursts.

Judd covered his ears. There had not been time to dig in, so he simply pressed himself as hard against the ground as he could. The barrage increased, and began to spread. They were covered in dust, each explosion creating a fresh shockwave that hit them, pushing at them, forcing the breath out of them. One of the batteries must have changed the fuse setting by twisting the cap of each shell, so that they drove into the earth, burying themselves before exploding. Trees were uprooted, ripped out of the ground by their roots and tossed aside.

Judd lay. His eyes were wide open because he was too terrified to close them. All he could see was a few inches of bank and coarse grass – and his left hand, which kept trembling. The skin seemed unnaturally white and his fingers were trying to claw into the soil, to do anything to get closer.

'Now that's nice!' Buchanan shouted. The Canadian was staring down the slope. Somehow, Judd managed to raise his head just enough to see. The Germans were coming up the slope, tanks and infantry, but a British barrage was flaying them. Smoke engulfed them, and more and more shells came, but the Germans were still pounding the orchard and after a moment Judd pressed his face into the dirt again.

Time passed – he did not know how much and perhaps it was only seconds. The shelling slackened, and Judd dared to peer out once more. The slope below them was blanketed in white smoke. A German tank drove out of the mist, a huge, wide tracked German tank with a round turret and an immense gun. Another followed to its left, and then two more to its right.

'Tigers,' Buchanan hissed. They certainly seemed even bigger than Panthers, and those damned things had been big enough.

There were no infantry with them.

'Get through to Company,' Buchanan said to the wireless operator.

'Set is U/S, sir.' A chunk of timber had buried itself in the radio. Well, Judd thought, better it than any of them. Miraculously, no one had been hit.

'Damn! Snafu again.' The lieutenant took out his pad and wrote a note, and gave it to the signalman. 'Go back to HQ. Tell them Tigers attacking and we need all the fire we can get.' The man ran off. Judd was not sure whether it was more dangerous running back into the orchard where shells were still falling now and then or staying here to face the tanks. Bit of a Hobson's choice, really.

One of the Tigers stopped, its turret swung and a massive crack sent an 88mm shell into the bank some ten yards from them. The ground erupted, but no one was there. The other tanks came up to it, forming a rough line about a hundred yards away and opened fire, spraying the bank and hedge of the orchard with machine gun bullets and now and then a shot from the big guns.

They had a PIAT, but the range was too long for any tank, let alone one of these monsters, and anyone popping up to shoot was unlikely to get a second chance.

No German infantry appeared, so Buchanan, Judd and the rest pressed themselves against the bank and hoped or prayed or cursed or did not think at all. After ten minutes, more British shells came down and the tanks wheeled about and drove away.

Buchanan crouched to see better. Someone was groaning. It was Protheroe, who had a big splinter driven into his back. Buchanan sent a man to fetch the stretcher bearers and then looked at the rest.

'Dig, boys, dig.'

21.55 hrs, at the foot of the northern slope of Hill 112

James could not see very well. The light was fading as the Sun went down. There was a noticeable difference from a couple of weeks ago, and the day was ending just a little earlier. Not that the night would be long, just a little less brief.

The Glamorgans were on the hill. They had the Orchard – the big one that was so neatly diamond shaped on the map. James could see it as a darker patch on the crest of the high ground. They might have taken other patches of woodland as well, but no one really seemed to know. The Germans were already putting in counter attacks, as they always did, but the infantry were holding firm. Some anti-tank guns had gone up to support them, and it sounded as if some had run into trouble and been caught by Tigers before they could get into action. Others had got through.

Everyone seemed pretty certain about the Tigers, and the bogeymen of all their nightmares did seem to be there this time.

'Baker Three Able to Baker Three, think something is moving on the right. About six fifty yards. Looks like a hornet.'

James raised his binoculars and studied the open slope and crest to the west of the Orchard. The troop of Churchills which had supported the attack had withdrawn, and the newly arrived B Squadron was spread in a line at the foot of the slope. If there was a tank prowling up there, then it was German, no doubt trying to attack the Orchard from the flank.

He could see plenty of dark, boxy shapes, but most, perhaps all, were the wrecks left by the earlier fighting.

'Baker Three to Three Able, I can't see anything. Engage with tracer and we will conform. Baker Three to Three Baker and Charlie. Shoot as soon as you spot the target.'

The co-axial Browning machine gun on Sergeant Dove's tank chattered into life, the red and orange tracer loping up the slope almost as if it was not in a hurry. Sparks flew as it struck one of the shapes, then Dove adjusted the aim onto a second square shape. His 75 boomed.

'Gunner, see the target. Fire an AP then an HE.'

Collins obliged. Sergeant Martin's Firefly gave off a particularly dazzling flash when it fired, making Corporal Bell's effort with the 75mm seem feeble.

'Baker Three to all stations, cease fire.'

'Three Able to Baker Three, I reckon we got him, over.'

'Well done, out.' James was not so sure, and they may simply have put some more holes into one of the wrecks. Still, Dove was good, with all the instincts a soldier should have and that James feared that he himself lacked. He might have been right, and they might have helped the Glamorgans up there. At the very least, it should show the infantry that they were not on their own and perhaps that would encourage them. Yet night was falling, and tanks could not operate in the dark, so very soon B Squadron would pull back to laager. The Glamorgans would still have the gunners to call in their storms of fire – that is if the observers could see anything.

James stared up at the barely visible line of the hill and worried about his friends – and all the men he did not know, but mostly about his friends. For a while it helped to distract him from worrying about himself.

23.10 hrs, in the Orchard, Hill 112

Mark and his men dug. When the shells came again, and came close, they cowered in the shelter they could find and the shallow holes they had already dug, until it slackened or moved away. He had already lost three men to shrapnel or vicious splinters of wood. None were critical and all had a decent chance, but they were out of the fight and on their way back to the aid station. The stretcher bearers were wonderful, slogging up and down the hill, dodging the shells as they went. Some were already dead, but the rest carried on.

The Glamorgans dug and hacked at the ground with picks. There were tree roots everywhere, writhing through the soil just inches beneath the grass. A few men had hatchets or machetes and they chopped at them, swearing foully as they worked. The easiest places to dig were the banks, because there was more space behind them without trees, and most of the Company was probably digging in there. In the dark it was so hard to tell. Mark had got lost more than once amid the trunks of the trees and on ground thick with fallen branches. It was hard to see far and his sense of direction soon got confused. In the end, he followed the sounds of digging and cursing, bumped into one of

Buchanan's sections, who said that they thought his 17 Platoon was on their right. That proved to be true, and he stumbled on to his own men.

No one really knew what was going on. C Company had vanished towards what they had been told was the Quarry Wood, not that it was marked properly on their maps. The CSM and his platoon had chased after the Germans and not come back. As far as Mark could tell, his Platoon and Buchanan's 9 Platoon were all or mostly in the Orchard, with some men from B Company, although he was not sure how many, and some from HQ and Support Company and various bits and bobs. He had no idea how many that made altogether, but feared that it was not enough.

Half an hour earlier the Germans had put in another attack, pushing closer this time, so that they could hear the roar of big engines in between the crashes of the shells. Explosions and muzzle flames lit up the night, then left a man blinking and struggling to see. Judd came running back with his section, Buchanan jogging along at the rear. The front hedge was being savaged by the Tigers and there was no point staying. Another of the big tanks came around the side of the Orchard and fired at them for a while.

Once again, the gunners saved them. For all the German shells tearing up the Orchard, the British sent back many times more. They could not stop the Tigers, not unless there was a fluke hit from a medium gun or bigger, but the panzer grenadiers coming with them were human not machines, and had frail bodies instead of thick armour. They bled and died or went to ground and in the end they gave up and fell back. Like petulant children, the Tigers kept on shooting for a while, before they too withdrew. No one had managed to knock a tank out with any of the six-pounders brought up, let alone a PIAT, but for the moment the threat was just enough to deter the monsters.

Mark dug, and wondered when the next attack would come.

D+35, Tuesday 11ᵗʰ July

02.45 hrs, in the Orchard, Hill 112

Major Fletcher had gathered Mark and Buchanan together, along with Will Grant, a subaltern with B Company, and an RA captain acting as FOO. It was not for a discussion, but to explain what he had done, in case he was put out of action and one of them took charge. As far as Fletcher could tell, he was the senior officer in the Orchard, so the decision was his and he had made it.

'I've given Major Foster' – this was the senior RA officer – 'a note for Brigade – SITUATION CRITICAL. PERMISSION TO WITHDRAW. He's taking it down the hill by carrier.' Fletcher pushed his helmet back a little and scratched at his hair. 'Unless we get more support, we'll bleed to death up here. Maybe that serves a greater purpose and maybe not. I just wanted you to understand in case I catch one. The order may come to pull back – or to stay.'

They were certainly bleeding. The German mortars were relentless, rarely stopping for more than ten minutes throughout the night. Big guns were less frequent, but when the barrages came, they were appalling. Mark had probably lost a third of his platoon already. The dead were left where they fell, or moved to the side if they were in the way. Stretcher bearers and even some carriers kept getting the wounded away fairly quickly.

'Take cover!' a voice shouted, and Mark caught the screech of shells coming in. The darkness split apart in great spurts of light as more trees were shredded. All the officers were on the ground, as flat as they could. More rounds came in, at least a dozen, and they were close. Someone screamed.

'Stretcher bearers! For Christ's sake, stretcher bearers!'

04.55 hrs, on the front edge of the Orchard

Dawn was close, but there was no need to order a stand-to because no one had slept, except those so stunned by the crashing of shells, the stifling gusts as they sent waves of pressure through the air, and the sheer appalling din, that they retreated into oblivion and passed out at the bottom of a trench.

'Poor bastards,' Davison said to Judd. They had been watching the other patch of woods, the Quarry Wood. C Company must have got there because for almost an hour there had been gunfire and grenades in and around the dark trees. It had stopped now, and in the rare gaps when no one was shooting, they could hear heavy engines from that direction. The Germans were there, in force, and massing to press on.

Judd's section was back at the forward edge of the Orchard. There were men from Mark's 17 Platoon on their left and others beyond them. Buchanan seemed to spend a lot of time on the move, checking on them, and then going around the other men of 9 Platoon, who were mostly back in the centre.

'We're staying put,' the Canadian told them. 'So, the Germans won't want that and will throw everything at us. But we've got some guns up and more men than we thought. Seen any more of C Company?'

'No, sir,' Judd told him.

Buchanan sighed. 'You're a praying man, aren't you, Judd?'

'Yes, sir.'

'Do a few extra!'

'Coop' grinned and walked along the line, crouching below the bank, saying a word or two to each man.

'He's getting chatty,' Davison said. 'We'll make a Welshman of him yet.'

The Sun came up, and through the hovering smoke that reeked of cordite, they were able to look around. There was barely a leaf or branch left on the rows of trees in the Orchard, and the remnants lay piled around on the ground. Healthy trees, many of them old, were left as little more than bare trunks, like giant toothpicks stuck into the ground. A good few were split or shattered into stumps and most had gouges across their bark. The Orchard was bleeding with the Glamorgans as it turned into a wasteland. There were craters everywhere, even though the Germans kept using a lot of airbursts.

Judd eased himself up to see over the bank. The slope ahead of him was worse, rent and torn like the pictures you saw from the Last War. Little was left of the golden wheat, and the line of trees a few hundred yards away were ragged and torn. That was the German front line, as near as they could make out, but his eye was drawn past it. This had not seemed like much of a hill when they had gone up its slope. It was not that high after all, not what you would call a proper hill back home.

Davison whistled through his teeth. 'Is that Caen?' He pointed over to the far left.

'Think so.'

'Shit, you can see for bloody miles. ... Bugger. They're not going to give this up in a hurry.'

The sound of tank engines grew louder and a Tiger appeared from behind the Quarry Wood. There was the whistle of approaching shells.

05.15 hrs, in the Orchard, Hill 112

Lt. Col. Dorking-Jones seemed to be everywhere, walking with his stiff Guardsman's gait, like some wading bird as he stepped over fallen branches and debris. He had come up before Major

Fletcher got a reply to his message. The colonel made it clear that they had to hold on as best they could, and later Brigade confirmed the order. 'Hopefully the rest of the Division can push up alongside us during the day,' he assured them. Mark knew that at the moment they had enemies on three sides. However, somehow they managed to bring up hot food just after dawn. So far only a few men had had the benefit of this, but hopefully more could be pulled back for a while whenever there was a lull.

The colonel wandered around the position as if he was having the time of his life. He chatted to the men, joked, laughed with them, especially if they made a joke about him.

'Gunners, hold your fire until you can't miss!' Dorking-Jones called over to the crew of a six-pounder, dug in as well as they could manage and with a rough embrasure carved out of the bank a few feet ahead so that they could shoot through. The low shield of the gun offered some scant protection to the front. Nothing could ward off the airbursts and one of the gunners lay dead, his helmet and head shattered by a lump of wood ripped from a tree and flung through the air. The other gun numbers waited, kneeling, and poised to do their job. They were covered in pale dust, but so was everyone else.

Mark heard a tank engine coming closer. They were attacking from a different direction this time.

'Where's my artillery?' Dorking-Jones called cheerfully to some gunners with a radio. The FOO was dead, sliced in two at the waist by a bursting shell.

'Don't have a target, sir.'

'Oh well, we'll soon solve that mystery. Hold my stick, David.' This was to his adjutant. Dorking-Jones tossed him his riding crop and bounded over to a tree that still had a few branches left. As eager as a schoolboy, the commander of the Glamorgans began to shin up, until he was a good twelve feet in the air. Gripping the trunk with one arm, he somehow managed to use his map in the other.

'Call this in,' he shouted down, and began to reel off coordinates.

Evans laughed. 'He's like a ruddy pigeon.'

'Come on,' Mark told him and headed over to check on his other sections.

The six-pounder fired with its high pitched crack. Mark turned back, and saw the lurking shape of a Tiger, perhaps three hundred yards away, moving diagonally across the field as if to outflank them. The shell whipped across just in front of the moving tank.

'Load sabot!' the gun's number one shouted. The shell was oddly slim, almost dartlike. In went the round, the breech slammed shut and a moment later the gun fired again, and again went in front of the panzer.

The Tiger halted, its turret turned, long gun swinging round. The gunners were loading again, but before they could fire, machine gun bullets flicked over the gap in the bank and struck the gun shield, screaming and flying off at all angles. One of the gunners leaned back and kept on leaning, and as he fell Mark saw a bloody mess where the man's left eye had been. The Tiger fired its big gun, striking the tree trunk in front and spreading shards of metal and fragments of wood over them, with one of the few branches left falling onto the gun. By the time the remaining crew had shifted it, the German tank had reversed out of sight.

'Splendid!' Dorking-Jones cried out, still up his tree. British shells were streaming over the Orchard to fall on the far slope.

06.03 hrs, the northern slope of Hill 112

The Glamorgans asked for help, so B Squadron drove forward, fourteen tanks in a staggered line – they were still understrength with just three troops and a couple of tanks for the Squadron HQ. With them went an RA tank with a wooden gun barrel as a decoy, so that the turret could be filled with powerful radio equipment.

'Baker to all stations Baker. Our little friends are under attack. Lots of infantry, plus all the hornets you could wish for – Tigers, SPs and Mark Fours...'

'And Uncle Tom Cobleigh and all,' Thomson sang over the intercom, 'and Uncle Tom Cobleigh and all.'

'Baker One, you go on the left, Baker Three in the middle and Baker Two on the right. Let's get up there. On the southern slope there is a wall and a line of trees. They want the Germans cleared from it, out.'

'Driver, advance,' James said. He was out of the hatch, and did not need his binoculars to see that the main Orchard was being hammered by the Germans. They went up the slope, towards the wrecks. There was a Mark IV he did not remember, so perhaps Dove had got one last night.

A few shells dropped around them, but only a few, and it may simply have been chance or bad aim, for the enemy continued to focus his malice on the Orchard.

'Baker Two to Baker, I can see hornets to my right, range one thousand.' The new commander of 1 Troop was called Peterson. James did not know him, but he was built like a prop forward, big for a tankman, and gave every impression of pugnacious enthusiasm. 'Suggest I halt and cover your flank.'

Static hissed for a while. 'Baker to Baker Two, I don't see them, over.'

'Think they've moved back into the trees. They're there, though, Baker. Permission to halt.'

'Denied, Baker Two. Keep going, out.'

The Shermans went steadily up the hill. They could not see over the crest and as usual there was no radio link to the Glamorgans to hear what the infantry could see.

Hector II bumped up and down a few times as they went over debris hidden in the grass. There were a few more shell holes than James remembered, but nothing too large. They were halfway up the slope, still not close enough to see very much.

'Baker to Baker Two, why have you stopped, over?'

'Bit worried about those tanks – I mean hornets, Baker.' Peterson had an oddly soft, rather high pitched voice, surprising in someone so heavily built. 'They're out there.'

'Baker Two, I see nothing.' James could sense Major Scott's puzzlement turning into anger. 'Continue to advance, Baker Two.'

The static hissed for a while.

'That's an order, Baker Two.'

James and the rest of the squadron were no more than a hundred yards from the crest. He turned the cupola to see to the right, rather than standing taller to see over the open hatch. Two Troop had been left behind. As he watched, three out of the four Shermans began to go forward.

'Baker to Baker Two, advance.'

The stationary Sherman shuddered and went forward a few yards then halted again. 'Baker Two to Baker, my engine is playing up.'

'No, it's not,' someone chipped in. 'He's...' The transmission garbled as several voices tried to speak at once.

'Baker to Baker Two Able, assume command of Troop. Baker Two, advance with your men. Fight alongside them if you cannot lead them. That's an order, Baker Two.'

'Oh Christ. ... I'm ill, my stomach's in agony. Oh Christ, I can't.'

James shifted his gaze back to the front. He was embarrassed, ashamed even to witness someone collapsing so suddenly and so completely. It could be me, he thought, and that thought made his revulsion all the stronger. Dear God, don't let that happen.

They were close to the crest, and in a few moments would be hull down if they stopped. James waited for the order.

'Baker to Baker stations, keep going. We need to help the

infantry. Baker Three and Baker Two Able, lead your tanks to the right side of the Orchard. I'll go left with Baker One. Good luck. ... And Baker Two, pull yourself together.'

'Will do Baker, Baker Two out.' The voice was not Peterson's.

'That sounds like Tommy Duggan,' Whitefield said.

'Yes, good old Tommy,' Collins agreed.

'Driver, steer to the left of that Churchill.' James guided them past the wrecks. As before, back in June, as soon as they came onto the flattish top of the hill, the world opened out in great vistas. 'This is Baker Three. Target line of trees to our left, seven hundred yards. Ten plus hornets. Halt and engage.'

James could not remember seeing so many German tanks before, even at Rauray. In the lead were five Tigers, big, thickset unmistakeable Tigers, and behind were Stugs and Mark IVs. The infantry were everywhere.

'Gunner, traverse left, left, on. Target the leading hornet. See if you can get him on the side before he turns. Fire when ready.'

Collins waited longer than he expected, then the 75mm boomed. The shell seemed to hit the Tiger, but at this range, even against its thinner side armour, they would be lucky to do much damage.

Other tanks were firing, and so were the Germans.

'Driver, take us up to that wrecked Mark Four. Baker Three to Able. I'm creeping forward, try to come round on my right. Three Baker and Charlie, cover us.'

Other commanders were issuing orders, the sergeant now in charge of 2 Troop doing a very good job.

'Baker to Baker stations, am in position ready to join the party.' Scott had had a longer route around the other side of the Orchard. 'Shelldrake is calling on his friends to help.' That was good. The artillery would hammer the German grenadiers if nothing else.

'Driver, halt, well done. Gunner, see if we can get that same tank.'

'Got 'im!' Collins yelled in triumph. The Tiger was reversing, black smoke coming from its rear. Still, that might just be fumes from its exhaust.

Sergeant Dove in Three Able belted forward, further than James had expected, then slewed to a halt, swinging to put the tank's front armour towards the enemy. A couple of seconds later his gun fired, close enough for James to feel the shockwave in the air. A Mark IV lurched, flames coming out of its engine.

'Bloody hell, that Dove's a boy!' Collins said admiringly. 'Got one already.'

'Gunner, traverse right, on. Hit that SP!'

Scott came on the air. 'Shelldrake has bought it. Keep laying into them. Oh God, I'm hit, bail out, bail out...'

'Think I got him,' Collins said.

'Hit him again,' James told him. The Stug was not moving, but the Germans always halted to shoot, so it could mean anything.

A lot of the wheat was flattened on this side of the hill, but James saw a patch that was still thick flip down to either side as a shell came through, coming at them – no, to their right.

An 88mm round drove through the hull armour of Dove's Sherman. The solid steel, red hot from momentum, decapitated the co-driver and kept going, through a shell locker and into the engine. The Sherman exploded, the turret ripped from its mounting and flying up ten, twenty feet into the air. James felt the heat on his face, and could smell the stench of burning ammunition and fuel.

'Poor Dove,' Thomson said under his breath.

'Gunner, hit that SP again – no, it's smoking. Traverse left, new target, Mark Four.'

Baker Two Charlie hit a Tiger square on before it was brewed in turn. Baker Two appeared, rushing forward, firing rapidly. Seconds later it was hit, and immediately caught fire, flames shooting up from the open turret hatch, burning whoever was commanding. No one got out.

'Baker to all stations, lay down smoke and pull back.' That

was Captain Morbey's voice, so Scott was dead or wounded, or at least unable to find a new mount.

'Understood, Baker,' James replied. 'Three Baker and Charlie, let's get going.' Each tank had small smoke dischargers, and the bombs from them gave off a little cloud when they landed. It was not much, not in such open country. James saw that the panzers were following, their blood up and eager for more slaughter.

Perhaps Morbey had requested it on another channel, or some FOO in the Orchard had understood the situation, for suddenly shells whistled in and the whole top of the hill was blanketed in thick white smoke as the phosphorus in the rounds flared.

B Squadron fled back down to where they had started. Six Shermans stayed on the hill, half of them burning like Roman candles.

07.30 hrs, the Orchard

Judd panted, trying to catch his breath. He had lost Kennedy, hit badly in both legs by shrapnel. They had tried to lift him back, but the man screamed in protest, and the panzer grenadiers were lobbing grenades and coming over the bank at the southern end of the Orchard. There was never any intention that the few men so far forward could hold a serious attack, so they had to retreat or surrender or be shot. They laid Kennedy down and ran for it. Bullets chased them, clipping bits of bark from the ravaged trees, but the rest of them all got back across the central track and joined the main line on its far side. Button became Clarke's N° 2 on the Bren, with Davison his only rifleman.

Mortar bombs dropped down, unhindered by any canopy. There were crashes and cries of pain.

'Stretcher bearers!'

'Wait, boys, they'll be here soon,' Reade yelled at 9 Platoon.

He was on his knees, crawling behind the line of men on the bank.

Judd watched. The Sten gun felt clumsy and uncomfortable. He knew that he had fired it, but could not remember how many rounds were gone. He unclipped the magazine and fitted a full one just to make sure.

He wished he had a Bren, if not old Bessie, then one as good. Better yet, he wished he had wangled a way into the ruddy RAF. If he had managed to make aircrew he would probably still be training now, maybe away in Canada with 'Coop' Buchanan's solid folk. Or he could have had a ground job, something nice and cushy, maybe even in an office, typing and making tea and probably failing to impress the WAAFs.

'Hold your fire, chaps, until you see the bastards' eyes.' Dorking-Jones appeared, strolling along as if he did not have a care in the world.

There was movement ahead, back from the bank on the other side of the track and amid the trees. Judd thought that he saw a helmeted head staring straight at him, before it vanished.

'Wait! Wait!'

A Spandau opened up, shooting from the flank, and bullets raced along the top of the bank. Judd slid back, then eased up again when they passed. Voices started shouting, German voices, and whether they were urging each other on or trying to frighten the defenders he could not tell.

Grenades landed on the track and on the bank. One came down just by Judd and he grabbed it and threw it forward before burying his face against the grass. It gave a dull boom, and something small pinged off his helmet.

The shouting was louder now, and the bare trees on the far side were suddenly swarming with men who ran forward; machine pistols chattered.

'Shoot the bastards!' Dorking-Jones yelled. The Glamorgans opened fire. Judd tried to fire three-shot bursts like he had with the Bren, but the Sten raced ahead, loosing off more than he had intended, and the damned thing kept trying to pull up and to the left. Germans were falling, writhing as the bullets struck them. He fired again, the gun once again pulling from his grip, and as it turned it put a couple of rounds into the chest of a grenadier who was almost across the track. The man fell flat onto the bank just in front of Judd.

Almost as suddenly as they had appeared, the Germans were gone, melting back into the southern side of the Orchard. The one who had fallen was moaning softly. He raised his eyes, giving Judd an almost puzzled look.

It went quiet.

'Give me a hand,' Judd said to Davison and crouched up on the bank to help the German. The Port Talbot lad was surprised, then shrugged and helped. They pulled the SS man over the bank and rolled him onto his back. The German's eyes were flickering, but they gave him a shot of morphine and put a dressing over each wound.

'I don't know, Judd-boy, make your bloody mind up,' Davison said after the stretcher bearers took the man away. 'Shoot him one minute and bandage him the next.'

'Blame Churchill.'

'I would, if they'd give me leave.'

08.40 hrs, the Orchard

Mark's rifle had its stock broken when a shell exploded right next to him. He could not hear for a while and his head still throbbed, but that was the only damage the thing had done. Sergeant Jenkins was less fortunate. The man who had walked unscathed through the field, spraying the enemy with rounds from his Bren, was killed in a shell scrape dug into the bank. A big shell, at least a 155mm, landed on top of him. The only thing left that was recognisable was his left leg, ripped off just below the knee. His well-polished boot was still on the foot.

Every twenty or thirty minutes, another charge would come somewhere along the line of the track. More often, tanks drove up to the side of the Orchard, and pumped shells and machine gun bullets into it. Evans had his head bandaged, having been clipped by a Spandau bullet from a Tiger. The boy swore that he was alright and refused to go back with the other wounded.

Whenever the infantry were busy getting ready and the tanks held back far enough, the guns and mortars resumed, shredding what was left of the trees, shrapnel searching blindly for the men cowering under them.

Half of Mark's platoon was gone, and even combined with what was left of 9 Platoon, there were barely twenty men left able to fight. Some were dead, far more wounded. One, a quiet unassuming man named Samuels who had been with the battalion for years, had stood up in the middle of one barrage and simply run off, howling like a beast. Goodness knows what had happened to him.

'Here they come,' Douglas shouted from close by. Even without any rank, the man was leading and Mark was glad to have him.

Spandaus opened up, trying to pin them down, and a howling charge followed. Grenades went off, and Mark had gathered a bag full of Mills bombs and armed and threw them one at a time. Evans was kneeling beside him, shooting the Sten. Germans were falling, but others were coming on, firing and screaming. Mark had run out of grenades and fumbled for his revolver.

A big SS man came up the bank and he and Douglas aimed and fired as the German sprayed with his sub machine gun. Both men fell. Mark had his revolver out and cocked it, raising it to shoulder height and searching for a target. The Germans were going back, some still shooting.

A grenade was in the air, coming towards them. Evans darted in front of him, dropping his Sten gun to catch the bomb in both hands. It was not a stick grenade, but one of the egg shaped ones, and as the lad raised it to throw, it went off. White smoke spouted everywhere, phosphorous spraying onto Evans' head and back, spreading, burning.

Evans fell, screaming. He tried to roll to put it out, but the movement only made the flames worse. His jacket and trousers were blazing.

'Oh Christ!' someone gasped. 'Oh Jesus God, oh Christ!'

'Shoot me, sir, please!' Evans' voice was distorted, but the words were clear. 'Shoot me, please! Please!'

Spandau rounds rattled along the bank, and one hit the boy's leg, but his agony was already too great to admit any more.

'Shoot me, please, shoot me!'

Mark aimed the revolver, his hand quivering. The boy's face no longer looked human, skin and flesh burned away. He pulled the trigger and the round went straight into Evans' chest.

'No, sir, in the bloody head! Please!'

Sergeant Reade of 9 Platoon appeared, took one look, and let off a single shot from his Sten. Evans jerked once and was still. The air was full with the foul scent of burning meat.

10.30 hrs, the Orchard

The Germans had not attacked for almost an hour. The shells came in, as did the mortar bombs, and more of the Glamorgans were killed or maimed. It was getting harder to take the wounded back, so instead, many lay in trenches at the rear of the position, sobbing, moaning or lying silent. Mostly the Germans let carriers and half-tracks come and go if they came alone and had a clear red cross flag or marking. Anything else was shot at, and sometimes the haze of battle meant that even the marked ambulances were smashed by shells.

In the Orchard, the Glamorgans continued to hold the northern half. Only one of the six-pounders was still in action, which meant that apart from in that one sector, the panzers and Stugs edged closer.

Dorking-Jones kept doing the rounds.

'Must be on bennies,' Davison suggested, as the spare figure of their commanding officer moved off. Mr Buchanan pretended not to hear. His platoon was now little more than a section, so he and Sergeant Reade were always close or sometimes helping 17 Platoon. A few waifs and strays, even some C Company men, had joined them, and if they were few in numbers they had more than the usual share of Brens, as well as a PIAT, not that the panzers were willing to come close enough for them to use it.

'Did you hear what happened to Evans?' Davison asked. 'Poor sod.'

'I saw it,' Judd said. He had simply happened to be looking in that direction at the time, searching for targets as the Germans pulled back, his fear turning to exhilaration so that he wanted to kill. That mood had passed as soon as he saw the boy on fire, and Mark shooting him. Poor sod, as Davison put it, and poor Mark too – to have to do what was right when it was also so terrible.

'Ammo check, boys,' Buchanan said, perhaps wanting them to change the subject. While they searched pouches and magazines, Reade went off to see what he could scrounge up.

'Still praying, Judd?' Buchanan asked.

Judd smiled. 'When I get a spare moment.'

'You a religious man, sir?' Davison asked, the ingrained nosiness of South Wales coming to the fore.

'No, son, not really. Begging Judd's pardon, I have always struggled with the idea of a kind God who says "Do what you're told or fry." As I say, no offence.'

'None taken, sir.'

'Still,' Buchanan conceded. 'Today I'll believe in anyone who'll help us!'

'Yup!' Davison said.

'Coop' Buchanan laughed.

11.00 hrs, on the slope below Hill 112

An HE shell from a 105mm should not harm a Sherman tank. The force generated was not enough to penetrate the armour, because howitzer shells came in slowly, lobbed onto the target from miles away. Even a direct hit should not do any real harm, beyond giving the crew one hell of a headache.

Yet war was never certain, and when Captain Morbey's Sherman was stuck on the glacis by such a round, the tank juddered to a halt. The engine was dead, not a spark from the battery, and it refused to come back to life. The captain dismounted to switch to another tank just as a single shell, not a salvo, but one shell, happened to land beside him and he was dead, his internal organs ruptured by the blast even though his skin was unbroken.

Soon afterwards, as they manoeuvred into a fresh position, another Sherman went over a mine. How this one mine had remained undetected and undetonated for so long as tanks and other vehicles churned across the field remained a mystery. No one ever knew, nor could anyone remember who had laid it. The track was broken, wheels damaged, and the tank was not going anywhere.

James Taylor was the only officer left in B Squadron, although since there were only seven Shermans still able to move, this was not the grandest of commands. C Squadron had come up, which meant that someone else was really in charge. They were on the left of the slope, covering as best they could the left of the Orchard and stopping the Germans from circling round behind it on that side. B Squadron's job was to watch the right, so James took them halfway up the slope and spread them out. Then they waited for targets or for fresh orders.

Thomson was singing again, this time 'If I Didn't Care'.

James did not know what had happened to Peterson. His crew had taken over, that at least was for certain, and perhaps the officer was still on board when they had charged forward and been killed. Maybe they had killed him beforehand.

From his nest in the co-driver's position, Thomson was giving the song all he had got. He was fond of the Ink Spots and might even do the deep, deep bass part when the mood took him, speaking rather than singing.

Perhaps Peterson was alive. James had not bothered to report what had happened, although someone may have heard it all on the regimental net. They could search for him if they liked. James did not care. Some men simply could not take it, even tough, very martial seeming men like Peterson. Best to get rid of them before they got others killed. Get them away, in case the contagion spread. Dear God, wasn't that true? James knew that his nerves were fraying. Disgust and pity for someone losing control like that had helped though. He felt a little better. Habit helped too. When they were busy in action there was simply too much to do. Only the waiting, like this, played on his mind.

Thomson had switched back from bass to what he was pleased to consider a tenor.

James realised he was clutching his pocket. Poor Penny. She was in love, and no doubt felt all the sentiment in songs like this.

Thomson kept ignoring a chorus of raspberries added by Whitefield.

James did not know about love, but he could not help remembering dancing with her. That would be something, with her in one of her preciously guarded long gowns and him in his uniform. She liked him in uniform. He clutched the pocket even harder. Yes, that would be something. When they danced it was all so simple.

Whitefield gave up before Thomson finished. Then they all sat in silence.

11.55 hrs, the Orchard

Mark had been sent to report to the colonel. There was the sound of engines and activity by the Quarry Wood, which might mean another attack, so it would be good to call on the artillery.

Finding Dorking-Jones was not easy, for he was rarely still. Men said that he had been here, but gone that way, so Mark walked for a while in circles. He kept thinking of Evans, and seeing the boy's eyes, somehow untouched by the flames, staring up at him as he begged to be killed. Poor kid, who had been dealt such a rough hand in life and now this. He hoped that at least the mother and sister would be kept free and safe from the father. Now there was someone who deserved to burn. Hell was waiting, if there was a Hell, but a phosphorus grenade could do the job straight away.

'Have you seen the colonel?' Mark asked a signalman working on a wireless set. The man pointed a finger upwards. Dorking-Jones was up a tree once again, hugging it with his legs and one arm, and reading from a map.

'Need me, young Crawford?' he asked.

Mark told him about the quarry.

'Ah, the vile Hun is up to his tricks again, eh? Thought there was something going on, that's why I'm up here – or did you think I had become some sort of hermit? What did they call them?'

'Stylites,' Mark said mechanically. It was a wonder how much useless information was tucked away in his brain.

'That's the chaps. Mad as hatters. Now, listen, Crosbie, and summon the thunderbolts of the gods for us!' He started to reel off the numbers and instructions. 'That'll spoil his hash.'

The call went in, the signalman giving the casing a bang at one point. 'Put together from bits of three smashed ones,' he explained to Mark. 'Wonder the bloody thing works at all.'

A Spandau gave its insane rattle, sending a stream of bullets through the dead trees to their left.

'Better come down, sir,' Mark called.

'Just want to check that they are on target,' Dorking-Jones shouted down. 'Although actually I am beginning to like it up here. Very airy, you know... ah, that's the ticket!'

Mark could hear the barrage coming down, although from ground level he could not see the shells landing.

The Spandau carved through the air again, closer this time. Dorking-Jones' head jerked back, his body shook, and he dropped onto the ground, his helmet spinning away. Half his face was gone, along with all of the back of his head. The machine gun was still firing, but the bullets were high and no danger.

'Who is next in command?' Mark asked the signalman. He felt detached, as if he was watching himself perform in a play.

'No idea, sir.'

'Can you get Brigade on that?'

The soldier tried, but at that moment the cobbled together radio decided that it had had enough. He tried again, and there was nothing.

'The fucking fucker is fucked,' he said bitterly.

Somewhere, not far away, but lost in the trees, a voice began to shout. 'Withdraw! Withdraw! Pull back!'

12.20 hrs on the northern slope of Hill 112

The Glamorgans ran. Someone had given the order and other voices took it up. It was not an organised retreat, not a withdrawal, but a slow-starting avalanche of men getting up and fleeing from the Orchard.

'Coop' Buchanan could sense his men's desperation to go, realised that there was no point in staying behind on their own, and took 9 Platoon back with the rest, but made sure that they stayed as a group.

Judd saw Davison hesitate.

'Shall we pack it in?' Davison asked.

Judd did not feel the same panic as at Rauray. He was tired, desperately tired, but at that precise moment the fear was a small thing, lurking in the shadows on the edge of his mind. There, but not the only thing that was there.

'What, give up?'

'Reckon we've already done our bit.'

'Move, you stupid bastards!' 'Rusty' Reade had come back and was glaring at them.

They moved, and were soon back with the rest of the platoon. It felt strange and exposed once they were over the rear bank and out into the open. There must have been a hundred, even two hundred men streaming down the slope. They all seemed to have their equipment and weapons, but there was no doubting the determination with which they fled. If anyone was trying to stop them, they were ignored.

Buchanan led and Reade kept at the back, like shepherd and sheepdog, keeping the twenty or so men together. Most were from their own platoon, some from Mark's, along with a few others, including a gunner from Support Company.

Most of the stream went straight down the slope, but Buchanan led them towards a line of Sherman tanks.

'What's up?' a commander called from the turret.

'Don't know,' Buchanan told him. 'Someone started shouting orders to pull back. Everyone was going and it didn't seem wise to hang about.'

'The Germans?'

'Weren't attacking. But once they realise, they'll be coming. Do you want some support?'

'Always glad of infantry,' James Taylor assured him, and then noticed Judd's big frame. 'Oh, hello, Bill.'

Judd nodded. You did not salute in the front lines, because that simply marked out the officers as targets for the enemy, so that solved the problem of whether or not he needed to salute an old friend. Buchanan glanced between the two, gave a wry smile, and said nothing. 'Get digging!' he yelled.

'Baker Three to Baker Stations, keep your eyes peeled,' James spoke into his microphone. 'An attack may be coming. Baker Three to Charlie Sunray, little friends have retreated. Repeat, they have retreated. They were not under attack.'

12.35 hrs, north of Hill 112

One of the other battalions of the Brigade was dug in at the foot of the slope. Men peeked out of fox holes and slit trenches, faces confused and nervous as the Glamorgans surged towards them. Mark had caught up, and then sprinted to try to get to the front and find out what was happening. Seeing an officer running, others began to go faster.

'Anyone move and I'll shoot them!' A stocky captain had run forward and was waving his revolver, pointing in turn at one trench after another. 'You hear me? Run and I'll kill you!'

'Hold your positions!' another voice shouted. 'Stay in your positions. No one is to move.'

'Stand fast, you bastards!' someone else was yelling.

Major Probert appeared. 'What the bloody hell is going on? Who ordered this?' The RSM came behind him, majestic and unperturbed as ever. ''Talion, halt!'

The Glamorgans slowed and then stopped, milling in a loose crowd. A few shells in the right spot could easily have massacred them all, but there was no sign that the Germans were taking an interest.

'You, Mr Crawford. Organise D Company.'

'D Company on me!' Mark tried to shout. His throat was dry and he managed to spit, and at last make some noise. 'D Company over here.' He held his hand up in the air. 'On me, D Company.'

Other voices rallied different groups. Seven men came over to Mark. He could not see any of Buchanan's 9 Platoon among them. Goodness knows where they were.

Major Fletcher appeared. 'Right, we're going back up, and fast, before the Hun realises what's happening. Mark, you take D. Get back to the positions you left. I'll see if I can get the tanks to come with us. Now go, go!'

Slowly, like children caught by a parent or teacher doing something forbidden, the Glamorgans went back up the hill. The few who lacked weapons searched the ground for replacements. Thirty reinforcements, only just arrived, went with them, the men uncannily fresh and tidy compared to the dirty, weary men who had held the Orchard.

12.45 hrs, on the slope of Hill 112

James led 3 Troop forward with the infantry, while the rest of B Squadron waited to cover them. He was not willing to go over the crest, not without specific orders from his own regiment, but this seemed the right thing to do. The Canadian officer and his men came with them, Judd striding along, the Sten gun looking rather small in his hands. There was a good chance that the Germans were there at the edge of the Orchard, crouched behind the bank, waiting for the British to get closer so that every shot would count. He could picture them, the camouflaged figures in their odd, coal scuttle helmets, Spandaus ready to set up, panzerfausts and bazookas in hand. Maybe they even had a gun up, one of the Paks, and in a moment they could wheel it forward, long barrel reaching over the earth bank. There would be a flash, at that range a fraction of a second while the shell was in the air, then a crash, the Sherman rocking, flames starting.

If they were there.

Whitefield kept in low gear, keeping pace with the infantry. In the last weeks James and the other tankmen had learned that the best thing was for the infantry to lead the tanks, flushing out the bazookas from their hiding places, killing those deadly men, so that the tanks could blast the MGs so lethal to the infantry. That was best, but today was not best and he felt that the Glamorgans needed a bigger show of support, so he kept up with them. If the Germans were already in the Orchard, then the Glamorgans would be cut down and a fair few of the Shermans brewed up. The rest might be able to flay the treeline just enough to keep the enemy's heads down and help the survivors of the infantry to escape. If the Germans were there.

They were close, no more than a hundred yards. That was a devastating range for machine guns. Perhaps they were not there? Or perhaps the panzer grenadiers were waiting until the tanks came within the very short range of the panzerfaust? Tank fist. It was a stupid name. Very Germanic, very crude. Looked like a tuba or a stubby trombone. A stick with a lumpen rocket head at the top. Shoot it, throw the stick away and get another. Cheap and nasty. And very deadly.

'Gunner, keep an eye on the bank. Ready with the co-ax.' Collins did not need to be told. Would he worry that James was nervous, even cracking up like Peterson?

'Can't see anything, sir.'

Nor could James. The Canadian officer called something and waved his arm and the infantrymen ran the last short distance, went over the bank and into the tortured remnants of the Orchard, its bare trees like rows of pillars.

No one fired.

Dear God, I'm still alive, James realised.

'Baker Three to Baker and Charlie, we will stay here, spread yourselves out, turret down below the crest.' That meant that the whole tank was hidden by the ground, but that the commander could see over the crest, at least if he stood up. 'Charlie on the left, then Baker, then me.' James was about to tell the Able tank to go to the flank, only to remember that Dove was dead and his Sherman probably still smoking. Poor Dove, the man had seemed indestructible. Best sergeant an officer could hope for. A damned fine man. Now burned beyond all recognition along with all his crew. The padre refused to let anyone who fought in a tank help get the remains from one that had brewed. Said they did not need to see it. James could imagine and his imaginings were terrible.

'Baker Three to Three Baker and Charlie, watch out for anything that moves up there, out.'

13.34 hrs, the Orchard, Hill 112

None of the Glamorgan's companies were as large as a platoon in normal times. Just under two hundred men went back into the Orchard. In barely an hour there were no more than one hundred and sixty left unwounded. Major Probert commanded the battalion for forty-seven minutes before a jagged piece of shell drove through his steel helmet and into his brain. The few remaining gunners for the six-pounders were killed or wounded, not that any of the guns were still working. Three new radios had been carried up the slope. One was already smashed, along with its operator.

The Germans had not attacked. As far as anyone could tell, the enemy had not even noticed that the Glamorgans had fled the wood and then come back.

'Snafu,' Buchanan said, 'just Hun Snafu this time rather than ours.'

'What's snafoo?' asked a replacement attached to them. Judd thought his name was Kitchener or Kendall or something like that.

'Somebody explain,' Buchanan told them.

'Situation normal, all fucked up,' Judd said. He did not usually swear, certainly not so strongly, at least out loud. His thoughts were different, at least since coming into the Army, and were the resentful, angry, complaining thoughts of a Tommy.

They did not talk much anymore. Although the Germans had not yet launched another assault, the mortar bombs and shells

kept coming in, short savage barrages that killed or wounded
a few more. They were not regular, and sometimes the minutes
of silence stretched out and for just a moment a man felt less
battered and terrified. Then the next shells would come.

Men clung to the side of the bank or shrank to the bottom of
the shallow trenches that was all it had been possible to dig. The
Orchard reeked of mutilated human beings and the foulness of
explosives. The air was thick with it, so that simply breathing
was unpleasant. Men coughed, until the explosions came close
and the very breath was knocked out of them, sometimes for
ever.

Fragments of men were everywhere. Limbs torn off, heads
missing or lying on their own, entrails scooped out and spread
wide across the ground. The flies were also everywhere,
seemingly immune to the hail of splinters and metal falling
around them. Some bodies were neat, almost like ones from
a painting, faces waxy, but bodies intact even if the features of
old friends were empty. Other corpses were hideous parodies of
the human form, recognisable only by the fragments of uniform
and equipment still clinging to them. Not far from where Judd
lay was a left hand, cut with almost surgical precision from the
arm. There was a ring on the third finger and the nails were
deeply engrained with dirt, just like the rest of them.

The shells kept on coming, followed by screams and calls
for stretcher bearers. They hugged the earth as a baby clings
to its mother, craving protection. They were scarcely aware of
each other anymore, save that when they could they huddled
together as if this would somehow make them safer.

'Coop' Buchanan talked. He moved among them, saying
little things to each one, making a joke, and shaking the men
who did not respond. Unless he got a word back, or at least a
smile, he kept at them until they did. 'Rusty' Reade followed
behind and made each man check his weapons.

Judd, so far as he was able, marvelled. The two men were

wonderful and he knew that he could not do what they were doing.

14.25 hrs, near the Orchard, Hill 112

'Baker Three Charlie to Baker Three, I can see hornets beside the wood on the right, over.'

James glanced to the side and noticed that Sergeant Martin was standing behind his turret, binoculars raised.

'I see them, Three Charlie. SPs. Looks like an attack. Prepare to move to hull down if we get a chance to engage, out.'

Shellfire redoubled on the Orchard, the explosions flashing in rapid succession. A thick cloud of dark smoke hung over the enclosure.

There were three Stugs rolling towards the south-west corner of the Orchard, infantry with them. Behind them loomed larger shapes. Tigers. A pair of them. James had always wondered about stories where the hero felt a cold sweat down his spine. It was now a very familiar sensation.

'Three Charlie to Baker Three, I see Tigers, over.'

'I see them. Wait for the order. We'll roll up, give them a few shots and then pull back. Understood, over?'

'Three Baker, acknowledged.'

'Three Charlie, acknowledged.' Martin was back in the cupola. Would he go when ordered, James wondered? The man had said he was not willing to take any unnecessary risks. How would he judge this? It ought to be safe. The Germans were pushing to the Orchard, not watching their flank. If they were quick, they might throw the attack off balance, even brew one or two and get out before anything nasty happened.

'Baker Three to Baker and Charlie. Go to hull down, engage at will, then pull back when I say, out. Driver, advance, just creep us up. That's it, that's it. Gunner, can you see?'

'Not yet, skip,' Collins told him. 'Bit more, bit more. That's it! Shit. Sorry, boss.' The wide open field ahead of the Orchard and by the smaller wood was alive with tanks and infantry.

'Gunner, traverse left, on. Target SP, the closest one, range three fifty yards. Fire when ready.'

Collins stamped on the button to start the co-axial Browning machine gun to the left of the 75mm. Red tracer flashed amid the stream of bullets, dropping just by the side of the Stug. There was something odd about the vehicle and it seemed longer than usual. Collins adjusted, elevating both guns, and the tracer splashed over the side skirts of the self-propelled gun. He stamped with his other foot and the 75 boomed, punching a neat hole through the thin side plate. It must have struck the hull, but James could not see. The Stug halted, which could mean a lot of things.

'Give him another!' James told Collins.

Three Baker shook as a round struck home and immediately began to burn. Crewmen came tumbling out. One was on fire.

Collins felt Blamey tap him on the leg to say that the gun was loaded; he checked the aim, not that it needed it, but just to make sure, and then stamped on the firing button. The second shell slammed into the Stug and black smoke started to rise from it.

Sergeant Martin was shooting with care. Another Stug had stopped, the whole vehicle sagging down like a camel on its knees. A round must have destroyed its suspension.

James searched for another target and saw it. A Tiger, a huge, terrifying Tiger was coming forward with surprising speed. How could something so huge go so fast? Martin's Firefly gave one of its great flashes as it fired, missing the German tank. The long gun on the Tiger started to swing towards it. At least that movement was slow, ponderous. It was still moving, and went behind an old wreck of a Churchill so that it was hard to see.

'Driver, advance.' James saw a chance. The Tiger was busy

with Martin, alert to the danger of the Firefly's gun. James could not see the panzer very well, which should mean that the same was true in reverse. If he dashed forward, he might just be able to get in a shot at the side or even the rear of the great behemoth.

What Whitefield and the rest thought, he could not say, for no one said anything.

'Take us right,' James said, 'then swing round past the brewed Shermans.' There were two, and at least one was one of their own, knocked out back in June.

Martin hit the front of the Tiger. A seventeen-pounder shell could go through the thickest armour, even a Tiger's front plate at this range – if it hit squarely. This one glanced on the corner, making a groove along the side, stripping off the strange criss-cross paste the Germans put on their tanks to stop magnetic mines from fixing on. The Tiger was still working, although the crew ought to have a devil of a headache.

'Three Charlie to Baker Three, it's getting hot. We need to pull back.'

'Nearly, Three Charlie, just a minute,' James replied. 'Gunner, can you see the Tiger.'

'No, skip, the wreck is in the way.'

'Keep going, driver.'

'Wait!' Collins almost shouted. 'I can see the end of the bastard.' There was a yard or two of big hull and round wheels visible past the destroyed hulk of the Churchill. Flat sides, flat back, with big exhausts giving off plumes of dirty smoke.

Collins pressed down with his boot on the co-axial button. Tracer struck the rear wheel of the Tiger and sprang away.

James saw the remnants of the wheat parting as the shell sliced through. Oh Sweet Jesus, there was another Tiger, in the smoke off to their right. *Hector II* rocked as if they had driven into a cliff at full speed.

They were hit. Shermans could brew in less than a second. Ammunition and fuel erupting like a volcano, burning everything it could reach. He had to get out – they all had to get out! Oh God, the flames could start now, throwing off the turret. James was panting. He pulled his headset free, let his binoculars fall and with both hands pushed himself up and over the side of the turret. His boot caught on the edge of the cupola, he unbalanced, tripped, and flew through the air to land hard on the ground beside the wheels and tracks of the Sherman. Collins jumped down beside him, landing on his left leg, which hurt like hell. Blamey came down onto the back of the hull, then juddered and shook as a round of tracer went into his back, followed by three more bullets as the Spandau chattered away. He fell, head and arms hanging down over the side of the tank.

James felt like a horse had thrown him. He could not quite focus, could barely breathe. Collins started to drag him back, behind the tank. Whitefield appeared, bareheaded, his forehead dripping blood and he helped the gunner get James away.

'It's alright,' James said, 'I can walk.' Bullets clattered against the hull of the Sherman. Then the aim changed, and stalks of wheat were shredded as the MG stitched a row through the field. Only behind the Sherman were they shielded and safe – unless *Hector II* caught fire.

'Where's Tommo?' Collins asked.

Whitefield shook his head.

14.48 hrs, the Orchard, Hill 112

Judd had a Bren gun once more. His section was down to just him and Clarke, so he was back as number one with 'Nobby' Clarke as his loader. Davison had gone to the rear, his thighs and backside riddled with shrapnel from a mortar round that went off just behind him as he lay against the bank. He had been cheerful, at least once they gave him morphine and wrote an M on his forehead to prevent him getting an overdose further back.

'Just my ruddy luck. "What did you do in the war, Daddy?" the kids will say. Well, son, I got my ruddy arse blown off in France!'

It was a Blighty wound, which meant that for all the pain he was out of it, at least for a good six months and perhaps forever.

When there was time, Judd envied him. Not that there was much time, for the Germans were pushing forward from the central track and shooting up the sides of the Orchard with MG and tank fire. Davison was gone, like so many, and unless you were here, then you did not really matter, not for the moment – and the moment was all there was. Davison was gone and perhaps had never existed at all. Nothing had, apart from the shells and the mortar bombs and bullets.

A wave of SS men came on, shooting as they charged. Judd squeezed the trigger, saw a man fall, and then another coming behind him. Clarke was throwing grenades, screaming at the top of his voice, just incoherent noises. Buchanan picked men off with his rifle and Mark was there with a revolver. Germans fell, but they kept coming. 'Nobby' Clarke whipped off the magazine, replaced it, tapped Judd to tell him that the gun was ready, and then slumped over with a sigh and died, a single bullet in his chest.

Judd stood, because the panzer grenadiers were among them. He shot a man, then swung the heavy gun like a club. Buchanan jabbed forward, his pig sticker bayonet punching between a man's ribs. It stuck and the Canadian officer let it go and a German dived at him, both men going down in a ball. Mark's cheek was flapping, blood flying, slashed open as a round grazed him.

'Rusty' Reade saved them. The misfit, the man from the back streets who had to fight as soon as he could walk, struggling in a tiny terraced house against the cold and the diseases and the brutality of poverty. The man who had fought at school, against teachers and the other boys, who had done time as a juvenile, as an adult, had rarely been able to get work, and who had fought in the pubs and outside them in the gutters. Then the Army had taken him and he had fought the Army as well. Now he fought the Germans.

His Sten gun chattered. Grenadiers fell. The magazine was empty. He clubbed a man with it, then threw it away. A German came at him, bayonet lunging. Reade dodged, grabbed the rifle, twisted, wrenched it from the SS man's hands, and used the swing to slam the butt into his chin. He reversed the rifle and jabbed down into the back of the man struggling with Buchanan. The German arched his back, gasping. Reade jerked the blade out, spraying blood, brought the rifle up to waist height, saw another enemy, worked the bolt and pulled the trigger, flinging the German back. Then he rammed the bayonet so hard into another grenadier that the tip of the blade came out of his back.

Judd swung at a German and missed, but the enemy was retreating.

'Mongrels!' Reade screamed after them. He bent down, found a grenade, pulled the pin and threw it after the enemy. When he could not see another, he found a lump of wood and threw that. 'Give me the Bren!' he shouted at Judd, who did as he was told. Sergeant Reade fired it after the enemy until the magazine was empty. 'Take the bloody thing,' he said, throwing it back at Judd.

A massive stonk of British artillery was savaging the field outside, as close to the Orchard as they dared. The German infantry, caught in the open, wilted, and they either fell back or dashed into whatever shelter was offered inside the Orchard. Protected by their armour, the tanks and SPs remained, prowling across the open ground. Several parked within fifty yards of the bank, firing at anything that moved among the dead trees.

Inside, the Glamorgans dealt with their wounded, and sorted out weapons and ammunition. Mark came over to Judd. He was carrying a PIAT in both arms. 'I could do with some help,' he said, although the words were distorted by his flapping cheek.

'Get back to the Regimental Aid Post, sir,' Judd said.

'Afterwards.' Mark spat, the saliva red. 'Sorry. There's a tank so close that it's asking for it. I want to kill it.'

Judd nodded and hefted the Bren. 'I can try to keep their heads down.'

'So can I,' Buchanan added, 'and I can carry the bombs.'

'What about here?' Mark asked.

'Rusty can manage.' The sergeant was sitting, carefully slipping bullets into Sten gun magazines.

They went to the edge, moving cautiously, waiting until the big gun fired into the trees before dashing a few more yards. It was not a panzer, but a Stug, with a fixed gun firing forward.

Judd went wide, and set up the Bren on the bank. The head of the SP's commander was just visible above the cupola. Judd fired, rounds pinging off the armoured top of the Stug. The commander's head vanished. Then something moved and he realised that there were twin periscopes. Typical damned Germans, they thought of everything. He gave it a few shots, missed, then managed to clip one of the scopes. That should give the fellow a shock. After that he aimed more at the front, hoping to smash the driver's vision block.

The Stug's engine revved, and it locked its left track so that the whole vehicle pivoted towards him. Well, I've got their interest, he thought. Now where the hell was Mark?

The PIAT banged from over on his left and he saw the bomb as it sailed through the air and went past the SP. Bloody Mark.

The Stug had a machine gun mounted behind a shield on its roof. Judd could not see anyone manning it, but the gun began to fire and spurts of muck flew up from the bank around him. He dived back to shelter behind it as the Spandau continued to tear into the earth.

15.05 hrs, outside the Orchard

'Reckon she'll still go?' James asked. *Hector II* continued to show no sign of catching fire.

Whitefield had already peeked around the corner to see. 'Not a hope, boss. Track's gone – and the front wheel. Engine's still on, though.' That meant there was power for the turret traverse. A man could turn it by hand even if there were no electrics, but it took much longer.

'You two go back,' James said. 'I'll follow.' The British artillery had scoured the top of the hill of infantry, but only a few of the tanks and SPs had gone. There was so much smoke drifting in the air that it was hard to see, but he knew they were there. Someone in the Orchard was shooting at a Stug, and he could see the low slung assault gun clearly, one hundred and fifty yards away and side on to them.

'You want to get back in the tank, sir?' Collins asked. 'Then you'll need us,' he added, without waiting for an answer.

'Too much of a risk,' James said. 'Go back. I'll be along.'

'Union rules, boss. Can't go without us,' Whitefield told him. 'Don't want to put Collie here out of a job, do you?'

'I can gun.'

'Don't you bloody touch my gun,' Collins said, and then added a 'sir.'

'I don't need a driver, the tank won't go.'

Whitefield grinned. 'Used to be a loader. And they're affiliated to the Drivers' Union, so no arguments. I will not tolerate a scab in my tank.'

James laughed. 'You're both bloody mad.'

'Hark who's talking.'

Collins hauled himself up onto the engine deck and went to the turret. Whitefield followed, then James, because that was the only way for everyone to get into position. Blamey was still draped over the hull.

Hector II stank. As he got down into the turret James was

assaulted by the smell of blood. He could not see well, but Thomson's body was leaning back from his seat. His shoulders and everything above had gone.

'Gunner, traverse left, on. Target SP, range one fifty yards.'

Collins had a trigger grip which allowed him to rotate the turret. The movement was smooth and easy. He stamped on the button, but the co-ax refused to work. 'Browning needs a new belt.'

James saw the Stug had turned to its left and was now shifting the other way. A PIAT shot from the wood, at the same moment that Collins fired the 75mm. The Stug shook with the strikes. There was no sign of any flames.

'Hit him with another AP.'

'Make your bleedin' mind up,' Whitefield said, having just put a new belt into the machine gun. He grabbed a dark topped AP round and slammed it into the breech. A slap told Collins the gun was loaded. He did not bother with tracer, because he could see that he was on target. Another PIAT bomb flew out of the wood. Collins fired as well and the Stug burst into flames.

15.12 hrs, inside the Orchard, Hill 112

Major Fletcher appeared. 'We're pulling out. How many have you got left in D Company?'

'About a dozen,' Buchanan answered. 'Give or take.'

Mark nodded, reluctant to speak. He felt a great wave of satisfaction for knocking out the Stug. That would show them. There were just two bombs left for the PIAT, and he had tucked them into his battledress blouse. He held the launcher low, reluctant to let anyone else have it.

'Get back to the MO,' Fletcher told him.

'I'm alright, sir,' Mark tried to say and sprayed the major with drops of blood.

Fletcher wiped his face, absent-mindedly, shifting a little of the blood, if less of the grime and filth plastered all over it. 'D Company to cover us, but don't hang about. They'll come forward again soon and I don't think we can hold another attack.'

The only protest came from 'Rusty' Reade when Buchanan told him.

'Fuckin' officers. We can hold this place to Hell and back.'

'We've bled them,' Buchanan assured him. 'And it's only a hill.'

15.15 hrs, near the Orchard

The wireless was still working, once Whitefield had adjusted it – and hit it a few times. Regiment was surprised when they called in. 'Thought you were goners, Baker Three.'

'Immobilised,' James explained. 'But the gun is still working.'

'Advise pulling out, Baker Three, our leek friends are doing so.'

'What the bugger?' Whitefield said. 'Who the 'ell are they.'

'The Welsh, you ignorant Londoner. They live off leeks.'

James ignored them. 'Will wait a little to see if I can give some cover, over.'

'As you wish.' There was a pause. 'Sorry to report that Sunray down. Out of his tank in a barrage.'

So Tim Leyne had come back only to be hit again.

'Bad?' James asked.

'Permanent.'

'Poor sod,' Whitefield said softly. 'He was a good 'un.'

15.25 hrs, near the Orchard

More than half of the Glamorgans had left before Major Fletcher gave his orders to D Company, and the rest had followed. Buchanan split his remaining men into two groups, put Reade in charge of one, and stayed with the other himself. Mark was in no fit state to give orders, but refused to leave them and was still clutching his PIAT. They went in bounds, just like the manual, one group ready to cover while the others moved, then switching round. Thankfully, the Germans were not yet ready to renew the attack.

Judd scrambled over the bank. He glanced back once at the ruined, shattered Orchard, dotted with smashed equipment and smashed men. There was no point trying to make sense of it all, and apart from that he was too tired. Buchanan led them past Reade's men, lying in the grass with their weapons ready. A mangled seventeen-pounder and the Lloyd carrier that had towed it lay twisted and smashed in the grass. He could not remember seeing them before, or the fly-ridden corpses of two gunners stretched untidily on the ground. The dead seemed to sprawl any old how, as if death undid all the body's joints.

Buchanan took them to the left, behind a couple of Shermans, because the slope fell away quicker in that direction and would make it harder for the enemy to see them. One of the Shermans blazed, even though the hull was scorched black. In the other, he was surprised to see a head move in the cupola. He could only see half of it, and the cupola shifted so that the semi-circular hatch blocked the man from view. Yet he knew it was James. There was just something about the slight lean forward and the eyes.

'Down!' Buchanan called. 'Judd, on the flank!' He pointed to where he wanted the Bren gun. They lay down, scanning the crest of the hill. It was close. James' Sherman was a little ahead, the others at the crest itself.

'Come on!' Buchanan called to Reade. Judd saw that Mark was with the other group.

Then the Tiger appeared, its big engine roaring.

15.28 hrs, Hill 112

'Oh f—' Collins began and did not finish.

'What?' asked Whitefield. The loader had no real way of seeing out.

'Tiger,' James said. 'But maybe it doesn't know we're here. Load AP.'

'Already done, boss.'

The German tank emerged from the smoke like a dragon from its lair, coming on steadily. James did not think that its crew could see the retreating Glamorgans, but it was heading straight for them.

'Let it get close,' James said. 'Gunner, traverse, but don't fire until I say. Traverse right, right, on.'

The panzer was a hundred and fifty yards away. They said a Sherman could not even scratch the paint at that range, not on a Tiger's front armour. Some said that the 75mm could not go through the front at any range, not even if you were parked in front of the ruddy thing.

'Let it get closer,' James said softly. 'Closer.' It was a hundred yards away. James wondered if it was worth a shot. No, wait a bit more.

Someone ran past the Sherman, carrying a piece of green pipe. He sprinted to the side, dodging behind one of the wrecks, then bounded to another. It was Mark.

Oh dear God, James thought, and wondered about firing, until the cold, trained military logic told him that if the panzer saw the man with the PIAT then it might turn to face – and then Collins could plug it in the side. I'm a bastard, he thought to himself.

'Permission to fire, skipper?' Collins asked.

James wondered, then made up his mind.

15.29 hrs, Hill 112

Mark knew what he was doing. He had just two bombs, but the PIAT was already cocked and all he needed to do was get down, put it in front of him, slip the protective cap off the detonator, put the bomb in the tray and shoot. Simple. If the first one did not do the job then the second bomb would – at least if the panzer was playing fair and keeping still.

He would do it. He had a sense, a rare, treasured sense, that at this moment he could do no wrong, that whatever he wanted to do would work. He had felt like this when he took a hat-trick for the only time in his life and the first time he reached a hundred. That was not his only century, but the feeling that absolutely everything was easy and bound to succeed was rare. Most of those other innings he had ground his way to the landmark, with a lot more ones and twos than boundaries.

All the wrecks helped a lot. An MG opened up from the Orchard and he ducked behind the hulk of some German tank knocked out last month. He crouched as he went along it, then crawled forward, trusting that there was enough wheat left to shield him from view. The machine gun lost interest, and he kept crawling, until he was close enough to spring up and dash to another burned out tank, this time one of ours.

Mark wanted to smile, but his torn cheek did not let him. There was not any pain. It was almost easy as he worked his way around the long hull of the Churchill. A PIAT could fire a hundred yards, but half that distance was better. With a Tiger, closer still was better, just to get through the hulking armoured plate.

He would do it. Mark the quite good, Mark the quite nice, Mark the quite handsome, knew exactly what he was doing and the whole Universe understood that at this moment, he was perfect in everything he did.

He crawled because here the crops and grass were flattened.

Dear God, the Tiger was big, no more than forty yards away, but it was blind, lumbering along, foolish in its pride.

This would do. Mark laid the PIAT in front of him and loaded it with the first bomb. His legs spread to brace against the vicious kick. The tank was coming closer, at an angle to drive past him. He could see its right side, and aimed for the black cross outlined with white near the front of the hull. The driver should be behind that plate, so serve the devil right. No, damn it, the bloody Continentals did everything backwards so it would be his assistant.

Mark pulled the trigger, the PIAT gave its confident bang, and the bomb flew over and struck inches from the cross. The Tiger juddered to a halt. Then it began to turn. Mark reached for his other bomb.

15.31 hrs, on Hill 112

James thought he heard the PIAT shoot, but could not see what happened. He could see Mark, who lay there, reloading. The Tiger was turning towards the lone man, more of its side now facing *Hector II*. That would do.

'Gunner, fire!'

Collins stamped on the button, the 75 thundered and the round grazed the Tiger's gun mantlet as it turned and skimmed past, missing the rest of the turret, the hull and the big gun itself.

'Bugger!' Collins muttered.

Whitefield was getting quicker and had a round in the breech in a matter of seconds. The Tiger's turret was turning towards them, slower than their own, but then it did not have far to go. They should beat it. Whitefield tapped Collins' leg, and could not resist shouting, 'Loaded!'

'Fire!' James yelled, his voice as loud.

Collins stamped his boot on the button for the 75mm. Nothing happened.

'Misfire,' he gasped.

'Oh fuck,' Whitefield added. The striker had not set off the propellant charge, at least not yet. It could go at any time, or never. The drill was to open the breech, unload the round, carry it like a parent carrying a sleeping infant and not wanting it to wake, and take it outside. The manual did not say what to do when a Tiger almost had you in its sights.

15.32 hrs, Hill 112

Mark saw the panzer begin to swing its turret away from him, but the hull was still going the other way, and the co-driver had his own Spandau. The long barrel was twitching as if trying to force the big tank around. He had a second or two at the most, but the bomb was in the tray. He waited, making sure of his aim.

In the Orchard the German MG team saw the Englishman in the open, hunting the tank, and thought him brave, but stupid. A new belt went on, the gunner pulled the bolt back, slid it forward, did it again and then fired.

Bullets threw up puffs of dirt as they ran in a line towards the prone figure. Something slammed into Mark's thigh, breaking the bone, and he rolled away and sat up in shock. Bullet after bullet drove into his body, making him twitch like a puppet pulled wildly. The MG 42 was pulling up and the next rounds went into his neck and head.

15.33 hrs, near the Orchard

'Oh Christ,' James said as the bullets seemed to shred his friend, but the 88mm, its muzzle a vast black circle at this range, was almost on them. 'Bail out!' he tried to say, but the words did not come and his limbs seemed frozen.

The Tiger's turret stopped.

Then there was a flash from the side, the faint shape of a missile and a glowing orange circle in the flat mantlet mounting the gun.

'Three Charlie to Baker Three, are you still there?' Sergeant Martin's voice came through James' headphones. Before he could answer, the Firefly sent another AP shell at the Tiger, this time going through the hull plate. Smoke, thin smoke, but smoke nonetheless began to rise from the back of its hull. Hatches opened, and men in camouflaged uniforms jumped out.

'Don't shoot them!' James said suddenly, for no reason other than it seemed unlucky after the escape they had just had. Whether Collins felt the same or not, he did not shoot with the co-axial. Neither did the Firefly.

'Baker Three to Three Charlie. Yes, we're here, but the tank is US.'

'Do you want a ride?'

'Tell him we'll walk,' Whitefield said quickly. 'Buggers tend to shoot at tanks, and on the back, you can't hide.'

'Thanks, Three Charlie, but we'll follow.'

'Okay, Baker Three.'

'Thanks again, Three Charlie.'

'All part of the service. Don't count on it next time.' AP shot struck the ground near the Firefly. Martin and his crew hastily reversed out of sight.

15.40 hrs, Hill 112

James and his remaining crew watched from the lip of the crest as Judd, unarmed, walked over to Mark. He had left the Bren behind, but he had no red cross armband and the laws of war gave the enemy free rein to shoot him. They did not, and the SS machine gunners and everyone else held their fire. So did the Tiger's crew, huddling behind the smoking tank, even though two had sub machine guns and the rest pistols.

Mark was dead, struck by so many bullets that the life had been shaken from him in an instant. His face was mangled, even worse than before, and Judd doubted that he would have recognised his friend if he had simply stumbled across the corpse. Poor Mark. He always did his best and was so sincere, even simple.

Judd knelt, lifting the body so that Mark was sitting again and then raised him onto his shoulder. He felt heavy, but loose, his limbs dangling. Judd could smell the blood, feel it seeping onto him. So much had come out in the moments before the heart stopped pumping.

Bill Judd stood, gave a nod in the direction of the enemy, turned and walked away, carrying his burden. At least Mark would get a proper grave, which he might or might not if left behind. He ought to get a ruddy medal.

15.45 hrs, on the northern slope of Hill 112

The fighting had slackened on the hill, for the moment, although it still raged along the front on either side. A message went back to Shelldrake, the most senior RA officer in the area, that the Glamorgans had pulled back and that the Germans had taken the Orchard. He called for a heavy stonk of the place, an Uncle Target with all of the Division's guns. They would fire five rounds apiece, which was not that many, for the batteries would soon move to other tasks, but it seemed right to make a point. The British had gone, but had not given up.

James heard the shells passing overhead and was glad that he was not wherever they were heading. He was walking beside Judd, who carried the dead Mark and refused to let anyone help him with the burden. Whitefield and Collins stayed with their officer, but no one was in the mood for talking.

In response to the British show of hate, a German FOO called in a battery of 120mm mortars on a preregistered target on the British slope of the hill. It felt like the natural thing to do. Compared to the British, ammunition was rare and precious, which meant that each tube only launched a single bomb.

Mortars were hard to hear in the air, the bombs coming slowly without the whine of artillery shells. That was what made them so dangerous, because there was less time to take cover. The Glamorgans, weary, walking in a daze, only began to dive down at the very last moment. Judd sank to his knees. The tankmen did not move.

Judd was slammed face first into the ground as if a sledge-hammer had hit him in the middle of the back. James Taylor was blown off his feet and did not know how he landed on his back staring at the sky. Whitefield was crouched nearby, face covered in blood, and he was screaming because he could not see. Collins, standing between the two of them, was knocked down, but did not have a scratch on him.

D+40, Sunday 16th July

12.35 hrs, Base Hospital, Basingstoke

JAMES HAD DRIFTED in and out of sleep for days. His memories were few, and confused. He had been hit, and badly, with shrapnel tearing into his left leg and all over his back and chest. He seemed to remember being lifted up then driven, perhaps on a stretcher mounted on a jeep. There was probably an aid post, and he thought that he could remember an Advanced Dressing Station, crowded, filled with all sorts of wounded and staff who somehow turned the chaos into some sort of order. Then there had been lights, electric lights in a tent, and nothing, until he woke, heavily bandaged. He seemed to remember a German in the bed next to his, an SS man, a hand and both legs gone, but very garrulous and with perfect English. Said he had gone to Winchester of all things. Then asked why the British were wasting their time and all this blood.

'You must know, my friend, that we will all have to join together soon to fight the Russians. Us, you English, and the Americans. Communism is the real threat, you must come to see that.'

Had that been real or just a morphine induced dream? Why would he have imagined something so mad? He could picture the fellow's face as clearly as anything, and his jacket hanging beside the bed, a jacket covered with the medals and badges the Germans loved. Odd that those had not been pinched as he came through the system.

James lay and stared at the ceiling. There was another bed in this little room, but no one was in it. He did not think that the German had been here anyway. That room had been poorly lit, but this was bright, the walls and ceiling a brilliant white. Was this Heaven? It smelled of disinfectant, which made that seem unlikely. He also hurt, and he did not think that was supposed to happen in the Blessed Realm. He hurt a lot. The slightest movement brought bouts of pain, but he felt stiff if he did not move. His left leg was held in traction above the bed.

'Awake, are we?' The voice was soft, feminine and Irish. It could be Heaven after all, hearing a voice like that. Still, he was not Catholic, which argued against that theory.

A face appeared, round, snub nosed, very pleasant and best of all smiling. The face had the cap of the Queen Alexandra's Nursing Yeomanry. James was almost disappointed to accept that this was not Heaven, somewhere where war could never come.

'How are you feeling, Lieutenant Taylor? You've made us work, haven't you?'

'Sorry,' he whispered. He was not sure what else he was expected to say.

The nurse laughed, an easy, genuinely happy laugh. He had not heard a sound so pure for longer than he could remember. 'Nothing to apologise for! It's just that you took a turn for the worse last night and we were worried. But a fresh X-ray showed the piece the surgeon in France had missed. Hiding behind your lungs it was, near the heart. Colonel Terry opened you up again, and got it all out. Says you made him miss his dinner! But he said to me, "Sister Jennings, don't let this one die after all the trouble he's caused." So, I won't.'

'I'm sorry,' he said again. Even he was not sure to whom he was apologising, or for what.

'Don't keep saying that or I'll get angry,' she said without a hint of any temper. 'Or I'll get Matron and she can really get angry. ... You're going to be alright. We were worried for a while, we all were, but you've done us proud. So, rest and get well. No more war for you, but you'll be alright in time.'

No more war. Was this another dream? Was the mad German about to wheel himself in and plan another march on Moscow?

'Are you hungry?'

James shook his head. It was bandaged and it hurt. He had a headache like the hangovers he had suffered at Bayeux. He was not sure whether that world or this felt more real. Neither really. This must be a dream and he would wake in the turret of a Sherman tank, the crackle of static in his ears.

'Hmm. Well, you'll need to eat soon. Have a drink now – and I won't take no for an answer.' Sister Jennings lifted his head and gave him some water. 'There'll be tea coming soon. Now is there anything else you would like?'

'What day is it?'

'Sunday, but since your card says you're a heathen Protestant I'll let you off for not knowing that. It's five days since you were hurt and two and a half since they got you back from France – in a plane, believe it or not.'

'So fast.' His mind was starting to work. So was his body. He managed to prop himself up and take another sip. It hurt, but was not unbearable.

Sister Jennings nodded. 'We're getting plenty back and have for weeks. There's a story doing the rounds that a major went to visit his men in a field hospital in France. He was tired and lay down for forty winks on an empty bed. The man woke up in England!'

'Thank you,' James said. 'Thank you.'

Sister Jennings smiled. She had a very good smile. 'You just get well. And I need to get on, or Matron will tear a strip off me!' She went to the door and then stopped. The look changed, part teacher showing affection for a wayward pupil and part conspirator.

'All your questions made me forget and run away talking. I have something for you.'

For a moment his mind went to one of Whitefield's bawdy stories. Surely not! Then he remembered his driver screaming. He could not remember any more because his own agony had engulfed him. No point asking the nurse. She would have no idea.

'Are you not a little curious? A strange woman says she has something for you and you don't ask what it is.'

'A kiss?'

'Ha! You soldiers are terrible, and me a good Catholic girl. No, it's not from me, but something of yours. They often get lost, of course, but there are some who try to make sure that a man's charm stays with him. Science is one thing, but these days we'll take all the luck we can get. These are yours, I think.' She pressed something into his right hand. He felt the softness and she must have seen the wonder on his face.

'Well, when I say yours, I mean I hope you don't wear them. Takes all sorts and all that, but that would be pushing it. You don't wear them, do you?'

'They were a present.'

'That doesn't answer my question.'

'From my fiancée.'

'Then that's alright and as I hoped. They're very nice. Lovely workmanship. P? I was very tempted to take them, rationing and all. Pamela Jennings. They'd suit me, don't you think – or you better not think, you cheeky devil! They will be safe in the drawer. Now rest, and get well. Call me if you need me.'

James went back to staring at the ceiling. The window blinds were drawn and even with the criss-cross of tape on the glass they let in a lot of light. Must be a nice day.

Penny. Penelope Stevens. Whimsical, poetry loving, romantic, pre-Raphaelite Penny. All those months ago or was it years? The proposal, the ring, the party her parents had held to celebrate the announcement. All those people, plenty of whom he did not know, and nearly all old or female because the men his own age were away.

How Penny had lured him away to be alone for a few short minutes, knowing that he had to catch the train in an hour and a half. She had taken him to the library. Trust the Stevenses to have a room called a library in the semi-detached house. It was a big house, true enough, but still a semi a mere twelve years old and scarcely the ancestral manor.

'In days of yore, a lady gave her knight a favour,' Penny had said, wholly serious, as only she could be when she spoke such lines.

'My lady,' he had said. She had looked beautiful that day. Her hair was long and gleaming gold. Her dress was a gentle blue, her high heeled shoes matching the colour as had her tiny hat. She had dark blue gloves and belt. Penny always said a lady never wore everything the same colour and shade. She was good with a needle and thread and careful with her clothes, but this was a special day so she had risked some of her surviving stockings – silk too, rather than the new-fangled nylons. She could have stepped out of a fashion magazine.

'Turn your back,' she said. That seemed odd, and James had hoped with all his heart that this did not mean that in a moment she would put her hands over his eyes and say 'guess who?' You never quite knew with Penny.

He obeyed and turned, facing a bookcase with glass doors. Cynically, he reckoned that Mr Stevens had bought most of the faded hardbacks in a second-hand shop. Probably had never opened a single one and just thought that they looked right as part of the furniture. Penny was the only reader in the family, even if her tastes were narrow and more than a little silly.

James could see her reflection in the glass and thought that she would have liked the transparent, almost ethereal appearance it gave her. Penny was twisting, almost doing a shimmy, both hands on her hips, easing down, almost crouching. Something appeared beneath the hem of her dress.

James' mouth hung open, which was the only thing that stopped him from swearing.

'You can turn around now.' Penny had the delighted expression of an infant doing something that they knew to be terribly naughty and dangerous. Her hands were behind her back now. The tip of her tongue flicked out, licking her neatly rouged lips. She was brimming over with mischief. 'Hold out your hands.'

She came over, emphasising each step. Her heels were very high, the shoes tying around each ankle. Expensive and pre-War, not that she would have been old enough to buy or wear them back then. He doubted that they had come from coupons, so goodness knows how she had got hold of them. The dress was fuller too than you could buy these days, when even the number of pleats was regulated. She must have made it herself. It clung tight and swayed in all the right places.

The naughty child and the maiden from Arthurian romance stood just in front of him. Her mother's voice was calling from somewhere. Not too close, but they probably had little time. She pressed her hands down onto his and he felt the smoothness of silk. He had already guessed, but it was still a shock to see that she was giving him a pair of knickers, the palest of pink, with white lace and an embroidered P for Penny. No, not knickers, she probably would not use the word. Step-ins or panties or something like that. Women had a large vocabulary when it came to clothes.

'Take these. I want to be close to you always and these have been close to me as ever can be. I want to give you my love and my luck.'

Then she had stood on tiptoe and put her hands on his shoulders, her eyes closing in anticipated ecstasy, and it was so natural to lean forward and kiss her, not that she could get too close, because he was still dumbly standing there, holding the pants.

The kiss was good. Very good, and long, and he smelled her perfume and felt the softness of her hair – and the netting on her hat. He could not see, but was sure her right leg came up, bending at the knee, pointing out straight behind her just like in the flicks.

'Ah, there you two love birds are!' Mrs Stevens said as she came into the room. 'I know how you feel, but we have guests.'

Penny pulled away and sighed. 'Oh, Mother.'

'I know, I know, but you and James will have a lifetime together.'

James frantically bunched up the lacy pants and shoved them into his trouser pocket before the girl's mother saw what he had. Penny was in front of him, and he just managed to stow the things away before the girl moved.

There was nearly an hour before he had to leave. James struggled to pay attention to anyone or anything, and kept having to beg someone's pardon and ask them what they had said, or pretend he had heard and give a vague answer. The vicar wanted to have a long talk with him, and throughout he had a nightmare vision of sneezing, reaching for a handkerchief and instead brandishing a pair of frilly knickers in front of the clergyman and his very proper wife.

Penny managed to be close a lot of the time, since, after all, this was meant to celebrate their betrothal. Whenever she could she took care to brush her hips against him. Her dress was quite thin. Presumably she had a petticoat, but otherwise was bare underneath. Dear God, it was an ordeal trying to appear unmoved and as disinterested in everything as a soldier and young English gentleman should. He was not sure whether she was teasing him or simply taking delight in being so very naughty. You really did never know with Penny.

'I love you, my prince,' she had said when he had to go. Her parents gave them a little distance, but not too much. 'I love you with all my heart. I'll be with you.' They had kissed, rather chastely, but what was a fellow to do when a girl's parents were watching. He pulled her close, that was surely acceptable – and apart from that what were they going to do at this stage? 'Keep them with you,' she whispered in his ear. 'And I'll be with you and keep you safe.' James smoothed her back. The dress was very soft and so was she. He let his hand wander a little lower onto her behind. Mrs Stevens noticed and arched an eyebrow. His heart was pounding, but that was the least of his worries.

Penny gave a little giggle, so like a child's and so unlike. She pushed herself closer for just a moment. At least he had had his folded greatcoat to hold out in front when she stepped away.

Well, she had brought him luck, he supposed, for he was not dead, even if it sounded as if he really ought to be. What's more, if Sister Jennings was right, he would not be going back, no matter how long the War lasted.

James was not sure that he believed the nurse, but he was alive and he ought to be out of it all for a few months at the very least.

'Thank you,' he murmured, not sure whether he was speaking to the nurse, to Heaven, or to the whimsical, passionate young woman who loved him with such fervour.

James realised that he was still clutching Penny's favour. He tried to sit up, but could not reach as far as the locker beside his bed, so kept hold of them.

Lucky knickers. It was not the sort of story that you could tell your grandchildren. Good God, was he going to have bloody grandchildren? Was it all over? No more 'Forming Up Points', no more 'No Move Before' and no more tanks with all their stench and discomfort. No more Baker Three.

No more fear. With that thought, James fell into a deep sleep.

D+59, Friday 4th August

19.45 hrs, south of Hill 112, Normandy

THE EVENINGS WERE starting to draw in and there was probably little more than a couple of hour's daylight left. 'Coop' Buchanan would have preferred to wait for darkness before leading the patrol, but Brigade had pressed Battalion and Battalion had pressed A Company, so out they went to get a sense of where the German positions were. After weeks spent in the Odon valley, fighting and dying for tiny strips of land, they were going forward. The Americans had begun it, pulverising the German front lines with heavy bombers and then fighting their way through. Almost two months after D-Day things were starting to move faster, but only starting. There were still plenty of Germans out there who showed no sign of packing it all in. The four men went carefully forward to see if they could find some.

Judd tried to remember how Hill 112 had looked all those weeks ago, but the ground was so tortured by high explosives that it resembled a wasteland. At least there were plenty of shell craters to offer cover, along with the wrecks and other debris of war. There were skeletons too, mostly of cattle and a few horses, but perhaps of other things as well.

Buchanan tapped the magazine of his rifle and they froze. Judd was the only other man apart from the lieutenant who had been with the Glamorgans in the Orchard. The other two were replacements, although three weeks in Normandy had

changed them from the raw, dangerously careless men being
sent to battalions these days. They were still alive, which was no
mean achievement. 'Coop' had chosen them a couple of times
to come on similar patrols.

That was one of the problems of doing a job well. 'Coop'
Buchanan was the only subaltern who had landed with them
in Normandy who was still left in charge of a platoon. The
rest were dead, wounded, or had cracked up and been sent
away lest they failed when it really mattered. 'Coop' was still
being sent out on patrols more often than anyone else. Another
CANLOAN officer had come to the Glamorgans, but the other
two originals were both dead. Buchanan had rested 'Rusty'
Reade this time, and for once the sergeant had not needed
persuading. They were all so tired.

Back in June and early July, Judd had thought that it was
not possible to become more exhausted and still to stand and
function when told. He was wrong. They were pulled back
after Hill 112, given replacements and a few quiet days. Then
they were back in the line. There had been other big offensives
since then, but the Glamorgans had not been involved, at least
not directly. Twice the Battalion had put in a set-piece attack
on a village. Half a dozen times the Company had assaulted a
farm or other cluster of buildings or swept a wood for snipers
and machine guns. Once 9 Platoon was sent to occupy a lone
house beside a brook. They did it, and lost half their number,
all replacements, in a vicious little fight against half a dozen
Germans who would not give up. Otherwise, the attacks usually
succeeded, and sometimes failed.

None of it seemed to matter. Judd was still alive and
unwounded, for otherwise he could not be sent on patrols, sit
in his slit trench under bombardments, and eat and drink tea
made from foul chlorinated water. The dead had rest and he did
not, although it was hard to tell the difference. Everything was
mechanical now, a mixture of training, experience and sheer
habit. He did what he had to do, and if he survived would do it

again. He wore the two stripes of a corporal and led a section of just five men, including himself. There were rarely as many as twenty men in 9 Platoon, and that was typical of the Glamorgans as a whole, although they had managed to go back to having four companies instead of three. None of his men were on this patrol; they were too raw or simply too clumsy. One even wore glasses, which was a surprise in the infantry. There was no sense in bringing him along and risking light glinting off the lenses.

Buchanan tapped his magazine again. Whatever had worried him, worried him no longer. Judd rose and led them, another man next, then 'Coop' and then a lance corporal who had been here long enough to be useful, but not long enough to have lost all his enthusiasm. The man was twenty-two and Judd felt ancient and broken by comparison.

Early on, they had passed the spot where Mark had died. The Orchard was in British hands again, as was Hill 112 itself, properly occupied soon after dawn that morning. Its wide vista no longer had much importance, for the main German line had pulled back and was not really overlooked. Instead, a few miles to the south, there was more high ground from which the German observers could spot. Those hills and ridges would need to be captured, just like this one, and no doubt the price would be high. A lot more men, much like Mark and others who had gone, would die or be maimed.

Poor Mark. Judd had felt a pang of sadness as he remembered his friend. He was too tired to think and feel any more than that, although he had written to Mark's mother. That had been weeks ago, and a reply had come back, thanking him.

And poor Mrs Crawford. She had never cared much for him, but she was so grateful and so sad. Judd had told her that Mark had saved his life, which was true, although he had not said how. When the mortar bomb landed, Mark's corpse had taken the brunt of the blast and the jagged metal, mutilating his body still further. Judd had not had a scratch, unlike James. That had looked bad, very bad. He had not had any news since then.

'Oh shit,' the man behind Judd gasped. He turned, saw the other man, white faced, his hands trembling as they held the Sten gun. His right boot was just above the ground and beneath it were the three metal prongs of an S mine. Whatever he did now, the mine would go off. The first charge would throw him, blowing off his leg, and throwing a cannister into the air, which the second charge would explode, sending hundreds of ball bearings spraying through the air all around.

'Oh my God,' the man said.

Judd struggled to remember his name. Dawkins, that was it, from Exeter. These days he struggled to remember anything new.

'Try to go in your footsteps,' Buchanan called. 'And get back.' They could do nothing to help Dawkins. He would die or perhaps just be blinded and crippled. There was no sense in the rest sharing his fate for the sake of it. The question was whether this was one isolated mine or whether they had strayed into a minefield.

'Easy, lad,' Buchanan called. 'When I say, throw yourself back as far as you can.' It sometimes worked. Not often, but sometimes it did, and a man escaped with just a few wounds. The pellets were not big, but they were flung at immense speed.

There was a crack, almost like a pistol shot, and a scream of pure agony. 'Coop' had taken a step backwards, onto another mine. Judd did not know what the Germans called it, but it was the smallest, and in some ways cruellest one they used, for it was a piece of pipe buried in the ground and when someone stepped onto it, it fired a rifle bullet up and at an angle. The British called it the debollocker.

With a much louder bang the S mine went off. Perhaps the surprise had made Dawkins shift his weight just too much. The charge ripped off his foot and leg beneath the knee and sent the cannister up. It burst and sent dozens of steel balls into the falling man, lacerating his face and chest. A couple more spread far enough to strike Buchanan as he lay on the floor, hands pressed against his crotch. Several hit the lance corporal.

Judd was not touched.

Either there were no more mines or he was just lucky, but he managed to get to Buchanan and carry him back to the RAP. The lance corporal was not much help, because some of the ball bearings had broken his arm. Judd lied when 'Coop' asked him whether it was bad.

At the Aid Post, Judd had sat down and then fallen asleep. When he woke, the MO gave him a shot and he slept some more.

Three days later he was sent back to the Battalion.

Historical Note

T HIS IS A novel based on fact, and it is only fair to give the reader a clearer idea of how close the story keeps to the events of the summer of 1944. Perhaps it will also be of interest to explain the origins of the story. One is very old. I attended a prep school in a small town on the Welsh side of the Bristol Channel. The school had changed hands, as such places often do, but for a while the former headmaster, who had been there since before the Second World War, stayed on to assist the new team. It was said that in his office he had a photograph of a class of boys from the Thirties. It was not a large school then or when I was there in the late Seventies, so this probably meant twenty or so youngsters at the most. The story went that none of them had survived the Second World War.

Times change, and with it the management of schools, and these days no one knew anything about this. I do not know whether or not the story is true. My suspicion, reinforced by years as a professional historian, is that the story is exaggerated, and perhaps *most* rather than *all* fell during the war. Certainly, small schools like this tended to suffer unusually heavy losses. Boys with this sort of education who became eligible for military service between 1939 and 1945 were likely to go into many of the most dangerous roles in the military, for instance as aircrew, and as subalterns in the Army, especially in the infantry.

The First World War remains in British memory as the worst war, most terrible for its losses where whole towns and villages were left to mourn after the Somme or Passchendaele or other terrible battles. There are plenty of reasons for this collective memory, and not least is the simple fact that the experience was appalling – made worse because this was the first war with conscription and mass mobilisation in Britain. Added poignancy comes from the widespread belief – which may or may not be justified – that the struggle from 1914 to 1918 was unnecessary, whereas few will doubt the need to defeat the Nazis and Imperial Japan in the Second World War.

British fatalities in the Second World War were about a third of the losses in the Great War. To a great extent this was because Britain did not field as large an army and play as central a role in ground warfare as it had done with the BEF in France and Flanders. Some of this was through technology. Modern armies needed far more men to support the teeth arms than had been the case in 1918. Yet for the ones actually doing the fighting, the risks were often as great and sometimes greater than those run by their predecessors in the earlier conflict.

The second thread in all this came from reading about the Second World War. Mine was a generation that grew up making plastic kits of fighters, bombers, ships and tanks and reading about 'the War' as it was still called. Films did a lot to shape my imagination, and I doubt that I am alone in admitting that my perception of D-Day had a lot to do with *The Longest Day*. Yet libraries offered more books than pocket money could afford, and the local library had a good history section with an especially good section on the Second World War. Many topics fascinated me, but the campaign in North-West Europe had a particular draw. Again, films helped, notably *A Bridge Too Far*, also based on a book by Cornelius Ryan, which I found mesmerising when I first saw it in the cinema.

As I read and learned more, the realisation came that the films, quite reasonably, only told part of the story. D-Day was important, its success to some extent hiding the incredible effort required to mount it and the risks involved. Yet the Battle of Normandy lasted for two and a half months after D-Day itself, and it was appallingly costly. This was an attritional battle fought against a determined enemy in a very confined space. The Germans did not give up ground as readily as they had done in Sicily and mainland Italy, so the same villages and features were fought over again and again. Senior officers, who had been young officers in Flanders, repeatedly compared some of the actions, such as those fought around Hill 112, to the likes of Passchendaele. Some even thought that the experience in 1944 was worse. Indeed, the average time a British or Canadian infantry subaltern spent at the front before becoming a casualty was lower than it had been on the Somme.

Over the years, I realised that this was a story I wanted to tell, in part because it does not seem to be as widely known as it should be. In 2024 the eightieth anniversary of D-Day will be – and should be – commemorated, even though the remaining ranks of veterans will be few. Yet it will be about D-Day, with much fanfare on or around 6th June and far less attention to what followed.

There are plenty of very good non-fiction studies of the Battle of Normandy in all its aspects, and others are far better qualified to make new contributions to the field. However, not everyone reads much non-fiction, especially fairly specialised stuff, and the idea grew that a novel might be the best way to make more people aware of the story. Historical fiction, when well done, can offer a quicker window into places and times in the past. Thus, the two ideas came together and this is the result. I wanted to write a story about men who were little more than boys in age, who had come from a sheltered, middle class background in a Britain still at the head of a massive world empire, who found themselves in the melting pot of the Army, and then in the middle of a prolonged and very savage battle.

Writing this sort of story invites clichés. If there are a fair few of them in the text, then that is because such things are common in real life, which is why they become clichés in the first place. Yet I have tried to avoid some of the more hackneyed tropes of military stories and dramas, where the main characters have to loathe each other until they earn respect, since this tends to come across as false and is not borne out by the sources.

This is not *the* story of the Battle of Normandy, let alone of *the* British experience of the Second World War. It is simply *a* story from those times, and one that I have tried to get as right as possible, drawing on the many personal accounts of those who were there as I could find. I was not there, and am fortunate to belong to a generation not required to endure bombing and rationing and blackouts, to face a very real fear of invasion, and then to be called upon to don uniform and fight. The modern tendency is to dub everyone who took part a hero, until the word loses most of its significance. To my mind the striking thing about most of those who took part is that they come across as very ordinary, even though they were called upon to suffer and to do extraordinary things. That was the aim of the book, to follow some pretty ordinary, if fairly sensitive, young men through some of this experience. They are meant to be representative of one section of society, with all that that entails in terms of their perspective and attitudes. I hope that I have come close to the reality – at least as far as that is possible for someone born when I was born, who did not experience those years.

As stated at the start, the characters are fictional, not simply James Taylor, Mark Crawford and Bill Judd, but all the others who feature in the story, with the obvious exceptions of the likes of Montgomery and Eisenhower, who are mentioned, but never really appear. In addition, the two regiments key to the story are fictional. There was no Glamorganshire regiment, but it seemed better to create a wholly invented unit rather than add a fictional battalion to the Welch Regiment or the South Wales Borderers. With more than a touch of vanity, I decided to use a regiment I invented some years ago for a series of novels set in the Napoleonic era. However, the Glamorgans' major actions in this story are based on ones fought by several actual units in 1944.

The 165th RAC is another invention. Britain pioneered the use of the tank in the First World War, then, with all the cutbacks, neglected its development between the wars, only to be rather taken in by the propaganda of the might of the panzers, so that they raised too many armoured units in the years that followed. Many of these were recruited from scratch or converted from Territorial units. The 165th in the story is part of a brigade which I have based on the actual 8th Armoured Brigade of 1944. Its other units are Dragoons – based on the real 4th/7th Dragoon Guards – and the Yeomanry – based on the Sherwood Rangers Yeomanry. My 165th take the place of the 24th Lancers for most of the story, although for Operation Epsom they take the place of the 23rd Hussars, part of the 11th Armoured Division. I have felt free to simplify, and occasionally change, details of these actions, to make them easier to follow and fit the story better. Similarly, I have simplified the details of supply and maintenance of the vehicles, and wireless procedure, where codenames changed more often than they do in the book. One major difference between men serving in tanks and infantry was that the former tended to have more idea of where they were and what everyone was doing, because of the constant radio traffic.

This book is aimed at showing what it was like for the young men who did the fighting in Normandy. Its focus is on the British, and on an average infantry battalion and armoured regiment. As stated at the start, this means that I cannot go into any real detail about the roles played by others. The British and Canadians sent more gunners to Normandy than they did infantrymen – numbers reflected in the overall proportions of the Army as a whole. Shellfire killed and wounded more Germans than any other single cause during the campaign, and I hope that the narrative reflects the appalling power and sophisticated use of Allied artillery, even though it never gives a gunner's perspective.

Instead, we see the campaign through the eyes of three British soldiers, which means that the focus is on what happened around them. This is not a book about the grand strategy of the Normandy campaign let alone of the wider war. Such matters are fiercely debated to this day, not least because central to it all is the role of Field Marshal Montgomery, who, whatever his military merits, had an unfortunate personality. Until more American troops arrived late in the campaign, Montgomery commanded all the land forces of every nationality. Over him was the Supreme Commander, General Eisenhower, a truly remarkable manager, whose tact and charm – and easy smile – did so much to keep together a team of prickly senior commanders.

Montgomery did not excel in tact or charm. None of this was helped by the wider picture. Britain was coming to the end of its resources of manpower and funds. In the early days of the Battle of Normandy, there was a rough parity between British and American troop numbers. Over time the former would shrink and the latter keep increasing, so that by the end of the year it was obvious to everyone that the USA was the senior partner. Montgomery's methodical style of warfare was predicated on the knowledge that heavy British losses could not be replaced. Before the end of the Battle of Normandy the British disbanded battalions, regiments and whole divisions to provide replacements. The Canadians, who did not introduce conscription and instead relied on volunteers, faced a similar, perhaps even worse, problem.

In essence, Montgomery's plan for the campaign was this. The Americans landed in the west and the British and Canadians in the east. Cherbourg was the major port closest to the landing beaches and it was in the American sector, hence a priority for them to take. The American sector also involved some of the most difficult terrain for mobile warfare. A lot of it was the bocage of small fields and high banked, thick hedges. While there was a significant amount of this in the British and Canadian sector it was even more extensive in the west. This meant that it was harder for the Americans to push forward quickly. In the east, especially closer to the city of Caen, there was rather more open country. This in turn meant that there seemed to be more chance of breaking through with armoured spearheads in this area – and conversely this was the place where the Germans were most likely to be able to drive to the sea.

D-Day is rightly remembered, but by the end of 6th June all five beaches had been firmly secured in spite of some heavy fighting, most famously on OMAHA, but reflected on a smaller scale on several other beaches. The critical phase was the build-up, as each side rushed reinforcements to the area. Everything brought by the Allies had to come by sea. The Germans were distracted by the deception plan threatening a second landing in the Pas de Calais, had a far less smooth command structure and were hindered by Allied airpower, but it was still easier to travel by land than water.

The broad Allied plan was to keep German attention focused on the eastern sector, allowing the Americans to take Cherbourg and eventually break out, unleashing the newly arrived US Third Army under Patton into Brittany and the rest of France. To facilitate this, the bulk of the German armour was to be drawn to the eastern sector and held there by the British and Canadians. It helped that the transport infrastructure and the starting point of the panzer divisions tended to mean that they reached this area first. In addition, the country there looked most promising for an armoured attack. However, this would not have mattered if the British and Canadians had not mounted attack after attack to focus the Germans' attention on this sector.

Most of these attacks produced disappointing results at very high cost in casualties. Much of the controversy surrounds whether Montgomery actually intended offensives like Operation Epsom to create a major breakout from the beachhead – as he claimed publicly at the time – or was far more sanguine and really aimed at keeping the German strength facing the British and Canadians – as he claimed subsequently. For instance, Caen was a D-Day objective, but in fact did not fall for almost a month. Yet the way the campaign played out was broadly according to the plan, which suggests that the truth is probably somewhere in the middle.

For the soldiers involved, these were gruelling battles of attrition, with some areas, such as Hill 112, fought over again and again. There were no spectacular breakthroughs – no equivalent of the vaunted Blitzkrieg of the early war years, where the panzer divisions had advanced far and fast. However, to set against this, those same panzer divisions utterly failed in all the offensives they launched. Local counter attacks often recaptured lost positions, but the Germans never made any significant progress in major attacks, none of which came close to breaking through to the sea. Air power, and especially the formidable power and skill of Allied artillery – backed for much of the campaign by the guns on ships – made any major German attack difficult. In addition, the Germans failed to coordinate their offensives, to a fair extent because they were never given much opportunity. Montgomery kept attacking, so that as each panzer division arrived it was sucked into the fight to plug a gap in the line, and slowly worn down as it tried to hold and retake ground. Almost never did a panzer division attack as a division with all its different components and troop types concentrated to support each other. By late June to early July there was the bulk of nine panzer divisions facing the British and Canadians, but their combat power could not be effectively focused.

For all the problems faced by the Germans when they attacked, we should acknowledge that an important reason for the failure of these attacks was that the British and Canadians defended well – as would the Americans when attacked in August. The reverse is true when looking at why Allied attacks yielded disappointing results. In the days immediately after D-Day, the Canadians played a vital role in stopping German attempts to drive to the sea. British troops were also involved, and we see some of this in the novel. The pattern was set early – British and Canadian attacks prompted German reinforcements to rush counter attacks rather than to prepare them properly, leading to vicious fighting and eventual stalemate.

This was essentially what happened around Point 103, and what happens in the story is based closely on the actions of the 24th Lancers. Similarly, the advance to Hill 112 mirrors the actual experience of the 23rd Hussars – including the accidental firing of a 75mm gun when a loose shell rolled onto the firing button. The Glamorgans act as part of the real 49th Division for their part in Epsom. On 27th June, when the six Panthers drive into their position, the story follows a real incident which actually happened on the 26th. In reality, six tanks from the newly arrived 2nd (Vienna) Panzer Division got lost and managed to drive through the rather porous front lines and arrive in the middle of 5 DCLI (5th Duke of Cornwall's Light Infantry). They caused chaos, but most of the tanks were stalked and destroyed. Lt. Col. Atherton, the battalion commander, was killed loading an anti-tank gun, as is Davis in the story. The fighting in July at Hill 112 also mirrors the experience of 5 DCLI, who occupied the Orchard, subsequently known as Cornwall Wood. Once again, their CO was killed, having climbed a tree to spot for the artillery, just as in the story. Afterwards, someone shouted an order to withdraw and they pulled out, only to go back up once the confusion was sorted out. No one knows who shouted the initial order, and the suggestion that it was a German remains possible, even though the enemy did nothing to take advantage of the retreat.

However, for the 1st July defence of Rauray, the Glamorgans take the place of the Tyneside Scottish, also of the 49th Division, and once again the 165th assume the role of the 24th Lancers. This action was part of the last real attempt by the Germans to launch a major counter offensive against the beachheads. Key to the plan was the recently arrived II SS Panzer Corps consisting of the 9th and 10th SS Panzer Divisions (the same units who in September would play a vital role in stopping Operation Market Garden). These units had come from Russia by train, but as was so often the case became sucked into the fighting in Normandy before they were ready. The counter offensive did not come off as planned and was largely improvised and poorly coordinated, which did not mean that it was not a desperate business for the troops in its path. German accounts here and elsewhere stress the appalling weight of firepower brought down on them by the British and Canadians, and repeatedly say that they had encountered nothing like it in Russia.

Normandy was a far more concentrated conflict than most of the eastern front battles, with far more German tanks per mile of front than was ever possible on the wide steppe. The Germans discovered that tactics that had worked in the different conditions and against a different opponent in the east did not work in Normandy. Similarly, many of the lessons learned in the Desert by the British proved unsuitable for the close country of much of Normandy. Tanks, and especially tank commanders, were far more vulnerable to enemy infantry in Normandy and especially in the bocage country.

Several divisions and individuals with experience in the Mediterranean were brought back for the Normandy campaign, only to be criticised for lacking drive by senior commanders. A lot of this was unfair, since the conditions of the battle simply did not make for grand, sweeping advances, no matter how experienced a unit was. However, many of the men who had already done a lot of fighting were understandably less eager to keep on running all the risks. In general, much of the army felt 'browned off' to use an expression of the time – disliking service and its bull, and seeing the war as an unpleasant task to get over with as soon as possible. A minority had done a lot of fighting before D-Day, while the rest had waited and waited. I felt it important not to have any of the characters landing in the first wave on D-Day itself and wanted to give some impression of what it was like for the vast majority of men who spent 6th June and many more days still waiting.

Normandy was a long battle, lasting well into August. The Allies expected most of the fighting to occur further inland than it did, because elsewhere the Germans had fought hard to inflict losses before disengaging and doing the same thing at the next line of defence and the next. It was not a strategy aimed at winning, more at making winning hard and very costly for the Allies in the hope that the fortunes of the war could be reversed somewhere else. In Normandy, Hitler insisted that the Germans fight for ground rather than give it up, and his commanders were only able to bend this rule to a limited extent. This concentrated everything into a slow, attritional battle. It was essentially a First World War battle fought with far more modern and lethal weapons. Viewed from a distance, it can seem inevitable that the Allies would prevail, but that was small consolation to the soldiers doing the fighting.

The Second World War was won by the Allies. Several weeks after D-Day the Red Army launched its major summer offensive, Operation Bagration. This took more ground and killed more Germans than the Battle of Normandy. It also succeeded so well because panzer divisions had been sent to face the western Allies so were not available as reserves. In the course of the war, the majority of German soldiers to die would die on the eastern front. The price paid by the Russians to achieve this was staggering and should never be forgotten. Nor should all the other fronts and types of warfare be neglected. If one of the reasons for writing this book was to remind people that the Battle of Normandy was far more than just D-Day, then Normandy in turn was one chapter in a much bigger war.

Memory varies from country to country, and the perception of the past can be shaped as much by film and television's presentation of what happened as the reality. The Canadians rarely receive sufficient attention for the part they played in Normandy – much as the British feel that their role is neglected in American accounts, and especially on screen. In most respects, such as equipment, organisation, tactics and training, the British and Canadian military were essentially the same, as was their experience of Normandy.

The story did not allow me to cover Canadian operations in any real detail, but the CANLOAN scheme at least permitted the inclusion of a Canadian in an important role. As described, by early 1944 the Canadians had more officers than they needed and the British too few. Volunteers were sought for temporary attachment and 673 accepted and were posted to British units. Of these, 623 went to infantry battalions, usually a handful to each unit. The scheme was a remarkable success, and CANLOAN officers won a very high reputation – while their accents sometimes confused the Germans, who became convinced that they were facing American rather than British troops. Some 75 per cent became casualties, which was a high rate even by the standards of junior leaders in North-West Europe. Around a hundred CANLOAN officers were decorated.

If I could not cover the wider role played by the Canadians – or indeed other groups such as the Poles, who in due course served under British command – this is even more true of the American contribution. Normandy, like the wider war, was an Allied victory, but much of the time the sheer scale of operations meant that the different contingents saw little of each other. However, early on I decided that James would serve in a regiment equipped with American-made tanks. The Sherman was the standard medium tank of the US army by 1944, and while the British-made Churchill and Cromwell were employed in considerable numbers in Normandy, more units had Shermans.

The virtues of the Sherman tank were considerable. It was reliable, easy to maintain, fairly fast and manoeuvrable. American factories were also able to turn them out in vast quantities. In the early days of the Normandy campaign things were more difficult, but by July replacement tanks arrived with units within a day or so of a vehicle being put out of action. However, military equipment is always a question of balance and compromise. The drawbacks of the Sherman were light armour compared to German tanks, a very high profile which made it easier to see, and a 75mm gun that could not penetrate the armour on the heavier German tanks, especially their front armour. It also caught fire quickly and more often than other tanks, a weakness at the time believed to be a combination of fuel and ammunition igniting. Later study suggested that it was really the ammunition – and crews' fondness for carrying even more than could easily be stored – that was the problem and the root of nicknames like Ronson and Tommy Cooker.

The Sherman was very good as an infantry support weapon, for its 75mm gun fired an extremely effective HE round. This type of fighting was probably the most common form for most crews. In tank to tank fighting it did less well, although Sergeant Martin's point that the key thing was to spot an enemy before he saw you was very true. The side that shot first and from the better position tended to win such encounters, and when the Germans attacked, Panthers and even Tigers could be engaged from the flank and destroyed, while the big gun on the Firefly made a huge difference. These were very new at the time of D-Day and many regiments had not yet worked out how to employ this extra firepower.

As part of the wider debate on strategy, there has been considerable discussion of the relative quality of the British/Canadian, American and German armies in Normandy, ranging from equipment to training and motivation. The question is complex, not least because the German army varied so much from the elite, mechanised panzer divisions to less well-equipped infantry, to poor-quality static divisions. Even within these categories, things varied a great deal. For instance, most of the infantry of the 17th SS Panzer Grenadier Division, which fought in the American sector, reached the front on foot or riding bicycles. The Allies did not land a single horse on the

Normandy beaches, whereas the Germans employed tens of thousands of the animals. German tanks had good armour and powerful guns, but this came often at the expense of reliability, ease of maintenance, and most of all cost and speed of manufacture, not simply of the vehicle itself, but the spare parts needed to keep it operational. Allied tankers would have liked a better protected and bigger gunned tank, like the British Comet, which only began to arrive in any numbers in 1945, but instead they did the job with the Sherman – or Cromwell and Churchill, which were similarly under-gunned compared to the panzers.

The basic truth of the Normandy campaign is that the Allies won, for many different reasons. Apart from the wider context, one central reason was that Allied soldiers fought well enough in the circumstances to defeat their German counterparts. The cost was appalling. Before D-Day, British Army planners worked with estimates of likely losses and on that basis worked out probable numbers of replacements that would be needed, as well as how to provide appropriate medical facilities to cope with the wounded. They had two scales – normal and intensive. During the course of the Normandy campaign they had to create a third – double intensive. Losses fell most heavily on the infantrymen in the rifle companies, and at a lower, although still serious, level on tank crews. Leaders, the men who had to go first and who had to move around a position to receive and give orders, suffered even more heavily than the rest. By May 1945, very few units had more than a handful of men left who had landed in Normandy. The cost of liberating Europe – and of the fighting in other theatres – was high, and concentrated among the smaller proportion of men serving in the teeth arms in the most dangerous roles.

All in all, Normandy was a grim attritional battle, and the novel aims to reflect something of its nature and something of the young men who fought there. The subject has fascinated me for so long that I cannot hope to list all the books I have read, let alone all the conversations I have had or heard over the years. However, I really cannot finish without suggesting some things that the interested reader will find profitable. A far more detailed list can be found on my website – adriangoldsworthy.com – including lists of personal accounts, unit histories and the like. There are also videos discussing these things on my YouTube channel: Adrian Goldsworthy. Historian and Novelist.There is a lot of very good stuff out there.

On the wider campaign, there is excellent coverage in James Holland, *Normandy '44*, Anthony Beevor, *D-Day. The Battle for Normandy*, Max Hastings, *Overlord*, and Rick Atkinson, *The Guns at Last Light*. Older, but a book that did much to develop my interest, is Alexander McKee, *Caen. Anvil of Victory*, which focuses on the British and Canadian experience. For D-Day itself, Cornelius Ryan, *The Longest Day* remains worth a read, although the most thorough treatment of the preparations and the landings themselves is Peter Caddick-Adams, *Sand and Steel. A New History of D-Day*.

For more detail on the actual events which provide the background of the novel see Tim Saunders, *Battle for the Bocage. Normandy 1944* and *Hill 112. The Key to Defeating Hitler in Normandy*, Ian Dalglish, *Over the Battlefield. Operation Epsom*, and J. J. How, *Hill 112*. For the defence of Rauray, see Kevin Baverstock, *Breaking the Panzers. The Bloody Battle for Rauray, Normandy, 1st July 1944*. Finally, after all this non-fiction, a novel – Alexander Baron, *From the City, From the Plough* offers one of the most vivid portraits of the British soldier of the time and the fighting in Normandy and cannot be recommended too strongly.

About the Author

ADRIAN GOLDSWORTHY studied at Oxford, where his doctoral thesis examined the Roman army. He went on to become an acclaimed historian of Ancient Rome. He is the author of numerous works of non-fiction, including *Philip and Alexander: Kings and Conquerors*, and *Hadrian's Wall*. He has also written six critically acclaimed novels featuring Roman soldier Flavius Ferox. *Hill 112* is his first novel set during World War II.